Praise for

Women with Big Eyes

"Masterful . . . Mastretta casts a beguiling spell . . . With soulful warmth and sly humor—and a deep respect for the earthy details of lives that center on husbands (and lovers), fathers, mothers, sisters, brothers, grandparents, cousins, and children both pure and perfidious—Mastretta gets an entire world into very few pages. Taking as title and subject 'women with big eyes,' she describes those blessed with the ability to see truly, responding to joys and troubles with open hearts and a quirky individuality that enchants and appeals. Yet there is nothing sentimental about these women, and the boundaries of their somewhat circumscribed lives are quite clear, set by society, the Catholic church, and macho men who brook no disobedience. But they talk back and they do as they please, whether in the wilder reaches of their imaginations or the everyday clatter of Puebla kitchens . . . There's no end of aunts, fortunately, or of stories, and each is the unique creation of a greatly gifted author. A remarkable collection." —*Kirkus Reviews* (starred review)

"[Her characters'] voices, their bantering, affectionate way with one another, the food they eat, the books they read, the houses they live in and cherish, all come wonderfully alive."

—*The Washington Post Book World*

"Mastretta's fiction is a kind of alchemy." —*Vogue* (Spain)

"A bestseller in Mexico, this short-story collection features colorful women zeroing in on their driving forces: passion, bravery, imagination, and vanity. Expect the unexpected from these vibrant and wise heroines." —*Lifetime*

continued . . .

"The women who come to life in Mastretta's engaging bilingual story collection are independent and passionate individuals, and she writes about them with compassion and, above all, humor . . . Part fable, part mysticism, the stories are tied together with details of everyday life in the author's native Puebla, Mexico . . . Autobiographical in its inception as Mastretta searched her family tree for strong, unique women, this collection became much more as her imagination and vibrant mysticism took over, turning it into what she calls 'a plane ticket to another world.' " —*Booklist*

"There is a passionate intelligence at work in Mastretta's fiction. You have only to read the opening pages in the life of one of her heroines to realize you have come upon a modern novelist in the grand tradition." —Laura Esquivel, author of *Like Water for Chocolate*

"Thirty-nine indomitable aunts are captured in a series of lyrical snapshots in this autobiographically inspired collection . . . Homing in on the essence of each aunt, Mastretta also captures the flavor of her native Puebla . . . [*Women with Big Eyes*] showcases Mastretta's engaging ability to capture the pivotal moments of a woman's life, when everything changes or begins to make sense for the first time." —*Publishers Weekly*

"While all of the characters are inhabitants of Puebla, Mexico, during the early twentieth century, that's where the similarity ends in these funny and sexy stories. Some of the women are devout, but others are atheists; some are beautiful, some homely. Each is her own person and reveals a unique force, be it passion, a nurturing soul, strength of will, or mystical knowledge." —*Library Journal*

ALSO BY ÁNGELES MASTRETTA

Tear This Heart Out

(*Arráncame la vida*)

Lovesick

(*Mal de amores*)

RIVERHEAD BOOKS

New York

WOMEN *with* BIG EYES

Ángeles Mastretta

TRANSLATED FROM THE SPANISH BY

Amy Schildhouse Greenberg

THE BERKLEY PUBLISHING GROUP
Published by the Penguin Group
Penguin Group (USA) Inc.
375 Hudson Street, New York, New York 10014, USA
Penguin Group (Canada), 10 Alcorn Avenue, Toronto, Ontario M4V 3B2, Canada
(a division of Pearson Penguin Canada Inc.)
Penguin Books Ltd., 80 Strand, London WC2R 0RL, England
Penguin Group Ireland, 25 St. Stephen's Green, Dublin 2, Ireland (a division of Penguin Books Ltd.)
Penguin Group (Australia), 250 Camberwell Road, Camberwell, Victoria 3124, Australia
(a division of Pearson Australia Group Pty. Ltd.)
Penguin Books India Pvt. Ltd., 11 Community Centre, Panchsheel Park, New Delhi—110 017, India
Penguin Group (NZ), Cnr. Airborne and Rosedale Roads, Albany, Auckland 1310, New Zealand
(a division of Pearson New Zealand Ltd.)
Penguin Books (South Africa) (Pty.) Ltd., 24 Sturdee Avenue, Rosebank, Johannesburg 2196, South Africa

Penguin Books Ltd., Registered Offices: 80 Strand, London WC2R 0RL, England

Cover design by Honi Werner
Book design by Amanda Dewey
Photograph of the author © Dora Franco

The translations of "Aunt Leonor," "Aunt Natalia," "Aunt Jose," and "Aunt Concha" appeared, in slightly different form, in *TriQuarterly* ("New Writing from Mexico" issue, ed. Reginald Gibbons, 1992) and in *The Vintage Book of Latin American Stories* (ed. Carlos Fuentes and Julio Ortega, 2000).

PRINTING HISTORY
First published in Mexico in 1990 by Cal y Arena, as *Mujeres de ojos grandes*
First Riverhead hardcover edition: November 2003
First Riverhead trade paperback edition: November 2004
Riverhead trade paperback ISBN: 1-59448-040-0

The Library of Congress has catalogued the Riverhead hardcover edition as follows:

Mastretta, Ángeles, date.
[Mujeres de ojos grandes. English]
Women with big eyes / Ángeles Mastretta;
[translated by Amy Schildhouse Greenberg].
p. cm.
ISBN 1-57322-346-8
I. Title.
PQ7298.23.A795M38913 2003 2003046818
863'.64—dc21

PRINTED IN THE UNITED STATES OF AMERICA

10 9 8 7 6 5 4 3 2 1

To Carlos Mastretta Arista,
who returned from Italy

TRANSLATOR'S NOTE

When I lived in Mexico City in the late 1980s, I traveled frequently to the city of Puebla, two hours southeast of my smog-choked adopted megalopolis. How could one not? Puebla was everything the Federal District wasn't: quaint, provincial, filled with aromas of chocolatey *mole poblano,* and rich with an air of times past. It was so even when I was there, near the end of the twentieth century. In fact, it was remarkably like the Puebla of the stories in *Women with Big Eyes*. I walked among the señoras in the bustling open-air markets, and behind señoritas down shaded streets in the late afternoons, listening to their chatter. Like the "aunts" in Ángeles Mastretta's stories, the women whose conversations I overheard seemed to lead lives every bit as complicated and filled with intrigue as their supposedly more sophisticated counterparts in the capital. Perhaps it was a longing to revisit the charming streets of Puebla and its fascinating women that drew me to translate Mastretta's collection.

I admire the women she has created in these stories. To me, they embody a particularly Mexican brand of feminism. They are strong, determined, and passionate. They pursue their dreams. Yet these women are and remain deeply involved in their close circles of family and friends. Mastretta refers to them warmly as "aunts," and in translating their stories, that is how I too came to see them. She captures their lives with humor, affection, and insight, using their unique local references and colorful expressions. I tried to mirror her expressive Spanish faithfully in English. This chance to return to Puebla and Pueblan women—albeit via the art of translation—rewarded me with a delightful challenge.

Aunt Leonor

Aunt Leonor had the world's most perfect belly button: a small dot hidden exactly in the middle of her flat, flat belly. She had a freckled back and round, firm hips, like the pitchers of water she drank from as a child. Her shoulders were raised slightly; she walked slowly, as if on a high wire. Those who saw them tell that her legs were long and golden, that her pubic hair was a tuft of arrogant, reddish down, that it was impossible to look upon her waist without desiring all of her.

At age seventeen she followed her head and married a man who was exactly the kind you would choose, with your head, to accompany you through life. Alberto Palacios, a wealthy, stringent notary public, had fifteen years, thirty centimeters of height, and a proportionate amount of experience over her. He had been the longtime boyfriend of various boring women who became even more tiresome when they discovered that the good notary had only a long-term plan for considering marriage.

Destiny would have it that Aunt Leonor entered the notary's office one afternoon accompanied by her mother to process a supposedly easy inheritance, which for them turned out to be extremely complicated, owing to the fact that Aunt Leonor's recently deceased father had never permitted his wife to think for even half an hour in her lifetime. He did everything for her except go grocery shopping and cook. He summarized the news in the newspaper for her and told her how she should think about it. He gave her an always sufficient allowance, which he never asked to see how she spent; he even told her what was happening in the movies they went to see together: "See, Luisita, this boy fell in love with the young lady. Look how they're gazing at each other—you see? Now he wants to caress her, he's caressing her now. Now he's going to ask her to marry him, and in a little while he will abandon her."

The result of this paternalism was that poor Aunt Luisita found the sudden loss of the exemplary man who was Aunt Leonor's papa not only distressing but also extremely complicated. With this sorrow and this complication they entered the notary's office in search of assistance. They found him to be so solicitous and efficacious that Aunt Leonor, still in mourning, married notary Palacios a year and a half later.

Aunt Leonor's life was never again as easy as it was back then. In the only critical moment, she had followed her mother's advice: Shut your eyes and say a Hail Mary. In truth, many Hail Marys, because at times her immoderate husband could take as long as ten Mysteries of the Rosary before arriving at the series of moans and gasps that culminated in the circus that inevitably began when, for some reason, foreseen or not, he placed his hand on Leonor's short, delicate waist.

Aunt Leonor lacked for nothing a woman under twenty-five should want: hats, veils, French shoes, German tableware, a diamond ring, a necklace of unmatched pearls; turquoise, coral, and filigree earrings. Everything, from underdrawers embroidered by Trinitarian nuns to a tiara like Princess Margaret's. She had whatever she might want, including the devotion of her husband, who little by little began to realize that life without precisely this woman would be intolerable.

From out of the affectionate circus that the notary mounted at least three times a week, first a girl and then two boys materialized in Aunt Leonor's belly. And as happens only in the movies, Aunt Leonor's body inflated and deflated all three times without apparent damage. The notary would have liked to draw up a certificate bearing testimony to such a miracle, but he limited himself to merely enjoying it, helped along as he was by the polite and placid diligence that time and curiosity had bestowed upon his wife. The circus improved so much that Leonor stopped getting through it with her rosary in her hands and even came to thank him for it, falling asleep afterward with a smile that lasted all day.

Life couldn't have been better for this family. People always spoke well of them; they were a model couple. The neighbor women could not find a better example of kindness and companionship than that offered by Señor Palacios to the lucky Leonor, and their men, when they were angriest, evoked the peaceful smile of Señora Palacios while their wives strung together a litany of laments.

Perhaps everything would have gone on in the same way if it

hadn't occurred to Aunt Leonor to buy medlars one Sunday. Her Sunday trips to market had become a happy, solitary rite. First she looked the whole place over, without trying to discern exactly from which fruit came which color, mixing the tomato stands with those that sold lemons. She walked without pausing until she reached an immense woman fashioning fat blue tacos, her one hundred years showing on her face. Leonorcita picked out one filled with pot cheese from the clay tortilla plate, carefully put a bit of red sauce on it, and ate it slowly while making her purchases.

Medlars are small fruit with intensely yellow velvety skin. Some are bitter and others are sweet. They grow in jumbled clusters on the branches of a tree with large, dark leaves. Many afternoons when she was a girl with braids and as agile as a cat, Aunt Leonor climbed the medlar tree at her grandparents' house. There she sat to eat quickly: three bitter ones, a sweet one, seven bitter, two sweet—until the search for and mixture of flavors became a delicious game. Girls were prohibited from climbing the tree, but her cousin Sergio, a boy of precocious eyes, thin lips, and a determined voice, induced her into unheard-of, secret adventures. Climbing the tree was among the easiest of them.

She saw the medlars in the market, and they seemed strange, far from the tree yet not completely apart from it, for medlars are cut while still on the most delicate, full-leaved branches.

She took the medlars home, showed them to her children, and sat the kids down to eat, meanwhile telling them stories of her grandfather's strong legs and her grandmother's snub nose.

In a little while, her mouth was brimming with slippery pits and velvety peelings. Then suddenly being ten years old came back, his avid hands, her forgotten desire for Sergio, up in the tree, winking at her.

Only then did she realize that something had been torn out of her the day they told her that cousins couldn't marry each other, because God would punish them with children who seemed like drunkards. And then she could no longer return to the days past. The afternoons of her happiness were muted from then on by this unspeakable, sudden nostalgia.

No one else would have dared ask for more: to add to her complete tranquility when her children were floating paper boats in the rain, and to the unhesitating affection of her generous and hardworking husband, the certainty in her entire body that the cousin who had made her perfect navel tremble was not prohibited, and that she deserved him for all reasons and forever. No one, that is, but the outrageous Leonor.

One afternoon she ran into Sergio walking down Cinco de Mayo Street. She was coming out of the Church of Santo Domingo, holding a child by each hand. She'd taken them to make a floral offering, as on every afternoon that month: The girl in a long dress of lace and white organdy, a little garland of straw, and an enormous, impetuous veil. Like a five-year-old bride. The boy with a girlish acolyte's costume that made him even at seven feel embarrassed.

"If you hadn't run away from our grandparents' house that Saturday, this pair would be mine," said Sergio, kissing her.

"I live with that regret," Aunt Leonor answered.

That response startled one of the most eligible bachelors in the city. At twenty-seven, recently returned from Spain, where it was said he had learned the best techniques for cultivating olives, cousin Sergio was heir to a ranch in Veracruz, another in San Martín, and one more in nearby Atzalan.

Aunt Leonor noticed the confusion in his eyes and in the tongue with which he wet his lips, and later she heard him say:

"If everything were like climbing the tree again."

Grandmother's house was on 11 Sur Street. It was huge and full of nooks and crannies. It had a basement with five doors in which Grandfather spent hours doing experiments that often soiled his face and made him forget for a while about the first-floor rooms and occupying himself playing billiards with friends in the salon constructed on the rooftop. Grandmother's house had a breakfast room that gave onto the garden and the ash tree, a jai-alai court that they'd always used for roller-skating, a rose-colored front room with a grand piano and a drained aquarium, a bedroom for Grandfather and one for Grandmother; and the rooms that had once been the children's were various sitting rooms that had come to be known by the colors of their walls. Grandmother, sound of mind but palsied, had settled herself in to paint in the blue room. There Leonor and Sergio found her drawing lines with a pencil on the envelopes of the old wedding invitations she'd always liked to save. She offered them a glass of sweet wine, then fresh cheese, then stale chocolates. Everything was the same at Grandmother's house. After a while, the old woman noticed the only thing that was different:

"I haven't seen you two together in years."

"Not since you told me that cousins who marry each other have idiot children," Aunt Leonor answered.

Grandmother smiled, poised above the paper on which she was sketching an infinite flower, petals upon petals without respite.

"Not since you nearly killed yourself getting down from the medlar tree," said Sergio.

"You two were good at cutting medlars. Now I can't find anyone who can do it right."

"We're still good," said Aunt Leonor, bending her perfect waist.

They left the blue room, almost ready to peel off their clothes, and went down to the garden as if drawn by a spell. They returned three hours later with peace in their bodies and three branches of medlars.

"We've lost our touch," Aunt Leonor said.

"Get it back, get it back, because time is short," advised Grandmother, her mouth full of medlar pits.

Aunt Elena

Arroyo Zarco plantation was a large strip of fertile land in the mountains north of Puebla. In 1910 its owners planted coffee and sugar cane, corn, beans, and other vegetables. The landscape was green year-round. It rained while the sun shone, while it didn't shine, and beneath the moon. The rain seemed so natural that no one thought twice about putting on a raincoat to go out for a walk.

Aunt Elena lived but a short time in this dampness. For one thing, there were no schools nearby, so her parents sent her to the Sacred Heart high school in Mexico City. She was three hundred kilometers away there—twenty hours by train, with a snack and a night's sleep in the city of Puebla, and a breakfast already governed by the nostalgia that ten months spent far from her mother's extravagant cooking and close to French and the caravans of barren nuns would provoke. Later, when she had completed her studies with honors in arithmetic, grammar, history, geography, piano, needlework, French, and calligraphy, and had returned to the country and the happy anxiety of living there, she had to leave again, because the Revolution came.

When the usurpers entered the plantation to take possession of its fields and waters, Aunt Elena's father put up no resistance. He handed over the house, the patio, the chapel, and the furniture with the same show of courtesy that had always distinguished him from the other plantation owners. His wife showed the soldiers the way to the kitchen, and he took out the titles that evinced his ownership of the plantation, and delivered them to the leader of the rebellion in the state.

Then he moved his family to Teziutlán, settled comfortably in a carriage and practically smiling.

They had always been famous for being half crazy, so when they showed up in town whole and at peace, the other landowners were sure that Ramos Lanz had something to do with the rebels. It could not be pure coincidence that they hadn't burned down his house, or that his daughters didn't seem terrorized, or that his wife was not in tears.

The Ramoses were viewed badly when they walked around town, talkative and happy as though nothing bad had happened to them. The father's demeanor was so steady and gentle that none of the family saw fit to upset him. After all, if he smiled it was merely because the next day and the next decade there would be food on the table and crinolines beneath the silk skirts. It was because no one would be left without hair combs, or without lockets, or clasps, or diamond earrings, or without port to drink.

They saw him worried only one afternoon. He passed several hours at the desk in the house in Teziutlán, drawing something that looked liked a map, which he could not leave alone. He threw sheet after sheet into the wastebasket, feeling as useless as one who tries to remember a route to treasures buried centuries earlier.

Aunt Elena watched him from an armchair without saying a word, without paying attention to anything but his actions. Suddenly she saw him relax and heard him speak to himself in a whisper, but not so softly that she missed his euphoria. He folded his paper in quarters and threw it into a bag.

"Is it suppertime yet?" he asked, looking at her for the first time, without revealing anything or speaking of what had kept him occupied all afternoon.

"I'll go see," she said, and she went to the kitchen, making up her mind about something. When she returned, her father was asleep in a very high-backed armchair. She slowly drew near and went to the wastebasket to salvage a few of the pieces of paper he had thrown away. She put them inside a book and then woke him to tell him supper was ready.

Everything was huge in the Ramos house. Even in these times of scarcity, Aunt Elena's mother got herself organized to make seven-course meals and dinner for at least five people. That night there was mushroom soup, *torta de masa,* pepper strips with tomatoes, and refried beans. The menu ended with chocolate water and shiny sugared breads that Aunt Elena never saw again until after the Revolution. With all this in their stomachs, the family went to sleep and to grow fat without a single regret.

Of the eight daughters Señora Ramos had borne, five had died of illnesses such as smallpox, whooping cough, and asthma, so the three who lived grew up overfed. According to popular belief, it was the good and plentiful food that helped them survive. But that night Aunt Elena's father surprised his family by not being very hungry.

"Eat, little bird, you're going to get sick," Doña Otilia begged her husband, a man of one hundred eighty centimeters from his feet to the tip of his head and ninety kilos who guarded her soul.

Elena asked for permission to leave the table before finishing the last bite of her sugared bread and went to shut herself up in the guest room with a candle. There she put together the pieces of paper and read the green ink in which her father wrote: the map had a footpath, which arrived at the plantation from somewhere behind the house and led directly to the underground room they had constructed near the kitchen.

The wines! The only regret her father had since the usurpers took Arroyo Zarco was the loss of his wines, his collection of bottles with labels in many languages, full of a beverage that she had sipped from the adults' cups since she was a small child. Her father, that steady and moderate man, could he be capable of returning to the plantation for his wines? Was it for this that she had heard him at midday asking Cirilo for a wagon with a horse and straw?

Aunt Elena grabbed a shawl and flew down the stairs. In the dining room, her father was still looking for excuses to explain to his wife the grave sin of not being hungry.

"It's not contempt, my love. I know all the trouble it takes you to prepare each meal so that we don't miss the previous one. But tonight I have something to take care of and I don't want to have a heavy stomach."

At the moment she heard her father say "tonight," Aunt Elena ran out to the patio in search of the carriage. The servant Cirilo had hooked it up to a horse and was watching in silence. Why hadn't Cirilo gone to fight in the Revolution? Why was he standing here silently, next to the horse, in the same soliloquy as always? Aunt Elena crept on tiptoe and climbed into the back of the carriage. After a short while, she heard her father's voice.

"Did you find good straw?" he asked the servant.

"Yes, master. Would you like to see it?"

Aunt Elena thought that her father had nodded, because she heard him move near the back of the carriage and lift a corner of the straw sleeping mat. She felt her father's hand move within three hand lengths of her body:

"The straw is very good," he said, moving away.

Then Aunt Elena regained her soul and loosened the stiffness in her neck.

"You are not coming, Cirilo," said Señor Ramos. "This is a folly of my body that, if it costs anyone, I want to cost only me. If I don't return, tell my wife that all the meals she made in my life were delicious, and tell my daughter Elena that I didn't seek her out to give her a kiss, because I want to keep owing it to her."

"Godspeed," Cirilo told him.

The carriage began to move slowly; slowly it left the town behind in darkness and moved along a road that must have been as straight as Aunt Elena imagined it when she saw it painted with a single line. There was no room on either side of the carriage, so the horse could not run the way it did when she drove it on a wide road.

It took them more than an hour to arrive, but because she fell asleep it seemed like a short time to Aunt Elena. She awoke as the carriage almost stopped moving, and she heard nothing in the air but the "Sss-sss" with which her father calmed the horse. She lifted her head to see where they were, and saw before her the back of the enormous house she had loved her whole life. Her father stopped the carriage and got down. She saw him tremble below the half-moon. Apparently no one was guarding the place. Her father walked to a door and opened it with a huge key. Then he disappeared. Aunt Elena got out from under the straw and followed him into the wine cellar, which was illuminated by a newly lit lantern.

"Can I help you?" she asked him in her hoarse voice. Her face was sleepy and her hair full of straw fibers.

She would never forget the horror she saw in her father's eyes. For the first time in her life she felt afraid, despite having him close by.

"I like port too," she said, controlling her own shaking. She picked up two bottles and went to put them in the straw of the carriage. Upon returning, she passed her father, who was carrying four others. They came and went like this in silence, until the carriage was full and there wasn't room in it for even one of those ports she had learned to drink on the knees of that man so prudent and faithful to his habits, who surprised her that night with his craziness.

He took two more bottles to pay his toll, and put them between his legs. Then he harnessed the horse to the carriage and made his way toward the narrow hidden road by which they had arrived. They would be hours in returning, but it was a miracle that they were about to leave without anyone's having seen them. Not one of the peasants who occupied Arroyo Zarco watched over the back of the plantation.

"Could they all have gone?" Aunt Elena asked her father, and jumped from the carriage without giving him time to grab her. She ran to the house, pressed herself against the darkness of a wall, and walked close to it until she turned the corner. Finally she bumped against a bench that once guarded the main door. There was no light in all that darkness. Not a voice, or a screech, or footsteps, or a single open window.

"There's no one here!" screamed Aunt Elena. "There's no one here!" she repeated, balling her hands into fists and jumping up and down.

They returned via the bog road. Aunt Elena hummed "An Old Love" with the nostalgia of an old lady. At eighteen, the loves of a day before are already old. And so many things had happened to her that night that suddenly she felt in her loves a hole impossible to mend. Who would believe her adventure? Her small-town boyfriend, not a word.

"Elena, for God's sake, stop talking nonsense," he told her, alarmed, when he heard her tale. "These are not times for fantasy. I know it hurts you to have left the plantation, but don't ruin your father's good name telling tales that make him look like an irresponsible drunkard."

But she had already lost her father, beneath the merciless moon of the previous night, and she didn't even try to convince her boyfriend. A week later, she climbed aboard the train car into which her mother was able to fit everything from the Louis XV parlor to ten hens, two roosters, and a cow with her bull calf. Aunt Elena carried with her no more baggage than the future and the early certainty that the most honorable of men had a screw loose.

Aunt Charo

She had a restless back and a porcelain nape. She had chestnut-colored subversive hair and a merciless, happy tongue with which she went through life and every last detail of the lives of whoever offered her theirs.

People liked to speak with her because her voice was like fire and her eyes converted to precise words the most insignificant gestures and the least obvious stories.

It wasn't that she invented evil acts more than others, or that she knew with greater precision the details of a bit of gossip. Above all, it was that she discovered the point of each tangle, the exact carelessness of God that made someone ugly, the tiny verbal imprecision that became unpleasant in a naive soul.

Aunt Charo liked to be in the world, to peruse it with her unmerciful eyes and sharpen it with her hurried voice. She wasted no time. While she spoke, she sewed her children's clothes, embroidered her husband's initials on his handkerchiefs, knit vests for all who were cold in winter, played jai-alai with her sister, made the most delicious corn cake, molded crullers on her knees, and figured out the assignments her sons and daughters didn't understand.

She might never have been ashamed of her passion for words if one June afternoon she had not agreed to go to some spiritual exercises in which the priest dedicated his speech to the commandment "Thou shalt not bear false witness against thy neighbor." For a while, the father spoke of the great false testimonies, but when he saw that this failed to frighten his sleepy parishioners, he was reduced to demonizing the small series of venial sins that originate in conversation about others and that together create gigantic mortal sins.

Aunt Charo left the church with remorse in the pit of her stomach. Would she be full of mortal sins, the end product of all those times she had said that the nose of this lady and the feet of that one . . . the sports jacket of this gentleman and the hunchback of that one . . . the money of a nouveau riche man and the wandering eyes of a married woman . . . ? Could she have a heart putrid with sins because of her knowledge of everything that passed between the skirts and trousers of the city, of all the foolishnesses that impeded others' happiness, and of so much of others' happiness that was nothing but foolishness? The horror inside her kept growing. Before going home she went to confess to the recently arrived Spanish priest, a small, meek man who traversed San Javier parish in search of the faithful who could trust him.

In Puebla, the people could love more forcefully than elsewhere, it just took a while. It was not the thing to see the first stranger and devote oneself as if one had known him forever. Nevertheless, in this Aunt Charo was not a typical Pueblan. She was one of the first clients of the Spanish father. The old priest who had given her first communion died, leaving her with no one to whom she could make her most secret confessions, those that she and her conscience alone distilled, those that involved her small deviations, the doubts of her most private skirts, the bubbles of her body and the dark crystal of her heart.

"*Ave María Purísima*," said the Spanish father in his crowded speech, more like that of a singer of Gypsy songs than a priest educated in Madrid.

"Conceived without sin," said Charo, and she smiled in the darkness of the confessional, as was her custom every time she affirmed that item.

"Are you laughing?" asked the Spaniard, guessing as if he were a wizard.

"No, Father," said Aunt Charo, fearing the bad habits of the Inquisition.

"I am," the little man said. "And you can, with my permission. I don't believe there could be a more ridiculous greeting. But tell me: How are you? What is happening that you are here so late today?"

"I'm wondering, Father," said Aunt Charo, "if it's a sin to speak of others. You know, tell what's happened to them, know what they feel, disagree with what they say, point out that the cross-eyed is cross-eyed, the lame one is lame, the shaggy one uncombed, and the woman who talks only about her husband's millions, conceited. To know where the husband got his millions, and who he spends them on most. Is that a sin, Father?" Charo asked.

"No, my daughter," the Spanish priest answered. "That is zest for life. What do the people here have to do? Work and say prayers? There's still a lot of day remaining. To see is not a sin, nor to comment on it, either. Go in peace. Sleep tranquilly."

"Thank you, Father," said Aunt Charo, and ran out to tell her sister all about it.

Free of sin since then, she continued living avidly the soap opera that the city presented to her. She had her head full of the comings and goings of others, and this was a clear guarantee of entertainment. For this reason she was invited to knit for all the charity bazaars, and people fought by the dozen to have her at their table when they played canasta. Those who could not see her by these means invited her to their homes or went to visit her. No one was ever disappointed by hearing her, and no one ever had a first juicy tidbit that did not come from her mouth.

And so her life went on, until one evening in the Guadalupe bazaar. Aunt Charo had spent the afternoon battling with the spangles on a belt, and since she had nothing new to report, she limited herself to listening.

"Charo, you know the Spanish father at the Church of San Javier?" a woman asked her, while finishing the border of a napkin.

"Why?" asked Aunt Charo, not accustomed to committing herself easily.

"Because they say he is not a priest, that he is a lying republican who arrived with those exiled by Cárdenas,* and since he couldn't find work as a poet, he fabricated a story that he was a priest and that his papers had been burned in a fire, along with the church in his town, when the communists came."

"How intractable some people are," said Aunt Charo, and added with all the authority of her prestigious position:

"The Spanish priest is a devoted man, a great Catholic, incapable of lying. I saw the letter in which the Vatican dispatched him to watch over the parish of San Javier. That the poor old man may have been dying when he arrived is not his fault—they gave him no time to present himself. But did they send him? They sent him. I'm not going to make a fraud of my confessor."

"He is your confessor?" asked someone from among the chorus of the curious.

"I have that honor, yes," said Aunt Charo, fixing her gaze on the flower of spangles that she was embroidering, and so ending the conversation.

The next morning she confined herself in the Spanish priest's confessional.

---

*Lázaro Cárdenas del Río (1895–1970), president of Mexico from 1934 to 1940.

"Father, I told lies," she said.

"White lies?" he asked.

"Necessary lies," she answered.

"Necessary for the good of whom?" the priest asked.

"Of an honorable person, Father," said Aunt Charo.

"The person you are helping is innocent?"

"I don't know, Father," Aunt Charo confessed.

"Doubly worthy are you," said the Spaniard. "May God preserve your clarity and good milk. Go with Him."

"Thank you, Father," said Charo.

"Thank *you*," the strange priest responded, causing her to tremble.

Aunt Cristina

Aunt Cristina Martínez wasn't pretty, but something about her slim legs and breathy voice made her interesting. Unfortunately, the men of Puebla weren't looking for interesting women to marry, and Aunt Cristina reached the age of twenty without anyone's so much as having proposed a courtship of good standing. When she turned twenty-one, her four sisters were married for better or worse, and she spent her entire days in humiliation, left to attend church an old maid. In no time at all, her nephews and nieces would call her "leftover," and she wasn't sure if she would be able to withstand that blow. It was after that birthday, which ended with her mother in tears by the time Cristina blew out the candles on her cake, that Señor Arqueros appeared on the horizon.

Cristina returned one morning from downtown, where she had gone to buy shell buttons and a meter of lace, telling of having met a Spaniard of good breeding at La Princesa jewelers. The jewels in the display window had made her enter to inquire about the cost of an engagement ring that was her life's dream. When they told her the price it seemed fair, and she lamented the fact that she was not a man, to buy it that instant with the idea of wearing it someday.

"Men can have the ring before they have the fiancée, until they can choose a fiancée who goes with the ring," she said to her mother during dinner. "We, on the other hand, have to just wait. There are those who wait their whole life long, and those who are forever burdened with a ring they dislike, don't you think?"

"You should no longer yearn for men, Cristina," her mother said. "Who will look after you when I die?"

"I will, Mama, don't you worry. I am going to look after myself."

In the afternoon, a messenger from the jewelry store showed up at the house with the ring Aunt Cristina had tried on, holding out her hand to view it from all sides while saying a great deal of things similar to those she later repeated to her mother in the dining room. The messenger also carried a sealed envelope with Cristina's first and last names on it.

Both these things Señor Arqueros had sent to her, along with his devotion, his respects, and his regret that he could not bring them to her personally, because his boat from Veracruz was leaving the next day, and he needed to travel part of that day and all night to arrive on time. In his message he proposed marriage: "Your concepts of life, of women and men, your delicious voice and the freedom with which you walk dazzled me. I will not return to Mexico for several years, but I propose that you catch up with me in Spain. My friend Emilio Suárez will come to see your parents within a short while. I leave with him my trust, and with you, my hope."

Emilio Suárez was the man of Cristina's teenage dreams. He was twelve years older than she, and was still single when she reached the age of twenty-one. He was as rich as the jungles were rich in rain and as intractable as the mountains in January. All the women of Puebla had chased after him, and the most fortunate among them merely obtained the trophy of an ice cream eaten with him in the city arcades. Nonetheless, he showed up at Cristina's house to ask, on behalf of his friend, for her hand in marriage, by the power vested in him by one he would very gladly represent.

Aunt Cristina's mother refused to believe that she had seen the Spaniard only that one time, and when Suárez disappeared with the answer that they would think about it, she accused her daughter of a thousand acts of a brazen young hussy. But such was the look of astonishment on her daughter's face that she ended up begging her pardon and asking permission of the heavens in which her husband resided to commit the foolish act of marrying her daughter off to a stranger.

When she recovered from her own anguish at the surprise, Aunt Cristina looked at her ring and began to cry for her sisters, her mother, her friends, her neighborhood, the cathedral, the main square, the volcanoes, the sky, the *mole,* the chalupas, the national anthem, the highway to Mexico City, the town of Cholula, the village of Coetzalan, the fragrant bones of her father, the casseroles, the bittersweet chocolates, the music, the smell of tortillas, the San Francisco River, the ranch of her friend Elena and the cattle pastures of her uncle Abelardo; for the moon of October and that of March, for February's sun, for her arrogant old-maidhood, and for Emilio Suárez, who in a whole life of looking at her never heard her voice or noticed, for God's sake, her walk.

The next day, she went out to the street with the news and her sparkling ring. Six months later, she married Señor Arqueros before a priest, a notary, and the eyes of Suárez. There was a mass, a banquet, a dance, and good-byes. All with the same enthusiasm as if the groom were from this side of the ocean. People said that a more radiant bride had not been seen in a long while.

Two days later, Cristina departed from Veracruz toward the port where Señor Arqueros, with all his chivalry, would pick her up and take her to live in Valladolid.

She sent her first letter from there, saying how much she

missed everyone and how happy she was. She used little space to describe the crowded landscape of small houses and cultivated land, but she did send her mother a recipe for beef with red wine, which was the local dish, and her sisters two poems by one Señor García Lorca, which they sent back to her. Her husband turned out to be a hardworking, careful man who laughed at his wife's way of speaking Spanish and her stories of ghosts, her blushing every time she heard the word *coño,* and her terror at the way the whole world here shit on God for any old reason and swore at the sacramental host without a single consideration.

A year of letters came and went before the one in which Aunt Cristina told her family of the unexpected death of Señor Arqueros. It was a brief letter, which seemed devoid of feeling. "That's how bad off she must be," said her sister, the second one, who knew of her emotional fickleness and her impulsive passions. Everyone was left sharing Cristina's pain and waiting for when she would recuperate from the upheaval and write with a bit more clarity about her future. Her family was speaking of this one Sunday after dinner, when they saw her appear in the dining room.

She bore gifts for all. The nieces and nephews would not leave her alone until she finished passing them out. Her legs had filled out and she wore very high heels, black like her stockings, her skirt, her blouse, her coat, her hat, and the veil she didn't have time to remove from over her face. When she finished handing out the presents, she pulled the veil off along with her hat and smiled.

"Well, I've returned," she said.

From then on she was Arqueros's widow. The pain of being an old maid did not fall on her, and she frightened away all other pain with her out-of-tune piano and her ardent voice. No one had to beg her to play the piano and accompany any song. She had in her repertoire every type of waltz, polka, folksong, aria, and *paso doble.* She put words to some Chopin preludes and sang them, evoking great romances that she never knew. At the end of her concerts she waited for everyone to applaud and after rising from the bench to make a deep curtsy, she extended her arms, displayed her ring, and then, pointing to herself with her aged and lovely hands, said conclusively, "And buried in Puebla."

The gossips said that Señor Arqueros never existed. That Emilio Suárez told the only lie of his life, persuaded by who knows which art of Aunt Cristina's. And that the money she called her inheritance she had taken from contraband hidden in the luggage of her trousseau.

Who knows? What is certain is that Emilio Suárez and Cristina Martínez were friends until their final days. Something for which no one ever forgave them, because friendship between men and women is an unforgivably good thing.

Aunt Valeria

There was an aunt of ours, loyal as no other woman had ever been. Or at least so everyone who knew her said. Never was there seen in Puebla a woman more in love or more solicitous than the ever radiant Aunt Valeria.

She did her shopping in La Victoria market. The old saleswomen tell that you could see her peacefulness even in the way she chose vegetables. She touched them slowly, she felt the shine of their rinds, and let them fall onto the scales. Then, while they were being weighed, she threw her head back and sighed, like someone who has just completed a fascinating chore.

Some of her friends believed her half mad. They did not understand how she went through life so enchanted, always speaking so well of her husband. She said that she adored him even when they were entirely alone, when they conversed to themselves in the corner of a garden or the atrium of the church.

Her husband was a common, ordinary man, with his indispensable attacks of ill humor, with his necessary lack of appreciation for the daily dinner, with his disagreeable certainty that the best time of day for making love was whenever he felt like it, with his matutinal euphorias and his nocturnal absences, with his perfect reasoning about and very prudent distance from those who are and must be his sons. A husband like any other. Because of this, the condition of everlasting love that shone from Aunt Valeria's eyes and smile seemed astounding.

"How do you do it?" asked her cousin Gertrudis one day, who was famous for changing her activities every week, putting into all the same unruly passion that great men spend on a single task. Gertrudis could knit five sweaters in three days, ride horseback for hours, bake pastries for all the charity bazaars, take a painting class, dance flamenco, sing *rancheros,* feed lunch to seventy invited guests on a Sunday, and fall in love with total impudence with three different men every Monday.

"How do I do what?" asked the placid Aunt Valeria.

"Never get bored," said cousin Gertrudis, while threading a needle and beginning to embroider one of the three hundred cross-stitch tablecloths that she would bequeath to her daughters. "At times I believe you have a secret lover full of audacity."

Aunt Valeria laughed. They say she had a clear, challenging laugh, the envy of many.

"I have one every night," she answered.

"As if there were somewhere to get them from," said cousin Gertrudis, hypnotically following the to and fro of her needle.

"There is," answered Aunt Valeria, crossing her smooth hands in her lap.

"In this town of only four available and appropriate guys?" asked cousin Gertrudis, making a knot.

"In my own head," asserted the other, as she threw back her head in that gesture which was so her own that from then on, her cousin was able to see it as something more than just a strange habit.

"You need only close your eyes," Aunt Valeria went on, not opening hers, "and make of your husband whoever most appeals to you: Pedro Armendáriz or Humphrey Bogart, Manolete or the governor, your best friend's husband or your husband's best friend, the merchant who sells squash or the millionaire benefactor of an old-age home. Whoever you want, to desire him in a different way. And you'll never be bored. The only risk is that at the end your lovers may notice the clouds in your eyes. But this is easy to avoid, because you scare them away with your hand and return to kiss your husband, who surely loves you as though you were Ninón Sevilla or Greta Garbo, María Victoria or the teenage girl blossoming in the house next door. You kiss your husband, you curl up against his body on dangerous nights, and you let yourself dream. . . ."

They say this is what Aunt Valeria always did, and because of this she lived a long, happy life. The truth is that she died in her sleep, with her head thrown back and an autograph of the singer Agustín Lara under her pillow.

Aunt Fernanda

Staring blankly at the patio on a rainy day like so many others, Aunt Fernanda finally figured out the exact cause of her being off balance: it was her rhythm. It was that, because she had all the rest where it should be. But it was that damned rhythm that put her off-kilter. The cadence, that indecipherable, insignificant something that makes someone walk a certain way, speak in a certain tone, look with a certain pause, caress with a certain exactitude.

If she had had a fifth of a brain to foresee this mess, she never would have entered into it. But who knows where her head was that day, or where her father got that rot about man's being, above all, a rational being. Or maybe it was that when he said "man," he meant only man and not woman.

She was very upset, because she had never anticipated such a commotion. Once she had dreamed of things that were beyond the peace of her thirty walls and her feather bed, but she never had the time to follow up on such frightful ideas. She had a lot to do, and when she didn't, she invented it. She had to teach catechism to poor children and sewing to their poor mothers; she had to organize the Red Cross charity drive and dance at the charity balls; she had to embroider napkins for when her daughters grew up and married, and until they married, she had to make them costumes to wear to the school masquerade parties. She had to take her son to look for lake salamanders in the afternoons, help with arithmetic homework, and know she failed when she helped with the English. Also, she had to play bridge with some girlfriends and go to lectures with others. And as if that were not enough, she made dessert for every meal, watched that the soup had enough white wine in it, that the meat wasn't overcooked, that the rice got fluffy but not sticky, that the sauces were neither too spicy nor too bland, and that the cheese was served alongside the grapes. In those days, husbands ate lunch at home and then took a nap, so that the eternity of the day did not weigh them down by midafternoon. Back then, there were unhurried breakfasts and nighttime delights like sugared bread and *café con leche.*

To manage all these things without confusion and be, incidentally, a good-natured woman was something that any husband had the right to ask of his wife. So Aunt Fernanda didn't even think herself heroic. She had protection, laughter, and sufficient pleasures. Frequently, when she watched her children sleep and her husband read, it seemed to her that she had *more* than her share of blessings.

Should she have wanted anything more than that tranquil well-being? Not on your life. To her, the rhythm had fallen from heaven. Or from hell? She wondered, furious with her disorder.

She spent the entire nine-o'clock mass arguing with God

about her disaster. It wasn't fair. So many old-maid cousins, and she with a mess in her whole body. She never asked forgiveness. What fault was it of hers that it had occurred to Divine Providence to exaggerate her infinite mercy? She didn't need another punishment. She was not afraid of anything; what was happening to her was already her penitence and her other world. She was sure that by the time she died, she would not have the energy for any type of life, let alone the eternal one.

Her encounters with the cadence left her worn out. It was so complicated to make love in basements and on rooftops, to meet in gloomy places and solitary nooks in this city so full of darkness and crannies that they could not have been there by chance. How were you to know if a church's stairs were safe, or the floor of a cave, when at any time it was possible that someone would feel like getting drunk or reciting a Rosary?

They were always in danger, always getting lost. First from the others, then from themselves. When they said good-bye, she was sure that she would not want to see him again, that she had used up all her need for him, that there was nothing better than to return home ready to love the others with all the vehemence that the craziness left inside her. And she went back home tolerant, incapable of teaching the children to brush their teeth, ready to tell them stories and sing songs until they entered into the peace of the guardian angel. She returned home enlightened, enlightened she got into bed, and everything, even her husband's desire, enlightened her.

Affection never gets used up, she thought. Who would have imagined that one could use up affection?

She was never as generous as in that time. In that time she stayed with the two children the cook left her with to go after her own cadence, in that time her cousin Carmen got sick with sadness and went to face an insane asylum from which Fernanda removed her, first to take care of her and later to cure her. In that time her cousin Julieta had the singular and terrifying idea to save the country, fighting in the mountains. Aunt Fernanda also took charge of cousin Julieta's children.

"We have divided up the work," she would say, when anyone tried to criticize the clandestine Julieta.

Aunt Fernanda had time for everything, even to listen to her husband plan another business and make his daily pronouncement on the destructive state in which the irresponsible, abusive, and corrupt government of the republic found itself.

"Their first mistake: being a republic," he said. "Instead of being grateful for the wisdom of Emperor Iturbide* and protecting it forever like a flourishing empire."

"Yes, my love," Fernanda knew to answer, with the voice of an angel. She was not going to discuss politics when her life was busy with much more important matters.

Little by little, she grew accustomed to her disorder. She gave up daily mass for the one on Sundays, she liberated the children from studying their catechism and left to her sister the responsibility for the sewing class. She spent afternoons with the nine children that her delirium had assembled, and the rest of her

*Agustín de Iturbide (1783–1824), Mexican revolutionary and self-declared emperor of Mexico in 1822.

obligations—including finding a good wine and scaling roofs—she fit perfectly into each day's work.

Who would have guessed it? She who so feared disorder was as grateful for it as for the sun. Even in her body one could note the generous chaos in which she lived.

"What have you got on your face?" her sister asked, when they saw each other in their father's house.

"Confusion," Aunt Fernanda answered, laughing.

"Be careful with the dose," her father said, sucking his cigar as though he did not have cancer. He was a cheerful man; he was the best protector.

"It isn't always up to me," she responded, hugging him.

And in truth, it wasn't always up to her. When the owner of the cadence had the good fortune to disappear, the overdose of confusion nearly killed her. One fine day, the gentleman entered in the curve of indifference and passed like vertigo from addiction to disenchantment, from necessity to abandon, from knowing her like the back of his hand to forgetting her like the back of his hand. Then her disorder lost its logic, and poor Aunt Fernanda's life fell into the horrifying chaos of days without a trace. One after another, they culminated in the biggest head cold any woman had endured. She spent hours with her head under a pillow, crying as though coughing, blowing her nose and cursing like a drunkard. Thank heavens it occurred to her husband just then to found a democratic party to oppose the insolent National Revolutionary Party—a party worthy of people like him and his distressed, very decent friends. Therefore it did not occur to him to look too deeply into the ills of his wife, whom he'd seen go crazy as a raccoon a short time before, anyway. He thus proved the theory that his father and grandfather, ardent readers of Schopenhauer, had discovered clearly in the philosopher: the causes and certainties of the lack of brains in women.

He thought about all this while his house, still governed by the inertia of the times in which Aunt Fernanda lived inflamed and fevered, ran smoothly and without a hitch. There were always towels on the towel racks and buttons on his shirts, Veracruz coffee for his breakfast and Cuban cigars in his desk drawer. The children had new uniforms and newly covered books. The cook, the chambermaid, the nanny, the servant boy, the chauffeur, and the gardener had recently filed away the asperities that living together creates, and even Felipita, the old hunchback who still believed herself Fernanda's nanny, was amused by the sweetness of the secrets she told her.

More than a month passed in this way. Aunt Fernanda's bedroom smelled of confinement and belladonna; she, of salt and bait. Her eyes had grown like toads, and four wrinkles appeared on her forehead. The children grew tired of doing as they pleased, the cook fought to death with the chauffeur, Fernanda's husband finished founding the party, and they started urging her to make conversation and go to bed early. The director of the Red Cross called to ask for financial help, her sister wanted to take a break from teaching the sewing classes, and as if that did not suffice, her papa sent someone to say that cancer patients end up dead, and that later she would miss him more than anyone. All this made Aunt Fernanda cry with the same ferocity as on the first day. She passed twelve consecutive hours amid snot and tears. Around seven at night, Felipita prepared her a tea of orange blossoms, linden blossoms, and valerian, in a dose for an extreme case, and put her to sleep until Divine Providence took pity on her.

One morning Aunt Fernanda opened her eyes and was surprised by relief. She had slept for nights without grinding her teeth, without dreaming of dead fish, without suffocating. Her eyes were dry and she wanted to pee, properly, for the first time in ages. She spent half an hour bathing, and upon emerging, with wet and lustrous skin, she saw her face in the mirror and winked. Later, she went down to have breakfast with her family, who, with pleasure, found it wise to forgive her that the bread may have been stale because the chauffeur had changed bread shops, to avoid the one the cook told him to go to, because who was she to send him?

Upon completing the early-morning chores, Aunt Fernanda went to mass as in the good old days.

"You are going to owe me eternal life," she told the Most Holy Trinity.

Aunt Carmen

When Aunt Carmen found out that her husband had fallen prisoner to other perfumes and another embrace, she promptly gave him up for dead. Because not in vain had she lived with him for fifteen years; she knew him inside out, and on the long and pointless list of his qualities and defects, his vocation as a womanizer had never appeared. Carmen was always sure that her husband would die before bothering to become one. That he would take the time to learn the habits, the birthday, the precise aversions and inescapable addictions of another woman seemed more than impossible. Her husband could waste time and stay out late playing cards and endlessly repairing the political conditions of politics itself, but waste it trying to understand another woman, please her, listen to her? This was as incredible as it was intolerable. Anyway, gossip is gossip, and that uncertain truth pained her like a curse. So after putting herself in mourning, acting as if she didn't see him, she started not worrying anymore about his shirts, his suits, the shine of his shoes, his pajamas, his breakfast, and little by little, even his children. She erased him from the world with such precision that not only her mother-in-law and her sister-in-law but even her own mother agreed they should take her to an insane asylum.

And there she ended up, without too much resistance. The children stayed at the home of her cousin Fernanda, who in those days had so many troubles in her heart that to air it out she left its doors open, and everyone could get in to ask for favors and affection without even knocking.

Aunt Fernanda was Aunt Carmen's only visitor at the insane asylum. The only one who might have stayed there herself apart from Carmen's mother, who couldn't stop crying about her grandchildren and biting her nails, at sixty-five years old, desperate because her daughter didn't have the courage and good sense to stay with them, as if all men didn't do the same thing.

Aunt Fernanda, who in those days lived in a trance of loving two gentlemen at the same time, went to the asylum sure that with the slight loosening of a screw she had more than four good reasons to stay there herself. In order not to run that risk, she always brought along many manual tasks to keep herself and her unhappy cousin Carmen busy.

At first, since Aunt Carmen was dazed and slow, the only thing they did was thread a string with one hundred beads and tie the necklace that would later be sold at a store designated to earn money for the poor crazies in San Cosme. The asylum was a horrible place, where no sane person could remain so for more than ten minutes. While they were counting beads, it happened that Aunt Fernanda couldn't stand it anymore and told Aunt Carmen of her equally frightful sorrow.

"You grieve because you have too many or too few. That which devastates is the norm. You are seen badly for having less than one husband, but for your consolation, you are seen worse for having more than one. As if affection could be used up. You can't use up your affection, Carmen," said Aunt Fernanda. "And you are no crazier than I am. So let's get out of here."

She took her out of the asylum that very afternoon.

That was how Aunt Carmen came to be installed in her cousin Fernanda's house and returned to the street and to her children. They had grown so much in six months that merely by seeing them she regained half her good sense. How could she have lost herself from these children for so many days? She played with them, being a horse, a cow, a queen, a dog, a fairy godmother, a bull, and a rotten egg. She forgot they were the offspring of The Deceased, as she called her husband, and at night for the first time she slept just like a teenager.

She and Aunt Fernanda talked in the mornings. Little by little Aunt Carmen began remembering how to cook red rice and how many cloves of garlic the spaghetti sauce took. One day she spent hours embroidering the saying that she had learned from a crazy woman in the asylum, and of which only that morning she had understood the meaning: "Don't ruin the present mourning the past or worrying about the future." She gave the embroidery to her cousin with a kiss filled with more compassion than pure gratitude.

"It must be debilitating to love twice as much," Carmen thought, when she saw Fernanda fall asleep like a cat in any corner at any hour of the day. One of these times, watching Fernanda sleep like one finally breathing for herself, Carmen revived her husband and found herself murmuring:

"Poor Manuel."

The next day, she awakened compelled to sing "To Love You," and after dressing the children and combing their hair with the same efficiency as back in her good days, she sent them to school and spent three hours putting on face cream, combing her hair, curling her lashes, choosing a dress from among the ten that Fernanda offered her.

"You are right," Carmen said. "Affection doesn't get used up. You don't use up affection. That's why Manuel told me he loved me as much as the other one. How ghastly! But also—what do I care? Why should I go crazy with gossip, if I'm in my house making good noises, not one more or less than those Divine Providence apportioned to me. If Manuel has room for more, God bless him. I don't want more, Fernanda. But neither do I want less. Not one less."

Carmen gave this entire speech while Fernanda gathered up her cousin's hair and inserted a gold wire into each earlobe. Then Carmen went to look for Manuel to let him know that in her house there would be soup at midday and at any hour of the night. Manuel then met the greediest mouth and the sanest gaze he had ever seen.

They ate soup.

Aunt Isabel

The day her father died, Aunt Isabel Cobián lost faith in all unearthly power. When the illness began, she went to ask the Virgin of the Sacred Heart for help, and a little while later, to ask Señor Santiago, who had in his parish a saint with such an efficacious appearance that he was riding on horseback. Since neither of the two obliged by interceding for the health of her father, Isabel visited Santa Teresita, who looked so good; Santo Domingo, who was so wise; San José, who, merely by dint of being chaste, should have everything granted to him; Santa Mónica, who suffered so with her son San Agustín, who suffered so with his mama; and even San Martín de Porres, who was as black as his disgrace. But since throughout the course of five days no one had interceded on her father's behalf, Aunt Isabel made her way to Jesus Christ and his selfsame father to pray for the life of her own. Anyway, her papa died as had been decided at his conception: on Wednesday, the thirteenth of February, 1935, at three in the morning.

Then, surprisingly to Aunt Isabel, the earth didn't open itself up, nor did the day cease to dawn, nor were the birds that made a daily scandal in the ash tree of the garden quiet. Her brothers and sisters were not left speechless; her mother didn't even stop moving with the grace of her lovely body. Worse still, Isabel herself remained perfectly alive, in spite of always having believed that this event would kill her. With time, she knew that the thing was worse, that this pain was going to pursue her through life with the same persistence with which men pursued her legs.

Her papa was handsome in death. His skin was whiter than ever and his hands were smooth as always. When everyone went down to eat breakfast, she stayed alone with him, and for the first time in her life, she did not know what to say to him. All she could do was settle into position against his body and place on her head the inert hands of the man who begat her.

"What an idea of yours to go and die," she told him. "I am never going to forgive you."

And as a matter of fact, she never did.

Twenty years later, upon seeing an old man, she thought that her father could be as alive as he, and she felt the need to have him near with the same urgency as the day after his burial.

At times in the middle of any random afternoon, because her husband hadn't liked the chicken with tomato, because her three children caught colds at the same time, or just because, she felt a razor-sharp pain in her whole body, and she began to curse her father's treason. Then she let loose a temper tantrum just like those she'd had as a girl, back when he advised her: "Save your tears for when I die, now I'm here to solve whatever's eating you."

She did not go to church. She married one of those men who

in those days was called a freethinker, and raised her children in the theological confusion stemming from a father who never mentioned God's name, not even to deny His existence, a grandmother and some relatives who did nothing but pray for the salvation of that father's soul, and a mother who, instead of praying to the saints like everyone else in the city, had long conversations with a photo of Grandpa and who on Sundays bought an armful of carnations and went to the cemetery.

For her own comfort, Grandma had Isabel's children baptized, taught them the sign of the cross and the catechism of Father Ripalda. Thanks to her, they received first communion and were not saddled with the problem of being seen as atheists. The children learned everything in the same way they learned from their mother to play Chinese checkers, read, and curse.

They were teenagers when Aunt Isabel fell off a horse. Nobody wanted to know why or where or with whom she had gotten on. They found her flung down by the military field, repeating a great deal of nonsense that her husband decided not to listen to. He devoted himself to kissing her as though she were a medal and staying near her all the time, when in the past he had been so busy.

Grandma called a priest; Isabel's older son became enraged by grief and spent the day kicking the furniture in the house. The younger son went to stay at the Church of Santa Clara, and the daughter took all of her seventeen years, lit a candle for her grandpa, and went to the cemetery with a wheelbarrow full of carnations. When she returned home, the doctor said that everything was in God's hands, and the whole family cried.

"Nothing bad is going to happen to her," said her daughter, with the smile of those who, in the middle of a downpour, find refuge in the corner of a doorway. "Grandfather just finished assuring me," she added, in response to the question in the others' eyes.

In a short while Isabel left her delirium and gulped from a glass of milk that her daughter had put near her.

"You are right, Mama," said the girl. "Grandpa is a saint."

"Really?" asked her mother.

"Really," the girl affirmed, recollecting the only Sunday she had accompanied her mother to the cemetery. She was six years old and knew half the national anthem. She wanted to sing it to her grandfather.

"You will do it well," Isabel had told her.

And while the girl sang, Aunt Isabel thrust her face in the carnations and whispered secrets upon secrets, pleas upon pleas.

"What are you asking him for, Mama?" the girl had asked.

"Delirious things, my daughter," Isabel Cobián had answered. "Delirious things."

Aunt Chila

Aunt Chila was married to a man whom she abandoned, to the scandal of the entire city, after seven years of life together. Without giving explanations to anybody. One day like any other, Aunt Chila awakened her four children and took them to live in a house that, with such good judgment, her grandmother had left to her.

Chila was a hardworking woman who had enough years' experience darning socks and preparing bean and bacon soup that setting up a clothing factory and selling in large quantities cost her no more effort than she had always expended. She became the purveyor of the two most important stores in the country. She never stopped bargaining, and once a year she traveled to Rome and Paris to look for ideas and free herself from her routine.

Most people did not agree with her behavior. No one understood how she had been able to abandon a man whose innocent eyes reflected his kindness. How could such an amiable husband, who kissed the women's hands and bowed affectionately to any good man, have bothered her?

"What it is—is that she's a whore," some said.

"Irresponsible," said others.

"A lizard." They shut an eye.

"Look at that—to leave a man who never gave you any reason to complain."

But Aunt Chila lived in the present and without complaints, as if she didn't know, as if she didn't realize, that even in the beauty salon there were those who did not approve of her strange behavior.

It was precisely in the beauty parlor, when she was surrounded by women who held out their hands to have their nails painted, their heads to have their hair curled, and their eyes to have their lashes brushed, that the husband of Consuelito Salazar entered with a pistol in his hand. He stood over his wife screaming, and fished her up by her mane of hair to shake her violently like the clapper of a bell, tossing off insults and recounting his jealousies, reproaching the lazy girl and cursing his in-laws, all with such ferocity that the calm women ran to hide behind the hair dryers, leaving Consuelito, who cried gently and fearfully, prisoner of her husband's tempest.

It was then that Aunt Chila, waving her just polished nails, came out of a corner.

"You get out of here," she told the man, approaching him as if she had spent her whole life disarming cowboys in saloons. "You don't scare anyone with your screaming. You coward, son of a bitch. We're fed up already. We're not afraid anymore. Give me the gun if you're such a man. Brave man of courage. If there's something you need to settle with your wife, tell it to me, because I am her representative. Are you jealous? Of whom? Of the three children Consuelo spends her time watching? Of the twenty pots among which she lives? Of her knitting needles, her housecoat? This poor Consuelito, who looks no farther than her own nose, who devotes herself to putting up with your nonsense? You came here to create a scandal in this place where we are all screeching now like frightened mice. Don't even dream of it. Throw your temper tantrum elsewhere. Get out of here—go, go, go!" said Aunt Chila, snapping her fingers and coming close to the man, who had turned purple with rage and who, without his gun, was on the verge of provoking a laughing attack in the salon.

"Until never, mister," finished Aunt Chila. "And if you need understanding, go find my husband. Good luck, and I hope you get the whole city to feel sorry for you."

She aimed him toward the door, pushing him along, and when she got him out on the sidewalk, she shut the door and locked it with three keys.

"These bastards," they heard Aunt Chila say, almost to herself.

She was applauded when she came back, and she made a very big curtsy.

"I finally said it," she later sighed.

"So you, too, eh?" asked Consuelito.

"One time," answered Chila, with a look of shame.

The news spread rapidly and liberally from Inesita's salon, like the smell of baking bread. And nobody spoke ill again of Aunt Chila Huerta, because there was always someone, or the friend of a friend of someone, who had been there that morning in the beauty parlor who was ready to prevent it.

Aunt Rosa

One afternoon Aunt Rosa saw her sister as something recently polished, still shining for a reason she could not imagine. She spent hours listening to her every word, trying to intuit where it came from, but she could not guess. She knew only that her sister was less brusque with her that night and acted as if she might finally forgive Rosa's vocation of prayers and stews, as if she would never again laugh at her unredeemed celibacy, her catechistic foolishness, her boring devotion to the Virgen del Carmen.

So she went to sleep in peace, after repeating the Rosary and dunking little butter cookies into chocolate milk.

Who knew what her first dream would be like that night? If anyone had seen her, plump and smiling in her nightdress, they would have compared her to a child of five. Nevertheless, that night an unsuspected dream entered into Aunt Rosa's curly head.

She dreamed that her sister was going to a masquerade ball, that she went out without making noise and returned the center of an outcry, the encouragement of a chorus of men who laughed with her, having no more to do than accompany the happiness that surrounded her whole body. The very happy one donned and doffed a mask like the kind made in Venice, one of many colors, with the moon at the crown of the head and a delirious mouth. Suddenly she began to dance before Aunt Rosa, who, seated in the main armchair of the parlor, stopped eating crackers. Such was the wonder that had entered her house.

Her sister lifted her legs to dance to a cancan that the men hummed, but instead of the knickers and lace of cancan dancers, she wore a tiny skirt that rose contentedly, showing her firm legs and her pubes. Above the hair she had painted a decoration of yellow, green, and brown leaves that throbbed as if at the center of the universe. And above a leg, shining and puffed up, was her tuft of pubic hair: wandering and free like the rest of her.

The next day Aunt Rosa saw her sister as though seeing her for the first time.

"I think I am beginning to understand you," she told her.

"Amen," her sister responded, moving her shining face near to plant on Rosa one of those kisses that women in love give because all the kisses no longer fit inside them.

"Amen," echoed Rosa, and she set about to mount her own dream.

Aunt Paulina

Paulina Trasloheros was twenty years old when she met Isaak Webelman, a musician who lingered in Puebla to await news from his Jewish relatives in New York.

He came from Poland and South America and was a different type of man from those among whom Paulina had grown up. A man with the smile of a woman and the eyes of an old man, the voice of a teenager and the hands of a pirate; capable of summoning enthusiasm like children do, and of chasing away happiness like the keel of a boat separates water. He was as ungraspable and attractive as his favorite music, to which he attributed an endless number of virtues, plus the principal one: to be called, and to be, Unfinished.

"In reality," he told Paulina, after knowing her a short time, "endings are unworthy of art. Works of art are always unfinished. Whoever creates them is never sure of having finished them. The same is true of all the best things in life. Goethe, even though he was a German, was right about this: 'Every beginning is beautiful, but one must stop at the threshold.'"

"And how does one know where the threshold ends?" Paulina asked him, thinking that even if she was being a stubborn nitpicker, she had no reason to withdraw her question. Later, while walking toward the piano, she began to whistle the main melody of Schubert's Seventh Symphony.

Webelman was known as a great musician, and when he arrived in Puebla, he accustomed himself to teaching a great number of students, a group commensurate in size to the veneration each townsperson had for anything foreign. Every time a maestro came from out of town, he had dozens of students by the first three days of his stay. Retaining them was the problem.

The musician Webelman presented himself as a teacher of piano, violin, flute, percussion, and cello. He had students for all of these, including one named Victoriano Alvarez, who started to learn percussion before becoming a politician as a more efficient means of making noise.

Paulina Trasloheros played piano with much greater understanding and style than any other female student; not in vain did her father lock her away in the upstairs parlor every afternoon of her childhood. At first, it was an obligation to stay there two hours, practicing scales until she died of boredom, but then later she liked the place. She grew used to the sparkling, stiff furniture that made itself comfortable in that parlor, waiting for callers who never came. She grew used to the embroidered shawl draped over the rear of the piano, the stenciled fans, the Saint John the Baptist who watched her from the door, and the pictures of remote landscapes that presided over the walls. She liked to spend time there, far from the bustle of the rest of the house, submerged in that environment that smelled of the preceding century and that allowed her the most modern of lucubrations and fantasies.

That was where Isaak Webelman came with his Unfinished, every evening, from six to eight. He liked to make speeches and Aunt Paulina liked to listen to them. At times he laughed in the middle of a thesis about why Mozart had used an E-flat major instead of a D minor in the Sinfonia Concertante.

"You are vain," said Paulina happily.

She had lived so long surrounded by overwhelming or irrefutable truths that she hated them.

"Better said, you are an unbeliever," answered Isaak Webelman. "Give me that D again that sounded like a leap."

Aunt Paulina obeyed.

"No, not like that. You are showing me what a virtuoso you can be, how clever, but not how artistic. It is one thing to create a sound with an instrument and something quite different to make music. Music has to have magic, and the magic depends on a few tricks, but more than anything else on good impulses. Look," he said, putting an arm around Aunt Paulina's waist, "you want to play this D with more emphasis, you don't know how. Apparently you have one finger and one key to do it with, but with the finger and the key you make no more than a noise—the rest you have to get from your head, from your heart, from your gut. Because that is where, with all exactness, the sound you wish for comes from. When you know it, you have to do no more than extract it. Pull it out!"

Hypnotized, Aunt Paulina obeyed. Grandma's piano played like never before the same "Für Elise" as always.

"You are learning," said Webelman, seated next to her. Then he kept looking at her as though she herself were Elise.

A shiver ran down Paulina Trasloheros's back. This man was horrible, excessive, outrageous. To exorcise him, she would have to commit a string of sins for which she could never repent. Not even when he decided to return to New York, where there lay success, a success that could not diminish the fury that would be the life of a great musician clogged up in a parlor in Puebla because of something as ethereal as love.

"You've always known which is my preferred symphony," said Webelman, traversing Paulina Trasloheros's back for the last time with the entreaty of his bold, heretical hand.

"And I always will know it," she answered while fastening her bodice, beginning to dress herself.

The musician left and found the success he sought. So much success that it was impossible to go through life without hearing his name on the lips of one foreigner or another. Paulina Trasloheros married, had children and grandchildren. She crossed more than one threshold during her life, yet she could never avoid the chill that ran down her back each time someone mentioned that name.

"What's wrong, Grandmother?" one of her granddaughters asked when she saw her tremble at the first chords of Schubert's Seventh coming from the record player—forty years after the afternoon on which she had first met Isaak Webelman.

"The same thing as always, my dear, but this time it must be caused by a virus, because nowadays everything is viral."

Then she shut her eyes and hummed, feverish and adolescent, the unfinished music of her whole life.

Aunt Eloísa

At a young age, Aunt Eloísa thought it wise to declare herself an atheist. It was not easy to find a husband who agreed with her, but by searching she found a man of noble feelings and gentle manners, whose childhood no one had threatened with such things as the fear of God.

They both raised their children without religion, baptism, or scapulars. And the children grew up healthy, handsome, and brave, despite their not having inside them the tranquility granted by knowing themselves to be protected by the Most Holy Trinity.

Only one of the daughters believed in the need for divine assistance, and during the years of her belated adolescence she sought help in the Anglican Church. When she learned of their God and of the hymns that others sang, the girl wanted to convince Aunt Eloísa of how beautiful and necessary that faith could be.

"Ay, daughter," her mother answered, caressing her as she spoke, "if I have not been able to believe in the true religion, how do you think I am going to believe in a false one?"

Aunt Mercedes

It was already late, and Aunt Mercedes continued searching for who knows what in the body of the man she recognized as the love of her life.

During childhood they had decided they would be together, but not even they themselves knew for sure where they had first lost the certainty that they were meant for each other. Often he wasted time lamenting that which he considered an unforgivable mistake. Nevertheless, Aunt Mercedes always told him that nothing could have been different, because even though no one wanted to believe it, destiny was destiny.

It was sometime after each of them had married, with fortune or misfortune, that they ran into each other again at one of those parties where, out of pure boredom, everyone might have wished to fabricate for himself another love. One of those parties filled with *pasos dobles* and cigarettes, one of those that inevitably ended with arguments between Arabs and Spaniards that were not about anything at all—the Spaniards having arrived in the city four centuries earlier and the Arabs eighty years back, so that their descendants, in reality, were all Pueblans in dispute.

The two saw each other from afar, they set about getting closer, and finally they met, at the table of some Spaniards who were already plotting to break a few chairs over the heads of the Arabs seated at the next table. In the middle of that chaos the two lost the use of words, held on to gestures once again, saw themselves connected unavoidably and unhurriedly, until who knew when.

Before that fight began, they left the party to go off in search of a path they had left pending twelve years earlier.

They found it. And they became old, going off to search for the path every time their lives grew narrow. Aunt Mercedes was always afraid that each encounter would be their last. For this reason she liked to converse, to steal from the other, so that she wouldn't forget it all when she returned home with an appeased body; to be able, during the unpredictable time they were apart, to reconstruct it all, not only her adventure but all their shared adventures since forever.

Each time she found out something new. In this way, she came to know even the color with which he lined his notebooks in first grade, how much he paid for the *perones con chile* that he bought outside the school building, and why he would have liked so much to call her Natalia.

One evening, almost nighttime, Aunt Mercedes Cuadra's greed was inflamed, and she wanted to know how it had been for him, that which men did for the first time on Ninetieth Street. He had never spoken of this with any woman, and he was slow in starting his story. But Aunt Mercedes ran her hand down his back as though he were a horse, and she got him to speak of that memory, just as she got him to undress sometimes when they had already dressed and were just about to leave.

Ninetieth Street was a filthy place, where even the streetlights seemed dirty. He went there for the first time with some friends who had already been once or twice, but no one was an expert. Some had gone one night with their older brothers or uncles; another was taken there by his papa because he had a face full of pimples, and to his father's way of thinking, there was no better way to get rid of them. Anyway, there were about seven of them, talking one another into being brave, woozy with that immoral, clandestine act.

They all went with the same one, a short, filthy-faced girl who never stopped chewing gum. She asked them: With clothes or without?

"Without clothes will cost you double," she advised.

They decided with clothing. He did not know how he even wanted to do anything when his turn came, but he went. The short girl chewed gum in his ear the whole time, and he swore he'd never return.

"And you never returned?" asked Aunt Mercedes, starting to dress, as jealous as if she had just heard the most impeccable love story.

"Yes, I returned," he said. "By afternoon I was already stealing money from my mama to go back. And I went back with the same one."

"Just like now?" Aunt Mercedes asked, falling onto him to bite and scratch.

"Only you don't chew gum" He hugged her. Then he tickled her ribs to make her laugh.

They remained like that for a while, a long while: laughing, laughing, until they ended up in tears.

Aunt Verónica

Aunt Verónica was a girl of intense eyes and thin lips. She was impatient, and the time spent in school seemed long to her. At times they punished her with her face against the wall, or made her sew the hem that, with a jump, had torn loose from her uniform.

Finally, in the afternoons, they let her play with her cat, Cassiopeia, an animal with the look of a queen and a disdainful attitude that contrasted with her gray stripes and commonplace coat.

At almost the same time that she stopped putting a bonnet on

Cassiopeia and turning her into the perfect mascot to climb trees, Aunt Verónica discovered the nights and their strange challenges. From the tip of a branch she went with all her brothers and sisters to a bathtub, and from there to a light meal and bed for each one.

She could not say exactly how it was that she fell into the nocturnal game that she associated with the ineffable Sixth Commandment. Perhaps because it was never clear, and it was grand, conceited, and dark like those very nights. The thing is, she stopped going to confession and stopped receiving communion on one First Friday or another.

No one gave herself the luxury of such things in the small community that was her school. Surely, she thought, because no one gave herself time for other luxuries.

They were taken to eleven-o'clock mass. They crossed Bravo Boulevard with shawls over their shoulders, in line, two by two, without permission to look at the obscenely smiling monkeys in their cages or to lift their heads to the top of the wheel of fortune and leave it there, spinning.

She always took advantage of this time to break her fast with a piece of gum, three peanuts, or whatever would signify a less grave punishment than the excommunication derived from taking holy communion with the Sixth Commandment abounding in one's whole body.

But after having made her fill a notebook, with "I must not break the fast," four times, Verónica's teacher walked next to her on the way to the park, watching carefully to see that she did not put anything in her mouth.

Then Verónica declared that she had not confessed, and she stopped at the end of the longest line near the confessional. Luckily for her, there were many girls anxious to confess the same things as always: deceiving their parents and fighting with their siblings. She let five of them take her place, and when the moment came for her to take communion, she freed herself from the confessional for lack of time.

She thought up these sorts of tricks for a year, but even with audacity like hers, she imagined she'd run out of them someday. For this reason, she felt a jolt of pleasure when she found out that a new little priest from the mountains had arrived at her neighborhood parish. He spoke a broken Spanish, and his uncombed hair inspired her trust.

The Church of Santiago was a plaster fright covered with half-chipped gilt and saints. The same mix of old rich and eternal poor piled up on its democratic and filthy benches. The confessionals were of carved wood and had three doors: the priest entered the middle one, the other two formed little hiding places in which a kneeling stool fit under the only window, a lattice directly above the ear of the confessor. There the girls kneeled, put their mouths against the foul grating, and cleared their consciences. Then they received a dose of Hail Marys and went on their way with the same restlessness, to continue fighting with their siblings and storming the pantry.

Aunt Verónica knew that the recent arrival was just in front of the confessional in which sat the eternal Father Cuspinera, who had baptized her, given her first communion, and who pinched her cheeks in the atrium while repeating always the same greetings to her mama. She could not allow herself to damage the ears of Father Cuspinera, the hoarse and round monsignor, domestic prelate of His Holiness, who was like a parent without children, like an uncle compelled to construct a church of the Virgin of Perpetual Help with the same stubbornness with which Verónica persisted in her nocturnal sins. The best one, she thought, would be the recent arrival. This way everything will stay between strangers.

She entered the confessional, dispensed with the Confiteor, and said:

"I sinned against the Sixth."

"Alone or with someone else?" the new vicar asked her.

Until then Aunt Verónica had understood that one could practice such a matter only with someone else. How could that be? she wondered, while answering, "Alone." Such was her surprise that she spared herself the disobedience and the other trifles and said softly, "Nothing more, Father."

Afterward she heard the penance: she had to leave the confessional, pray the Confiteor and then go home, stopping on the way in front of every pole she encountered, to give herself a bump to the sound of a *"Salve."*

She could not have imagined a more horrendous penance. She was ready for any pain that was as clandestine as her sin, but to go along bumping into every post with the mob of her laughing siblings behind her gave her more fright than going to tell everything to Father Cuspinera.

She saw him sitting in the facing confessional with the expression of a bored child, fed up that the afternoon was so much the same as other afternoons, sleeping between one devout woman and another. Suddenly he pushed open the door that hid half of him, and looked at the line of women waiting their turns.

"All of you," he told them, "you already confessed yesterday. If you are not bringing me anything new, kneel down, because I am going to give you absolution."

Without getting up from his seat, he began to bless them while murmuring something in Latin. Then he sent them home and reduced his work as confessor to the separate line of men kneeling before him.

When he finished with the last one, he heard the women's door open slowly. He felt a short body fall onto the kneeler stool and a young breath against the latticed window. He sighed when he heard the Confiteor recited by a voice that sounded like the crystal of his German wineglasses.

"I have sinned against the Sixth," said the sound, on the point of breaking.

He needed no more than to rise from his seat and walk to the adjoining door. He opened it. There stood the slender figure of Aunt Verónica, with her enormous dark eyes, her mouth like a challenge, her long neck, her short mane of hair.

"You, creature?" said Father Cuspinera, his voice like a church bell. "You don't know what you are saying."

Then he took her hand, brought her to sit next to him on an empty bench, pinched her cheeks, slapped her shoulder, smiled from the depths of his chaste past, and told her:

"Take a little look at the Holy Sacrament and go to sleep. Tomorrow, on First Friday, you'll take communion."

From that time on, Aunt Verónica slept and sinned like the blessed one she was.

Aunt Eugenia

Aunt Eugenia did not get to know San José Hospital until she gave birth to her fifth child. After fighting for twenty hours with the help of her whole family, she accepted the dangers of going to a hospital, since no one knew what to do to remove the child stuck in the middle of her belly. Aunt Eugenia was terrified of hospitals, because she was sure it was impossible that a bunch of strangers would care about people they were seeing for the first time.

She was a good friend of her midwife; her midwife always arrived on time, as clean as a just washed glass, smiling and gentle, competent and quick like no doctor. She arrived with her thousands of bleached-out rags and her pails of boiled water to contemplate the effort with which Aunt Eugenia brought her children into the world.

The midwife knew that she was not the protagonist of the story, and she limited herself to being a presence full of apt pieces of advice and even more apt silences.

Aunt Eugenia was the first one to touch her children, the first one to kiss and lick them, the first one to check whether they were whole and well made. Doña Telia comforted her afterward and managed the creature's first bath. All with a contagious calm that made each delivery an almost pleasant event. There were no screams or races or fear with Doña Telia as helper.

But unfortunately, this wonderful woman was not eternal, and she died two months before Aunt Eugenia's last delivery. Nevertheless, Eugenia installed herself in her bedroom as always and asked for her sister, her mother, and the cook. All would have gone well if it hadn't occurred to the child to take a swing that left it with its head facing up.

After some hours of Eugenia's pushing and cursing in private, all who dared passed between her legs to see if with their advice it was possible to convince the stubborn fool that life would be better far from his mama. But no one hit on the solution to that confusion. So then Aunt Eugenia's husband got energized and loaded her up and took her to the hospital. There the poor thing fell into the hands of three doctors who put chloroform to her nose to end the discussion, and do with her what best suited them.

It was only several hours later that Aunt Eugenia recovered her soul, asking for her child. They told her he was in the nursery.

There are still those at the hospital who can remember the scandal that ensued. Eugenia had the strength to strike the nurse, who took off running in search of her supervisor. The supervisor also received a shove and a string of insults. While walking down the halls in search of the nursery, Aunt Eugenia called her tasteless, pedantic, ridiculous, dim-witted, despicable, crazy, demented, possessive, high-handed, and exceedingly, exceedingly stupid.

She finally entered the little room full of cribs and went with no trouble toward her child. She thrust her face into the basket and began to speak of matters that no one understood. She talked and talked of a thousand things, embracing her child until she considered the dose of murmurs sufficient. Then she undressed him to count his toes and check his belly button, knees, weenie, eyes, and nose. She sucked one of his fingers and put it near her mouth, calling it finicky. And she breathed easily only when she saw him move his head and stretch his lips in search of a nipple. Then she cradled him, gave him kisses, and put him to her left breast.

"That's it," she told him. "You've got to come into the world on the right foot and the left breast. Isn't that right, my love?"

The head nurse had four or five years, five children, and one husband less than Aunt Eugenia. From the immense wisdom of her virginal twenty-five years, she judged that the new mama was going through one of the many critical moments of hyperactivity and arrogance that a mother needs in order to survive the first few days of nursing, so she decided to take up the offense with the woman's husband. She swallowed the insults and asked Aunt Eugenia if she might like her help in returning to her room. Aunt Eugenia told her that she didn't need any more help than her own two legs, and she walked like a ghost to room 311.

Eugenia's husband was a man whose eyes denied his incurable forty years, whose intelligence was evident even in his manner of walking, and who had such a love of life in his laugh and words that at times he seemed immortal.

He arrived one afternoon to visit his wife, laden with flowers as always, a drawing from each child, some chocolates sent by her mother, and the two boxes of cigars that he would distribute among the visitors to celebrate that the baby was a boy. He walked through the halls, amusing himself just thinking of the thousands of particular defects there were in hospitals, which his wife had surely encountered, this woman who was, in his opinion, strange and fascinating, and with whom he'd sworn to live his whole life, not only because at a certain moment she seemed to him the most beautiful woman in the world, but also because he always knew that with her, it would be impossible to become bored.

In the middle of the hall he was detained by the unpredictable mouth of Georgina Dávila. He'd heard her spoken of once, badly, of course. People thought she was half crazy, rich like all the people who were gossiped about excessively, and extravagant, because it could be only an extravagance to go study medicine instead of looking for a husband who would give her a reason to exist. Even the threat of losing the beautiful Vicencio property didn't matter to her, nor did the infinite pain it caused her mother to know she was amid the pus and wounds of a hospital, as though her family had nowhere to let her rest her bones. In truth, she was vainly determined to have a profession, as if she didn't already have everything. Even Father Mastachi had spoken to her about the risks of pride, but she didn't want to listen to anyone.

She only smiled, showing the straight teeth of a princess, keeping her eyes steady like those of a beauty who had broken so many hearts. She attained a soft, careful smile that she wielded against those bent on convincing her of what a lovely, altruistic profession marriage was, and a laugh that wanted to say something like:

"You don't understand anything, and I'm not going to bother explaining it to you."

It was clear that it cost Georgina Dávila too much effort to maintain herself in the place she sought for her life, for her to go and lose it before a vulgar new mother. So as soon as she saw the husband, she fell on him with a list of Eugenia's disrespectful behavior, and ended her speech by requesting that he control his wife.

"Look," said the man, with the brilliance of irony, "don't ask me to do the impossible."

She consented with her icy blue eyes to understand him, and Aunt Eugenia's husband fell in love with her coldness with the same inopportune force with which he had always loved his wife's warmth.

"I am going for your son," Dr. Dávila managed to say, extending a hand that did not feel like her own.

She had a palpitation in the site that she had taken care of with such devotion in other women, and she suffered the horrible pain of the arrival of desire in that same place.

Shortly thereafter she entered Eugenia's room, carrying a child with the baked-potato face that all newborns have, but which she suddenly saw as a luminous, adorable being. She put him in his mother's arms.

"He is perfect," she said.

"Forgive me for this morning's commotion," said Aunt Eugenia, looking affably at Georgina Dávila.

"There's nothing to forgive," Georgina was heard to say.

"I would do it again," Aunt Eugenia concluded.

"You'd have good reason to," Georgina answered her.

Then she turned and left swiftly to examine the sensation of ignominy that traveled through her body. She'd exchanged four words with that woman's husband and already it seemed like torture to leave him with her.

"I am a fool. I need to get some sleep," Georgina told herself while walking toward the room of a woman who instead of a womb had a painful volcano.

Near midnight she returned to where Aunt Eugenia searched for the baby that the man so like her maternal grandfather had engendered. Georgina's grandfather was the only adult she had seen naked in the shower where they used to wash together, her long-legged grandfather who showed her his penis with the naturalness with which he let her touch the large veins that hardened in his hands; her grandfather who counted her vertebrae under the water.

"You are a pile of little bones," he told her. "You should call yourself 'Little Bones.'"

When Georgina entered room 311, Aunt Eugenia was sleeping like an exhausted angel. Her husband hadn't dared to move his arm, on which she'd spent a long time unloading her untiring vehemence, until she lost it in sleep.

Georgina took the child from his lap and looked at it so as not to look at the man who was stealing her patience.

"They are a miracle," she heard his voice say in the semi-darkness.

"Completely," she agreed, hugging the child she carried.

Three days later, Aunt Eugenia left the hospital with her fifth child and half her husband.

From one day to the next, that man had lost the certainty of his solid bliss, the force that at one time made him immortal, the control of his days and his dreams.

From then on he lived in the hell that it is to pretend one love in front of another, and now nothing seemed any good to him, he felt comfortable nowhere, and an unpardonable nostalgia established itself in his eyes.

All the passion with which at one time he had walked through life left him, just like that, and he was no longer happy, and he could make others happy no longer.

For this reason, in the middle of a family dinner, his weakened heart could not continue life separated from those years, and Aunt Eugenia took him without the slightest hesitation to San José Hospital. Because that is where Georgina would be.

"Is he going to die?" she asked as soon as she and Georgina were alone.

"Yes," Georgina answered.

"When?" asked Aunt Eugenia.

"Soon, tomorrow, Thursday," said the doctor, biting her bottom lip.

Aunt Eugenia walked the four paces between them to embrace her. Georgina Dávila let her rock and caress her like an orphan.

One week later, the changing of nurses surprised the two

crying over the same cadaver. Between them they had stood vigil over his last dreams, they had taken off his tattered clothes as his eyes followed them, they had put calm in his hands and words of amnesty in his ears. As her final consolation to him, each had given him the certainty that it was impossible not to love the other.

"No one could be better company. No one was as unhappy as I, except Georgina," recounted Aunt Eugenia years later, recalling the origins of her long sisterhood with Dr. Dávila.

Aunt Natalia

One day Natalia Esparza, she of the short legs and round breasts, fell in love with the sea. She didn't know for sure at what moment that pressing wish to know the remote and legendary ocean came to her, but it came with such force that she had to abandon her piano school and take up the search for the Caribbean, because it was to the Caribbean that her ancestors had come a century before, and it was from there that what she'd named the missing piece of her conscience was calling relentlessly to her.

The call of the sea gave her such strength that her own mother could not convince her to wait even half an hour. It didn't matter how much her mother begged her to calm her craziness until the almonds were ripe for making nougat, until the tablecloth that they were embroidering with cherries for her sister's wedding was finished, until her father understood that it wasn't prostitution, or idleness, or an incurable mental illness that had suddenly made her so determined to leave.

Aunt Natalia grew up in the shadow of the volcanoes, scrutinizing them day and night. She knew by heart the creases in the breast of the Sleeping Woman and the daring slope that capped Popocatépetl.* She had always lived in a land of darkness and cold skies, making sweets over a slow fire and cooking meats hidden beneath the colors of overly elaborated sauces. She ate off decorated plates, drank from crystal goblets, and spent hours seated in front of the rain, listening to her mother's prayers and her grandfather's tales of dragons and winged horses. But she learned of the sea on the afternoon when some uncles from Campeche passed through during her snack of bread and chocolate, before resuming their journey to the walled city surrounded by an implacable ocean of colors.

Seven kinds of blue, three greens, one gold—everything fit in the sea. The silver that no one could take out of the country, whole under a cloudy sky. Night challenging the courage of the

*The Sleeping Woman (Iztaccíhuatl), a dormant volcano, and Popocatépetl, an active one, are both visible from Puebla.

ships, the tranquil consciences of those who govern them. The morning like a crystal dream, midday brilliant as desire.

There, she thought, even the men must be different. Those who lived near the sea that she'd been imagining without respite since Thursday snack time, would not be factory owners or rice salesmen or millers or plantation owners or anyone who could keep still under the same light his whole life long. Her uncle and father had spoken so much of the pirates of yesteryear and those of today, of Don Lorenzo Patiño, her mother's grandfather, whom they nicknamed Lorencillo between gibes when she told them that he had arrived at Campeche in his own brig. So much had been said of the callused hands and prodigal bodies that required that sun and that breeze, so fed up was she with the tablecloth and the piano, that she took off after the uncles without a single regret. She would live with her uncles, her mother hoped. Alone, like a crazed she-goat, guessed her father.

She didn't even know the way, only that she wanted to go to the sea. And at the sea she arrived, after a long journey to Mérida and a terrible long trek behind the fishermen she met in the market of that famous white city.

They were an old man and a young one. The old man, a talkative marijuana smoker; the youth, who considered everything madness: How would they return to Holbox with this nosy, well-built woman? How could they leave her?

"You like her too," the old man had told the young one, "and she wants to come. Don't you see how she wants to come?"

Aunt Natalia had spent the entire morning seated in the fish stalls of the market, watching the arrival of one man after another who'd accept anything in exchange for his smooth creatures of white flesh and bone, his strange creatures, as smelly and as beautiful as the sea itself must be. Her eyes lingered on the shoulders and gait, the insulted voice of one who didn't want to "just give away" his conch.

"It's this much, or I'll take it back," he had said.

"This much or I'll take it back," and Natalia's eyes followed him.

The first day they walked without stopping, Natalia asking and asking if the sand of the seashore was really as white as sugar, and the nights as hot as alcohol. Sometimes she paused to rub her feet, and the men took advantage of the chance to leave her behind. Then she put on her shoes and set off running, repeating the curses of the old man.

They arrived on the following afternoon. Aunt Natalia couldn't believe it. She ran to the sea, propelled forward by her last remaining strength, and began to add her tears to the salty water. Her feet, her knees, her muscles were aching. Her face and shoulders stung from sunburn. Her wishes, heart, and hair were aching. Why was she crying? Wasn't sinking down here the only thing she wanted?

Slowly it grew dark. Alone on the endless beach, she touched her legs and found that they had not yet become a mermaid's tail. A brisk wind was blowing, pushing the waves to shore. She walked the beach, startling some tiny mosquitoes that feasted on her arms. Close by was the old man, his eyes lost on her.

She threw herself down on the white bed of sand, in her wet clothes, and felt the old man come nearer, put his fingers in her matted hair, and explain to her that if she wanted to stay, it had to be with him because all the others already had women.

"I'll stay with you," she said, and she fell asleep.

No one knew how Aunt Natalia's life was in Holbox. She returned to Puebla six months later and ten years older, calling herself the widow of Uc Yam.

Her skin was brown and wrinkled, her hands callused, and she exuded a strange air of self-confidence. She never married, yet never wanted for a man; she learned to paint, and the blue of her paintings made her famous in Paris and New York.

Nevertheless, her home remained in Puebla, however much, some afternoons while she watched the volcanoes, her dreams would wander out to sea.

"One belongs where one is from," she would say, painting with her old-lady hands and child's eyes. "Because like it or not, wherever you go, they send you back home."

Aunt Clemencia

Clemencia Ortega's boyfriend did not know the vial of craziness and passions that was uncorked that night. He opened it like marmalade, but from that point on, his whole life, his tranquil coming and going about the world with his English suit or his jai-alai racquet, filled up with that perfume, that atrocious potion, that poison.

Aunt Clemencia was pretty, but beneath her brown curls she had ideas, and in the end, that became a problem. Because in the short run it was her ideas and not just her fancies that carried her easily to the clandestine bed she shared with her boyfriend.

In those times, not only did well-educated Puebla girls not sleep with their boyfriends, but it didn't occur to the boyfriends to even suggest the possibility. It was Aunt Clemencia who unfastened her brassiere when, from being secretly pawed so much, she felt that her breasts were tapering to a point like two weenies. It was she who put her hands under his pants, into the cave where men guard the mascot they carry everywhere, the animal that they give to one when they feel like it, and which later they carry, indifferent and peaceful, as if it had never seen a woman. It was she who, without anyone's asking her, placed her hands near the irregular vigor of that devil; it was she, the temptress, who wanted to see it.

Therefore her boyfriend never felt the shame of the abuser or the duty of those who make promises. They made love in the pantry while the whole world's attention was on Aunt Clemencia's cousin, who that morning had donned a wedding gown to marry as God commands. Once the banquet ended, the pantry was dark and silent. It smelled of spices and nuts, of Oaxacan chocolate and ancho peppers, of vanilla and olives, of sponge cake and codfish. Music could be heard from afar, punctuated with shouts that the newlyweds should kiss, that the bouquet should go to a poor ugly girl, that the in-laws should dance. It seemed to Aunt Clemencia that there could not be a better spot in the world for what she had chosen to have that afternoon. They made love without taking oaths, without the heavy responsibility of knowing they were cautious. And they were happy for a while.

"You have oregano in your hair," her mother told her when she saw her dance by the table where she and Aunt Clemencia's father had been sitting for five and a half hours.

"It must be from the bouquet that fell on my head."

"I didn't see the bouquet fall on you," her mother said. "I didn't even see you when they threw the bouquet. I was yelling for you."

"I caught another bouquet," answered Clemencia, with the nimbleness of a trickster child.

Her mother was used to this kind of answer. Even though they all sounded crazy to her, she attributed such answers to the mental disorder that the fevers of a strong case of measles had left in her child. She also knew that in these cases it was best not to ask more questions, to keep out of a mess. She limited herself to conjecturing that oregano was a precious herb, to which little justice had been done in the kitchen.

"No one has thought of using it in dessert," she said in a high voice, by way of ending her meditation.

"How beautifully Clemencia dances," her seatmate commented, and they began to converse.

When the boyfriend to whom she had given herself in the pantry wanted to marry Aunt Clemencia, she answered that that would be impossible. And she told him so with such seriousness that he thought she was angry because instead of having asked her earlier, he had waited a year of furtive perfumes, during which he built up his bakery business until he had a chain of six stores offering white and sweet breads and two others that sold cakes and gelatins.

But it was not for this that Aunt Clemencia refused him, but rather for all the reasons that she never had either time or need to explain to him.

"I thought you had understood for a long time," she told him.

"Understood what?" her boyfriend asked.

"That it was never in my plans to get married, not even to you."

"I don't understand you," said the boyfriend, a common, vulgar man. "Do you want to be a whore all your life?"

When Aunt Clemencia heard that, within a second she regretted all the hours, the afternoons, and the nights that she'd given to this stranger. She didn't even have the energy to feel offended.

"Go," she told him. "Go before I charge you for the fortune you owe me."

He was afraid, and he left.

A little while later, he married the daughter of some Asturians, then baptized six children and let time pass over his memories, rusting them like the stagnant water in the walls of a fountain. He became a furious cigar smoker, an every-afternoon drinker, an insomniac who knew not what to do with the dawn hours, an insatiable hunter of business deals. He spoke little, and had two friends with whom he went to the shooting club on Saturday afternoons and to whom he was unable to confide anything more intimate than the infantile rage that paralyzed him when more than two pigeons were left alive. He grew bored.

One Tuesday morning, nineteen years after the man had lost the perfume and the mouth of Aunt Clemencia, a Yucatec Indian showed up to offer for sale the best-supplied food store in the city. The man went with him to see it. They entered through the storeroom at the back, an enormous space filled with seeds, sacks of flour and sugar, cereals, chocolate, fragrant herbs, chili peppers, and other products for stocking pantries.

Suddenly the man felt turmoil through his entire body; he pulled out his checkbook to buy the store without having seen the whole place, paid the Yucatec his asking price, and took off running to the house with three patios where Aunt Clemencia still lived. When they told her there was a man at the door looking for her, she ran down the stairs to a patio filled with flowers and birds.

He saw her come near, and he wanted to kiss the floor upon which stepped that goddess of harmony the thirty-nine-year-old woman who was Clemencia had become. He saw her approach, and might have wished to disappear, thinking how old and ugly he was. Clemencia took note of his embarrassment, felt pity for his belly and balding head, for the bags beginning to grow beneath his eyes, for the convulsive, bored grin he might have liked to erase from his face.

"We've grown old," she told him, including herself in the same disaster to take some of the stress off him.

"Don't be good to me. I've been an idiot and you can see it all over me."

"I didn't love you for your intelligence," Aunt Clemencia said with a smile.

"But you stopped loving me for my stupidity," he said.

"I never stopped loving you," she said. "I don't like to waste anything—least of all my feelings."

"Clemencia," said the man, trembling with surprise. "You had twelve boyfriends after me."

"I continue loving all twelve," said Aunt Clemencia, removing the apron she wore over her dress.

"How?" asked the poor man.

"With all the shivers of my heart," Aunt Clemencia answered, coming close enough to her ex-boyfriend to feel him tremble as she knew he trembled.

"Let's go," she said then, taking his hand to go out to the street. So he stopped trembling and took her quickly to the store he had just bought.

"Turn off the light," she requested, when they entered the storeroom and the smell of oregano swaddled her head. He extended an arm behind himself and in the darkness retraced the twenty years of absence that had just stopped weighing him down.

Two hours later, combing oregano from Aunt Clemencia's dark curls, he begged her again:

"Marry me."

Aunt Clemencia kissed him slowly and dressed quickly.

"Where are you going?" he asked when he saw her walk toward the door, opening and closing her hand to tell him good-bye.

"To the morning," Aunt Clemencia said, looking at her watch.

"But you love me," he said.

"Yes," agreed Aunt Clemencia.

"More than any of the others?" he asked.

"The same," Aunt Clemencia said.

"You are a—" he began, but Clemencia stopped him.

"Be careful what you say, because I'll charge you, and even with thirty bakeries you won't have enough money."

Then she opened the door and left without hearing more.

The following morning, Clemencia Ortega received at her house the deeds to thirty bakeries and a grocery store. They came in an envelope, together with a card that said: "You are a stubborn one."

Aunt Fátima

Fátima Lapuente was José Limón's girlfriend for ten years. Before he asked her, she pledged her body full of fireflies to the man who had sent them into flight.

Everything started the night of a party in the country. At the end of the afternoon, they lit an enormous bonfire in the center of the house, one of the patios that four-sided houses have, with latticed balconies and railings greedy for light and fearful of the open country. The guests were seated around the fire after having tolerated a bullfight.

José Limón had a guitar. He began singing the story of a horseman who roamed about alone in search of his beloved, and that was all Aunt Fátima needed to fall in love with him. She had never liked the happy guys, so his overflowing sorrow fascinated her. She was seated opposite his voice, and she saw him move behind the bonfire, skipping: "All your life you wanted, my love, to play with two cards," he sang.

"You cannot play with one, my love, but you want to play with two," chorused Fátima, and José walked around the bonfire to plant himself next to her.

The party was at a ranch where, once a year, all the friends of the Limón family were invited, with all their children and if necessary their parents, to celebrate the birthday of the old grandfather, a man with both an accurate aim and a precise memory. Besides his grandson José, he was the only inhabitant of the only ranch left to his family after the recent revolution. That day the old man and his grandson made up beds in all the rooms and even in the stable, where the youngest children slept with the drunkards.

They set out dinner on the patio, and the guests ate with their fingers, snatching at the barbecued animals cooked between fleshy leaves of agave, under the earth. There was also *mole* and stuffed peppers, cactus leaves with onions, colored sauces, pulque, and *curados* of pineapple and celery. The old Limón sisters spent several days making little Santa Clara cookies, nougat, and sweet milk candy, to get rid of the taste of the peppers and salt before the afternoon, with its cockfights and bullfights, became euphoric and slow with blood, liquor, and curses. That night even the Knights of Columbus forgot their manners and, in the confusion, came close to allowing the women to stay awake the whole night, singing with any old man without having to marry him the next day.

For this reason, José and Fátima could go watch as a cow that didn't respect the night off gave birth. José and three laborers pulled out the calf, to the insurmountable horror that Fátima felt in her throat. It was still dark when they left the stable for the house. The stars crowded together in the sky, and she curled up beneath the arm of this surly man whom the dawn had converted into a warm, persuasive refuge.

Who knows what his exact charm was? Aunt Fátima could never clearly explain it, but she always knew that this thing of her fireflies had no cure, and that the vertigo they caused was worth watching her girlfriends all get married, have children, sew, and use the beds in their bedrooms full of lace and pillows merely to occasionally attempt the game that she and Limón devoted themselves to many afternoons on the untidy cot he kept in the ranch house.

"José Limón is unmarriageable," her mother said all day long.

"I already know that," she answered all day.

People said that he was aloof and distant, wrapped up in himself, irascible, egotistical, and arrogant. They also said that he had a strong body and very large hands, that he looked like someone who kept secrets, and that as the proprietor of factories and stores, he was bent on living with the obligation of taking care of the ranch and tolerating his grandfather's follies, as though life might not have offered him more comfortable and less dangerous paths.

So his courtships were long, but never as long as that of Aunt Fátima. After the first two years following his grandfather's death, which seemed like the only excuse for José not to get rid of the ranch and return to the city in search of a tranquil life and the girlfriend who had waited for him so many years, everyone began to wonder and ask when the wedding would be.

Only Aunt Fátima always knew that there was no "when" and that Limón was inaccessible, that he would never make a home for her or anyone else, that he had another battle in life, that she should not even lament having loved him undeniably since the beginning, because had it not been like this, it may never have been at all. Begging would have been useless—it would perhaps mean the loss of everything they had gone through. Because things happened to both of them together—things that had to do not at all with peace or the good sense that others aspired to, but rather with the war that makes a few solitary and restless souls.

They had scandalized everyone with their ten years of eternal courtship when the agrarians killed José Limón. At least that is what they said in the city. That it had been the agrarians, and no one but the agrarians, who hated him because he had divided the ranch among all his relatives.

"It was not the agrarians," Aunt Fátima said firmly, before going to kiss the cadaver that no one had moved from the floor yet. She kneeled next to him on the dampness of the tiles, caressing him with one hand and supporting him with the other. She lifted him with no one's help, as though she were used to the weight of that enormous body. She brushed his hair, shut his eyes, caressed his frozen cheeks for a long while. She asked the laborers to dig a grave under the ash tree near the house. She sent one to buy a straw sleeping mat in which to wrap her treasure, and she kept vigil over it as though she were an Indian, surrounded by candles and tears all night long.

The next day, she walked in front of the friends who carried him and threw him into the dark earth, as if the commands of the girlfriend were those of a widow with all her rights. No one—not his brothers or his uncles, not even his mother—could intervene in the order of such a ceremony.

Later Aunt Fátima wrote in her diary:

"Today we buried José's cadaver, crying and crying, as if his death were possible. By tomorrow we will know that he has never been more alive and that he could not die before me. Because there is not enough soil to cover the light of his body at midafternoon, or the strongest gale to quiet his low-speaking voice, José belongs to me. I entwined my life with his, and there will never be anyone who can take him away from my sight or my soul. Even though he pretends to be dead, no one can kill the part of him that he has made live on in others."

She never married. She did not want anyone else, and it never occurred to anyone to try wanting her. To children she seemed strange and enchanted. She had no offspring, took no part in arguments; no one ever heard her scream or laugh heartily. They never saw her cry—not in church, not at funerals, not at the theater, not at Christmas. On the other hand, they often heard her sing. May afternoons people took their children to leave floral offerings at church, and Aunt Fátima sang from the choir in her sad, intense voice. What might have been a run-of-the-mill ritual made the children hit the youngsters in front of them in line with their flowers; her singing turned it into a ceremony for the privileged. Even now, upon evoking her voice, the fireflies in other bodies take flight.

When Aunt Fátima died, fifty years after José Limón, they buried her under the same ash tree where he was buried. The night of the day on which she lay down to die, she wrote in her diary:

"I believe that love, like eternity, is a yearning. A beautiful human yearning."

Aunt Magdalena

One day Aunt Magdalena's husband opened the door to a courier with a letter addressed to her. Aunt Magdalena and her husband had never kept secrets, and the symbiosis of their marriage was such that either of them opened letters even if they were addressed to the other. Neither of them considered this a violation of privacy, much less a lack of breeding. So when he received that envelope—so white, so pressed, with the name of his wife written in a bold hand—he opened it. The message read:

Magdalena:

Since whenever we speak of the subject we end up crying and you get confused by the madness of loving the two of us with the same intensity, I have decided not to see you again. I don't think it will be impossible to get rid of my desire for you; sometimes one has to stop dreaming. I am sure you will not have a hard time forgetting me. Putting a stop to this turmoil will do us both good. Return to the duty you chose, and do not call or try to convince me of anything.

Alejandro.

P.S. You are right, it was beautiful.

Aunt Magdalena's husband saved the letter; he resealed the envelope and left it on the mail tray with the telephone bill and the bank statements. He was furious. Rage turned his ears red and made his eyes damp. He went into his office so that no one would see him, even though there was no one else in the house. His wife, the nannies, and the children had gone to the Cinco de Mayo parade, to celebrate the day on which "the Zacapoaxtla took away Napoleon's prestige."

Seated in the chair in front of his desk, the man breathed violently through his mouth. He had his hands over his forehead and his arms around his face. If there was anything in life he loved and respected above all else, it was the body and erudition of his wife. How could anyone dare to write to her in that manner? Magdalena was a queen, a treasure, a goddess. Magdalena was sustenance, a tree, a sword. She was generous, honorable, brave, perfect. And if at one time she had told someone I love you, then that someone should have prostrated himself at her feet. How was it possible he had made her cry?

He drank a whiskey and then two more. He hit a golf club against the floor until he ruined it. He stood under the shower for twenty minutes and when he got out put the most hopeless Beethoven symphony on the record player, and when his wife and children came home two hours later, he was feigning calm.

They had gotten sun, their hair was a little messy, and their cheeks were boiling red. Aunt Magdalena took off her hat and went to sit beside her husband.

"Can I get you another whiskey?" she asked after kissing him like a brother.

"Not now, because we're going to eat at the Cobiáns', and I don't want to get drunk."

"We're eating at the Cobiáns'? You never told me."

"I'm telling you right now."

"'I'm telling you right now.' You always do this to me."

"And you never get mad; you're a perfect wife."

"I never get mad, but I'm not a perfect wife."

"Yes, you are a perfect wife. And yes, bring me another whiskey."

Aunt Magdalena went for the bottle and the ice, poured the whiskey, moved it aside, wanting one for herself. When she had poured it, she returned to her husband, a glass in each hand. Magdalena was truly lovely. She was one of those pretty women who required nothing more to be that way than to get up in the morning and go to bed at night. To top it off, Aunt Magdalena went to bed at other hours full of passion and guilt, which most recently had given her a steadiness of gait and a trembling in her lips, the kind with which her type of angel earned exactly the touch of evil necessary to appear divine. She went to sit at her husband's feet and told him about the bustle of the parade. She gave him a complete list of who sat in the stands at the Spanish social club. Later she drew for him on a piece of paper a new design for a set of Talavera pottery that could be made at the factory. They spoke for a long while of the problems caused by the bean black-marketeers in La Victoria market. During all this time, Aunt Magdalena felt herself being observed in a new manner by her husband. He interrupted her frequently while she spoke, to caress her forehead or cheeks, as though he wanted to linger over her expression of joy.

"You are looking at me strangely," she once told him.

"I am looking at you," he answered.

"Strangely," Aunt Magdalena repeated.

"Strangely," he admitted, and continued the conversation. How could anyone in the world allow himself to lose this woman? He must be crazy. He began to get furious all over again at whoever had sent that letter, and also at himself, who hadn't even hidden the letter from her until the next day. His wife should find it during the morning, when neither he nor the children would disturb her sadness. Then he rose from the armchair, contending that it was already late, and while Aunt Magdalena went to put on lipstick, he walked to the foyer and took the letter from the mail tray. The table it sat on was an antique that had belonged to Aunt Magdalena's great-grandmother. It had a drawer in the middle into which a moth frequently sneaked. He put the letter there and sighed, happy to postpone the problem for his wife. Thanks to this, they had a cheerful and placid midday meal.

On Monday, before going to the factory, he put the letter on top of the others.

Aunt Magdalena had awakened radiant.

It must be because I am leaving, her husband thought.

And actually, Aunt Magdalena liked workdays. Who knew at what time or how she would meet that clumsy oaf, but surely it was on workdays. When they said good-bye, her husband said, as usual, "I'll be at the factory if you need anything," and kissed her on the head. She took a last sip of her coffee and a bite of the buttered slice of bread of which she always left a little piece behind, following who knows what diet regimen. Then she got up and went to look for the mail.

She found the letter. She took it to the bathroom adjoining her bedroom, still a chaos of wet towels and just torn-off pajamas. She sat on the floor and opened it. There were not enough towels to dry the quantity of tears that poured out. She was upset for so long and so vigorously that if the cook had not pulled her from the precipice to ask what to make for the midday meal, she might have turned into a pond. She answered that they should make mushroom soup, cold meat, salad, French fries, and cheesecake, without doubting or second-guessing herself and with such speed that the cook could not believe it. They usually spent hours putting together the menu, and she had infected the girl with her manias.

"The soup is brown, and so is the meat," said the cook, sure there would be a change.

"It doesn't matter," Aunt Magdalena answered, still possessed by the grief of a wake.

Her husband returned early from work, as when they were newlyweds and she got a head cold. He came looking for her, sure that the pain would have her prostrate, pretending something bad. He found her sitting in the garden, waiting her turn to jump rope in a contest in which her two daughters and a cousin granted her Olympic standing. She was counting her daughter's jumps, which were up to one hundred three. The other two girls held the ends of the rope and moved it while counting in perfect unison.

"Women's play," said her husband, who had never seen the point of jumping rope.

Aunt Magdalena rose to kiss him. He put his arms around her shoulders and heard her continue counting the girl's jumps:

"One hundred twelve, one hundred thirteen, one hundred fourteen, one hundred fifteen, one hundred sixteen—you stepped on it!" she screamed, laughing. "My turn."

She separated from her husband and flew to the center of the rope. Her eyes shone, her lips were enraged, and her cheeks redder than ever. She started to jump silently, with her mouth pressed shut and her arms suspended in air, hearing only the voices of the girls counting in unison. When she reached one hundred, their voices began to come out like a whisper, which she relied on to keep jumping. Her husband joined the chorus when he saw Aunt Magdalena reach one hundred seventeen without stepping on the rope. Cradled by that song, Aunt Magdalena jumped faster and faster. She passed two hundred like a flash, and kept jumping and jumping, until she reached seven hundred five.

"I won!" she screamed then. "I won!" And she let herself fall to the floor, rising a second later with the spirit of a flame. "I won! I won!" she screamed, running to her husband.

"Lucky in play, unlucky in love," he said.

"Lucky in everything," she panted. "Or are you too going to tell me that you don't love me anymore?"

"Me too?" said her husband.

"Husband, you are a trespasser of correspondence, and you used a terrible glue to conceal it," said Aunt Magdalena.

"You, on the other hand, hide things very well. Aren't you very sad?"

"A little," said Aunt Magdalena.

"If I left, would you be able to jump rope?" he asked.

"I don't think so," said Aunt Magdalena.

"Then I'll stay," answered her husband, regaining his soul. And he stayed.

Aunt Cecilia

An old lady died in the house next to Aunt Cecilia's. Aunt Cecilia saw the old one leave that box of a stone mansion so like her own, and remembered her conversing with her cats and covered in filth, as she had lived during her last years. The little old lady scratched her head, where at one time she had combed the bright curls still brilliant in the sepia portraits in the parlor.

She came and went from her house, crammed with ornamental Chinese vases and Baccarat crystal, viceregal paintings, lacerated saints, lamps of blue crystal, French oil lamps, little gilded chairs and armchairs with stiff seats and wide arms, glass cabinets full of porcelain, thousands of little tablecloths knitted in her bored youth, Persian rugs, china, brass beds with their feather pillows smelling of the dust of three generations, wardrobes of carved wood, Bull bureaus and inlaid tables, chairs of Austrian wicker, and the corridor with its stained-glass windows, the large collection of clocks with bells of all eras assembled in the parlor to mark time.

There, in front of the clocks, she passed many hours. There Aunt Cecilia found her more frequently than anywhere else, and there she stayed to talk with her about the things passing through her head, things that made the most attractive collection of tales that Aunt Cecilia had heard in her life. Many times they were tales without end that began with her narrating the frightful treatment the cook gave her plates, and ended with her describing the great beauty of the Emperor Maximilian or the idiocy of a boyfriend who called a painting of Adam and Eve, hung among the pictures in the anteroom to disguise its identity as a sixteenth-century treasure and perhaps one of the foremost pictures painted in New Spain, a "useless thing."

There were tales that spoke of things Aunt Cecilia had never heard the sane members of her family mention. Cecilia liked to hear one tale in particular that made the little old lady red with fury: the one about the misguided brother who got mixed up with a brazen hussy who bore him three daughters whom the lady had never seen and never hoped to see.

The little old lady spoke of this tall, very handsome brother who had made the great mistake of getting entangled with a girl from the streets, whom, of course, he didn't bring home. The brother died regretting his ruination, a prisoner to the frightful pains with which God barely punished him for his waywardness.

The old lady never would have allowed an evil passion to disturb her. One got rid of evil passions with cold water, with a rope tied around the legs during early-morning mass, and in the best of cases—she laughed through her two teeth—with fish soup and a glass of fresh oysters before breakfast.

"You end up nauseated by everything."

Aunt Cecilia's mother thought the little old lady something the devil had forgotten on earth, and prohibited visits to her house. One time Aunt Cecilia tried to change her mother's mind, describing how abandoned and purulent the old lady was, but she did not incite even a whit of compassion in her mother.

"It is scarcely what she deserves," was all her mother, a pious and charitable woman like few others, said.

In any case, Aunt Cecilia took advantage of every opportunity to escape to the little old lady's house and go through it, sticking her nose under the beds, trying to find out what could be kept in the armoires that made it so worthwhile to sit and guard them so. She could never find out, but the little old lady lived to guard them. She finally died, at the age of ninety-seven, from so much filth, so much pain, and so many belongings.

Her dusty bones went out one door, and by the same door her brother's daughters and their husbands entered, with their children and grandchildren, to take out everything to sell to antique dealers from all over within twenty-four hours.

"It was all her fault," Aunt Cecilia's mother said, enumerating someone's sins for the first time in her life: "For intimidating her brother. For driving her sister crazy. For saving and saving and saving, as though one could carry large vases into purgatory."

"No, Mama," said Aunt Cecilia, remembering the only time she had seen the little old lady cry, "it was the fault of the guy who didn't know how to recognize a painting from the sixteenth century."

With the passing of years and the changing times, Aunt Cecilia, an only daughter, married a talkative and generous man who turned out to be a disaster at business and a genius at fertility, so that in less than a decade he gave her six children and spent her inheritance. When all they had left was the house on Reforma, they moved to the outskirts of town and Aunt Cecilia opened an antique shop. She started by selling her family's antiques to the hordes of nouveaux riches in search of patrimony who devastated the city, and she ended up with a chain of bazaars throughout the entire republic.

When she began buying items to open a branch in San Francisco, California, an adolescent girl with bright curls arrived at her shop on Reforma, carrying in the trunk of her car a collection of old clocks, a blue glass lamp, a frame with the sepia figure of a woman, and the *Adam and Eve* from the sixteenth century.

Aunt Cecilia watched her arrive and felt like the oldest forty-year-old on earth.

"How much will you give us for these trinkets?" asked the boy who held the girl around her waist and kissed her every so often.

"Where did you get the 'trinkets'?" asked Aunt Cecilia, addressing herself to the girl.

"They were in my grandmother's house," said the girl. "I think they belonged to a crazy aunt. I don't know. I've heard her spoken of a little, and badly. That's why I want to sell them, they don't have good vibes."

"But you'll pay well, right?" asked the boy.

"Yes, I'll pay well," answered Aunt Cecilia.

"Should I keep them?" the girl asked, with a hint of indecision.

"No, child," said Aunt Cecilia, and she wanted to add, but only thought, Better in bad company than alone.

Because she recalled the image of the little old lady, among her paintings and cats, dirty and forgetful, promising her with the greed of a beggar: "If you come back tomorrow, I'll give you the little blue clock."

The brilliant little blue clock that she now held in her hands.

Aunt Mari

Aunt Mari had so much foresight that she bought a lacquered trunk from Olinalá, in which they were to put her ashes. And there it was, in the middle of the parlor, until all those who loved her had arrived to think about her.

Aunt Mari had a friend of her heart. A friend with whom she voiced her sorrows and wisecracks, with whom she shared several secrets and a great many memories, a friend who was seated next to the small chest without speaking to anyone during the entire day and night of Aunt Mari's wake. Upon awakening, the friend got up slowly and went over to the chest. When she was close, she took a vial and a spoon from her purse, lifted the lid of perfumed wood, and with the spoon took two bits of ashes and put them in the vial. She did everything with such discretion that those who were in the parlor imagined she had gotten close to pray.

It was discovered by only one pair of eyes; seeing them open in surprise, the friend gave an explanation to their owner.

"Don't be frightened," she told him. "She gave me permission. She knows it will do me good to have a little of her aroma in the box where the ashes of the others are. Whenever I can, I take a little of the beings whom I will continue to love after their deaths, and mix them in with the previous ones. She gave me the inlaid box where I save them all as a gift. When I die, they'll put me inside there and I'll be blended with them. Later, they can bury us or throw us to the wind, but we'll be together."

Aunt Rebeca

At one hundred three years of age, Rebeca Paz y Puente had never in her life had any sickness but the one that, from its beginning, seemed it would be her last.

Of the thirteen children she had borne between the ages of seventeen and thirty, five remained alive. She had buried her husband nearly half a century before, and seventy-two grandchildren now came and went around her bed. She was so ill for six months that every night they said it would be impossible for her to make it until morning, every morning that she would die by four in the afternoon, and every afternoon, that it would be a miracle if she lasted until midnight. There was nothing left of the luxuriant and smiling old woman she had become except the pale covering of a skeleton. She had been more beautiful than any woman of the Juarist* epoch, but there was no one left from that time who remembered, because all her contemporaries had died before the revolution against Porfirio Díaz. So she alone daily recalled the perfume of her liberal body—every day, and with the same spirit that, during the siege of the city, took her from her house to fire a pistol from night until morning and until the surrender.

She breathed ten times a minute, and seemed to have left weeks earlier. Nevertheless, a force kept her alive, fleeing from death as though from something much worse.

From time to time, her children spoke in her ear, looking for her diminished face in the midst of a head of white hair that was more abundant each day.

"Why don't you rest, Mama?" they asked her, exhausted and filled with pity.

"What do you want? What are you still waiting for?"

Aunt Rebeca did not answer. She fixed her stare on the colored leaded glass of the balcony railing in front of her bed and smiled as though she feared causing injury with her words.

---

*Referring to the patriot and statesman Benito Juárez (1806–1872), president of Mexico from 1861 to 1863 and, after deposing the French-installed emperor Maximilian, from 1867 to 1872. The revolution against the autocratic Díaz (1830–1915) began in 1910.

Among the grandchildren was the woman who sat next to her every afternoon enumerating her troubles, as if talking about them to herself.

"You no longer hear me, Grandmother. Or better, to hear bitterness, you do well to be deaf. Or do you hear me? At times I am sure that you hear me. Did I already tell you that he left? I already told you. But for me, it is like he is still here, because I go on carrying him. Is it true you lost a lover in the war? I would have liked it if they had killed him for me before he had the notion of killing me himself. In place of his hatred, I would have the pride of having lived with a hero. Because your lover was a hero, right? Grandmother, how were you able to live so long after losing him? How are you still alive even though they killed your man, even though my grandfather sent you back by blows from the place where your lover bled to death? They forced you to marry my grandfather, true? I never dared to ask you about it before, you who were so eloquent, so beautiful. Now what good is it? Now I will never know if the gossip they spoke about you was true, if you really abandoned your whole family to follow a Juarist general. Whether he was killed by a Frenchman or by your husband a little before the siege ended."

Aunt Rebeca did not answer. She concentrated on breathing and breathed long, disorderly sighs. Twice the bishop had come to hear her confession, four times to give her extreme unction, until from so much wandering in the throes of death her descendants grew accustomed to living with her dying.

"She is getting better," said the granddaughter. The thought that her grandmother might die made her panicky. She would be left without a confidante, and when love fails, the only cure is confidences.

"Ay, Grandmother," she told her one afternoon, "I have a dry body: dry eyes, mouth, crotch. The way I am, I'd rather die myself."

"Fool," said the old lady, breaking a year's silence. "You don't know what you're talking about." Her voice sounded like it was shaken from another world.

"Do you know death, Grandmother? Do you really know it?"

As her only reply, Doña Rebeca lost herself between breaths and troubled respirations.

"Why do you fight, Grandmother? Why haven't you died? Do you want your reliquary? Do you want to change the inheritance? What worry do you have?"

The old lady moved one of her hands to ask her to come close, and her granddaughter put an ear next to her stammering mouth.

"What's wrong?" she asked, caressing her.

The old lady let herself be like that for a while, feeling her granddaughter's hand come and go on her head, her cheek, her shoulders. Finally, in her broken voice, she said:

"I don't want them to bury me with the man I married."

Half an hour later, the sons and daughters of Doña Rebeca Paz y Puente promised to bury her as she pleased, in a tomb for her alone.

"I am leaving indebted to you," she told her granddaughter before dying the final time.

The following day, her celestial influence made her granddaughter's lost husband return. The man entered his house with a parade of roses, a litany of excuses, oaths of eternal love, elegies and entreaties.

All the gossips had told him that his wife was a wretch, that her ears touched her mouth, and that her breasts had been consumed by tears; that from so much crying she had fish eyes and from so much suffering she was as skinny as a neighborhood dog. But he found a woman as slim and luminous as a candle, her eyes sadder yet more alive than ever, with a smile like a magic spell and the aplomb of a queen as she walked, looking at him as though she did not have four children of his and telling him:

"Who called you to a funeral? Take your flowers and go. I don't want to be buried with you."

Aunt Laura

Laura Guzmán's husband liked that his bedroom gave onto the street. He was a man of careful habits and pertinent schedules who went to bed a little after nine and arose a little before six. He had only to put his head on the pillow and his unconsciousness carried him to a place where he remained mute all night long, because if there was anything that man bragged about, it was that he did not tire his busy noggin with unbridled dreams. He had never dreamed in his life, and he was certain that insane surprise would never befall him. He awoke a little before six and turned toward the Swiss alarm clock that he set with precision each night:

"I beat you another time," he told it, proud of the interior mechanism his mother had installed in his body. Then he heard the whistle of the fellow who delivered the newspaper, the broom of the man who swept the sidewalk, the early conversation of two workers on their way to the Mayorazgo factory, the gossip of women who'd gone out for tortillas, the screams of the neighbor across the street seeing her sons off to school, and the passing of the morning's first automobiles. All of this awakened Laura Guzmán from her recent agony and without mercy damaged all the dreams that she missed having before eleven in the morning.

In contrast to her husband, she was a professional insomniac. She liked to do errands when the house was finally quiet; to come and go between cellar and kitchen, kitchen and sewing room, sewing room and pantry, where every night she wrote a detailed diary account of what went on in her life. She had bought a series of notebooks, which she kept next to the cookbooks, to end the ritual of every day's work. Then it might occur to her to cut her nails, brush her hair, listen to a recording of the popular songs—played low—that her husband had prohibited her from playing within the walls of his house, make sure that each child was in bed and well covered, sit down to determine that no rats moved between the kitchen and the dining room, go out to the patio to bathe in the moonlight, or ruminate in an armchair next to the cat. The thing was to go to bed late, never before three in the morning; stir up as much as possible in the time of solitude that the night presented to her. Of course, at six in the morning she was a wretch who lacked nearly four hours of sleep to convert herself into a wife. But by seven it was impossible to keep sleeping, and then she swore on all the Bibles that from now on she would always go to bed by nine and bury her head beneath the pillow, trying to fortify herself while counting to seventy.

Not even that minute was peaceful, however. Outside, the war had begun at five in the morning and no god existed who was capable of halting it. Many times she had followed it from its first noise. One or two hours after going to bed, she awoke from the fright of a dream not written the day before, and she could not go back to sleep until after midday, bent like a pretzel under the sun of her shelter on the roof. In the bedroom, never. The bedroom seemed like a marketplace all day long; everything that passed by in the street passed on top of her bed; car, dog, child, vendor, drunk, whatever—one could hear it on the pillow like a public proclamation. And only she knew this, because only she had wasted time trying to sleep in that room during the day.

In the sum of all these times she learned an alternative vocabulary that she had been taught neither in her home nor in school, which was used by neither her husband nor her parents nor her friends nor any of the people with whom she lived. A vocabulary she learned to use so correctly that at night it gave her notebooks a tone of audacity and redemption.

In that language fools were called dumbasses, and only because of this they were greater fools, in the same way that bastards were worse, and worst of all, were sons of bitches. The language was not merely one of words but one of inflections. She lived in a world where the worst insults were spoken with gentleness, and for that seemed less vulgar expressions. In the street, on the other hand, anything could sound insolent, even the name of He who should not be mentioned in vain. Laura could not forget the sharp cry of a drunk at daybreak that she had in her ears: "Ay-ay-ay, my God!" The voice of that man entered into dream after dream of hers like the most burning nightmare. It was a strident, desperate, furious voice. The voice of an unhappy person sick of being so who, when he called to God, insulted Him, protested against Him. That memory caused Aunt Laura fear: fear and ecstasy. "Ay-ay-ay, my God!" It resounded in her head and she felt shame, because that sound produced an extraordinary joy in her.

"I am horrible," she said aloud, and filled her time with noisy errands.

Why did she live with that tedious, disciplined husband? Who knows? She did not know and, according to her nocturnal reflections, didn't have much cause to investigate it. She was going to stay there with him because she had promised to in church, because she was devoted to his children, and because it had to be so. She was no Joan of Arc, nor did she want to be burned alive. After all, it was only in her dreams that she found a better place than her house. And her house was her house only because the man she slept with gave it to her.

Among the various problems that this marriage of convenience caused her, one of the worst was to receive praise in public. Her husband was an expert at that. He could spend weeks away, visiting businesses or tidier women, he could live day after day in her house without speaking of anything important, mute from the bed to the dining room and from the dining room to the office.

He presided pensively over dinner while his children elbowed one another to ask for the salt without making noise; then went to play dice at the Spanish social club; and from there returned home to set the alarm clock and get into bed, culling a miserable "Good night" from his silence. Identical days could pass without his noticing even the color of his wife's dress. But God forbid when there was one of those dinners the men agreed would be "with wives," because then he watched her carefully as she slowly brushed her hair, imagining a good hairdo. He watched her put on a lace petticoat, peruse the wardrobe looking for a dress, put on the stockings he bought for her as a tithe for his stays in the capital, rouge her cheeks and paint her lips red and her lashes blue. He watched her grow taller in high heels of dark silk, and search for the little holes in her ears to put in the earrings he took out of the safe. Then, having finished the task of preparing herself, she heard him say:

"You could not have chosen better, you are perfect."

He covered her shoulders with a raincoat and took her by the arm until she climbed into the car.

On the ride there he told her how much he loved her, about his desire to travel with her to Italy, of the enormous problems created by fortunes, how pleasant her company was that night. That was just the beginning, and Aunt Laura was already almost used to bearing it patiently. The hard part came later: to be liberal with the liberals and conservative with the conservatives, anticommunist in front of Don Jaime Villar and pro-Yankee at the Adames'. Placid at the Pérez Rivero home and active at the Uriartes'. In every case, her husband declaimed her virtues in public, and depending on the preferences of the lady of the house, she was an excellent reader and a sensitive pianist, or a great pastry cook, a sacrificing mother, a wife of gentle and aristocratic habits.

Her husband always knew which of her qualities to exalt before whom. It was not hard. The city was dominated by a lazy, conservative spirit, and the people who were born in one flock almost never learned what was going on in another. In some homes it may have been impossible to accept the invention of lay education, just as in others the idea of speaking badly of General Calles* would be considered crazy.

One night they dined at the Rodríguez home, to meet some people from the bishop's office with whom Aunt Laura's husband had several business deals planned.

The Rodríguezes enjoyed the great prestige of having the archbishop, the bishop, the domestic prelate of His Holiness, and all the other mystic investors assembled there. They went to daily mass at the cathedral with their whole family, and had three children and were prepared to keep on having as many as God in

---

*Plutarco Elías Calles (1877–1945), president of Mexico from 1924 to 1928, whose administration was known for its revolutionary, and anti-Catholic, zeal.

his infinite mercy wished to send to the fertile womb of Señora Rodríguez, who, in addition to being a firm believer, was an exemplary mother who lived with a smile like a flower amid diapers, sleepless nights, and fervent prayers.

Despite the exhaustion inherent to such a new Christian, Señora Rodríguez had prepared an opulent dinner for the older Christians, and took great pains to dutifully kiss the rings perched on the hands of the representatives of the Holy Mother. She was of a sweetness that bordered on idiocy or, as Aunt Laura thought, an idiocy disguised by sweetness, so typical of her kind.

Aunt Laura heroically put up with the conversation about the holiness of His Holiness the Pope, and the theological explanations that made plausible the sale of some properties and the purchase of others that appeared to be owned by her husband, so that the government, which was so perverse, would not take them from the Church. The Church could not have anything but that the government would want to take it away. For that favor, which more properly should have been considered a pious work, the Church furnished her husband with a papal benediction, three rosaries of rose petal, a splinter from Jesus Christ's cross, a nail from the headdress of sacred nails, and five hundred meters of the twenty thousand that would be put in his name.

Aunt Laura's spouse was so enchanted by the business deal that night that he exaggerated his wife's virtues. She listened with great patience to the inventory of her Christian qualities, and in a few moments was even pleased to know that her husband noticed how generous she was in her dealings with others, the infinite devotion with which she attended obligatory mass, and the time she dedicated to charitable work. However, that which during the soup and meat courses described someone more or less like Aunt Laura had by the time of the strawberries and cream become an insufferable prig. According to her husband, she went to mass twice daily, prayed the Rosary at five in the morning and again at six in the evening, taught catechism, took care of one hundred poor children, visited a hospital and an insane asylum, had become the guiding light of an old-age home, and had so great a devotion to the Blessed Sebastián de Aparicio that sometimes the Blessed One visited her at night while everybody else was sleeping. Her husband knew of this last item because the celestial light of a halo illuminated the kitchen and in his bedroom he could hear the voice of the saint blessing his wife.

By this time, the cognacs had empowered the devoted throats of the bishops, and they were all ready to be dazzled by Aunt Laura's discreet piety. So having decided to put up with this torture until the end, she took refuge in dessert as the only possible hiding place. But unfortunately for her, the hostess's busy pregnancy had kept her from realizing that the cream was rancid, and a pigsty taste came from that dessert, under which Aunt Laura could not hide.

"Ay-ay-ay, my God!" she screamed, spitting out the strawberries, throwing her spoon, and filling the air with the furor and ecstasy that cry produced.

Doña Sara Rodríguez fell to her knees with tearful eyes:

"Forgive her, Lord," she said, overcome with emotion.

"He has nothing to forgive me for," explained Aunt Laura,

who with her now loosened mouth carried forth with the street vocabulary that had been tying her tongue all night.

Without pausing to take a breath, she shot holes through the list of her pious attributes and described her husband, the Rodríguezes, and the bishops with every single one of the memorable adjectives that the irreverent vantage point of her bedroom had lodged in the center of her entrails. Then she fled to her house and went to sleep in that room full of affronts and hubbub, not lifting her head during ten hours of oblivion.

The only business deal that the bishop's office agreed to conduct with her disconcerted spouse was the expensive negotiation of his matrimonial annulment.

Aunt Pilar and Aunt Marta

Aunt Pilar and Aunt Marta came across each other some years, children, and husbands after finishing elementary school. And they set about conversing as though they'd received their diplomas as studious girls just the day before.

The same people had transmitted to each of them the same habits, the same values, and the same fears. Each in her own way had made something different out of all this. Merely by seeing each other, the two discovered the size of their worth and the quality of their manias; they took all this for granted and began recounting what they had done with their fears. Aunt Pilar had the same transparent eyes through which she had looked at the world when she was eleven, but Aunt Marta found in them the lifelong vigor of those who have undergone a great many troubles yet not stopped to bemoan a problem but rather looked for its solution.

Aunt Marta thought her friend was beautiful, and told her so. She told her so because she had not heard it enough, because of the time she had doubted it, and because it was true. Then she sat down in an armchair, thankful that women have the privilege of praising one another without offending. That the woman with three children and two husbands who had turned her kitchen into a business to free herself from the husbands and stay with the children, that this lady of nearly forty whom she could not stop seeing as a girl of twelve, her friend Pilar Cid, provoked a devilish tenderness in her.

"Do your brothers still 'operate' on lizards?" Marta Weber asked. She had dedicated herself to singing. She had an ironic, passionate voice that garnered her fame on the radio and aches in the head. Singing had always been her relief and her play. When she turned it into work, everything began to hurt her.

She told her friend Pilar about this. She told her also how much she loved this man and how much that one, how much she loved her children, how much her destiny.

Then Aunt Pilar looked at Marta's wild hair, at her eyes like those of someone recently frightened, and she touched her affectionately on the head:

"You have no idea how much good you have done me. I feared that you might have overwhelmed me with the joy of power and glory. Can you imagine? How boring that would have been."

They embraced. Aunt Marta felt in her body the aroma of being twelve.

Aunt Celia

They met in the vestibule of the Palace Hotel in Madrid. Aunt Celia was asking for her room key and felt him at her back. Something was in the air when he cut through it, and for fifteen years she hadn't forgotten that.

She heard his voice as though it were carried by a sea snail. She was afraid.

"Who are you studying with your eyes?" he asked, touching her shoulders lightly. And again she felt the shiver that at twenty had pushed her toward him.

It was a Sunday. Aunt Celia was sucking on a lemon ice, just like all the other women with whom she fluttered around the plaza, making the sound of birds. He came near with the boyfriend of one of them and remained, introduced as Diego Alzina, the Spanish cousin who was passing through Mexico for a few weeks. He greeted each woman dazzlingly with a kiss on the hand, but upon reaching Aunt Celia, he tripped over her gaze and said to her: "Who are you studying with your eyes?"

So she held them high and answered in the glowing voice nature had given her:

"I still haven't discovered who."

They became friends. They went to play jai-alai every day at the Guzmáns' and danced until dawn at the wedding of Georgina Sánchez and José García (he of the García groceries). They danced so well that, after the newlyweds, they were the most talked-about couple at the wedding, and by the following day, the most talked-about couple in the city.

Back then Spaniards were like diamonds, even when they may have arrived with one hand behind them and the other holding a cheap valise, kicking quarters together to make a dollar, working at the counters they slept on at night. So when Diego Alzina arrived, unlike the typical Spaniard rich and noble (or so his cousins said), he put the city in suspense, depending on whether he departed or stayed with one of the girls who had learned to pronounce *s*'s like *th*'s when they were children, to distinguish the quality of their origins.

Aunt Celia began to weave a chimera, and Alzina forgot to return to Spain in three weeks. He was very happy with that faultless Sevillana who, by chance, had been born among Indians. This made her even more charming, because she had eccentric habits, like crying while she sang and eating with a heap of chilis nearby, which she bit between mouthfuls. "Gypsy," he called her, and he made himself hers.

They went out walking for entire mornings in the countryside that circled the city. Aunt Celia made him climb to the top of bald hills that, according to her, would turn into pyramids if only the crusts were removed. She was obsessed with a place called Cacaxtla, upon which one stopped to imagine the existence of a beautiful destroyed civilization.

"Devastated by your savage, irresponsible, and stubborn ancestors," she told Diego Alzina furiously one midday.

"Don't say it was my ancestors," he responded. "Because I am the first member of my family to visit this country. My ancestors have never moved from Spain. *Your* ancestors, on the other hand, Gypsy, were the destroyers. Starving Andalusians who, so as not to die amid rocks and olives, came to see what of America they could tear up."

"My ancestors were Indians," said Aunt Celia.

"Indians?" Alzina replied. "And where did you get your Andalusian nose from?"

"Diego is right," said Jorge Cubillas, a friend of Aunt Celia's, who was walking near them. "We are Spaniards. We have never mixed with Indians. Nor is it likely that we ever will. Or are you planning to marry your servant Justino, Celia?"

"That one's not an Indian, he's a drunk," Aunt Celia said.

"Because he's an Indian, pretty girl, because he's an Indian he's a drunk," Cubillas retorted. "If he were like us, he would be a wine sampler."

"You always have to contradict me. You're exasperating," Aunt Celia reproached him. "You and all the others infuriate me when you come out with your idiotic veneration of Spain. Spain is a country, not the moon. And we Mexicans are just as good in every way as the Spaniards."

"We agreed that they were your ancestors," said Alzina, "but why don't we agree that if something was destroyed it's a shame, and then give me a goodwill kiss to change the subject?"

"I don't want to change the subject," Aunt Celia said after a long laugh. Then she gave many kisses to that man who, for being so refined, seemed a Hungarian and not a Spaniard.

The following day, Jorge Cubillas and the other guests in the countryside predicted that the next wedding would be Celia and Alzina's.

So Aunt Celia's mama thought that however Spanish the boy might be, it would be better to send along her younger daughters to chaperone each time Celia went out with him. It was not difficult to station the girls at the Reforma cinema with three bags of popcorn each, and walk who knows where every afternoon.

"How well the Indian women blow without bellows!" Alzina said once in the bell tower of the Church of the Most Holy Trinity.

From then on, every day they found the nook they needed in the belfries. And they walked there holding hands and kissing in public the way all young people would do forty years later.

But in that era, even in the farthest corners of Puebla, people began to talk of Alzina's abuses and Aunt Celia's lack of inhibition.

One day Cubillas found Celia's mother mourning her daughter like a dead person, after receiving a visitor who, with the best of intentions and knowing that she was a poor widow without support, had the kindness to inform her of some of the stories that were spreading throughout the city, ruining Celia's reputation and laying waste to her future.

"It is difficult for people to endure someone else's happiness," Cubillas told Celia's mother, to console her. "And if the happiness comes from what seems to be a pact with another, then it is simply unbearable."

This is how things were when war broke out in Spain. The celebrated Spanish Republic was in danger, and Alzina could not find a better reason to escape from the happiness than that mishap calling him to war, as if to a less difficult pastime than love.

He told Aunt Celia suddenly and without offense, without hiding the relief he felt at fleeing from the need she provoked in him. Because his need for her was making him obsessive and jealous, so much so that, against everything he believed, he might have fully married her in less than a month, when in less than six months the routine would have changed him into a domestic bureaucrat who, from so much time spent keeping a woman in bed, ends up viewing her like a pillow.

He would do well to leave, and he told Aunt Celia so. She first looked at him like he was crazy and later had to believe him, as one believes in earthquakes during the minutes of an earthquake.

She went at him biting and scratching, with insults and kicks, in tears, bawling and begging. In any event, Diego Alzina succeeded in fleeing from the ecstasy.

And after that, nothing. For three years she heard talk of the famous war without anyone's ever mentioning Alzina's participation. Sometimes she remembered him well. She walked slowly through the streets interrupted every so often by a church, and she went into every church to pray a Hail Mary to relive the euphoria of each belfry. The horror provoked upon seeing her kneel before the Holy Sacrament, reciting strange prayers while smiling with a serenity unworthy of the mystics, became part of her ill repute.

"He might have done better staying," said Aunt Celia. "He just went to jinx a noble cause. Who knows what has become of him? Surely they killed him like so many others, for nothing. But it's my fault, because I let him go alive. How is it possible I didn't take out an eye, or pull out his hair, or his patriotism?" she said, crying.

Thus the time passed, until a Hungarian pianist, owner of beautiful hands and a tepid, distracted expression, arrived in the city.

When Aunt Celia saw him come onto the stage at the Teatro Principal, dragging the thinness of his childlike body, she said to her friend Cubillas:

"That poor man, he is like my soul."

Ten minutes later, Liszt's violent music had changed him into a great man. Aunt Celia closed her thirty-four-year-old eyes and wondered whether there would still be time for her. When the concert was over, she asked Cubillas to introduce her to that man. Cubillas was one of the founders of the Concert Society of Puebla. To tell the truth, he and Paco Sánchez *were* the Concert Society. His friendship with Aunt Celia was one more of the oddities everybody found in the two of them. They were different sexes, yet their brains functioned in the same way; they were such good friends that they never ruined it all with the baseness of falling in love. What's more, Cubillas had felt compelled to hire the Hungarian, whom he had met in Europe, because he was sure he would be a good husband for Celia.

And he was right. They married twenty days after meeting each other. Aunt Celia did not want the wedding to take place in Puebla, because she couldn't stand the smell of its churches. So she vexed her mother one last time, by leaving the city with the pianist she had known for only a week.

"Do not suffer, Señora," Cubillas told Aunt Celia's mother, caressing her hand. "They'll be back in six months, and the last of the loafers will have given up worrying about Celia's reputation and her future. The future disappears for married women. For that reason alone, it was good to get her married."

"You could have married her," said Celia's mother.

"I love everything but fighting, Señora. Celia is the person I love most in the world."

Aunt Celia and the Hungarian returned after a while. They spent the summer beneath the volcanoes and rains of Puebla and then resumed his work, traveling to theaters all over the world.

Not even in her wildest fantasies had Aunt Celia dreamed of something like this.

In November they arrived in Spain, where Jorge Cubillas awaited them with a list of the latest baptisms, wakes, and broken engagements that had shaken Puebla in their four months' absence. They went to dinner at Casa Lucio and returned to the hotel around one in the morning. At that hour the good Hungarian kissed his wife and asked Cubillas to forgive him for not staying to hear about the tiniest details of the lives of so many people he didn't know.

Jorge and Celia stayed up gossiping until dawn. Around six in the morning the pianist saw his wife come in, shining with memories and satisfied nostalgia.

In the beginning they had communicated in French, but the two of them knew that they would never know anything profound about each other until each spoke the other's language. Aunt Celia, who had great recall, learned a lot of words in a short time and spoke in sentences and brief, badly constructed discourses with which she seduced the Hungarian, who had nearly always concentrated on learning scores. They were a couple who possessed genteel manners and vast understanding. Aunt Celia discovered that there was another way to look for sustenance in the world:

"Let us say, less emphatic," she confessed to Cubillas when at nearly four in the morning the conversation finally arrived at the only topic they had wanted to ask each other about and talk about all night.

"I don't miss him with this or this," said Aunt Celia, pointing first to her heart above and then to that below. "When I find out where he's buried I'm going to go see him, just to insult him by not shedding a single tear. I have peace, I don't want magic."

"Ay, friend," Cubillas said. "Where there's a grudge, there's memory."

"You look happy," the Hungarian said when she got into bed, moving close to his thin body.

"Yes, my love, I am happy. I am very happy. *Boldog vagyok*," she said, bent on translating.

Twelve hours later Aunt Celia returned from shopping, toting an abundance of packages and frivolous emotions, when she heard Alzina's voice behind her. Her father used to say that time was an invention of mankind; she never believed that aphorism as strongly as she did now.

"Who are you studying with your eyes?" she felt the voice behind her.

"Don't get any closer," she said without turning to see him. Then she dropped her packages and ran, as though chased on horseback. If you turn to look back you will become a statue of salt, she thought while running up the stairs to Cubillas's room. She woke him from the deepest refuge of his nap.

"He's there," she told him, trembling. "He's there. Get me out of here. Take me to Fátima, Lourdes, Saint Peter's. Get me out of here."

Cubillas did not have to ask whom she was speaking about.

"What shall we do?" he asked, as horrified as Aunt Celia. "What can I do for you?"

While they trembled, Alzina collected the bundles she had thrown down, asked for her room number, and went to find her.

The Hungarian opened the door with his customary calm.

"How may I help you?" he inquired.

"Celia Ocejo," said Alzina.

"She is my wife," answered the Hungarian.

Only then did Alzina realize that his love for the Gypsy had endured in silence for years, and that it was more or less logical that she might have found a husband.

"I offered to carry up her packages. We are friends. We were."

"She may be with Cubillas. Do you know Cubillas?" asked the Hungarian in Spanish. "He is a friend of ours from Puebla who arrived just yesterday. I believe they still haven't finished gossiping," he added in French, in hopes of being understood.

Alzina understood *Cubillas* and asked the Hungarian to write the room number on a piece of paper. Then he gave him the packages, smiled, and ran off.

He knocked on the door of room 502 as though there were deaf-mutes inside. Cubillas opened it, grumbling.

"What a commotion! You are gone fifteen years and you want to return in two minutes," he said.

Alzina hugged him, seeing Aunt Celia over his shoulders, behind Cubillas with her eyes shut and her hands covering her face.

"Go away, Alzina," she said. "Go away. If I see you I'll damage what's left of my life."

"You must be Indian," Alzina told her. And that was enough to make her go at him, kicking and scratching with the same ferocity as if they had slept together for fifteen years.

Cubillas escaped. A horrible uproar came from the room, shaking the corridor. He sank to the floor with his back to the wall and his legs tucked under him. He didn't understand much, because the screams rose above him. At times Aunt Celia's voice was an avalanche of insults, and at others a whisper trampled by Alzina's Hispanic fury.

About an hour later, the screams were extinguished and a peaceful breeze began to seep from under the door. Cubillas considered it indiscreet to remain listening to the silence, and he went down to the second floor in search of the pianist.

The Hungarian was putting on his tails, he could not find his jabot, and he felt incapable of tying his tie.

"This woman has turned me into a good-for-nothing," he told Cubillas. "You are my witness that before meeting her I used to go out well dressed for my concerts. I have become a good-for-nothing. Where is she?"

Cubillas found the pianist's jabot and knotted his tie for him.

"Don't worry," he lied. "She went out with her friend Maicha, and with her, there's never enough time. If they don't get back soon, they'll catch up with us at the concert."

The pianist listened to Cubillas's excuse as one listens to a Latin mass. He combed his hair without saying a word and went wordlessly the whole way to the concert. Cubillas assumed the responsibility of filling the silence. Years later, he still remembered with embarrassment the parrot-like feeling that came to paralyze him.

The pianist was playing the final Prokofiev when Celia Ocejo slipped into the box where Cubillas sat. Seconds later, the whole theater applauded.

"A thousand thanks," Aunt Celia told her friend. "How can I ever repay you?"

"You can tell me everything," answered Cubillas. "That will be a good repayment."

"But I can't," Aunt Celia responded with her mouth afire, who knows why.

"Tell me," Cubillas insisted. "Don't be difficult."

"No," said Aunt Celia, rising to applaud her husband.

They never again touched the subject for forty years. Not until recently, when anthropologists discovered the ruins of a civilization buried in the valley of Cacaxtla. Celia told her friend during a stroll through the past:

"Write to Diego Alzina and tell him how right I was."

"Diego who?" asked her Hungarian husband, in perfect Spanish.

"A friend of ours who has since died," answered Cubillas.

Aunt Celia kept on walking as though she hadn't heard him.

"How did you know?" she asked after a while with her head full of belfries.

"You two," said the Hungarian, "will die fighting over a scrap of gossip."

"Don't you believe it," Aunt Celia told him, in perfect Hungarian. "I just lost the war."

"What did you tell him?" Cubillas asked Aunt Celia.

"I cannot tell you," she answered.

Aunt Mónica

Sometimes Aunt Mónica wanted desperately not to be herself. She detested her hair and her belly, her way of walking, her limp lashes and her need for things besides the peace hidden in flowerpots or the time passing with busyness, and so quickly that it scarcely allowed anything more important to happen than the baptism of some nephew or the strange discovery of a new flavor in the kitchen.

Aunt Mónica might have liked to be one of those balloons that children release to the sky, to cry over later as though they'd taken some care not to lose it. Aunt Mónica might have liked to ride horseback until she fell off some afternoon and lost half her head; she might have liked to travel to exotic countries or visit the towns of Mexico with the same curiosity as a French anthropologist; she might have liked to fall in love with a boatman in Acapulco, to be the bride of the first aviator, the girlfriend of a suicidal poet, or the mother of an opera singer. She might have liked to play the piano like Chopin and have someone like Chopin play her as though she were a piano.

Aunt Mónica wanted it to rain in Puebla like it did in Tabasco; she wanted the nights to be longer and more irregular; she wanted to swim in the sea at dawn and drink the moon rays like chamomile tea. She wanted to sleep one night in the Palace in Madrid and bathe without a brassiere in the Trevi Fountain, or at least in the Fountain of San Miguel.

No one ever understood, because she was never still for more than five minutes. She had to keep moving, because otherwise her fantasies would overtake her. And she knew very well that one is punished for them, that from the moment one begins to act them out, the punishment arrives, because there is no worse punishment than the clear sensation that one is dreaming of prohibited pleasures.

For this reason she very determinedly had a house built with three patios; for this reason she thought to put in two fountains and convert the back area into a guesthouse; for this reason she had a sewing machine that she pedaled until all her nieces could show up dressed alike on Sundays; for this reason she knitted caps and mufflers in winter for every family member, respectable or not; for this reason one afternoon she cut her own waist-length hair, which her loving husband so liked. So loving was he that to maintain her he worked well into the night, to return home with sick and tired eyes and the beatific but useless smile of a man who upholds his responsibilities.

No one has ever made as many or as delicious cheese biscuits as Aunt Mónica. They were tiny and big; she spent hours kneading, then baked them over a slow fire. When they were finally done, she covered them in sugar and, after contemplating them for half a second, ate all of them at one sitting.

"The bad thing," she once confessed, "is that when I finish them I still have room for an unfulfilled fantasy and I go to sleep with it. I shut my eyes to see if I can escape it, but no. So I speak with God: 'You left it with me, I swear to you that I've put up with a whole day of fighting. This one is going to beat me, and let's see if tomorrow you'll want to forgive me.'"

Then she went to sleep with temptation still between her eyes, like a saint.

Aunt Teresa

Aunt Teresa's lover was a man of smooth manners and stern eyes. He used one or the other, as the situation required.

He was as correct as midday or as unrestrained as the night sea. He had a winsome smile that almost never matched his eyes. He focused his eyes elsewhere because they were thinking about other things. Only once in a while did they join the radiance of his look, and then he was irresistible.

At least this is what Aunt Teresa believed. She avariciously collected each of these magnificent alliances, each sign of nearness, to contemplate them later like great treasures: the precarious moment in which he had said her name with need; the occasional sentence he spoke about the son they shared; the desperation with which he wanted to touch her one rainy night; the longing with which he kissed her after a trip.

She tried to figure him out for one hundred nights. He seemed ungraspable. Who knows, perhaps at one time she grasped him fully and didn't realize it. It would have been a blessing if she had known it at age eighty, when she deliriously searched the whole house for keys and ties.

They rendezvoused in a secret spot near what was then the outskirts of the city. Aunt Teresa Gaudín Lerdo was one of five women in Puebla who owned and drove cars. So while crossing the bridge of the highway to Cholula, she silently apologized to the other four for risking the good name of all five.

Her lover was named Ignacio Lagos, and he had a chauffeured Packard in which he traveled examining papers.

For the rest of her life, Aunt Teresa could not forget how she trembled when she got out of her blue Chrysler to enter the room in the Resurrección colony. She was fearful like a good Gaudín and wild like a good Lerdo. She was going to meet the man of her obsessions, dying of fright and feigning aplomb. When the door opened and behind it he stood ready to give up his gaze and his mouth to her at the same time, all risks ceased being that and the world was a scarab until both had protested their absences, their distrust, their hatred, their rocky out-and-out love.

Later, when she had just begun to cover herself in her abandon, he decided to go because it was already late. He had to catch up with the eternal enemy that stalked the minds of others: time. But Teresa stayed in bed while he—whatever the weather—took a bath that made her feel filthy inside. When he reappeared, shining and perfumed, Aunt Teresa jumped from the bed to collect the clothing she had strewn about the room, and dressed quickly, feeling the once again distant gaze of that man.

They went out to the street separately, trying to pretend that they had never seen each other. He had the keys to the place; he used them to undo the seven turns of the bolt and let her leave with slow steps that at this hour drove him to despair. He left two minutes after her, shut the door and got into his automobile with the speed of a fugitive.

One night they lost the keys.

"You have them," he said, looking at the ones she dangled from her hand.

"These are the keys to my car," she explained, shaking them before his eyes.

Ignacio looked so handsome fooling with his tie, with his expression of perturbed efficiency, that Aunt Teresa might have begun all over again.

"So where are they? Watch this for me," Ignacio said, draping over Aunt Teresa's shoulder the tie that had been a bother in his hands. It was a blue silk tie that felt like a public embrace around her neck.

His hands free, Ignacio rummaged quickly through his pants pockets and then among the tumbled sheets. There he found the keys, which he had dropped upon arriving, when no other future mattered to him but the fervent covering of Teresa. He made her leave. His car waited patiently like a horse at the disposition of its master. Ignacio waved a silent good-bye and stayed to lock up while Aunt Teresa walked to her Chrysler, passing through the darkness with the same fear as always. Not even the luminous memory of the sky at dawn, which she saved for that very moment to think about, took away her fear. She trembled. The party was over and she didn't dare hum a song. She saw her car still far away when she heard a voice behind her. A voice of metal calling her. She pretended not to hear it. With the very last chink of her inflamed body she regretted being there.

He can kill me, she thought, but this will happen to me because I am such a fool.

She was overwhelmed by a vision of her body flung into the middle of the street: inert, stripped, cold. She had never felt colder than when she imagined that cold. Her car was three endless steps away. The voice kept calling her. She felt hands on her shoulders. A vomit of horror rose in her throat.

"My tie, love," said Ignacio's voice behind her. "You have my tie."

He pulled the tie off carelessly, and Aunt Teresa felt it run over her neck like a whip. Then, without saying or noticing anything else, Ignacio Lagos returned to his car, which was stopped in front of them, and left.

Aunt Teresa reached her car, shivering as though she were naked. She drove toward the city, crossed the bridge, and went into her house. That night there was no greater loneliness than hers.

She never met Ignacio Lagos again. Many years later, when the good sense vanished from her restless old head, she began to dream of the Resurrección colony, of the eyes and demanding mouth of that insensitive lover. So she went searching for keys in all the sheets of the house, and there was no wardrobe that her desperate hands did not rummage through in pursuit of a tie. Her daughters agreed to put keychains and old ties nearby, and those who went to visit her knew they could not bring a better gift than a bundle of keys and a tie of pure silk.

"Now yes, sir," old Aunt Teresa would rant, with the two items in her hand. "Now we can leave together."

Aunt Mariana

It was very difficult for Aunt Mariana to understand what life had dealt her. She said "life" to give some kind of name to the mountain of coincidences that had settled on her bit by bit, although the total might have presented itself like a fulminating tragedy, in the exhausted condition she had to contend with each morning.

To all the world including her mother, almost all her friends, and her mother's friends—not to mention her mother-in-law, her sisters-in-law, the members of the Rotary Club, Monsignor Figueroa, and even the municipal president—she was a lucky woman. She had married an upright man who was engaged in the common good, the depository of ninety percent of the modernizing plans and activities of social solidarity that Puebla society counted on in the 1940s. She was the famous wife of a famous man, the smiling companion of an illustrious citizen, the most beloved and respected of all the women who attended mass on Sundays. Her husband was entirely as handsome as Maximilian of Hapsburg, as elegant as Prince Philip, as generous as Saint Francis, and as prudent as the provincial of the Jesuits. As if that were not enough, he was rich like the landowners of yesteryear and a good investor like the Lebanese of today.

Aunt Mariana's situation was such that she could live gratefully and happily all the days of her life. And it may never have been otherwise if, as only she knew, she had not crossed paths with the immense pain of spying on happiness. Such idiocy could have happened only to her. She who had proposed so much to live in peace, why did she have to let herself get in the way of war? She would never stop regretting it, as though one could regret something one did not choose. Because the truth is that the vortex inserted itself deep into her, the way cooking aromas from the kitchen enter the whole house, the way the unforeseeable stabbing pain of a toothache comes on and stays. And she fell in love, she fell in love, she fell in love.

Overnight she lost the smooth tranquility with which she

used to awaken to dress the children and let herself be undressed by her husband. She lost the slow lust with which she drank her juice and the pleasure she felt sitting for half an hour to plan the dinner menus every day. She lost the patience with which she listened to her impertinent sister-in-law, the desire to spend an entire afternoon baking pastries, the ability to sink, smiling, into the tedious sameness of the family dinners. She lost the peace that her pregnant bellies rocked and the hot, generous sleep that overtook her body at night. She lost the discreet voice and ecstatic silences with which she surrounded her husband's opinions and plans.

Instead, she acquired the terrible talent for forgetting everything, from keys to names. She became as inattentive as a deaf student and as difficult as people who are ill advised by indifference. She no longer had a purpose. She who thought herself made to solve minor problems and who bet she'd been created merely to fulfill the desires of others, she who enjoyed herself noiselessly with the plants and the aquarium, the unfolded socks and the orderly drawers!

Suddenly she lived in the chaos that comes from permanent excitement, in the jumble of words that hides an enormous fear, jumping for joy in the face of unhappiness with the feverish obsession of those who are obsessed by a single cause. She asked herself constantly how this could have happened to her. She could not believe that the recently met body of a man she had never anticipated might have put her in that state of confusion.

"I hate it," she said, and after saying so, devoted herself to the pitiful care of her nails and hair, to exercises to shrink her waist, and to plucking out the down on her legs, hair by hair, with eyebrow tweezers.

She bought herself the smoothest-ever silk underclothes and surprised her husband with a collection of shiny briefs, she who had spent her life touting the virtues of cotton!

"Who could have told me?" she murmured while walking in the garden or trying to water the plants in the corridor. For the first time in her life, she had used up the large sum of money her husband put away for her each month in his wardrobe safe. She had bought three dresses in the same week, when she used to debut one each month so as not to appear ostentatious. And she had gone to the jeweler for a long chain of twisted gold whose price scandalized her.

"I am crazy," she told herself, using the qualifier she always used to disqualify those who did not agree with her. And it was true that she did not agree with herself. To whom would it occur to fall in love with her? What folly! Nevertheless, she let herself reach the foolish precipice of needing someone. Because she had an insubordinate need for that man who, in contrast to her husband, spoke very little, did not explain his silence, and had irreplaceable hands. For these alone it was worth risking all her days to be dead. Because dead she would be if her craziness were known. Even though her husband was as good to her as he was to everyone else, nothing would save her from facing the collective lynching. All the adorers of her adorable husband would burn her alive in the atrium of the cathedral or in the public square.

When she came to this conclusion she kept her eyes on the infinite and little by little, started feeling the guilt leave her body, to be replaced by an enormous fear. Sometimes she spent hours prisoner of the intense heat that would destroy her, hearing even her girlfriends' voices call her "whore" and "ingrate." Then, as if she'd had a celestial premonition, a smile opened in the middle of her tear-stained face and she covered her arms with bracelets and her neck with perfumes before going to hide herself in the joy she had not used up yet.

Aunt Mariana's lover was a gentle, silent man. He made love to her without hurry or orders, as though he and Mariana were equals. Then he asked: "Tell me something."

So Mariana told him about the children's colds, the menus, her forgetfulness, and with total precision, every one of the things that had happened to her since their last meeting. She made him laugh until his whole body recovered the boisterous frolics of a twenty-year-old.

"I rightfully dream they are burning me in the middle of the street. I deserve it," Aunt Mariana murmured to herself, shaking off a piece of straw from a stable in Chipilo. The refrigerator in her house was always stocked with the cheeses she went to look for in that village, full of flies and blond peasants, descendants of the first Italian sowers of anything in Mexico. Sometimes she thought that her grandfather might have approved of her proclivity for a man who could have been born like him in the hills of Piedmont. She returned while it was still daylight, in her auto without a chauffeur.

Upon coming home one afternoon she passed her husband's Mercedes-Benz. It was the only Mercedes in Puebla, and she was sure she saw two heads inside when she watched it pass. But when it stopped in front of her car, the only head she saw was the upright one of her husband, returning alone from the ranch in Matamoros.

"How clear is my conscience?" Aunt Mariana asked herself, and followed her husband's car on the highway.

They traveled one car behind the other the whole way, until arriving at the entrance to the city. One turned right and the other left, both waving their hands out the car window to say good-bye, in agreement that at seven in the evening each still had obligations to take care of alone.

Aunt Mariana thought that her children would be just about ready to request a snack, and that she never left them alone at that hour. Regardless, guilt hit her suddenly as she thought of her hardworking spouse, capable of spending the day alone among the melon and tomato fields he visited as far away as Matamoros on Thursdays, only to go back to the store and the Rotary Club, without allowing himself the slightest break. She decided to turn around and catch up with him at that moment to tell him of the evil that had overtaken her heart. In two minutes she had caught up with the cruising Mercedes in which was her husband's elegant head. With trembling hands and tears welling in her eyes she neared his car, feeling that she would put her final force in the hand that waved, calling to him. Her entire expression begged forgiveness before she even opened her mouth. Then she saw the beautiful head of a woman reclining on the seat, very close to her husband's legs. And for the first time in a very long while she felt relief; pain turned into surprise, and then surprise into peace.

For years the city talked about the sweetness with which Aunt Mariana had endured the romance between her husband and Amelia Berumen. What no one could ever understand was how not even during those months of grief did she interrupt her absurd habit of going all the way to Chipilo to buy the weekly cheeses.

Aunt Inés

There had been a half-moon the night that Aunt Inés Aguirre's orderly feelings became unhinged forever. A scheming, burning moon laughed at her. And the sky surrounding it was so black that it was anyone's guess why Inés did not think of escaping that bewitched thing.

Perhaps even if the moon hadn't been there, even if the sky had pretended to be transparent, everything would have turned out the same way. But Aunt Inés blamed the moon, so as not to feel that she herself was the sole cause of her disgrace. Only under that moon could the sorrow that had overtaken her body have begun. An unhappiness that, as nearly always happens, inserted itself inside her, pretending to spring from the same origin as her joy.

Because that night, under the moon, the man gave her a kiss on the nape of the neck like one who drinks a glass of water, and it was a night so far from sorrow that no one could have imagined it as the beginning of the slightest misfortune. Electric lights had just come to town, and the houses below the hill seemed like stars. The moon had to take revenge on someone for the pain that the lit-up houses gave her, the streets under cover of purchased, lying light, the ingratitude of a whole city growing dark tranquilly, without seeking the help of her brilliance. She had to be useful for something; someone would have to remember her light when saying good-bye to the afternoon, and that someone was Inés Aguirre: the moon pushed her deep into the arms that would enclose her forever, even though they might be leaving early.

The next day Aunt Inés did not remember a request, much less an order, but she had a light between her eyes that darkened her entire existence. She could not forget the breath that cooled her shoulders, or detach from her heart the pain that tied it to the sacred will of the moon.

She grew absentminded and forgetful. She asked for help to find the pencil she carried in her hand, the glasses she was wearing, the flowers she had just cut. From the way she walked one could tell she was going nowhere, because after the first step she almost always forgot her destination. She confused her right hand with her left and never remembered a name. She ended up calling her uncles by her brothers' names and her sisters by the names of her girlfriends. Every morning she had to figure out which drawer she kept her underwear in and what the round fruit was called that she used to make juice for breakfast. She never knew what time it was, and on several occasions she was almost run over.

One afternoon she baked the most delicious chocolate pastry, but the following week she could not find the recipe or recall which pastry people were talking about. She went to the market and returned without onions, and all at once even forgot the Our Father. Sometimes she stood looking at a vase, a chair, a fork, a comb, a ring, and asked with all the ingenuousness of her soul: "What is this for?"

Other times she wrote down in notebooks all kinds of stories that later she could not read because by the ends of the sentences she forgot the letters.

In one of these notebooks she wrote, the last time she knew how: "Each moon is different. Each moon has her own story. Lucky are they who can forget their best moon."

Aunt Ofelia

There are people upon whom life vents its cruelty, people who suffer not through a bad streak but rather through an endless succession of torments. These people nearly always become lachrymose. When anyone runs into them, they start recounting their misfortunes until another of their misfortunes is that no one wants to run into them.

This never happened to Aunt Ofelia. Although several times life touched her with its arbitrariness and miseries, she never wearied anyone else with the story of her troubles. They were said to be many, but no one knew how many, and even less their causes, because she took care to erase them from the memories of others every morning.

She was a woman of strong arms and a playful expression; she had a clear, contagious laugh that she knew to let out always at the right moment. No one ever saw her cry.

At times she was pained by the very air and the earth she walked on, the rising sun, her eyesockets. Memory pained her like vertigo, and the future pained her like the worst possible threat. She awoke at midnight with the certainty that she would split in two, sure that the pain would consume her. But as soon as there was light enough for all, she rose, put on her laugh, painted mascara on her lashes, and went out to meet the others as if her troubles made her float.

No one ever dared feel sorry for her. Her fortitude was so unusual that people began seeking her out to ask for help. What was her secret? Who protected her from afflictions? Where did she get the talent that kept her standing tall in the face of the worst misfortunes?

One day she told her secret to a young lady whose troubles seemed to have no solution:

"There are many ways to categorize human beings," she said. "I separate them into those who become wrinkled up and those who wrinkle down, and I want to belong to the first group. When I am old I want my face not to be sad. I want to have laugh lines and take them with me to the other world. Because who knows what we'll have to face there?"

Aunt Marcela and Aunt Jacinta

Those two women were like the locks of hair in a braid. From when they went to a school run by nuns, hidden under a tunnel and several stairs during the time of the persecution of the Cristeros,* until the 1940s when they went to their first university dance and met those strange, remote beings called men. Not the men of their home, who were at times like furniture and at other times like blankets, but rather those who looked at them with covetous, curious eyes. Those who thought about them with everything and their legs, about them with everything and the hollows below their waists, about them as something both unpredictable and disturbing.

On the same night, the two met the burning hearts who would take their lives and wombs and fill them with their surnames, their obsessions, their children. The two followed more

*Catholic rebels who suffered persecution during and after the presidency of General Plutarco Elías Calles, and led an armed uprising, 1927–1929.

or less proper engagements. The two ended up marrying during more or less the same years. The two shared the uneasiness of their impregnated bellies for the first time. The two had infernal fights before spending two days of honeymoon, and the two learned that later, after the sorrow of the fatal appearance of each fight, came hours of glory and intimate phrases that gave the conjugal pact its pathetic characteristic of irreversibility—the feeling that one could not have made a better pact in life. The two cooked with very similar spices and even their cakes gave off the same smell, despite the fact that they were baked in very different ovens at very different times. Not resigned to merely all that, the two of them had five children each.

They spent the afternoons sewing dresses in bulk and watching the ten children together, like shepherdesses of the same flock. The Gómez twins were identical, distinguished only by the precision of some of their expressions. Nevertheless, the difference in their faces was the exact measure of the difference in their spirits. Aunt Marcela had in her eyes the light of those who search for the best side of life, the light of those who, unfortunately, do not accept the happiness that only fools can enjoy, but who are ready to even pretend so, just to hold on to the very tip of joy. For that reason she always sang softly when getting the children to sleep and when waking them, when threading a needle, when beseeching the heavens that the breakfast eggs not stick to the frying pan, when asking her husband to look at her the way he did at the beginning, and even when accompanying the soliloquy of her long walks.

From her mother, Aunt Jacinta inherited a debilitating melancholy. At times she stood looking off into space as if she had lost something, as if space itself would not be enough for her limitless yearning. Other times she would grow sad about not having been born in Norway on a stormy night, about never having been to the Congo or never knowing whether she was capable of traveling through India. She was sure she would never see Egypt, never be able to travel the hills of Chihuahua; that the sea with all its betrayals and promises would never be her companion every dawn. From the time she was a young girl she had read with passion, but for every story she read she never came away with that certainty many readers feel of being inside the story. On the contrary, each story, setting, and character served merely to drown her in the nostalgia of being only herself. She would never be a suicide like Anna Karenina, or a drunk like Ava Gardner, a madwoman like Joan of Arc, an invader like Carlota Amalia, or a wild singer like Celia Cruz.

She had five children, and she would never know what it was like to have two or what it would be like to have ten. She had a medium-size house and a businessman husband; she would never know palaces or hunger. Her husband's hair was brown and docile; she would never understand what it was to caress coarse black hair like Emiliano Zapata's, a golden head like Henry Ford's, or a completely bald one like Bishop Toríz's.

Sometimes her sister interrupted a song to ask what she was thinking about, because in the past fifteen minutes she had not made a backstitch. Then Aunt Jacinta answered with responses like:

"Wouldn't you have liked to have painted the Mona Lisa? Can

you imagine if we had learned to dance with Fred Astaire? Will Evita Perón turn out to be a liar? What size shoe do you think Pedro Infante wears? They say there is a beach in Oaxaca called Huatulco and that it's paradise. And you and I are stuck here."

"I like it here," said Aunt Marcela, looking at the countryside around her and the volcanoes in the distance. This countryside was never the same. Every season changed its colors, and only because custom dictated that these mountains were always named the same was it possible to see them as the same, when at times they shone green and at others drought left them gray and dusty.

In that season when everything became bone-dry, even the skin on hands and eyelids, in that time when the sun burned hot in the mornings and set early to let a freezing wind pass by, in those afternoons when the children had atrocious fevers, when their throats ached until they coughed like dogs, in those days close to Christmas but after the anticipation for parties was as long as a mass with three priests and as hateful as Lenten sermons, Aunt Marcela discovered a little lump in her left breast.

They were sewing white dresses with red polka dots that their girls would receive on Easter Sunday.

"I don't know why we came up with this idea to make these smocked," said Aunt Jacinta, lingering over a pleat.

"I have a sort of strange little lump in my left breast," responded her sister.

"What?" asked Jacinta, letting a dress fly. "Let me see, let me see." She pulled up her sister's sweater and stuck her hand in to touch the breast: there it was, hard as a mushroom, without being exactly circular. Feeling around for the evidence, Aunt

Jacinta touched higher up and felt another one like it, and another one, lower. Her entire body trembled with terror at the mere idea that this could be bad. Her sister saw her grow pale while trying to use an unworried tone of voice:

"I don't think it is anything important, but you'll have to go to the doctor," she said. "Don't tell your husband. You know how noisy and disgraceful men are."

"Why did you turn pale? They seem like Mama's, right?" asked Aunt Marcela.

"I don't remember now. That was nearly twenty years ago."

"I do remember," said Aunt Marcela, spreading out a smile so beautiful that it made her look evil. "They were the same."

"You wouldn't think of dying before getting to see Egypt?" said Aunt Jacinta, playing with the pleat on a dress.

"No way," answered Aunt Marcela.

They went to the doctor's the following afternoon. He was a man of about fifty, who enjoyed good wine and the music of Brahms. They had known him as long as they could remember. He had once had a full head of brown hair, but it was only now that Aunt Jacinta came to know the look of compassion on his face that suddenly made his eyes beautiful.

While Aunt Marcela let him examine her breasts, she tried to concentrate on the idea that they were her knees, so she didn't need to feel ashamed, because even little girls displayed the bruises on their knees without blushing. The poor man looked at Aunt Jacinta, asking her pardon for being the one who had to tell her. Aunt Jacinta bit her lip. By then, Aunt Marcela had opened her eyes and saw her sister's expression. With the speed of a young girl she lifted her back from the examining table and told her, wielding the same evil smile as the day before:

"Don't you worry. We'll have enough time to see Alexandria."

Aunt Jacinta looked at her as though she herself were the infinite. Aunt Marcela kept talking; she got up and went to dress in the adjoining room. She heard them whispering.

"Don't pull any tricks on me," she said, coming out with the last buttons of her blouse undone. "I want to be in the movie of my death doing something more than dying behind everyone's back."

"Jaime proposes an operation for you," said Aunt Jacinta. "Perhaps it hasn't spread."

"Would you leave me flat?" Aunt Marcela asked the doctor.

"Yes," said the man.

"And you want me to reach my fortieth birthday without breasts?"

"Sister, if not, you might not reach it," said Aunt Jacinta.

"That would be a relief," answered Aunt Marcela. "It's enough to have to have cancer, but to also have to reach forty . . ."

From then on, Aunt Jacinta did not leave her sister alone for even a minute. She accompanied her to the operation and the treatments, to the homeopathic therapist, to the herbal-water doctors, to the witches in the mountains, to the churches, and to Rochester.

"You are going to know what it is to have ten children," Aunt Marcela told her one afternoon upon leaving Santo Domingo. "I don't know why God is bent on taking me from the party."

Aunt Jacinta heard her repeat this during the Sanctissima, as they were next to each other before the altar, on the kneelers covered in red velvet: "God, God, God, why are you bent on taking me from the party?" Her body, with its erect shoulders and long legs, had been shrinking. She learned to walk with a cane and had lost the freshness of her skin and the vigor of her eyes, but the inexorable kindness of her smile still governed her face.

Only nine months had passed since the afternoon they had visited the doctor. And October was upon them, with the inevitable forty years.

"Why don't we have our party in the lodge at the volcano?" asked Aunt Marcela, on one afternoon of noisy kids.

"Wherever you want," answered Aunt Jacinta, who had lost her everlasting condition of pining for something else. She no longer wasted even a second wanting other places. She took care of ten children, two houses, a husband, a brother-in-law, and a blind hope. This was her way of exorcising the slow ceremony of death. But she knew that Aunt Marcela was tired and sick, that hundreds of small and large pains entangled her, that it was no longer worthwhile even to dissemble, and that soon she would be tired of pretending. She went through the streets pointing out to herself the people who could die in place of her sister, singling out the perverse, the useless, the undesirable, until after so much singling out she ended up singling out herself as the most unfair hussy of all. In the beginning she played with her sister by speaking of the future—they made plans to travel, to go shopping, to sign up for Madame Girón's French classes, to learn to swim before going to Cozumel. With time they stopped doing so, as if each had agreed to spare the other that torture. Then Aunt Marcela spent many hours describing the virtues and weaknesses of her children, describing them so many times and in so many ways that her sister could have recognized them and predicted even the smallest detail.

"Remember that Raúl pretends toughness to hide his sorrow, don't forget that Mónica is timid, don't neglect Patricia's artistic calling, don't let Juan grow up fearful, touch Federico tenderly very often. You know how, right?"

"Yes, sister. I already know. Even though I also know that you would be a much better mother than I and that God is crazy."

"Don't say that, sister," responded Marcela, who also had thought many times that God was crazy, that he wasn't even there, but she knew perfectly well what the lack of something like God would do to her sister when she died. "God knows why He does things. He writes straight in twisted lines of words, He loves us, He takes care of us, He protects us.

"Yes, sister, yes. That's why you are going to die when you are most needed. There's no need to deceive oneself. What for?"

"What for? Sister, for you to keep on living, for me to die without so much distress. Don't deny yourself the ideas of your time. And don't even think of teaching my children one bit of your nonsense."

They had a party in the snowy shelter at the volcano. The sisters blew out their forty candles, and the adolescent children thought of going for a long walk. Aunt Marcela got ready to follow them.

"Where are you going, Marce? You are still not well," said her husband, with whom she still played that she'd get better someday.

"Only where the air hits me."

"I'll go with you," Aunt Jacinta said, helping her up. Outside it was the kind of cold that gets in your nose and travels to the farthest part of your body.

"He's going to hate me for betraying him," said Aunt Marcela. "For him I'll always be the woman who left him in the middle of the journey. And what do I tell him? Don't be unfair, feel sorrier for me than you feel for yourself, forgive me, it's not my fault, please don't forget me, marry someone else, tell me how attractive I look, call me 'my life' for the next month instead of 'Hey, Marce'?"

Aunt Jacinta put an arm around her shoulder and didn't answer. They remained that way until their husbands came over. For a while they spoke about the beauty of the volcano, of how it made the snow shine, of the first morning they were together. Then the children returned, ruddy and burning, recounting their exploits.

"Let's go, forty-year-olds," said Aunt Marcela's husband, caressing her neck. He helped her down to the car and installed her inside, wrapping her up like a child.

Aunt Jacinta came over to give her a kiss.

"You see, I *was* with you on your birthday," Aunt Marcela told her.

The following day she did not want to get up. "My forty years are weighing me down," she teased Aunt Jacinta when she saw her enter the room with courage mixed with anguish.

Two days later the doctor decided to give Aunt Marcela morphine.

"Yesterday I dreamed of Alexandria," Aunt Marcela told Aunt Jacinta when she awoke from one of her drug-induced trances. "You are right to want to go. What are you going to do with your hopes and desires, sister?"

"I am going to leave them as my inheritance," said Aunt Jacinta, sorrow on her lips.

"One must go to Denmark and Italy, to Morocco and Seville, to Cozumel and China," Aunt Marcela went on. "I'm becoming like you. Tell me, what are you going to do with your hopes and desires?"

For the past year all Aunt Jacinta's wishes had come down to the one wish not to lose her sister. It had been a long time since she had dreamed about Paris and New York, Istanbul and the Greek isles, that long list of impossibilities with which she'd tortured her life.

The night of the day on which they buried her sister Marcela, Aunt Jacinta, exhausted from her months-long vigil and possessed by a sorrow that was now part of her body, fell asleep in an armchair in the parlor. After a short while she awoke, cold, with a strange smile making her mouth quiver.

"What's going on?" asked her husband, who stood nearby looking at her.

"I dreamed of Marcela," Aunt Jacinta said. "She's in heaven."

"And what does she say?" asked the man, knowing the risks of disturbing that sorrow.

"She says she likes it there and that she's content. You know that she never liked to travel," answered Aunt Jacinta, walking toward her room. "Let's go. Come to bed. We have to go to sleep to see what else we can see."

Aunt Elvira

As a child, Aunt Elvira was afraid of the dark. Her sisters thought it was because you can't see anything in the dark, but the reason for her fear was exactly the contrary: In the dark she saw everything. From the dark came spiders and huge vampires, from the dark came her mother wearing a slip and hanged on a crucifix, her father on all fours contemplating a green comet while her grandfather and uncles passed above him at full speed, opening their purple mouths to howl without anyone's hearing them. In the dark was a girl tied to the stair railing with a satin ribbon that made her bleed. Aunt Elvira said nothing, but moved her lips as if to say: "There are lions and birds floating dead in their fishbowls."

"Don't make things up, Elvira," her sisters told her. "In the darkness there is nothing more than what there is when there is light."

Nevertheless, even when there was light, Elvira did not see the same things as her sisters. She was able to turn the piano into a lizard, the pantry into Ali Baba's cave, the fountain into the Black Sea, and the hibiscus tea into the blood of the executed.

It was said that Aunt Elvira was always a little removed from reality, but during the periods she dedicated to it, she learned to embroider like any other respectable young lady, to play the piano without mistreating it, and to sing the entire song collection decently, including the nine loveliest versions of the "Ave Maria."

She cooked everything except codfish. Her maternal grandmother had taken care that her daughters and granddaughters did not learn to prepare that dish, because in Spain it was poor people's food, and if she had gone through so much to be able to live in Mexico, it would not be so that her descendants ended up eating dried fish, like any old starving Andalusian.

Aunt Elvira had her mother's black eyes and her father's indiscreet mouth. A talkative, pettifogging mouth without which she could have been married before she was twenty to any Creole whose family had been in the country for fifty generations, or to one of those recently arrived impoverished Spaniards who made it in America with such good fortune. Or else, in case of an unavoidable love affair and given that her father practiced a racial tolerance that was in reality indifference, to a hardworking and abusive Lebanese. Any of these men hoped, like all others, to reside with a woman who did not go around giving opinions, or butting into men's conversations, or giving advice on how to solve the trash problem or the epidemic of governors. Women were not meant to talk about nondomestic subjects, and the less they spoke overall, the better. For the women: sewing and singing, cooking and praying, sleeping and getting up when necessary.

It was known throughout the city not only that Aunt Elvira was full of more opinions than an opposition newspaper, but also that she had strange ways. Some as strange as staying awake until three in the morning and not being able to get up in time to go even to nine-o'clock mass, which was the last one. At nine and at ten, Aunt Elvira slept in the fetal position like a baby, precisely because it didn't matter to her in which position she slept. The ladies of those days took great pains to get themselves to mass at eight and return home as soon as it was over, so that no one would think they just strolled around like yapping little dogs. From then until dinnertime, they cooked or gardened, helped their mothers or wrote chaste letters to perfect their handwriting. The more dissipated of them gossiped or memorized an emotional poem.

In contrast, Aunt Elvira woke her belly around eleven. She spent the morning reading novels and social theory until the fierceness with which her belly felt hunger indicated it was time to dedicate herself to pitchers and basins, and to go about washing her whole body in a scattered but meticulous manner. First her crotch and its little hairs, as she was horrified by the thought that a louse might have arrived there from some corner during the night; then her armpits, from which she shaved the down with the same obstinacy as any woman; next the valley of her belly button; and finally her feet and knees. Once bathed, she put on rose lotion in the ten spots she considered fundamental, and beetroot on her cheeks. She did this last with such skill and from so young an age that even her mother was sure her daughter had a splendid natural blush.

She arrived at the dining room always at the last moment, but always in time.

"Good morning, pretty little girl," said her mama, who anxiously endured the behavior of this child of hers who she, like everyone else, saw destined for loneliness.

"Good morning," Aunt Elvira responded, with the tranquil soul of one who gets up to eat breakfast at six in the morning. Midday dinner was always her first meal of the day, and although destiny placed her in unfortunate and awkward situations, she never learned to eat earlier than two-thirty in the afternoon. At that hour each day, her papa returned from undertaking business deals and failures.

Aunt Elvira liked to steer the conversation to her father's world. It was full of projects and mirages, and she was happy to get everyone in the family to navigate that sea. There was no unlucky business that her father didn't undertake. He'd bought a failed factory that cost him as much as a new one and that owed the National Treasury more taxes than it cost. The governor eventually decided that it should pass into the hands of the workers, and Aunt Elvira's papa accepted that decision without uttering a word. With what he had left he bought the stocks of a salt mine, which was really a company formed by two geniuses who failed in their attempts to desalinize seawater. Then he imported German and Chinese tableware. To sell it, he opened a store that quickly became the city's most attractive conversation center. There were always coffee and cigars for everyone who showed any interest in the buying, selling, or use of porcelain. Within a year of its being established, the business went bankrupt and her papa had to close it, but people had grown so used to passing the time there with coffee and gossip that a Turk bought it to turn it into a taco stand, and became rich under the good Don José Antonio Almada's nose.

In the face of that disappointment, Señor Almada traveled to the state of Guerrero in search of land, and returned the owner of some plots along the coast near a port called Acapulco that, according to him, would become one of the most famous beaches in the world. This time his wife intervened, and she, who might never have dared mention the word, threatened divorce if her husband did not immediately sell the five hectares of that desolate beach. With things put to him that way, Elvira's papa sold his beach and lost what may have been the only good business deal of his life.

"Something bad will come of all this," he said the afternoon he sold his land. "You can't turn down such a marvelous thing without paying for it later."

His business fantasies all spent, Señor Almada entered politics with the same vehemence and the same ignorance with which he'd gone into the business world. As if the entire world didn't know that it was better not to get involved with the government, Aunt Elvira's papa did the good deed of dusting off his career as a lawyer to defend a bullfighter who had not been able to collect from the governor for his work at a fight in which he'd battled six horned beasts without a scratch and made one after another of a series of passes in honor of the brave men of Cinco de Mayo.*

To Aunt Elvira's father, who had watched bullfights with the same devotion with which others listen to mass or go to the bank, that seemed like the last straw. It was one thing for the governor to carry the authority of his investiture as far as managing the public finances as though they were his own, and another to calmly deny an artist his salary because he hadn't killed the last bull on his first try.

"The circus is free here," the governor told the bullfighter. "I can give you food or women, but as far as money, don't even dream of it. What's more, you behaved like a butcher."

The bullfighter had demonstrated his bravery for three hours in a row and did not know how to save any of it for himself. He took to calling the governor tyrant, assassin, thief, and the governor in turn, ordered him to be locked up.

Aunt Elvira's father wasted no time in taking off for the jail and offering his services to the bullfighter.

Señor Almada filed suit against the head of the government, accusing him of robbery and abuse of authority. By dinnertime, he was almost sure he would win the lawsuit. He'd been helped

*May 5, 1862, the date of the Battle of Puebla, in which a vastly outnumbered Mexican army defeated the French forces of Napoleon III. Now a holiday celebrating Mexican unity and patriotism.

by his friends in the press, who owed him so much coffee and to whom it seemed a tolerable-sized dispute to have with the governor. They dedicated large amounts of prose to doubting whether so magnanimous a gentleman and such an aficionado of bullfights as the governor was capable of mistreating a bullfighter. Surely it was not so, but if there had been a misunderstanding, there was that good gentleman named Don José Antonio Almada.

The family was eating dessert when an assistant arrived with the message that the bullfighter was free to go. Aunt Elvira took three more spoonfuls of her cream custard and went running after her father. They arrived just in time to witness the signing of the release, and her father was so pleased that he took Aunt Elvira to a saloon, where the other celebrants arrived, one by one. There ensued a party of brandy and anisettes, music and vulgar remarks, from which Aunt Elvira's reputation never recovered. She had danced with the bullfighter until they both collapsed on top of a table, broken down from exhaustion. She had drunk *chinchón* and used men's words with such brazenness and skill that all present forgot that among them was one of the reserved young Señoritas Almada. They did not remember that she was she until the following morning. Then Aunt Elvira and her father returned home, humming "Little Star" and declaring their love for each other.

"Hear me well, girl," her father told her. "I am the only man in your life who will love you without asking something from you."

"And I the only woman who will keep loving you when you're an old man who pees in his pants," Aunt Elvira responded.

Laughing, they entered the patio illuminated by a tepid sun. In the center of it, halted like a ghost, stood Aunt Elvira's mother.

"Do you realize what you've done?" she screamed at her husband.

She was covered by the shawl she had worn to church. She had been crying; she didn't understand what that pair of irresponsible fools could be laughing at. It was clear that they didn't realize what they had done. The happy man is blind and deaf.

"I got the bullfighter out of jail," said the man. "Did you sleep poorly? You don't look well."

Then he gave his wife a cheek-to-cheek kiss and went upstairs, thinking about his pillow.

Aunt Elvira knew that if she remained alone with her mother one second, the sky could fall on her head, so she ran to the kitchen in search of a cheese tortilla with epazote.

For several days the woman spoke to neither her daughter nor her husband, but later she was reconquered by both of them, and their existence once again became temperate and pleasant. Aside from her husband's incapacity for business, life had been kind to Aunt Elvira's mama. But her scant imagination allowed her to believe a little in the Salesian version that the world is bad when it's not good. And ever since she was a small child, Aunt Elvira had had an enormous propensity not to respect whatever the whole world considered good.

As people correctly guessed, it was not Señor Almada's legal diligence or journalistic moves that had set the bullfighter free, but the simple fact that the day after the bullfight, the citizen governor remembered with pleasure the moments of valor the man had shown; his frame of mind improved, and he considered it unjust to keep the fighter locked up solely for having extended his bravura to him. He even ordered him to be paid what he was owed, and once again shared with the bullfighter something that is difficult to call friendship but that somehow seems like it.

Anyway, as in his business deals, the only one who had fared badly was Aunt Elvira's papa, who of course did not learn anything. Because of this, a short while later he became enthused about a request for help from some striking workers whom the government had urged to return to work willingly, which simply meant to return empty-handed. What salaries? What loans? What . . . nothing! The important thing was to reestablish productivity.

As though he needed an additional reason to take up the workers' cause with passion, the part about productivity fueled Aunt Elvira's father. No good person should be productive by force, much less insist that others be. He railed to the journalists as much as he could against those who claimed that productivity was the only criterion by which to judge human beings; he took advantage of the opportunity to criticize those whose only quest in life was for power and money; and he once again put a restraining order against the governor and his allies.

All these things, said at home or among his friends, won him the praise and admiration of half the world. But on paper they sounded crazy, suicidal, the worst deal that Don José Antonio Almada could have undertaken in his entire warm and generous existence.

The governor had heard the story of the celebration with the bullfighter. The person who told him had described Aunt Elvira as the best of the best, the most magnificent, the height of passion and beauty that radiated forth that night.

"To each where he hurts," said the governor, dying of laughter, "and that man Almada makes it easy, because he puts his pain in freedom. Only a blockheaded good man like him would have this idea."

After dinner, Aunt Elvira and her sister Josefina usually walked along La Paz Avenue in the direction of San Juan Hill. They were two women who seemed like opposites, and perhaps they adored each other for precisely that reason. Josefina was going to marry the best catch in the city, a prudent and rich man who, according to Aunt Elvira, would have even been handsome if he hadn't had such a mean expression.

Out past the middle of the roadway, almost where the city ended, stood the fiancé's big house. It appeared even larger because it was adjacent to the flour mill from which part of his family's fortune derived. Josefina stopped at the house to visit awhile with her future mother-in-law, who waited for her in the doorway and spent the next two hours training the girl in the exact housekeeping and precise domestic tastes of the family, which she would have to enter with all her smoothness, her intelligence, and her perfect waist.

Aunt Elvira normally continued alone as far as the hill, climbing like a young goat biting the stem of some flower and submitting itself to the pasture and the earth with its expert, steady feet. Upon reaching the top, she stretched out to watch the setting sun with the devotion of one who knows prayers of privilege. A Cholultec ancestor pushed her to this rite of contemplating the sun and the volcanoes.

One afternoon she was robbed of this ceremony. They bound her eyes and began to bring her down from the hill, as she shouted out screams that no one heard. Her sister was two kilometers away, learning fine open-work embroidery, her mama was baking orange cookies, her papa had lit a cigar over a cup of Lebanese coffee and was commenting to his friends about the disaster of going on living in a Manichaean society like Puebla's, which was like Mexico City's, which in the end was the same as one anywhere else.

It was not until nightfall that her sister Josefina began wondering about Aunt Elvira's delay. She was a daring, crazy girl, but as everyone knew, she did not like to walk in the dark. At first Josefina hid her distress because she was embarrassed to bother her future in-laws, worrying them with the craziness of her sister, who hadn't been able to stay out of trouble at least until after the wedding. But when she drove up and down the hill with her fiancé and mother-in-law, visually undressing all the surroundings and yelling Elvira's name from the car without the slightest response, an anguish like putrefaction ran from her stomach to her mouth and she stopped talking. She had to give in to the certainty that Elvira was not in the outskirts of the city, and she returned to the house next to the hill holding back tears like a beaten child.

Arriving there, she found her fiancé's whole family assembled. The father-in-law, the aunts, the sister-in-law, the brother-in-law and his mama—they abandoned their customary prudence, and in a gesture of cordiality and good judgment started to baste together stories of women who had been kidnapped, raped, killed, and quartered during the past thirty years. In the Revolution, Josefina's mother-in-law had lost all the property her husband had obtained in that same time. She blamed the government for each and every one of those barbaric incidents, including that of the girl who went down a well while her mother was distracted for a second.

Don José Antonio Almada arrived home at eight o'clock and found his wife decorating little cookies and repeating "The Magnificent One" with a smile. When Señor Almada asked about the girls, she interrupted her oration to affirm that they had not arrived, and he went at her, telling her that she was nuts too, that she should no longer say that Elvira's craziness came from his side of the family only—had she not realized what time it was?

"Yes, I already noticed it," said the woman, "but I didn't make a scene, because you always tell me I exaggerate. I've resolved not to scream, so it doesn't seem like I'm exaggerating, okay?"

"Manichaean, wife, Manichaean. But they are never this late."

"I agree. But I've always said that I don't like them walking alone in the afternoon, that Elvira might lean back off the mountain, that night could fall. And you tell me that I'm possessive, that it's like this in New York, that it's been a while since the twentieth century began, that . . ."

She could not continue and began to cry, terrified.

"I am going to look for them," Don José Antonio informed her, trembling.

All afternoon long in the café, he had heard warnings much

more exaggerated than those his wife ever dared make about how dangerous it was to confront authority when one had daughters.

He set off down the street in the direction of the mill, spewing insults at his daughters, who were surely there, calmly eating fritters; at his wife, who always turned out to be right and who, just to be contradictory, had let him allow his daughters to walk through the world like people and not like the jewels that they were. And also at the bullfighter and the striking workers, at the governor, and above all, at himself.

It was the last cold wave of March and he trembled, resenting that chill more than any other. When he arrived at the mill, his older daughter hugged him as though he too must be certain that Aunt Elvira had been lost forever.

Josefina's fiancé approached to greet him with the mixture of kindness and perfection that his wife would later detest.

"I know it's an indiscretion to remind you, but I warned you against the danger of getting yourself involved in defending rebellious workers," he told Señor Almada.

"If you know it, why remind me of it?" asked Señor Almada, apparently recovered from his initial fear. He had his arm around the shoulders of his daughter, who on hearing the exchange wondered whether she was choosing a good husband.

Before anyone might have worried about her, Aunt Elvira had begun to descend the hill with her hands tied and her mouth free. After her first screams she stopped resisting her kidnapper. Contrary to what might have been expected, she restrained her throat as soon as she realized that no one would hear her. Ever since they told her at school about the tragedy of Saint Maria

Goretti, an adolescent who let herself be killed rather than be possessed by a villain, she had thought that the saint committed a tremendous mistake. And that if at any time her body ran a similar risk she would do everything but resist her life's designs. So when she found herself trapped by that youth with strong arms and a brutal expression, she said to him:

"If what you want is to take me away, I'll go with you. But don't hurt me."

The fellow thought about it a second and then asked her to stick out her hands so he could tie them up.

"You're not going to cover my mouth, because I'll become distressed and I'll faint," Aunt Elvira informed him. "I promise you I won't scream. But don't worry if I break my promise. In any case, there's no one around to hear me."

The guy was less of a brute than he looked, and he accepted Elvira's proposal so as not to have to carry her unconscious to the car where his immediate boss waited, a man in his fifties, lazy and eternally hungover, who had made him go up alone because, he said, he was sick and tired of carrying scared old broads.

They started to descend.

"Who do you work with?" Aunt Elvira asked after a while.

"With Tiger," said the boy, who couldn't help bragging.

"And that one—what does he want with me?" she asked.

"How should I know?"

"Are you one of those people who obey without question?" asked Aunt Elvira.

"I heard you're the daughter of some guy Almada," the boy answered, irritated.

"And what of it? How much are they paying you?"

"A lot. What do you care? It's not as if I'm going to take care of you. I'm just bringing you down and leaving you there with them."

"Who is going to take care of me?"

"It depends. You are pretty. You have to guess who wants you. All you see there are pretty ones."

"*You* will see them. Others will do more than just see them."

Furious, the boy approached her; he pinched her arms and kissed her like in the movies.

"You are brave like that with a tied-up girl," said Aunt Elvira. "Are you alone, or did they send you with someone else?"

"Of course I came with someone else. The other guy has the car and the gun," said the youth, his eyes searching for his boss's car in the foothills.

Another car came up the road, and the old guy would have to move away so no one would suspect anything. That was planned. If anyone approached, the boy would have to hide Almada's daughter in the little cave that opened up mid-hill on the other side of the trail that people usually climbed, and precisely the one that Aunt Elvira and her captor were descending. She knew it as well as she knew the whole mountain, but she had never entered it, because it was a dark, foul-smelling place full of spiderwebs and rats.

The youth covered Elvira's mouth and dragged her into the cave without encountering much resistance.

The girl wanted to flee as much as he did. She threw herself onto the floor, signaling that he too should drag himself in, and she got into the little cave with more speed and skill than the boy.

It grew dark. Elvira heard Josefina's shouts from afar and felt sorry for her. But she thought that if the Mirandas found her tied to a foul-smelling vagrant, the life her sister had dreamed of in the afternoons would end up in the garbage without great formality. Finally the shouts subsided. The boy looked at Elvira. Night was falling, but her body illuminated the growing darkness.

"Why didn't you scream?" he asked her.

"So they wouldn't hurt you," answered Aunt Elvira.

"Damned old lady, you want to get me in trouble," he said, approaching to touch her slowly.

"If I stole something, I would steal it for myself," said Aunt Elvira.

Night had closed over them, and she felt it would be better to take refuge in the idea that she was dreaming. The fellow resumed kissing her and rubbing himself against her, on fire.

"This way, cowardly one," said Aunt Elvira, crawling again toward the mouth of the cave. The youth followed her. They felt the air hit their bodies like another caress. He untied her hands and she threw them around his neck. His skin smelled strange. It occurred to Aunt Elvira that she had never been so close to skin not related to hers. Then she shut her eyes and caressed the stranger with her free hands as though she had to engrave him on the depths of her memory. She unbuttoned his shirt slowly, until she took it off him. Then she covered his eyes affectionately and went for his belt with a nimbleness that would make anyone say she'd performed this action many times before. She touched everything skillfully, even his toes, which she massaged like someone preparing a floral arrangement. She didn't leave a single doubt in his body. She pacified him by saying things into his ears and into all the parts of him that passed her lips.

"I knew that rich women were idiots about this," said the boy, from his pacified and fervent nakedness.

"We are," Elvira said when she felt him move his hand between her intrepid virgin's legs. "We are, we are," she murmured, wrenching free to run like a frightened cat. Leaving behind her the first naked body fate had sent her way.

She grabbed the pile of the boy's clothes and ran vehemently and desperately toward the mill. In the foothills was the car with the fat man and his gun, sleeping like the angel he never was. He had returned after the car carrying Josefina and her fiancé abandoned the site, and when he saw that his pupil was late in descending, he imagined that something good was happening to him, and he gave himself permission to take a nap. It seemed right to wait until the boy completed his job, robbing a little bit of woman from his employers.

Aunt Elvira passed close to the car without turning to look at it. An unknown excitement moved her. "What might have come next?" she asked her body for an instant. But instead of answering, she kept running.

She entered the mill with moonlike eyes and the mouth of a dead woman. The doorman watched her ascend the stairs still like a hunted animal. Then she entered the parlor and hugged her papa, who upon seeing her alive felt his heart burst and his body swoon.

"This was all because of selling Acapulco," Señor Almada said several times in his agonizing delirium the following days.

"Why did I quit business?" he asked everyone who came to visit him in the hospital.

Aunt Elvira kissed and kissed his face, wilted by weeping and despair.

"Don't upset yourself, Papa. We'll buy it again. Just don't die on me. Don't die."

She went on begging him not to die for a long time after they had buried him. Because in reality Aunt Elvira never buried her father. She spent the rest of her long life doing business deals in his honor. Her mother turned over to her the administration of the Xonaca brickworks factory, the last thing they had left, to see if making her feel needed would pull her out of the pit into which she had flung herself.

And that kept her entertained forever. She began by convincing half the builders in the state that her partition walls were better made than any others, and she ended up owner of a real salt mine, two of the first five airplanes to cross the Mexican sky, and three of the first twenty skyscrapers in Mexico, as well as four hotels on the coast of Acapulco.

"Now you see, Papa," she said every afternoon in front of the sea, toward the end of her life. "We bought Acapulco again."

Aunt Daniela

Aunt Daniela fell in love the way intelligent women always fall in love: like an idiot. She had seen him one morning, his gait serene, his shoulders puffed with pride. She thought: This man thinks he's God. But a short while after hearing him tell stories about unknown worlds and strange passions, she fell in love with him and his arms. It was as though since childhood, she hadn't spoken Latin, hadn't understood logic, hadn't surprised half the city copying the games of Góngora and Sor Juana de la Cruz like one who responds to a song at recess.

She was so wise that no man wanted to get involved with her, no matter how like honey were her eyes, how brilliant her mouth, no matter how much her body caressed the imagination, waking the desire to see her nude, no matter that she was beautiful like the Virgin of the Rosary. It made one afraid to desire her, because there was something in her intelligence that always suggested a disdain for the opposite sex and its confusions.

But that man who knew nothing of her and her books approached her as he would any other woman. So Aunt Daniela endowed him with dazzling intelligence, the virtue of an angel, and the talent of an artist. She viewed his head from so many angles that in twelve days she believed she had met one hundred men.

She wanted him, convinced that God could walk among mortals, involved up to her fingernails in the wishes and notions of a fellow who never understood a single one of all the poems that Daniela wanted to read to him to explain her love.

One day, in the same way he had come, he left without even saying good-bye. And there was not then in Aunt Daniela's entire intelligence a single clue to understand what had happened.

Hypnotized by a nameless, directionless sorrow, she became the stupidest of the stupid. Losing was a pain as prolonged as insomnia, a centuries-old age, a hell.

In vain hopes for some days of clarity, for a sign, for the eyes of iron and supplication that he lent her one night, Aunt Daniela buried her will to live and was losing the shine of her skin, the force in her legs, the intensity in her forehead and innards.

She was blind in three months' time, a hump grew on her back, and something happened to her internal thermostat so that despite walking in a beam of sunlight wearing an overcoat and socks, she shivered with cold as though living in the very middle of winter. They took her out for fresh air as if she were a canary. They placed fruit and cookies nearby for her to nibble, but her mother carried them away intact while she remained, silent despite everyone's best efforts to distract her.

At first they invited her to the street to see whether by looking at the doves or watching the people come and go some part of her would again show signs of an attachment to life. They tried everything. Her mother took her on a trip to Spain and made her visit all the street theaters in Seville without getting more than a tear out of her, and that only on the night the singer was happy. The following morning, her mother sent her husband a telegram saying: "She is beginning to get better; she cried for a second." Aunt Daniela had become a dry tree, she went where they took her, and as soon as she could, she fell into bed as if she had worked for twenty-four hours picking cotton. Finally she had only enough strength left to throw herself in a chair and tell her mother: "I beg of you, let's go home."

When they returned, Aunt Daniela could barely walk, and soon she didn't want to get up in the morning. Nor did she want to bathe, comb her hair, or pee. One morning she couldn't even open her eyes.

"She's dead!" she heard someone near her say, and she didn't have the strength to deny it.

Someone suggested to her mother that her behavior was blackmail, a way to get revenge on others, the pose of a spoiled child who, if she suddenly lost the tranquility of a home and a sure meal, would manage to get better overnight. Her mother tried to believe this and followed the advice to abandon her at the door of the cathedral. They left her there one night in hopes of seeing her return the next day, hungry and furious, as she once had been. On the third night they retrieved her from the cathedral door with pneumonia and took her to the hospital, amid the whole family's tears.

Her friend Elidé went to visit her there. She was a girl with shining skin who spoke without stopping to catch her breath and who said she knew cures for heartache. She asked that they leave her in charge of the soul and stomach of that shipwreck. Elidé was a happy, avid creature. They listened to her give her opinion. According to her, the error in the treatment of her intelligent friend lay in the advice that she forget. Forgetting was an impossible matter. What had to be done was to guide her memories so that they did not kill her, so that they obliged her to continue living.

Daniela's parents listened to Elidé with the same indifference that any attempt to cure their daughter provoked in them by now. They saw it as a given that it would not work, yet nonetheless they allowed it, as though they had already lost hope.

They put the two girls to sleep in the same room. Every time they passed by the door, they heard Elidé's untiring voice talking about the matter with the same obstinacy with which a doctor cares for a dying person. She was never silent. She never let up. One day and the next, one week and the next.

"How did you say his hands were?" she asked. If Aunt Daniela did not answer, Elidé came back at her from another angle.

"Did he have green eyes? Brown? Big?"

"Little," Aunt Daniela answered her, speaking for the first time in thirty days.

"Small and turbid?" asked Elidé.

"Small and fierce," responded Aunt Daniela, and she fell silent for another month.

"Surely he was a Leo. Leos are like that," said her friend, pulling out a book of horoscopes to read to her. She told of all the horrors that could befall a Leo. "They are hopeless liars. But you needn't lose heart; you are a Taurus. Taurus women are strong."

"Those were lies he told," Daniela said one afternoon.

"Which ones? Don't you forget. Because the world isn't so large that we won't meet up with him, and then you are going to remember his words. One by one, those you heard and those he made you say."

"I don't want to humiliate myself."

"He'll be the one humiliated. As if everything were not as easy as sowing words and leaving."

"They enlightened me," protested Aunt Daniela.

"You sure seem enlightened," said her friend when they arrived at points like this.

By the third month of talking and talking, Elidé made Daniela eat as if God commanded it. Elidé did not even realize how it happened. She took Daniela for a stroll in the garden. She carried a basket filled with fruit, cheese, bread, butter, and tea. She spread a tablecloth on the grass, took out the food, and kept talking, while starting to eat without offering Aunt Daniela anything.

"He liked grapes," said the sick one.

"I understand that you miss him."

"Yes," said the sick girl, bringing a cluster of grapes near her mouth. "He was a great kisser. And the skin of his shoulders and waist was smooth."

"How was it, exactly? You know," prompted her friend, as though she had always known what tortured the girl.

"I'm not going to tell you," Aunt Daniela answered, laughing for the first time in months. Then she ate cheese and tea, bread and butter.

"Yummy?" Elidé asked her.

"Yes," answered the sick one, beginning to be herself again.

One night they went down to supper. Aunt Daniela wore a new dress and had shining, clean hair, finally free of the dusty braid that she had not combed in such a long while.

Twenty days later she and her friend had gone over the memories from top to bottom until they turned into trivia. Everything Aunt Daniela had tried to forget by forcing herself not to think about it became unworthy of remembering after being repeated so many times. She punished her good judgment, hearing herself speak one after another of the one hundred twenty thousand foolishnesses that had made her both happy and wretched.

"I don't even want to avenge myself anymore," she told Elidé one morning. "I am bored to death of this subject."

"What? Don't go getting intelligent on me," said Elidé. "The whole time this has been a matter of stupid reasoning. Are you going to turn it into something brilliant? Don't. We haven't gotten to the best part yet. We haven't yet looked for the man in Europe and Africa, in South America and India, we haven't found him and created a scandal to justify our trips. We haven't gotten to know the Pitti Palace, see Florence, fall in love in Venice, or throw a coin in the Trevi Fountain. Aren't we going to track down that man who fell in love with you like someone falls for an imbecile, and then left?"

They had planned to travel the world in search of the guilty party, and this new idea that vengeance might not be of great importance in her friend's cure devastated Elidé. They were going to miss out on India and Morocco, Bolivia and the Congo, Vienna and, above all, Italy. She never thought she'd be able to change Daniela into a rational being after having seen her paralyzed and nearly crazy four months before.

"We have to go look for him. Don't become reasonable again before it's time to," she told her.

"He arrived yesterday," Aunt Daniela told her one midday.

"How do you know?"

"I saw him. He knocked at the balcony door like before."

"And what did you feel?"

"Nothing."

"And what did he say to you?"

"Everything."

"And how did you answer him?"

"I shut the door."

"And now?" asked her therapist.

"Now let's go to Italy. The absent are always wrong."

And they went to Italy because of what Dante had written: *Poi piovve dentro a l'alta fantasia.**

---

*"Then poured into my soaring fantasy" (*Purgatorio,* xvii, 25; translation by Mark Musa).

Aunt Amalia

Amalia Ruiz found her life's passion in the body and voice of a forbidden man. For more than a year, she watched him come feverishly as far as the hem of her skirt, which billowed beneath their embrace. They didn't speak much; they knew each other as though they had been born in the same room, and they provoked trembling and happiness in each other merely by touching each other's overcoat. Their passion came out of their fortunate bodies with such ease that after a short while of being together, their love room sounded like the Pastoral Symphony and smelled of perfume as if it had been invented by Coco Chanel.

Their glory kept their lives uncertain and turned their deaths into an impossibility. For this reason they were as beautiful as an enchantment and as promising as a fantasy.

Until one October night when Aunt Meli's lover arrived late to their assignation, and talking about business. She let him kiss her without putting up a fuss, and she felt his breath devastate her mouth as always. She held back her reproaches, but then took off running to her house and no longer wanted to know anything of that love.

"When the impossible becomes routine, it is time to give it up," she explained to her sister, who was unable to understand so radical an attitude. "One cannot get involved in the mess of loving something prohibited, feeling it at times like a blessing, wanting it above all else—because it's impossible, because it's hopeless—and then turning oneself into the annex of an office. I can't allow myself to do it, I am not going to let myself do it. If in the name of God something is forbidden, for that reason it is blessed."

Aunt Amanda

For a long time it was said that Amanda Rodoreda was the daughter of Antonio Sánchez, her father's close friend. And not even her own mother seemed to know whence came to her womb that child who so little resembled the two men who, to her misfortune, crossed her life. They said that when she gave birth to her daughter, her heart was still burning in the mouth and hands of Antonio Sánchez, even though her head rested as always on the lap of the gentle Rodoreda.

For many years Amanda's mother had lived with both of them from morning until night, listening to them think up and start businesses, watching them succeed and fail amid eternal conversations and debilitating drinking bouts. She had picked one and then the other up off the floor like bundles, she had put them to bed and covered them at the coming of dawn. She had prepared *chilaquiles* and black coffee for the two of them; she had packed their bags when they went to look over the ranch in Tlaxcala, and with one and the other she had sung in the nights without electric light that hovered above the environs of La Malinche Hill. She was very happily married to one of them, and she had always loved him as she should. She started loving the other one as an extension of that love and ended up falling in love with his voice and the things he said with it. But it was not her fault. In reality, it was no one's fault. Such things happen at times, and it's not worth losing sleep trying to figure out why.

Supposedly Antonio Sánchez thought about some of that when he decided to go who knows where without leaving a note or asking for one cent of all the money he had in the partnership with Rodoreda. He left the morning after the night that his friend told him that his wife was pregnant, and he left everything—even the scissors he used to cut off the tips of his cigars. Only three shirts and a pair of pants were missing from his drawers, so that Daniel Rodoreda thought something urgent had come up and he would return by week's end. But more than six months passed without their hearing from Sánchez, and Rodoreda began to miss him like a dog. He missed his smiling, bold presence; he missed his observations, his cleverness, the full-time company he had grown used to; his complicity. Especially in those final months of the pregnancy, which turned his happy, alert wife into a statue who hardly spoke, who could go for hours without saying a word, and who cried at every question and with difficulty ate three tablespoons of soup to feed the wonder she carried inside her.

Amanda had not yet been born when her future paternal grandfather had the tact to ask his son whether he was sure that only Rodoreda sperm had entered his wife's womb. With that single question, he demolished the tower of cards that was by then the husband's life, as he tried to avoid seeing the sadness in his wife's eyes. Rodoreda returned home to throw himself in bed and try to die. He had a fever for two weeks, his skin ashen and his hairs going gray one by one, but so quickly that when he came to, his whole head was white. His wife was beside him, and she saw him open his eyes for the first time to look, not just to lose himself in an unreachable horizon.

She saw him look at her, and a peace she had never imagined possible made her smile as if for the first time.

"Forgive me," she said.

"I have nothing to forgive you for," he answered.

They never spoke again of the subject.

One month later a little girl was born whom Daniel Rodoreda baptized as his own and with whose birth he stopped losing the little sense he still had. He was sure it would be impossible to find anything more beautiful in the world, and he watched her grow, in love with even the ire that filled her eyes at any setback.

Amanda was ten years old when her mother died, and for months more fury than sadness took up residence in her eyes. The same happened to Rodoreda, so they lived together more than a year without speaking to each other. One day Rodoreda stood watching while she wrote out her homework, tilted over her notebook.

"Who do you look like?" he asked, caressing her.

"Myself," Amanda answered. "Who do you want me to look like?"

"My grandmother," Rodoreda said, and told her about his grandmother in Asturias until conversation reestablished itself in the house.

Ten years later Antonio Sánchez returned to the city, as handsome and devastating as ever. At forty-five, he was so identical to his former self that he once again fascinated Rodoreda. Sánchez had sought him out and asked forgiveness for having left without warning. Sánchez also had given him a generous hug and had not asked for an accounting when he inquired about the state of the ranches and the store, which he called "your" businesses, never "our." Only when he spoke of Amanda did Rodoreda notice in Sánchez's voice something more than the interest of an absent, negligent uncle. Then Rodoreda sent for her, happy and fearful to show him that treasure.

Amanda entered the parlor with a head of curls and a pencil in her mouth.

"Papa, I'm studying," she said in the hurried, annoyed voice that he found so amusing.

"You'll pardon her manners," Rodoreda asked of Antonio Sánchez. "She enters the university in February, and she's a very obsessive girl."

"She's going to the university?" questioned Antonio Sánchez, overwhelmed by that monster who smiled with the same sly impatience as her papa.

"Yes," said Rodoreda. "Finally someone in this family will be able to be a full-time intellectual."

"And what are you studying?" Antonio Sánchez asked the arrogant angel before him.

"Law," she answered. "And who are you?"

"My name is Antonio Sánchez," he said, looking at her as though all of her were the Milky Way.

"Oh, at last. You're whose daughter I supposedly am," said Amanda in the tone one uses to comment on nice weather. "And why have you come back? To marry me? Because I have neither the looks nor the desire to be your daughter."

Daniel Rodoreda took off his glasses and chewed one of the earpieces until he broke it.

"What are you saying?" he asked his daughter.

"I'm not saying it, Papa. Everyone talks about it. Why not us? Did this gentleman beget me? No way? Who knows?"

"Who knows," said Antonio Sánchez.

"Who knows?" asked Rodoreda. "I know. You are my daughter because you resemble my maternal grandmother down to the creases of your neck, because you know how to sing like my father and get angry like me alone."

"Very well. What a blessing. I am your daughter. So then I want to marry your friend."

"Amanda, you are driving me crazy."

"What? What I'm after is for you to stop being crazy. Prove to me once and for all that you can truly believe with all your soul that which you so loudly proclaim: 'Amanda is my daughter.' Of course I am your daughter! Daniel Rodoreda, your wife never slept with your friend, true?"

"True," said Sánchez.

"And Amanda is not a gift from God, or a stroke of luck, or an angry person who took in your generosity. Amanda is your daughter, and for this reason she is going to marry her other papa. So that the gossip ends, so that my schoolmates' parents, my nannies, my grandmothers, my teachers, the vicar of San Sebastián, the archbishop, and the dog on the corner eat their words."

"You came back for this?" Rodoreda asked his friend.

One year later, Daniel Rodoreda paraded down the center aisle of the Church of Santo Domingo, holding the arm of his daughter Amanda. He gave her away in marriage to Don Antonio Sánchez, his best friend.

The three of them spent the wedding night at the ranch in Atlixco, dying of laughter and peace.

Aunt Jose

Aunt Jose Rivadeneira had a daughter with eyes like two moons, as big as wishes. The first time she was placed in her mother's arms, still damp and unsteady, the child opened her eyes, and something in the corner of her mouth looked like a question.

"What do you want to know?" Aunt Jose asked her, pretending to understand that expression.

Like all mothers, Aunt Jose thought there had never in the history of the world been a creature as beautiful as her daughter. Aunt Jose was dazzled by the color of her skin, the length of her eyelashes, and the serenity of her sleep. She trembled with pride imagining what her daughter would do with the blood and chimeras that pulsed through her body.

Aunt Jose devoted herself to contemplating the girl with pride and joy for more than three weeks. Then unassailable fate caused the child to fall ill with a malady that within five hours turned her extraordinary liveliness into a weak and distant dream that seemed to be sending her toward death.

When all of her own curative talents failed to make the child any better, Aunt Jose, pale with terror, took her to the hospital. There they tore the child from Aunt Jose's arms, and a dozen doctors and nurses fussed over her in agitation and confusion. Aunt Jose watched her child disappear behind a door barred to her, and she let herself sink to the floor, unable to control herself or bear that pain like a steep hill.

Her husband, a prudent, sensible man (as most men pretend to be), found her there. He helped her up and scolded her for her lack of hope and good sense. Her husband had faith in medical science and spoke of it the way others speak of God. He was disturbed by the state of foolishness into which his wife had settled, unable to do anything but cry and curse fate.

The doctors isolated the child in intensive care, a clean, white place that mothers could enter for only half an hour daily. So it filled up with prayers and pleas. All the women made the sign of the cross over their children's faces, they covered their little bodies with prayer cards and holy water, they begged God to let them live. All Aunt Jose could do was make it to the crib where her daughter lay, barely breathing, and beg: "Don't die." Afterward she cried and cried without drying her eyes or moving an inch, until the nurses told her she had to leave.

Then she'd return to sit on the benches near the door, her head in her hands, without appetite or voice, angry and surly, fervent and desperate. What could she do? Why should her daughter live? What could she ever offer that tiny body full of needles and catheters that might interest her enough to stay in this world? What could she say to convince the child that it would be worthwhile to make the effort, rather than to die?

One morning, without knowing why, enlightened only by the ghosts in her heart, she went near her daughter and began to tell her tales about her ancestors. Who they had been, which women wove their lives together with which men before she and her daughter were united at mouth and navel. What they were made of, what sort of work they had done, what sorrows and frolics the child now carried as her inheritance. Who sowed, with intrepidity and fantasies, the life it was up to her to extend.

For many days she remembered, imagined, invented. Every minute of every available hour Aunt Jose spoke ceaselessly into her daughter's ear. Finally, at dawn one Thursday, while she was implacably telling one of those stories, the child opened her eyes and looked at her intently, as she would for the rest of her long life.

Aunt Jose's husband thanked the doctors; the doctors thanked the advances in medical science. Aunt Jose hugged her daughter and left the hospital without saying a word. Only she knew whom to thank for the life of her daughter. Only she knew that no science was capable of doing as much as that element hidden in the rough and the subtle discoveries of other women with big eyes.

Aunt Concha

Near the end of her life she cultivated violets. She had a bright room that she filled with flowers. She learned how to grow the most extravagant strains, and she liked to give them as gifts so that people had in their houses the inescapable aroma of Concha Esparza.

She died surrounded by inconsolable relatives, reposing in her brilliant blue silk robe, with painted lips and enormous disappointment because life didn't want to grant her more than eighty-five years.

No one knew why she hadn't tired of living; she had worked like a mule driver for almost all her life. But those earlier generations had something that made them able to withstand more. Like all earlier things: like the cars, the watches, the lamps, the chairs, the plates and skillets of yesteryear.

Concepción Esparza had, like all her sisters, thin legs, huge breasts, and a hard smile, absolute disbelief in the plaster saints, and blind faith in spirits and their clownish jokes.

She was the daughter of a physician who participated in the

Revolution of Tuxtepec,* who was a federal deputy in 1882, and who joined the anti-reelection movement of 1908. A wise and fascinating man who filled his life with his taste for music and lost causes.

However, as fate likes to even the score, Concha had more than enough father but less than enough husband. She married a man named Hiniesta whose only defect was that he was so much like his children that she had to treat him like just another one of them. He was not much good at earning money, and the idea that men support their families, so common in the thirties, didn't govern his existence. To put food on the table, keep house, and buy coverlets for the beds, to pay for the children's schooling, clothe them, and take care of other such trifles was always up to his wife, Concha. He, meanwhile, thought up big business deals that he never pulled off. To close one of these deals, he had the bright idea of writing a check on insufficient funds for a sum so large that an order was issued for his arrest and the police came looking for him at home.

When Concha learned what it was all about, she said the first thing that popped into her mind:

"What's happened is that this man is crazy. Totally nuts, he is."

With this line of reasoning she accompanied him to his trial, with this line of reasoning she kept him from mounting his own defense—which might have really done him in—and with this line of reasoning she kept him from being thrown in jail. Instead

---

*An uprising led by General Porfirio Díaz in 1876, which led to the overthrow of the Mexican government.

of that horrible fate, with this same argument Concha Esparza arranged for her husband to be put in an insane asylum near the pyramids of Cholula. It was a tranquil place run by friars at the foot of the hills.

Grateful for the medical visits of Concha's father, the friars agreed that Señor Hiniesta could stay until the incident of the check was forgotten. Of course, Concha had to pay for the monthly maintenance of that sane man within the impregnable walls of the asylum.

For six months she made an effort to pay for his stay. When her finances would allow no more, she decided to retrieve her husband, after first having herself declared his legal guardian.

One Sunday she went to get him in Cholula. She found him breakfasting among the friars, entertaining them with a tale about a sailor who had a mermaid tattooed on his bald spot.

"One wouldn't look bad on you, Father," he was saying to the friar with the biggest smile.

While Señor Hiniesta was talking, he watched his wife coming down the corridor to the refectory. He kept talking and laughing the whole time it took Aunt Concha to arrive at the table where he and the friars were talking with that childish joy men seem to have only when they know they're among themselves.

As if unaware of the rules of such a gathering, Concha Esparza walked around the table in the clickety-clacking high heels she wore on occasions she considered important. When she was in front of her husband, she greeted the group with a smile.

"And you, what are you doing here?" Señor Hiniesta asked her, more uncomfortable than surprised.

"I came to get you," Aunt Concha told him, speaking as she did to her children when she met them at school, pretending to trade them the treasure of their freedom in exchange for a hug.

"Why?" asked Hiniesta, annoyed. "I'm safe here. It's not right for me to leave. What's more, I'm having a good time. There's an atmosphere of gardens and peace here that does wonders for my spirit."

"What?" asked Concha Esparza.

"What I'm telling you is that I'm fine right where I am. Don't worry. I have some good friends among those who are sane, and I don't get along badly with the loonies. Some of them have moments of exceptional inspiration, others are excellent speakers. The rest has done me good, because in this place even the screamers make less noise than your kids," he said, as though he'd had nothing to do with the existence of those children.

"Hiniesta, what am I going to do with you?" Concha Esparza inquired of the empty air. Then she turned and walked toward the exit with its iron grille.

"Please, Father," she said to the friar accompanying her. "You explain to him that his vacations cost money, and I am not going to pay for one day more."

One can only guess what the father told Señor Hiniesta, but in fact, that Monday morning the latch on Aunt Concha's front door made a slow sound, the same leisurely noise it used to make when her husband pushed it open.

"I came home, Mother," Hiniesta said with a mourner's sadness.

"That's good, son," answered his wife, without showing any surprise. "Señor Benítez is waiting to see you."

"To offer me a business deal." He brightened, and his voice recovered some liveliness. "You'll see. You'll see what a deal, Concha. This time you'll see."

"And that's the way this man was," Aunt Concha commented many years later. "All his life he was like that."

By then Aunt Concha's guest house had been a success and had provided her with earnings with which she opened a restaurant, which she closed sometime later to get into real estate, and which even gave her the opportunity to buy some land in Polanco and some more in Acapulco.

When her children were grown, and after Señor Hiniesta's death, she learned how to paint the waves at La Quebrada and how to communicate with the spirit of her father. Few people have been as happy as she was then.

That is why life really infuriated her, leaving her just when she was beginning to enjoy it.

MUJERES *de* OJOS GRANDES

para Carlos Mastretta Arista,
que regresó de Italia

Tía Leonor

La tía Leonor tenía el ombligo más perfecto que se haya visto. Un pequeño punto hundido justo en la mitad de su vientre planísimo. Tenía una espalda pecosa y unas caderas redondas y firmes, como los jarros en que tomaba agua cuando niña. Tenía los hombros suavemente alzados, caminaba despacio, como sobre un alambre. Quienes las vieron cuentan que sus piernas eran largas y doradas, que el vello de su pubis era un mechón rojizo y altanero, que fue imposible mirarle la cintura sin desearla entera.

A los diecisiete años se casó con la cabeza y con un hombre que era justo lo que una cabeza elige para cursar la vida. Alberto Palacios, notario riguroso y rico, le llevaba quince años, treinta centímetros y una proporcional dosis de experiencia. Había sido largamente novio de varias mujeres aburridas que terminaron por aburrirse más cuando descubrieron que el proyecto matrimonial del licenciado era a largo plazo.

El destino hizo que tía Leonor entrara una tarde a la notaría, acompañando a su madre en el trámite de una herencia fácil que les resultaba complicadísima, porque el recién fallecido padre de la tía no había dejado que su mujer pensara ni media hora de vida. Todo hacía por ella menos ir al mercado y cocinar. Le contaba las noticias del periódico, le explicaba lo que debía pensar de ellas, le daba un gasto que siempre alcanzaba, no le pedía nunca cuentas y hasta cuando iban al cine le iba contando la película que ambos veían: "Te fijas, Luisita, este muchacho ya se enamoró de la señorita. Mira cómo se miran, ¿ves? Ya la quiere acariciar, ya la acaricia. Ahora le va a pedir matrimonio y al rato seguro la va a estar abandonando".

Total que la pobre tía Luisita encontraba complicadísima y no sólo penosa la repentina pérdida del hombre ejemplar que fue siempre el papá de tía Leonor. Con esa pena y esa complicación entraron a la notaría en busca de ayuda. La encontraron tan solícita y eficaz que la tía Leonor, todavía de luto, se casó en año y medio con el notario Palacios.

Nunca fue tan fácil la vida como entonces. En el único trance difícil ella había seguido el consejo de su madre: cerrar los ojos y decir un Ave María. En realidad, varias avesmarías, porque a veces su inmoderado marido podía tardar diez misterios del rosario en llegar a la serie de quejas y soplidos con que culminaba el circo que sin remedio iniciaba cuando por alguna razón, prevista o no, ponía la mano en la breve y suave cintura de Leonor.

Nada de todo lo que las mujeres debían desear antes de los veinticinco años le faltó a tía Leonor: sombreros, gasas, zapatos franceses, vajillas alemanas, anillo de brillantes, collar de perlas disparejas, aretes de coral, de turquesas, de filigrana. Todo, desde los calzones que bordaban las monjas trinitarias hasta una diadema como la de la princesa Margarita. Tuvo cuanto se le ocurrió, incluso la devoción de su marido que poco a poco empezó a darse cuenta de que la vida sin esa precisa mujer sería intolerable.

Del circo cariñoso que el notario montaba por lo menos tres veces a la semana, llegaron a la panza de la tía Leonor primero una niña y luego dos niños. De modo tan extraño como sucede sólo en las películas, el cuerpo de la tía Leonor se infló y desinfló las tres veces sin perjuicio aparente. El notario hubiera querido levantar un acta dando fe de tal maravilla, pero se limitó a disfrutarla, ayudado por la diligencia cortés y apacible que los años y la curiosidad le habían regalado a su mujer. El circo mejoró tanto que ella dejó de tolerarlo con el rosario entre las manos y hasta llegó a agradecerlo, durmiéndose después con una sonrisa que le duraba todo el día.

No podía ser mejor la vida en esa familia. La gente hablaba siempre bien de ellos, eran una pareja modelo. Las mujeres no encontraban mejor ejemplo de bondad y compañía que la ofrecida por el licenciado Palacios a la dichosa Leonor, y cuando estaban más enojados los hombres evocaban la pacífica sonrisa de la señora Palacios mientras sus mujeres hilvanaban una letanía de lamentos.

Quizá todo hubiera seguido por el mismo camino si a la tía Leonor no se le ocurre comprar nísperos un domingo. Los domingos iba al mercado en lo que se le volvió un rito solitario y feliz. Primero lo recorría con la mirada, sin querer ver exactamente de cuál fruta salía cuál color, mezclando los puestos de jitomate con los de limones. Caminaba sin detenerse hasta llegar donde una mujer inmensa, con cien años en la cara, iba moldeando unas gordas azules. Del comal recogía Leonorcita su gorda de requesón, le ponía con cautela un poco de salsa roja y la mordía despacio mientras hacía las compras.

Los nísperos son unas frutas pequeñas, de cáscara como terciopelo, intensamente amarilla. Unos agrios y otros dulces. Crecen revueltos en las mismas ramas de un árbol de hojas largas y oscuras. Muchas tardes, cuando era niña con trenzas y piernas de gato, la tía Leonor trepó al níspero de casa de sus abuelos. Ahí se sentaba a comer de prisa. Tres agrios, un dulce, siete agrios, dos dulces, hasta que la búsqueda y la mezcla de sabores eran un juego delicioso. Estaba prohibido que las niñas subieran al árbol, pero Sergio, su primo, era un niño de ojos precoces, labios delgados y voz decidida que la inducía a inauditas y secretas aventuras. Subir al árbol era una de las fáciles.

Vio los nísperos en el mercado, y los encontró extraños, lejos del árbol pero sin dejarlo del todo, porque los nísperos se cortan con las ramas más delgadas todavía llenas de hojas.

Volvió a la casa con ellos, se los enseñó a sus hijos y los sentó a comer, mientras ella contaba cómo eran fuertes las piernas de su abuelo y respingada la nariz de su abuela. Al poco rato, tenía en la boca un montón de huesos lúbricos y cáscaras aterciopeladas. Entonces, de golpe, le volvieron los diez años, las manos ávidas, el olvidado deseo de Sergio subido en el árbol, guiñándole un ojo.

Sólo hasta ese momento se dio cuenta de que algo le habían arrancado el día que le dijeron que los primos no pueden casarse entre sí, porque los castiga Dios con hijos que parecen borrachos. Ya no había podido volver a los días de antes. Las tardes de su felicidad estuvieron amortiguadas en adelante por esa nostalgia repentina, inconfesable.

Nadie se hubiera atrevido a pedir más: sumar a la redonda tranquilidad que le daban sus hijos echando barcos de papel bajo la lluvia, al cariño sin reticencias de su marido generoso y trabajador, la certidumbre en todo el cuerpo de que el primo que hacía temblar su perfecto ombligo no estaba prohibido, y ella se lo merecía por todas las razones y desde siempre. Nadie, más que la desaforada tía Leonor.

Una tarde lo encontró caminando por la 5 de Mayo. Ella salía de la iglesia de Santo Domingo con un niño en cada mano. Los había llevado a ofrecer flores como todas las tardes de ese mes: la niña con un vestido largo de encajes y organdí blanco, coronita de paja y enorme velo alborotado. Como una novia de cinco años. El niño, con un disfraz de acólito que avergonzaba sus siete años.

—Si no hubieras salido corriendo aquel sábado en casa de los abuelos, este par sería mío —dijo Sergio, dándole un beso.

—Vivo con ese arrepentimiento —contestó la tía Leonor.

No esperaba esa respuesta uno de los solteros más codiciados de la ciudad. A los veintisiete años, recién llegado de España, donde se decía que aprendió las mejores técnicas para el cultivo de aceitunas, el primo Sergio era heredero de un rancho en Veracruz, de otro en San Martín y otro más cerca de Atzalan.

La tía Leonor notó el desconcierto en sus ojos, en la lengua con que se mojó un labio, y luego lo escuchó responder:

—Todo fuera como subirse otra vez al árbol.

La casa de la abuela quedaba en la 11 Sur, era enorme y llena de recovecos. Tenía un sótano con cinco puertas en que el abuelo pasó horas haciendo experimentos que a veces le tiznaban la cara y lo hacían olvidarse por un rato de los cuartos de abajo y llenarse de amigos con los que jugar billar en el salón construido en la azotea.

La casa de la abuela tenía un desayunador que daba al jardín y al fresno, una cancha para jugar frontón que ellos usaron siempre para andar en patines, una sala color de rosa con un piano de cola y una exhausta marina nocturna, una recámara para el abuelo y otra para la abuela, y en los cuartos que fueron de los hijos varias salas de estar que iban llamándose como el color de sus paredes. La abuela, memoriosa y paralítica, se acomodó a pintar en el cuarto azul. Ahí la encontraron haciendo rayitas con un lápiz en los sobres de viejas invitaciones de boda que siempre le gustó guardar. Les ofreció un vino dulce, luego un queso fresco y después unos chocolates rancios. Todo estaba igual en casa de la abuela. Lo único raro lo notó la viejita después de un rato:

—A ustedes dos, hace años que no los veía juntos.

—Desde que me dijiste que si los primos se casan tienen hijos idiotas —contestó la tía Leonor.

La abuela sonrió, empinada sobre el papel en el que delineaba una flor interminable, pétalos y pétalos encimados sin tregua.

—Desde que por poco y te matas al bajar del níspero —dijo Sergio.

—Ustedes eran buenos para cortar nísperos, ahora no encuentro quién.

—Nosotros seguimos siendo buenos —dijo la tía Leonor, inclinando su perfecta cintura.

Salieron del cuarto azul a punto de quitarse la ropa, bajaron al jardín como si los jalara un hechizo y volvieron tres horas después con la paz en el cuerpo y tres ramas de nísperos.

—Hemos perdido práctica —dijo la tía Leonor.

—Recupérenla, recupérenla, porque hay menos tiempo que vida —contestó la abuela con los huesos de níspero llenándole la boca.

Tía Elena

La hacienda de Arroyo Zarco era una larga franja de tierra fértil en la cordillera norte de Puebla. En 1910 sus dueños sembraban ahí café y caña de azúcar, maíz, frijol y legumbres menores. El paisaje era verde durante todo el año. Llovía con sol, sin sol y bajo todas las lunas. Llovía con tanta naturalidad que nadie tuvo nunca la ocurrencia de taparse para salir a caminar.

La tía Elena vivió poco tiempo bajo esas aguas. Primero porque no había escuelas cerca y sus padres la mandaron al Colegio del Sagrado Corazón en la Ciudad de México. A 300 kilómetros,

20 horas en tren, una merienda con su noche para dormir en la ciudad de Puebla y un desayuno regido ya por la nostalgia que provocarían diez meses lejos de la extravagante comida de su madre y cerca del francés y las caravanas de unas monjas inhóspitas. Luego, cuando había terminado con honores los estudios de aritmética, gramática, historia, geografía, piano, costura, francés y letra de piquitos; cuando acababa de regresar al campo y al desasosiego feliz de vivirlo, tuvo que irse otra vez porque llegó la Revolución.

Cuando los alzados entraron a la hacienda para tomar posesión de sus planicies y sus aguas, el papá de la tía no opuso resistencia. Entregó la casa, el patio, la capilla y los muebles con la misma gentileza que siempre lo había distinguido de los otros rancheros. Su mujer les enseñó a las soldaderas el camino a la cocina y él sacó los títulos en los que constaba la propiedad de la hacienda y se los entregó al jefe de la rebelión en el estado.

Luego se llevó a la familia a Teziutlán acomodada en un coche y casi sonriente.

Siempre habían tenido fama de ser medio locos, así que cuando aparecieron en el pueblo intactos y en paz, las otras familias de hacendados estuvieron seguros de que Ramos Lanz tenía algo que ver con los rebeldes. No podía ser casualidad que no hubieran quemado su casa, que sus hijas no se mostraran aterradas, que su mujer no llorara.

Los veían mal cuando caminaban por el pueblo, conversadores y alegres como si nada les hubiera pasado. Era tan firme y suave la actitud del padre que nadie en la familia veía razones para llamarse a tormento. Al fin y al cabo si él sonreía era que al día siguiente y al siguiente decenio habría comida sobre el mantel y crinolinas bajo las faldas de seda. Era que nadie se quedaría sin peinetas, sin relicarios, sin broches, sin los aretes de un brillante, sin el oporto para la hora de los quesos.

Sólo una tarde lo vieron intranquilo. Pasó varias horas frente al escritorio de la casa de Teziutlán dibujando algo que parecía un plano y que no lo dejaba contento. Iba tirando hojas y hojas al cesto de los papeles, sintiéndose tan inútil como quien trata de recordar el camino hacia un tesoro enterrado siglos atrás.

La tía Elena lo miraba desde un sillón sin abrir la boca, sin asomarse a nada que no fueran sus gestos. De repente lo vio conforme y lo escuchó hablar solo en un murmullo que no por serlo perdía euforia. Dobló el papel en cuatro y se lo echó en la bolsa interior del saco.

—¿Ya estará la cena? —le preguntó, mirándola por primera vez, sin enseñarle nada ni hablar de aquello que lo había mantenido tan ocupado toda la tarde.

—Voy a ver —dijo ella, y se fue a la cocina dirimiendo cosas. Cuando volvió, su padre dormitaba en un sillón de respaldo muy alto. Se acercó despacio y fue hasta el cesto de los papeles para salvar algunos de los pedazos que él había tirado. Los puso dentro de un libro y luego lo despertó para decirle que ya estaba la cena.

Todo era vasto en casa de los Ramos. Incluso en esos tiempos de escasez su madre se organizaba para hacer comidas de siete platillos y cenas de cinco personas cuando menos. Esa noche había una sopa de hongos, torta de masa, rajas con jitomate y frijoles refritos. Terminaba el menú con chocolate de agua y unos panes azucarados y brillantes que la tía Elena no volvió a ver después de la Revolución. Con todo eso en el estómago, los miembros de la familia se iban a dormir y a engordar sin ningún recato.

De los ocho hijos que había parido la señora De Ramos, cinco se habían muerto de enfermedades como la viruela, la tosferina y el asma, así que los tres vivos crecieron sobrealimentados. Según un acuerdo general, fue la buena y mucha comida lo que los ayudó a sobrevivir. Pero esa noche el padre de la tía sorprendió a su familia con que no tenía mucha hambre.

—Come pajarito, que te vas a enfermar —le suplicó doña Otilia a su marido, que era un hombre de uno ochenta entre los pies y la punta de la cabeza y de noventa kilos custodiándole el alma.

Elena pidió permiso para levantarse antes de terminar la última mordida de su pan con azúcar y fue a encerrarse con una vela en el cuarto de los huéspedes. Ahí puso juntos algunos pedazos del papel y leyó la tinta verde con que escribía su papá: el plano tenía pintada una vereda llegando al rancho por atrás de la casa, directo al cuarto bajo tierra que habían construido cerca de la cocina.

¡Los vinos! Lo único que su padre había lamentado desde que tomaron Arroyo Zarco fue la pérdida de sus vinos, de su colección de botellas con etiquetas en diversos idiomas, llenas de un brebaje que ella sorbía de la copa de los adultos desde muy niña. ¿Su papá, aquel hombre firme y moderado, sería capaz de volver a la hacienda por sus vinos? ¿Por eso lo había oído al mediodía pidiéndole a Cirilo una carreta con un caballo y paja?

La tía Elena cogió un chal y bajó las escaleras de un respingo. En el comedor, su padre todavía buscaba razones para explicarle a su mujer el grave delito de no tener hambre.

—No es desprecio, mi amor. Ya sé el trabajo que te cuesta construir cada comida para que no extrañemos lo de antes. Pero hoy en la noche tengo un asunto que arreglar y no quiero tener el estómago pesado.

En el momento en que oyó a su padre decir "hoy en la noche", la tía Elena salió corriendo al patio en busca de la única carreta. Cirilo el mozo la había colgado de un caballo y vigilaba en silencio. ¿Por qué Cirilo no se habría ido a la Revolución? ¿Por qué estaba ahí quieto, junto al caballo, en el mismo soliloquio de siempre? Tía Elena caminó de puntas a sus espaldas y se metió en la carreta por la parte de atrás. Al poco rato, oyó la voz de su padre.

—¿Encontraste buena brizna? —le preguntó al mozo.

—Sí, patrón. ¿La quiere ver?

La tía Elena pensó que había asentido con la cabeza porque lo oyó acercarse a la parte de atrás y levantar una punta del petate. Sintió moverse la mano de su padre a tres manos de su cuerpo:

—Está muy buena la brizna —dijo mientras se alejaba.

Entonces ella recuperó su alma y aflojó la tiesura de su cuello.

—Tú no vienes, Cirilo —dijo el señor Ramos—. Esta es una necedad de mi cuerpo que si a alguien le cuesta quiero que nada más sea a él. Si no regreso, dile a mi señora que todas las comidas que me dio en la vida fueron deliciosas y a mi hija Elena que no la busqué para darle un beso porque se lo quiero quedar a deber.

—Vaya bien —le dijo Cirilo.

La carreta empezó a moverse despacio, despacio abandonó el pueblo en tinieblas y se fue por un camino que debía ser tan estrecho como lo había imaginado la tía Elena cuando lo vio pintado con una sola línea. No había lugar ni a un lado ni a otro porque la carreta no se movía sino hacia adelante, sin que el caballo pudiera correr como lo hacía cuando ella lo guiaba por el camino grande.

Tardaron más de una hora en llegar, pero a ella se le hizo breve porque se quedó dormida. Despertó cuando la carreta casi dejó de andar y no se oía en el aire más que el murmullo de las eses con que su papá sosegaba al caballo. Sacó la cabeza para espiar en dónde estaban y vio frente a ella la parte de atrás de la enorme casa que añoró toda su vida. Ahí su padre detuvo la carreta, y se bajó. Ella lo vio temblar bajo la luna a medias. Al parecer, nadie vigilaba. Su papá caminó hasta una puerta en el muro y la abrió con una llave gigantesca. Luego desapareció. Entonces la tía Elena salió de entre la paja y fue tras él a meterse en la cava alumbrada por una linterna recién encendida.

—¿Te ayudo? —le dijo con su voz ronca. Tenía la cara somnolienta y el pelo lleno de brizna.

El horror que vio en los ojos de su padre no se le olvidaría jamás. Por primera vez en su vida sintió miedo, a pesar de tenerlo cerca.

—A mí también me gusta el oporto —dijo sobreponiéndose a su propio temblor. Luego cogió dos botellas y fue a dejarlas en la paja de la carreta. Al volver se cruzó con su padre, que llevaba otras cuatro. Así estuvieron yendo y viniendo en el silencio hasta que la carreta quedó cargada y no hubo en ella lugar ni para un oporto de esos que ella aprendió a beber en las rodillas de aquel hombre prudente y fiel a sus hábitos, que esa noche la sorprendió con su locura.

Cargó dos botellas más y se las puso en las piernas para pagar su peaje. Luego arreó al caballo y la carreta se dirigió al camino angosto y escondido por el que habían llegado. Tardarían horas en volver, pero era un milagro que estuvieran a punto de irse sin que nadie los hubiera visto. Ni uno solo de los campesinos que ocupaban Arroyo Zarco vigilaba la parte de atrás.

—¿Se habrán ido? —preguntó la tía Elena a su padre y saltó de la carreta sin darle tiempo de asirla. Corrió a la casa, se pegó a la oscuridad de una pared y caminó junto a ella hasta darle la vuelta. Por fin topó contra una de las bancas que custodiaban el portón del frente. No había una luz en toda esa oscuridad. Ni una voz, ni un chillido, ni unos pasos, ni una sola ventana viva.

—¡No hay nadie! —gritó la tía Elena—. ¡No hay nadie! —repitió, apretando los puños y brincando.

Volvieron a buen paso por el camino grande. La tía Elena tarareaba "Un viejo amor", con la nostalgia de una anciana. A los dieciocho años los amores de un día antes son ya viejos. Y a ella le habían pasado tantas cosas en esa noche, que de golpe sintió en sus amores un agujero imposible de remendar. ¿Quién le creería su aventura? Su novio del pueblo ni una palabra:

—Elena, por Dios, no cuentes barbaridades —le dijo alarmado, cuando escuchó la historia—. No están los tiempos para imaginerías. Entiendo que te duela dejar la hacienda, pero no desprestigies a tu papá contando historias que lo hacen parecer un borrachín irresponsable.

Lo había perdido ya bajo la despiadada luna del día anterior y ni siquiera trató de convencerlo. Una semana después, se trepó al tren en que su madre fue capaz de meter desde la sala Luis XV hasta diez gallinas, dos gallos y una vaca con su becerro. No llevaba más equipaje que el futuro y la temprana certidumbre de que el más cabal de los hombres tiene un tornillo flojo.

Tía Charo

Tenía la espalda inquieta y la nuca de porcelana. Tenía un pelo castaño y subversivo, y una lengua despiadada y alegre con la que recorría la vida y milagros de quien se ofreciera.

A la gente le gustaba hablar con ella, porque su voz era como lumbre y sus ojos convertían en palabras precisas los gestos más insignificantes y las historias menos obvias.

No era que inventara maldades sobre los otros, ni que supiera con más precisión los detalles de un chisme. Era sobre todo que descubría la punta de cada maraña, el exacto descuido de Dios que coronaba la fealdad de alguien, la pequeña imprecisión verbal que volvía desagradable un alma cándida.

A la tía Charo le gustaba estar en el mundo, recorrerlo con

sus ojos inclementes y afilarlo con su voz apresurada. No perdía el tiempo. Mientras hablaba, cosía la ropa de sus hijos, bordaba iniciales en los pañuelos de su marido, tejía chalecos para todo el que tuviera frío en el invierno, jugaba frontón con su hermana, hacía la más deliciosa torta de elote, moldeaba buñuelos sobre sus rodillas y discernía la tarea que sus hijos no entendían.

Nunca la hubiera avergonzado su pasión por las palabras si una tarde de junio no hubiese aceptado ir a unos ejercicios espirituales en los que el padre dedicó su plática al mandamiento "No levantarás falsos testimonios ni mentirás". Durante un rato el padre habló de los grandes falsos testimonios, pero cuando vio que con eso no atemorizaba a su adormilada clientela, se redujo a satanizar la pequeña serie de pecados veniales que se originan en una conversación sobre los demás, y que sumados dan gigantescos pecados mortales.

La tía Charo salió de la iglesia con un remordimiento en la boca del estómago. ¿Estaría ella repleta de pecados mortales, producto de la suma de todas esas veces en que había dicho que la nariz de una señora y los pies de otra, que el saco de un señor y la joroba de otro, que el dinero de un rico repentino y los ojos inquietos de una mujer casada? ¿Podría tener el corazón podrido de pecados por su conocimiento de todo lo que pasaba entre las faldas y los pantalones de la ciudad, de todas las necedades que impedían la dicha ajena y de tanta dicha ajena que no era sino necedad? Le fue creciendo el horror. Antes de ir a su casa pasó a confesarse con el padre español recién llegado, un hombre pequeño y manso que recorría la parroquia de San Javier en busca de fieles capaces de tenerle confianza.

En Puebla la gente puede llegar a querer con más fueza que en otras partes, sólo que se toma su tiempo. No es cosa de ver al primer desconocido y entregarse como si se le conociera de toda la vida. Sin embargo, en eso la tía no era poblana. Fue una de las primeras clientas del párroco español. El viejo cura que le había dado la primera comunión, murió dejándola sin nadie con quien hacer sus más secretos comentarios, los que ella y su conciencia destilaban a solas, los que tenían que ver con sus pequeños extravíos, con las dudas de sus privadísimas faldas, con las burbujas de su cuerpo y los cristales oscuros de su corazón.

—Ave María Purísima —dijo el padre español en su lengua apretujada, más parecida a la de un cantante de gitanerías que a la de un cura educado en Madrid.

—Sin pecado concebida —dijo la tía, sonriendo en la oscuridad del confesionario, como era su costumbre cada vez que afirmaba tal cosa.

—¿Usted se ríe? —preguntó el español adivinándola, como si fuera un brujo.

—No, padre —dijo la tía Charo temiendo los resabios de la Inquisición.

—Yo sí —dijo el hombrecito—. Y usted puede hacerlo con mi permiso. No creo que haya un saludo más ridículo. Pero dígame: ¿Cómo está? ¿Qué le pasa hoy tan tarde?

—Me pregunto, padre —dijo la tía Charo —si es pecado hablar de los otros. Usted sabe, contar lo que les pasa, saber lo que sienten, estar en desacuerdo con lo que dicen, notar que es bizco el bizco y renga la renga, despeinado el pachón, y presumida la tipa que sólo habla de los millones de su marido. Saber de dónde sacó el marido los millones y con quién más se los gasta. ¿Es pecado, padre? —preguntó la tía.

—No, hija —dijo el padre español—. Eso es afán por la vida. ¿Qué ha de hacer aquí la gente? ¿Trabajar y decir rezos? Sobra mucho día. Ver no es pecado, y comentar tampoco. Vete en paz. Duerme tranquila.

—Gracias, padre —dijo la tía Charo y salió corriendo a contárselo todo a su hermana.

Libre de culpa desde entonces, siguió viviendo con avidez la novela que la ciudad le regalaba. Tenía la cabeza llena con el ir y venir de los demás, y era una clara garantía de entretenimiento. Por eso la invitaban a tejer para todos los bazares de caridad, y se peleaban más de diez por tenerla en su mesa el día en que se jugaba canasta. Quienes no podían verla de ese modo, la invitaban a su casa o iban a visitarla. Nadie se decepcionaba jamás de oírla, y nadie tuvo nunca una primicia que no viniera de su boca.

Así corrió la vida hasta un anochecer en el bazar de Guadalupe. La tía Charo había pasado la tarde lidiando con las chaquiras de un cinturón y como no tenía nada nuevo que contar se limitó a oír.

—Charo, ¿tú conoces al padre español de la iglesia de San Javier? —le preguntó una señora, mientras terminaba el dobladillo de una servilleta.

—¿Por qué? —dijo la tía Charo, acostumbrada a no soltar prenda con facilidad.

—Porque dicen que no es padre, que es un republicano mentiroso que llegó con los asilados por Cárdenas y como no encontró trabajo de poeta, inventó que era padre y que sus papeles se habían quemado, junto con la iglesia de su pueblo, cuando llegaron los comunistas.

—Cómo es díscola alguna gente —dijo la tía Charo y agregó con toda la autoridad de su prestigio—: El padre español es un hombre devoto, gran católico, incapaz de mentir. Yo vi la carta con que el Vaticano lo envió a ver al párroco de San Javier. Que el pobre viejito se haya estado muriendo cuando llegó, no es culpa suya, no le dio tiempo de presentarlo. Pero de que lo mandaron, lo mandaron. No iba yo a hacer mi confesor a un farsante.

—¿Es tu confesor? —preguntó alguna en el coro de curiosas.

—Tengo ese orgullo —dijo la tía Charo, poniendo la mirada sobre la flor de chaquiras que bordaba, y dando por terminada la conversación.

A la mañana siguiente se internó en el confesionario del padre español.

—Padre, dije mentiras —contó la tía.

—¿Mentiras blancas? —preguntó el padre.

—Mentiras necesarias —contestó la tía.

—¿Necesarias para el bien de quién? —volvió a preguntar el padre.

—De una honra, padre —dijo la tía.

—¿La persona auxiliada es inocente?

—No lo sé, padre —confesó la tía.

—Doble mérito el tuyo —dijo el español—. Dios te conserve la lucidez y la buena leche. Ve con él.

—Gracias, padre —dijo la tía.

—A ti —le contestó el extraño sacerdote, poniéndola a temblar.

Tía Cristina

No era bonita la tía Cristina Martínez, pero algo tenía en sus piernas flacas y su voz atropellada que la hacía interesante. Por desgracia, los hombres de Puebla no andaban buscando mujeres interesantes para casarse con ellas y la tía Cristina cumplió veinte años sin que nadie le hubiera propuesto ni siquiera un noviazgo de buen nivel. Cuando cumplió veintiuno, sus cuatro hermanas estaban casadas para bien o para mal y ella pasaba el día entero con la humillación de estarse quedando para vestir santos. En poco tiempo, sus sobrinos la llamarían quedada y ella no estaba segura de poder soportar ese golpe. Fue después de aquel cumpleaños, que terminó con las lágrimas de su madre a la hora en que ella sopló las velas del pastel, cuando apareció en el horizonte el señor Arqueros.

Cristina volvió una mañana del centro, a donde fue para comprar unos botones de concha y un metro de encaje, contando que había conocido a un español de buena clase en la joyería *La Princesa*. Los brillantes del aparador la habían hecho entrar para saber cuánto costaba un anillo de compromiso que era la ilusión de su vida. Cuando le dijeron el precio le pareció correcto y lamentó no ser un hombre para comprarlo en ese instante con el propósito de ponérselo algún día.

—Ellos pueden tener el anillo antes que la novia, hasta pueden elegir una novia que le haga juego al anillo. En cambio, nosotras sólo tenemos que esperar. Hay quienes esperan durante toda su vida, y quienes cargan para siempre con un anillo que les disgusta, ¿no crees? —le preguntó a su madre durante la comida.

—Ya no te pelees con los hombres, Cristina —dijo su madre—. ¿Quién va a ver por ti cuando me muera?

—Yo, mamá, no te preocupes. Yo voy a ver por mí.

En la tarde, un mensajero de la joyería se presentó en la casa con el anillo que la tía Cristina se había probado extendiendo la mano para mirarlo por todos lados mientras decía un montón de cosas parecidas a las que le repitió a su madre en el comedor. Llevaba también un sobre lacrado con el nombre y los apellidos de Cristina.

Ambas cosas las enviaba el señor Arqueros, con su devoción, sus respetos y la pena de no llevarlos él mismo porque su barco salía de Veracruz al día siguiente y él viajó parte de ese día y toda la noche para llegar a tiempo. El mensaje le proponía matrimonio: "Sus conceptos sobre la vida, las mujeres y los hombres, su deliciosa voz y la libertad con que camina me deslumbraron. No volveré a México en varios años, pero le propongo que me alcance en España. Mi amigo Emilio Suárez se presentará ante sus padres dentro de poco. Dejo en él mi confianza y en usted mi esperanza".

Emilio Suárez era el hombre de los sueños adolescentes de Cristina. Le llevaba doce años y seguía soltero cuando ella tenía veintiuno. Era rico como la selva en las lluvias y arisco como los montes en enero. Le habían hecho la búsqueda todas las mujeres de la ciudad y las más afortunadas sólo obtuvieron el trofeo de una nieve en los portales. Sin embargo, se presentó en casa de Cristina para pedir, en nombre de su amigo, un matrimonio por poder en el que con mucho gusto sería su representante.

La mamá de la tía Cristina se negaba a creerle que sólo una vez hubiera visto al español, y en cuanto Suárez desapareció con la respuesta de que iban a pensarlo, la acusó de mil pirujerías. Pero era tal el gesto de asombro de su hija, que terminó pidiéndole perdón a ella y permiso al cielo en que estaba su marido para cometer la barbaridad de casarla con un extraño.

Cuando salió de la angustia propia de las sorpresas, la tía Cristina miró su anillo y empezó a llorar por sus hermanas, por su madre, por sus amigas, por su barrio, por la catedral, por el zócalo, por los volcanes, por el cielo, por el mole, por las chalupas, por el himno nacional, por la carretera a México, por Cholula, por Coetzalan, por los aromados huesos de su papá, por las cazuelas, por los chocolates rasposos, por la música, por el olor de las tortillas, por el río San Francisco, por el rancho de su amiga Elena y los potreros de su tío Abelardo, por la luna de octubre y la de marzo, por el sol de febrero, por su arrogante soltería, por Emilio Suárez que en toda la vida de mirarla nunca oyó su voz ni se fijó en cómo carambas caminaba.

Al día siguiente salió a la calle con la noticia y su anillo brillándole. Seis meses después se casó con el señor Arqueros frente a un cura, un notario y los ojos de Suárez. Hubo misa, banquete, baile y despedidas. Todo con el mismo entusiasmo que si el novio estuviera de este lado del mar. Dicen que no se vio novia más radiante en mucho tiempo.

Dos días después Cristina salió de Veracruz hacia el puerto donde el señor Arqueros con toda su caballerosidad la recogería para llevarla a vivir entre sus tías de Valladolid.

De ahí mandó su primera carta diciendo cuánto extrañaba y cuán feliz era. Dedicaba poco espacio a describir el paisaje apretujado de casitas y sembradíos, pero le mandaba a su mamá la receta de una carne con vino tinto que era el platillo de la región, y a sus hermanas dos poemas de un señor García Lorca que le habían vuelto al revés. Su marido resultó un hombre cuidadoso y trabajador, que vivía riéndose con el modo de hablar español y las historias de aparecidos de su mujer, con su ruborizarse cada vez que oía un "coño" y su terror porque ahí todo el mundo se cagaba en Dios por cualquier motivo y juraba por la hostia sin ningún miramiento.

Un año de cartas fue y vino antes de aquella en que la tía Cristina refirió a sus papás la muerte inesperada del señor Arqueros. Era una carta breve que parecía no tener sentimientos. "Así de mal estará la pobre", dijo su hermana, la segunda, que sabía de sus veleidades sentimentales y sus desaforadas pasiones. Todas quedaron con la pena de su pena y esperando que en cuanto se recuperara de la conmoción les escribiera con un poco más de claridad sobre su futuro. De eso hablaban un domingo después de la comida cuando la vieron aparecer en la sala.

Llevaba regalos para todos y los sobrinos no la soltaron hasta que terminó de repartirlos. Las piernas le habían engordado y las tenía subidas en unos tacones altísimos, negros como las medias, la falda, la blusa, el saco, el sombrero y el velo que no tuvo tiempo de quitarse de la cara. Cuando acabó la repartición se lo arrancó junto con el sombrero y sonrió.

—Pues ya regresé —dijo.

Desde entonces fue la viuda de Arqueros. No cayeron sobre ella las penas de ser una solterona y espantó las otras con su piano desafinado y su voz ardiente. No había que rogarle para que fuera hasta el piano y se acompañara cualquier canción. Tenía en su repertorio toda clase de valses, polkas, corridos, arias y pasos dobles. Les puso letra a unos preludios de Chopin y los cantaba evocando romances que nunca se le conocieron. Al terminar su concierto dejaba que todos le aplaudieran y tras levantarse del banquito para hacer una profunda caravana, extendía los brazos, mostraba su anillo y luego, señalándose a sí misma con sus manos envejecidas y hermosas, decía contundente: "Y enterrada en Puebla".

Cuentan las malas lenguas que el señor Arqueros no existió nunca. Que Emilio Suárez dijo la única mentira de su vida, convencido por quién sabe cuál arte de la tía Cristina. Y que el dinero que llamaba su herencia, lo había sacado de un contrabando cargado en las maletas del ajuar nupcial.

Quién sabe. Lo cierto es que Emilio Suárez y Cristina Martínez fueron amigos hasta el último de sus días. Cosa que nadie les perdonó jamás, porque la amistad entre hombres y mujeres es un bien imperdonable.

Tía Valeria

Hubo una tía nuestra, fiel como no lo ha sido ninguna otra mujer. Al menos eso cuentan todos los que la conocieron. Nunca se ha vuelto a ver en Puebla mujer más enamorada ni más solícita que la siempre radiante tía Valeria.

Hacía la plaza en el mercado de la Victoria. Cuentan las viejas marchantas que hasta en el modo de escoger las verduras se le notaba la paz. Las tocaba despacio, sentía el brillo de sus cáscaras y las iba dejando caer en la báscula.

Luego, mientras se las pesaban, echaba la cabeza para atrás y suspiraba, como quien termina de cumplir con un deber fascinante.

Algunas de sus amigas la creían medio loca. No entendían cómo iba por la vida, tan encantada, hablando siempre bien de su marido. Decía que lo adoraba aun cuando estaban más solas, cuando conversaban como consigo mismas en el rincón de un jardín o en el atrio de la iglesia.

Su marido era un hombre común y corriente, con sus imprescindibles ataques de mal humor, con su necesario desprecio por la comida del día, con su ingrata certidumbre de que la mejor hora para querer era la que a él se le antojaba, con sus euforias matutinas y sus ausencias nocturnas, con su perfecto discurso y su prudentísima distancia sobre lo que son y deben ser los hijos. Un marido como cualquiera. Por eso parecía inaudita la condición de perpetua enamorada que se desprendía de los ojos y la sonrisa de la tía Valeria.

—¿Cómo le haces? —le preguntó un día su prima Gertrudis, famosa porque cada semana cambiaba de actividad dejando en todas la misma pasión desenfrenada que los grandes hombres gastan en un sola tarea. Gertrudis podía tejer cinco suéteres en tres días, emprenderla a caballo durante horas, hacer pasteles para todas las kermeses de caridad, tomar clase de pintura, bailar flamenco, cantar ranchero, darles de comer a setenta invitados por domingo y enamorarse con toda obviedad de tres señores ajenos cada lunes.

—¿Cómo le hago para qué? —preguntó la apacible tía Valeria.

—Para no aburrirte nunca —dijo la prima Gertrudis, mientras ensartaba la aguja y emprendía el bordado de uno de los trescientos manteles de punto de cruz que les heredó a sus hijas—. A veces creo que tienes un amante secreto lleno de audacias.

La tía Valeria se rió. Dicen que tenía una risa clara y desafiante con la que se ganaba muchas envidias.

—Tengo uno cada noche —contestó, tras la risa.

—Como si hubiera de dónde sacarlos —dijo la prima Gertrudis, siguiendo hipnotizada el ir y venir de su aguja.

—Hay —contestó la tía Valeria cruzando las suaves manos sobre su regazo.

—¿En esta ciudad de cuatro gatos más vistos y apropiados? —dijo la prima Gertrudis haciendo un nudo.

—En mi pura cabeza —afirmó la otra, echándola hacia atrás en ese gesto tan suyo que hasta entonces la prima descubrió como algo más que un hábito raro.

—Nada más cierras los ojos —dijo, sin abrirlos— y haces de tu marido lo que más te apetezca: Pedro Armendáriz o Humphrey Bogart, Manolete o el gobernador, el marido de tu mejor amiga o el mejor amigo de tu marido, el marchante que vende las calabacitas o el millonario protector de un asilo de ancianos. A quien tú quieras, para quererlo de distinto modo. Y no te aburres nunca. El único riesgo es que al final se te noten las nubes en la cara. Pero eso es fácil evitarlo, porque las espantas con las manos y vuelves a besar a tu marido que seguro te quiere como si fueras Ninón Sevilla o Greta Garbo, María Victoria o la adolescente que florece en la casa de junto. Besas a tu marido y te levantas al mercado o a dejar a los niños en el colegio. Besas a tu marido, te acurrucas contra su cuerpo en las noches de peligro, y te dejas soñar . . .

Dicen que así hizo siempre la tía Valeria y que por eso vivió a gusto muchos años. Lo cierto es que se murió mientras dormía con la cabeza echada hacia atrás y un autógrafo de Agustín Lara debajo de la almohada.

Tía Fernanda

Con la vista perdida en el patio, un día de lluvia como tantos otros, la tía Fernanda dio por fin con la causa exacta de su extravío: era la cadencia. Eso era, porque todo lo demás lo tenía del lado donde debía tenerlo. Pero fue la maldita cadencia lo que la sacó de quicio. La cadencia, esa indescifrable nimiedad que hace que alguien camine de cierto modo, hable en cierto tono, mire con cierta pausa, acaricie con cierta exactitud.

Si hubiera tenido un cinco de cerebro para intuir ese lío, no hubiera entrado en él. Pero quién sabía en dónde había puesto la cabeza aquella vez, ni de dónde había sacado su papá aquello de que por encima de todo el hombre es un ser racional. O sería que al decir hombre, no quería decir mujer.

Vivía alterada porque nunca esperó tal disturbio. Alguna vez había ensoñado con cosas que no eran la paz de sus treinta paredes y su cama de plumas, pero nunca se dio tiempo para seguir tan horrorosas ideas. Tenía mucho quehacer y cuando no lo tenía, se lo inventaba. Tenía que enseñar catecismo a los niños pobres y costura a sus pobres mamás, tenía que organizar la colecta de la Cruz Roja y bailar en los bailes de caridad, tenía que bordar servilletas para cuando sus hijas crecieran y se casaran y mientras se casaban, tenía que hacerles los disfraces de fantasía con los que asistir a las fiestas del colegio. Tenía que llevar al niño a buscar ajolotes en las tardes, hacer la tarea de aritmética y saberse reprobada cuando hacían la de inglés. Además, tenía juego de bridge con unas amigas y encuentros de lectura con otras. Por si fuera poco, hacía el postre de todas las comidas y cuidaba que a la sopa no le faltara vino blanco, la carne no se dorara demasiado, el arroz se esponjara sin pegarse, las salsas no picaran ni mucho ni poco y los quesos fueran servidos junto a las uvas. Por ese tiempo, los maridos comían en sus hogares y luego dormían la siesta para que la eternidad del día no les pesara a media tarde. Por ese tiempo, en las casas había desayunos sin prisa y delicias nocturnas como el pan dulce y el café con leche.

Lograr que todas esas cosas sucedieran sin confusión, y ser de paso una mujer bienhumorada, era algo que cualquier marido tenía derecho a esperar de su señora. Así que la tía Fernanda ni siquiera pensaba en sentirse heroica. Tenía con ella la protección, la risa y los placeres suficientes. Con frecuencia, viendo dormir a sus hijos y leer a su marido, hasta le pareció que le sobraban bendiciones.

¡Cómo iba a querer algo más que ese tranquilo bienestar! De ninguna manera. A ella, la cadencia le había caído del cielo. ¿O del infierno? Se preguntaba furiosa con aquel desorden.

Pasaba toda la misa de nueve discutiendo con Dios aquel desastre. No era justo. Tanta prima solterona y ella con un desbarajuste en todo el cuerpo. Nunca pedía perdón. ¿Qué culpa tenía ella de que a la Divina Providencia se le hubiera ocurrido exagerar su infinita misericordia? No necesitaba otro castigo. No tenía miedo de nada, lo que le estaba pasando era ya su penitencia y su otro mundo. Estaba segura de que al morirse no tendría fuerzas para ningún tipo de vida, menos la eterna.

Sus encuentros con la cadencia la dejaban extenuada. Era tan complicado quererse en los sótanos y las azoteas, dar con lugares oscuros y recovecos solitarios en esa ciudad tan llena de oscuridades y recovecos que nunca eran casuales. ¿Cómo saber si eran seguras las escaleras de una iglesia o el piso de una cava cuando ahí a cualquier hora era posible que alguien tuviera el antojo de emborracharse o llamar a un rosario?

Estaban siempre en peligro, siempre perdiéndose. Primero de los demás, luego de ellos. Cuando se despedían, ella respiraba segura de que no querría volver a verlo, de que se le había gastado toda la necesidad, de que nada era mejor que regresar a su casa dispuesta a querer a los demás con toda la vehemencia que la locura aquella le dejaba por dentro. Y volvía a su casa tolerante, incapaz de educar a los niños en la costumbre de lavarse los dientes, dispuesta a decirles cuentos y canciones hasta que entraran en la paz del ángel de la guarda. Volvía a su casa iluminada, iluminada se metía en la cama, y todo, hasta el deseo de su marido, se iluminaba con ella.

—Es que el cariño no se gasta —pensaba—. ¿Quién habrá inventado que se gasta el cariño?

Nunca fue tan generosa como en ese tiempo. En ese tiempo se quedó con los dos niños que le dejó su cocinera para irse tras su propia cadencia, en ese tiempo su prima Carmen enfermó de tristeza y fue a dar a un manicomio del que ella la sacó para cuidarla primero y curarla después. En ese tiempo fue cuando su prima Julieta tuvo la peregrina y aterradora idea de salvar a la patria, guerreando en las montañas. También de los hijos de la prima Julieta se hizo cargo la tía Fernanda.

—Estamos dividiéndonos el trabajo —decía, cuando alguien intentaba criticar a Julieta, la clandestina.

Le daba tiempo de todo. Hasta de oír a su marido planear otro negocio y hacer el dictamen cotidiano del devastador estado en que se encontraba el irresponsable, abusivo y corrupto gobierno de la república.

—Primer error: ser república —decía él—. En lugar de haber agradecido la sabiduría del emperador Iturbide y guardarse para siempre como un imperio floreciente.

—Sí, mi vida —sabía contestar la tía con voz de ángel. No iba a discutir ella de política cuando la vida la tenía ocupada en asuntos mucho más importantes.

Poco a poco se había acostumbrado al desbarajuste. Resumió la misa diaria en la de los domingos, liberó a los niños del catecismo y le dejó a su hermana la responsabilidad de la clase de costura. Dedicó las tardes a los nueve hijos que había juntado su delirio y las demás obligaciones, incluída la de encontrar buen vino y escalar azoteas, le cupieron perfecto en cada jornada.

Quién lo diría: ella que tanto le temió al desorden, le estaba agradecida como al sol. Hasta en el cuerpo se le notaba la generosidad del caos en que vivía.

—¿Qué te echas en la cara? —le preguntó su hermana, cuando se encontraron en casa de su padre.

—Confusión —le respondió la tía Fernanda, riéndose.

—Ten cuidado con las dosis —dijo su papá, chupando el cigarro como si no tuviera cáncer. Era un hombre risueño, era el mejor cobijo.

—No siempre dependen de mí —respondió, abrazándolo.

Y de veras no dependían de ella. Cuando el dueño de la cadencia tuvo a bien desaparecer, la sobredosis de confusión estuvo a punto de matarla. Un buen día, el señor entró en la curva del desapego y pasó como vértigo de la adicción al desencanto, de la necesidad al abandono, de conocerla como la palma de su mano a olvidarla como a la palma de su mano. Entonces aquel desorden perdió su lógica, y la vida de la pobre tía Fernanda cayó en el espantoso caos de los días sin huella. Uno tras otro se amontonaban sobre el catarro más largo que haya padecido mujer alguna. Pasaba horas con la cabeza bajo la almohada, llorando como si tosiera, sonándose y maldiciendo como un borracho. Gracias al cielo, a su marido le dio entonces por fundar un partido democrático para oponerse al insolente PNR, un partido digno de gente como él y sus atribulados y decentísimos amigos. No se le ocurrió, por lo tanto, investigar demasiado en los males de su señora, a la que de cualquier modo hacía rato que veía enloquecer como a un mapache. El comprobaba así la teoría que su padre y su abuelo, ardientes lectores de Schopenhauer, habían encontrado en él con toda claridad, las causas y certidumbres filosóficas de la falta de cerebro en las mujeres.

Todo esto lo pensaba mientras su casa, regida todavía por la inercia de los tiempos en que la tía Fernanda vivía encendida y febril, caminaba sin tropiezos. Siempre había toallas en los toalleros y botones en sus camisas, café de Veracruz en su desayuno y puros cubanos en el cajón de su escritorio. Los niños tenían uniformes nuevos y libros recién forrados. La cocinera, la recamarera, la nana, el mozo, el chofer y el jardinero, tenían recién limadas todas las asperezas que hace crecer la convivencia, y hasta Felipita, la vieja encorvada que seguía sintiéndose nana de la tía, estaba entretenida con la dulzura de las confidencias que ella le iba haciendo.

Pasó así más de un mes. Su cuarto olía a encierro y a belladona, ella a sal y cebo. Los ojos le habían crecido como sapos y en la frente le habían salido cuatro arrugas. Los niños empezaron a estar hartos de hacer lo que se les pegaba la gana, la cocinera se peleó a muerte con el chofer, su marido acabó de fundar el partido y empezaron a urgirle conversación y cama tempranera. El director de la Cruz Roja llamó para pedir auxilio económico, su hermana quería dejar un tiempo las clases de costura y como si no bastara su papá le mandó decir que los enfermos de cáncer terminan por morirse, y que luego lo extrañaría más que a cualquiera. Todo esto puso a la tía Fernanda a llorar con la misma fiereza que el primer día. Doce horas seguidas pasó entre mocos y lágrimas. Como a las siete de la noche, Felipita le preparó un té de azar, tila y valeriana con dosis para casos extremos, y la puso a dormir hasta que la Divina Providencia le tuvo piedad.

Una mañana, la tía Fernanda abrió los ojos y la sorprendió el alivio. Había dormido noches sin apretar los dientes, sin soñar peces muertos, sin ahogarse. Tenía los ojos secos y ganas de hacer pipí, correctamente, por primera vez en mucho tiempo. Estuvo media hora bañándose y al salir con el pelo mojado y la piel lustrosa vio su cara en el espejo y se hizo un guiño. Después, bajó a desayunar con su familia que del gusto tuvo a bien perdonarle que el pan supiera rancio porque el chofer había cambiado de panadería con tal de no ir a la que le ordenó la cocinera, que quién era para mandarlo.

Al terminar el trajín mañanero, la tía Fernanda se fue a misa como en los buenos tiempos.

—Me vas a deber vida eterna —le dijo a la Santísima Trinidad.

Tía Carmen

Cuando la tía Carmen se enteró de que su marido había caído preso de otros perfumes y otro abrazo, sin más ni más lo dio por muerto. Porque no en balde había vivido con él quince años, se lo sabía al derecho y al revés, y en la larga y ociosa lista de sus cualidades y defectos nunca había salido a relucir su vocación de mujeriego. La tía estuvo siempre segura de que antes de tomarse la molestia de serlo, su marido tendría que morirse. Que volviera a medio aprender las manías, los cumpleaños, las precisas aversiones e ineludibles adicciones de otra mujer, parecía más que imposible. Su marido podía perder el tiempo y desvelarse fuera de la casa jugando cartas y recomponiendo las condiciones políticas de la política misma, pero gastarlo en entenderse con otra señora, en complacerla, en oírla, eso era tan increíble como insoportable. De todos modos, el chisme es el chisme y a ella le dolió como una maldición aquella verdad incierta. Así que tras ponerse de luto y actuar frente a él como si no lo viera, empezó a no pensar más en sus camisas, sus trajes, el brillo de sus zapatos, sus pijamas, su desayuno, y poco a poco hasta sus hijos. Lo borró del mundo con tanta precisión, que no sólo su suegra y su cuñada, sino hasta su misma madre estuvieron de acuerdo en que debían llevarla a un manicomio.

Y allá fue a dar, sin oponerse demasiado. Los niños se quedaron en casa de su prima Fernanda quien por esas épocas tenía tantos líos en el corazón que para ventilarlo dejaba las puertas abiertas y todo el mundo podía meterse a pedirle favores y cariño sin tocar siquiera.

Tía Fernanda era la única visita de tía Carmen en el manicomio. La única, aparte de su madre, quien por lo demás hubiera podido quedarse ahí también porque no dejaba de llorar por sus nietos y se comía las uñas, a los sesenta y cinco años, desesperada porque su hija no había tenido el valor y la razón necesarios para quedarse junto a ellos, como si no hicieran lo mismo todos los hombres.

La tía Fernanda, que por esas épocas vivía en el trance de amar a dos señores al mismo tiempo, iba al manicomio segura de que con un tornillito que se le moviera podría quedarse ahí por más de cuatro razones suficientes. Así que para no correr el riesgo llevaba siempre muchos trabajos manuales con los que entretenerse y entretener a su infeliz prima Carmen.

Al principio, como la tía Carmen estaba ida y torpe, lo único que hacían era meter cien cuentas en un hilo y cerrar el collar que después se vendería en la tienda destinada a ganar dinero para las locas pobres de San Cosme. Era un lugar horrible en el que ningún cuerdo seguía siéndolo más de diez minutos. Contando cuentas fue que la tía Fernanda no soportó más y le dijo a tía Carmen de su pesar también espantoso.

—Se pena porque faltan o porque sobran. Lo que devasta es la norma. Se ve mal tener menos de un marido, pero para tu consuelo se ve peor tener más de uno. Como si el cariño se gastara. El cariño no se gasta, Carmen —dijo la tía Fernanda—. Y tú no estás más loca que yo. Así que vámonos yendo de aquí.

La sacó esa misma tarde del manicomio.

Fue así como la tía Carmen quedó instalada en casa de su prima Fernanda y volvió a la calle y a sus hijos. Habían crecido tanto en seis meses, que de sólo verlos recuperó la mitad de su cordura. ¿Cómo había podido perderse tantos días de esos niños? Jugó con ellos a ser caballo, vaca, reina, perro, hada madrina, toro y huevo podrido. Se le olvidó que eran hijos del difunto, como llamaba a su marido, y en la noche durmió por primera vez igual que una adolescente.

Ella y tía Fernanda conversaban en las mañanas. Poco a poco fue recordando cómo guisar un arroz colorado y cuántos dientes de ajo lleva la salsa del spaguetti. Un día pasó horas bordando la sentencia que aprendió de una loca en el manicomio y a la que hasta esa mañana le encontró el sentido: "No arruines el presente lamentándote por el pasado ni preocupándote por el futuro". Se la regaló a su prima con un beso en el que había más compasión que agradecimiento puro.

—Debe ser extenuante querer doble— pensaba, cuando veía a Fernanda quedarse dormida como un gato en cualquier rincón y a cualquier hora del día. Una de esas veces, mirándola dormir, como quien por fin respira para sí, revivió a su marido y se encontró murmurando:

—Pobre Manuel.

Al día siguiente, amaneció empeñada en cantar *Para quererte a ti*, y tras vestir y peinar a los niños, con la misma eficiencia de sus buenos tiempos, los mandó al colegio y dedicó tres horas a encremarse, cepillar su pelo, enchinarse las pestañas, escoger un vestido entre diez de los que Fernanda le ofreció.

—Tienes razón —le dijo—. El cariño no se gasta. No se gasta el cariño. Por eso Manuel me dijo que a mí me quería tanto como a la otra. ¡Qué horror! Pero también: qué me importa, qué hago yo vuelta loca con los chismes, si estaba yo en mi casa haciendo buenos ruidos, ni uno más ni menos de los que me asignó la Divina Providencia. Si Manuel tiene para más, Dios lo bendiga. Yo no quería más, Fernanda. Pero tampoco menos. Ni uno menos.

Echó todo ese discurso mientras Fernanda le recogía el cabello y le ensartaba un hilo de oro en cada oreja. Luego se fue a buscar a Manuel para avisarle que en su casa habría sopa al mediodía y a cualquier hora de la noche. Manuel conoció entonces la boca más ávida y la mirada más cuerda que había visto jamás.

Comieron sopa.

Tía Isabel

El día que murió su padre, la tía Isabel Cobián perdió la fe en todo poder extraterreno. Cuando la enfermedad empezó ella fue a pedirle ayuda a la Virgen del Sagrado Corazón y poco después al señor Santiago que había en su parroquia, un santo de aspecto tan eficaz que iba montado a caballo. Como ninguno de los dos se acomidió a interceder por la salud de su padre, la tía visitó a Santa Teresita que tan buena se veía, a Santo Domingo que fue tan sabio, a San José que sólo por ser casto debía tener todo concedido, a Santa Mónica que tanto sufrió con su hijo, a San Agustín que tanto sufrió con su mamá, y hasta a San Martín de Porres que era negro como su desgracia. Pero ya que a lo largo de cinco días nadie había intercedido para bien, la tía Isabel se dirigió a Jesucristo y a su mismísimo Padre para rogar por la vida del suyo. De todos modos su papá murió como estaba decidido desde que lo concibieron: el miércoles 13 de febrero de 1935 a las tres de la mañana.

Entonces, para sorpresa de la tía Isabel, la tierra no se abrió ni dejó de amanecer, ni se callaron los pájaros que todos los días escandalizaban en el fresno del jardín. Sus hermanos no se quedaron mudos, ni siquiera su madre dejó de moverse con la suavidad de su hermoso cuerpo. Peor aún, ella seguía perfectamente viva a pesar de haber creído siempre que aquello la mataría. Con el tiempo, supo que la cosa era peor, que esa pena iba a seguirla por la vida con la misma asiduidad con que la seguían sus piernas.

Estaba guapo su papá muerto. Tenía la piel más blanca que nunca y las manos suaves como siempre. Cuando todos bajaron a desayunar, ella se quedó a solas con él y por primera vez en la vida no supo qué decirle. Nada más pudo acomodarse contra aquel cuerpo y poner sobre su cabeza las manos inertes del hombre que la engendró.

—Qué idea tuya morirte —le dijo—. No te lo voy a perdonar nunca.

Y en efecto, nunca se lo perdonó.

Veinte años después, al ver un viejo pensaba que su padre podría estar tan vivo como él y sentía la necesidad de tenerlo cerca con la misma premura que al día siguiente del entierro.

A veces, en mitad de cualquier tarde, porque a su marido no le había gustado el pollo con tomate, porque a sus tres hijos les daba gripa al mismo tiempo, o porque sí, ella sentía una pena de navajas por todo el cuerpo y empezaba a maldecir la traición de su padre. Entonces arrancaba un berrinche como los que hacía de niña mientras él le recomendaba: "Guarda tus lágrimas para cuando yo muera, que ahora estoy aquí para solucionar lo que se te ofrezca".

No iba a la iglesia. Se casó con uno de esos hombres que entonces se llamaban librepensadores y creció a sus hijos en la confusión teológica venida de un padre que jamás nombró a Dios, ni para negarlo, una abuela y unos parientes que no hacían sino rezar por la salvación del alma de tal padre, y una madre que en lugar de rezarles a los santos, como lo hacía todo el mundo en la ciudad, mantenía largas conversaciones con la foto del abuelito y los domingos compraba un abrazo de claveles y se iba al panteón.

Para consuelo propio, la abuelita los bautizó, les enseñó la señal de la cruz y el catecismo del Padre Ripalda. Gracias a ella hicieron la primera comunión y no cargaron con el problema de ser vistos como ateos. Los niños aprendieron todo del mismo modo en que aprendieron de su madre a jugar damas chinas, a leer y a maldecir.

Eran adolescentes cuando tía Isabel se cayó de un caballo al que nadie quiso saber ni por qué ni dónde ni con quién se había subido. La encontraron tirada por el campo militar repitiendo un montón de necedades que su marido decidió no escuchar. Se dedicó a besarla como si fuera una medalla y a permanecer junto a ella todo el tiempo que siempre tenía tan ocupado.

La abuelita llamó a un sacerdote, el hijo mayor enfureció de pena y estuvo todo un día pateando los muebles de la casa. El menor se fue a meter a la iglesia de Santa Clara y la niña de en medio cogió sus diecisiete años, le prendió una vela al abuelito y se fue al panteón con una carretilla de claveles. Cuando volvió a la casa, el médico había dicho que todo estaba en manos de Dios y la familia entera lloraba de antemano a Isabel.

—No le va a pasar nada —dijo la hija de en medio, al volver del panteón con la sonrisa de quienes en mitad de un aguacero encontraron refugio en el quicio de una puerta—. Me lo acaba de asegurar el abuelo —completó, para responder a la pregunta que había en los ojos de todos.

Al poco rato, Isabel dejó el delirio y se bebió de golpe la taza con leche que la hija le había acercado.

—Tienes razón, mamá —dijo la niña—. El abuelito es santo.

—¿Verdad? —contestó su madre.

—Verdad —afirmó la niña, recordando el único domingo que acompañó a su madre al panteón. Tenía seis años y sabía a medias el Himno Nacional. Quiso cantárselo al abuelo.

—Harás bien, hija —le dijo Isabel.

—Y mientras la niña cantaba ella metió la cara en los claveles y murmuró secretos y secretos, ruegos y ruegos.

—¿Qué le pides, mamá? —había preguntado la niña.

—Delirios, hija —había contestado Isabel Cobián—. Delirios.

Tía Chila

La tía Chila estuvo casada con un señor al que abandonó, para escándalo de toda la ciudad, tras siete años de vida en común. Sin darle explicaciones a nadie. Un día como cualquier otro, la tía Chila levantó a sus cuatro hijos y se los llevó a vivir en la casa que con tan buen tino le había heredado su abuela.

Era una mujer trabajadora que llevaba suficientes años zurciendo calcetines y guisando fabada, de modo que poner una fábrica de ropa y venderla en grandes cantidades, no le costó mas esfuerzo que el que había hecho siempre. Llegó a ser proveedora de las dos tiendas más importantes del país. No se dejaba regatear, y viajaba una vez al año a Roma y París para buscar ideas y librarse de la rutina.

La gente no estaba muy de acuerdo con su comportamiento. Nadie entendía cómo había sido capaz de abandonar a un hombre que en los puros ojos tenía la bondad reflejada. ¿En qué pudo haberla molestado aquel señor tan amable que besaba la mano de las mujeres y se inclinaba afectuoso frente a cualquier hombre de bien?

—Lo que pasa es que es una cuzca —decían algunos.

—Irresponsable —decían otros.

—Lagartija —cerraban un ojo.

—Mira que dejar a un hombre que no te ha dado un solo motivo de queja.

Pero la tía Chila vivía de prisa y sin alegar, como si no supiera, como si no se diera cuenta de que hasta en la intimidad del salón de belleza había quienes no se ponían de acuerdo con su extraño comportamiento.

Justo estaba en el salón de belleza, rodeada de mujeres que extendían las manos para que les pintaran las uñas, las cabezas para que les enredaran los chinos, los ojos para que les cepillaran las pestañas, cuando entró con una pistola en la mano el marido de Consuelito Salazar. Dando de gritos se fue sobre su mujer y la pescó de la melena para zangolotearla como al badajo de una campana, echando insultos y contando sus celos, reprochando la fodonguez y maldiciendo a su familia política, todo con tal ferocidad, que las tranquilas mujeres corrieron a esconderse tras las secadores y dejaron sola a Consuelito, que lloraba suave y aterradoramente, presa de la tormenta de su marido.

Fue entonces cuando, agitando sus uñas recién pintadas, salió de un rincón la tía Chila.

—Usted se larga de aquí —le dijo al hombre, acercándose a él como si toda su vida se la hubiera pasado desarmando vaqueros en las cantinas—. Usted no asusta a nadie con sus gritos. Cobarde, hijo de la chingada. Ya estamos hartas. Ya no tenemos miedo. Deme la pistola si es tan hombre. Valiente hombre valiente. Si tiene algo que arreglar con su señora diríjase a mí, que soy su representante. ¿Está usted celoso? ¿De quién está celoso? ¿De los tres niños que Consuelo se pasa contemplando? ¿De las veinte cazuelas entre las que vive? ¿De sus agujas de tejer, de su bata de casa? Esta pobre Consuelito que no ve más allá de sus narices, que se dedica a consecuentar sus necedades, a ésta le viene usted a hacer un escándalo aquí, donde todas vamos a chillar como ratones asustados. Ni lo sueñe, berrinches a otra parte. Hilo de aquí: hilo, hilo, hilo —dijo la tía Chila tronando los dedos y arrimándose al hombre aquel, que se había puesto morado de la rabia y que ya sin pistola estuvo a punto de provocar en el salón un ataque de risa. —Hasta nunca, señor —remató la tía Chila—. Y si necesita comprensión vaya a buscar a mi marido. Con suerte y hasta logra que también de usted se compadezca toda la ciudad.

Lo llevó hacia la puerta dándole empujones y cuando lo puso en la banqueta cerró con triple llave.

—Cabrones éstos —oyeron decir, casi para sí, a la tía Chila.

Un aplauso la recibió de regreso y ella hizo una larga caravana.

—Por fin lo dije —murmuró después.

—Así que a ti también —dijo Consuelito.

—Una vez —contestó Chila, con un gesto de vergüenza.

Del salón de Inesita salió la noticia rápida y generosa como el olor a pan. Y nadie volvió a hablar mal de la tía Chila Huerta porque hubo siempre alguien, o una amiga de la amiga de alguien que estuvo en el salón de belleza aquella mañana, dispuesta a impedirlo.

Tía Rosa

Una tarde la tía Rosa miró a su hermana como recién pulida, todavía brillante por alguna razón que ella no podía imaginar.

Durante horas oyó cada una de sus palabras tratando de intuir de dónde venían. No adivinó. Sólo supo que esa noche su hermana fue menos brusca con ella. Se portó como si al fin le perdonara su vocación de rezos y guisos, como si ya no fuera a reírse nunca de su irredenta soltería, de su necedad catequística, de su aburrida devoción por la virgen del Carmen.

Así que se fue a dormir en paz después de repetir el rosario y sopear galletitas de manteca en leche con chocolate.

Quién sabe cómo sería su primer sueño esa noche. Si alguien la hubiera visto, regordeta y sonriente dentro de su camisón, la habría comparado con una niña menor de cinco años. Sin embargo, a la cabeza rizada de tía Rosa entró aquella noche un sueño insospechado.

Soñó que su hermana se iba a un baile de disfraces, que salía sin hacer ruido y regresaba en el centro de una alharaca. Era el aliento de una comparsa de hombres que se reían con ella, sin más quehacer que acompañar la felicidad que le rodaba por todo el cuerpo. La muy dichosa se quitaba y se ponía una máscara de esas que hacen en Venecia, una de muchos colores con la luna en la punta de la cabeza y la boca delirante. De pronto empezó a bailar frente a la tía Rosa que, sentada en el sillón principal de la sala, dejó de comer galletas. Tal era la maravilla que había entrado en su casa.

Su hermana levantaba las piernas para bailar un can cán que los demás tarareaban, pero en lugar de los calzones y los encajes de las cancaneras, ella llevaba una falda diminuta que subía complacida enseñando sus piernas duras y su pubis cambiado de lugar. Porque sobre el sitio en el que está el pubis, ella se había pintado una decoración de hojas amarillas, verdes, moradas que palpitaban como si estuviera en el centro del mundo. Y arriba de una pierna, brillante y esponjado, iba el mechón de pelo de su pubis: viajero y libre como todo en ella.

Al día siguiente, la tía Rosa miró a su hermana como si la viera por primera vez.

—Creo que te estoy entendiendo —le dijo.

—Amén —contestó la hermana, acercando a ella su cara brillante, para darle un beso de los que regalan las mujeres enamoradas porque ya no les caben bajo la ropa.

—Amén —dijo Rosa, y se puso a brincar su propio sueño.

Tía Paulina

Paulina Traslosheros tenía veinte años cuando conoció a Isaak Webelman, un músico que se detuvo en Puebla a esperar noticias de sus parientes judíos en Nueva York.

Venía de Polonia y Sudamérica y era un hombre distinto al común de los hombres entre los que creció Paulina. Un hombre con sonrisa de mujer y ojos de anciano, con voz de adolescente y manos de pirata. Capaz de convocar al entusiasmo como lo hacen los niños y de ahuyentar la dicha como separa el agua la quilla de un barco. Era inasible y atractivo como su música preferida, a la que él atribuía un sinnúmero de virtudes, más la principal: llamarse y ser Inconclusa.

—En realidad —le dijo a Paulina, al poco tiempo de conocerla—, los finales son indignos del arte. Las obras de arte son siempre inconclusas. Quienes las hacen, no están seguros nunca de que las han terminado. Sucede lo mismo con las mejores cosas de la vida. En eso, aunque fuera alemán, tenía razón Goethe: "Todo principio es hermoso pero hay que detenerse en el umbral".

—¿Y cómo se sabe dónde termina el umbral? —le preguntó Paulina pensando que, si era cosa de ponerse pesados, ella no tenía por qué ir atrás. Luego, mientras caminaba hacia el piano, empezó a silbar la tonada principal de la Séptima Sinfonía de Schubert.

Webelman tenía fama de ser un gran músico, y en cuanto llegó a Puebla se hizo de una cantidad de alumnos sólo comparable al tamaño que tenía en cada poblano la veneración por lo extranjero. Cada vez que llegaba un maestro de fuera, obtenía decenas de alumnos durante los primeros tres días de estancia. Conservarlos era lo difícil.

El músico Webelman se presentó como maestro de piano, violín, flauta, percusiones y chelo. Tuvo alumnos para todo, hasta uno de nombre Victoriano Alvarez que intentó aprender percusiones antes de convertirse en político como un modo más eficaz de hacer ruido.

Paulina Traslosheros tocaba el piano con mucho más conocimiento y elegancia que cualquiera de las otras alumnas, no en balde su padre la había encerrado todas las tardes de su infancia en la sala de arriba. Primero, era una obligación estarse ahí dos horas practicando escalas hasta morirse de tedio, pero después le tomó cariño a ese lugar. Se acostumbró a los muebles brillantes y tiesos que se acomodaban en aquella sala, esperando visitas que nunca llegarían. Se acostumbró al mantón de manila sobre la cola del piano, a los abanicos enmarcados, al San Juan Bautista que la miraba desde la puerta y a los cuadros de paisajes remotos que presidían las paredes. Le gustó pasar el tiempo ahí, lejos del trajín de toda la casa, sumida en aquel ambiente que olía al siglo antepasado y en el que se permitía las más modernas elucubraciones y fantasías.

Hasta ahí llegaba Isaak Webelman con su Inconclusa todas las tardes, de seis a ocho. Le gustaba hacer discursos y a la tía le gustaba escucharlos. A veces se reía en mitad de una tesis sobre las causas por las que Mozart había puesto un Mi bemol mayor, en lugar de un Re menor, para regir la Sinfonía Concertante.

—Eres un fantasioso —dijo Paulina agradecida.

Tanto tiempo había vivido rodeada de verdades contundentes o irrefutables, que las odiaba.

—Mejor dicho, tú eres una incrédula —contestó Isaak Webelman—. Vuelve a darme ese Re que sonó a brinco.

La tía Paulina obedeció.

—No, así no. Así estás demostrándome cuán virtuosa puedes ser, cuán hábil, pero no cuán artista. Una cosa es hacer sonar un instrumento y otra muy distinta hacer música. La música tiene que tener magia y la magia depende de algunos trucos, pero más que nada de los buenos impulsos. Mira —dijo, pasando un brazo por la cintura de la tía—: Tú quieres dar este Re con más énfasis, no sabes cómo. En apariencia no tienes más que un dedo y una tecla para hacerlo, pero con el dedo y la tecla no haces más que un ruido, lo demás tienes que sacarlo de tu cabeza, de tu corazón, de tus entrañas. Porque ahí es donde está, con toda exactitud, el sonido que deseas. Cuando lo sabes, no tienes más que sacarlo. ¡Sácalo!

La tía Paulina obedeció hipnotizada. El piano de la abuelita sonó como nunca antes con el mismo *Para Elisa* de toda la vida.

—Aprendes —dijo Webelman sentado junto a ella. Luego se la quedó mirando como si ella misma fuera Elisa.

Por la espalda de Paulina Traslosheros corrió un escalofrío. Ese hombre era un horror, un exceso, un desafuero. Para exorcizarlo, ella cometería una hilera de pecados de los que nunca pudo arrepentirse. Ni siquiera cuando él decidió volver a Nueva York, porque ahí estaba el éxito y el éxito no podía cedérsele a la furia que sería la vida de un gran músico atorado en una sala poblana por culpa de algo tan etéreo como el amor.

—Tú supiste desde siempre cuál es mi sinfonía predilecta —dijo Webelman, al recorrer por última vez la espalda de Paulina Traslosheros con el conjuro de su mano audaz y hereje.

—Hasta siempre lo voy a saber —contestó ella, mientras se abrochaba el corpiño empezando a vestirse.

El músico se fue y tuvo el éxito que buscaba. Tanto éxito, que era imposible ir por la vida sin escuchar su nombre en boca de cualquier extraño. Paulina Traslosheros se casó, tuvo hijos y nietos. Cruzó más de un umbral durante la vida, pero nunca pudo evitar el frío bajando por su espalda cada vez que alguien mencionaba aquel nombre.

—¿Qué te pasa, abuela? —le preguntó una de sus nietas cuando la vio estremecerse con los primeros acordes de la Séptima de Schubert saliendo del tocadiscos. Cuarenta años después de la tarde en que había conocido a Isaak Webelman.

—Lo de siempre mi vida, pero ahora debe ser culpa de un virus, porque ahora todo es viral.

Después cerró los ojos y tarareó, febril y adolescente, la música inconclusa de toda su vida.

Tía Eloísa

Desde muy joven la tía Eloísa tuvo a bien declararse atea. No le fue fácil dar con un marido que estuviera de acuerdo con ella, pero buscando, encontró un hombre de sentimientos nobles y maneras suaves, al que nadie le había amenazado la infancia con asuntos como el temor a Dios.

Ambos crecieron a sus hijos sin religión, bautismo ni escapularios. Y los hijos crecieron sanos, hermosos y valientes, a pesar de no tener detrás la tranquilidad que otorga saberse protegido por la Santísima Trinidad.

Sólo una de las hijas creyó necesitar del auxilio divino y durante los años de su tardía adolescencia buscó auxilio en la iglesia anglicana. Cuando supo de aquel Dios y de los himnos que otros le entonaban, la muchacha quiso convencer a la tía Eloísa de cuán bella y necesaria podía ser aquella fe.

—Ay, hija —le contestó su madre, acariciándola mientras hablaba—, si no he podido creer en la verdadera religión ¿cómo se te ocurre que voy a creer en una falsa?

Tía Mercedes

Ya era tarde y la tía Mercedes seguía buscando quién sabe qué cosas en el cuerpo del hombre al que reconocía como el amor de su vida.

Desde jóvenes se tenían vistos, pero ni ellos mismos supieron bien a bien dónde se les había perdido la primera certidumbre de que estaban hechos para juntarse. Muchas veces él gastaba el tiempo en lamentar lo que consideraba un error inperdonable. Sin embargo, la tía Mercedes le dijo siempre que nada hubiera podido ser distinto, porque aunque ya nadie quisiera creerlo, el destino es el destino.

Fue tiempo después de casarse cada quien con fortuna o desventura, cuando se volvieron a encontrar en una de esas fiestas en las que de puro tedio todo mundo hubiera querido inventarse otro amor. Una de esas fiestas llenas de pasos dobles y cigarro, de esas que sin remedio terminaban en pleitos de árabes contra españoles, que no eran ni una cosa ni la otra: los españoles habían llegado a la ciudad hacía cuatro siglos y los árabes hacía ochenta años, así que sus descendientes, en realidad, eran poblanos en litigio.

Se miraron de lejos, se fueron acercando y por fin se encontraron en la mesa de unos españoles que ya estaban planeando cómo romper unas sillas en las crismas de los árabes sentados en la mesa más próxima. En medio de aquel caos, ellos perdieron las palabras, volvieron a prenderse de los gestos, se vieron enlazados sin remedio y sin prisa, hasta quién sabía cuándo.

Antes de que empezara la pelea, abandonaron la fiesta para irse en busca de una derrota que habían dejado pendiente hacía doce años.

La encontraron. Y se hicieron viejos yendo a buscarla cada vez que la vida se angostaba. La tía Mercedes tenía siempre miedo de que cada encuentro fuera el último. Por eso le gustaba conversar, para robarse al otro, para que no se le escapara del todo cuando volvía a su casa con el cuerpo apaciguado, para poder, en el impredecible tiempo que los desuniera, reconstruirlo todo, no sólo su aventura, sino todas las mutuas aventuras desde siempre.

Cada vez indagaba alguna cosa. Así llegó a saber hasta de qué color había él forrado los cuadernos cuando entró a primero de primaria, cuánto le costaban los perones con chile que compraba a la salida del colegio y por qué le hubiera gustado tanto que ella se llamara Natalia.

Una tarde, casi noche, la tía Mercedes Cuadra tenía la codicia encendida y quiso saber cómo había sido para él eso que los hombres hacían por primera vez en la calle noventa. El nunca había hablado de eso con ninguna mujer y tardó en empezar su historia. Pero la tía Mercedes le pasó la mano por la espalda como si fuera un caballo y lo fue haciendo hablar de aquel recuerdo, igual que lo hacía desnudarse algunas veces, cuando ya se habían vestido y estaban a punto de irse.

La calle noventa era un mugrero en el que hasta las luces parecían sucias. El fue ahí por primera vez con algunos amigos que ya habían estado dos o tres veces, pero nadie era un experto. Algunos habían ido uno noche con sus hermanos mayores o con sus tíos, a otro lo había llevado su papá porque tenía la cara llena de barros y a decir suyo no había mejor manera de quitárselos. Total, eran como siete dándose valor, atarantados con aquella clandestinidad impúdica, muertos de risa y pánico.

Pasaron todos con la misma, una chaparrita de gesto inmundo que no dejaba de mascar chicle. Les preguntó si con vestido o sin vestido.

—Sin vestido, les cuesta el doble —advirtió.

Acordaron que con vestido. El ya no sabía cómo tuvo ganas de nada cuando le tocó pasar, pero pasó. La chaparrita le mascó el chicle en la oreja todo el tiempo y él juró no volver.

—¿Y no volviste? —preguntó la tía Mercedes, empezando a vestirse, celosa como si acabara de oír la más impecable historia de amor.

—Sí volví —dijo él—. En la tarde ya le estaba robando a mi mamá dinero para regresar. Y regresé con la misma.

—¿Igual que ahora? —dijo la tía Mercedes, dejándose caer sobre él para morderlo y rasguñarlo.

—Sólo que tú no mascas chicle —contestó él abrazándola. Le pellizcó después las costillas para hacerla reír.

Así estuvieron un rato, un rato largo: riéndose, riéndose, hasta que acabaron llorando.

Tía Verónica

La tía Verónica era una niña de ojos profundos y labios delgados. Miraba rápido, y le parecía largo el tiempo en el colegio. A veces la castigaban con la cara contra la pared o la ponían a coser el dobladillo que de un brinco le había desbaratado al uniforme.

En las tardes, por fin, la dejaban jugar con su gata Casiopea, un animal con mirada de reina y actitud desdeñosa, en contraste con sus rayas grises y su pelambre corriente.

Casi al mismo tiempo en que dejó de ponerle gorro a Casiopea y la convirtió en la mascota ideal para trepar árboles, la tía Verónica descubrió las noches y sus extraños desafíos. De la punta de una rama pasaba con todos sus hermanos a una tina y de ahí a la merienda y a una cama para cada quien.

Ella no cuenta exactamente cómo fue que cayó en el juego nocturno que asoció al inefable sexto mandamiento. Quizá porque nunca estuvo claro, y era grande, fantasioso y oscuro como las mismas noches. El caso es que dejó de confesarse y dejó de comulgar uno y otro Viernes Primero.

Nadie se daba esos lujos en la pequeña comunidad que era su colegio. Seguramente, pensaba ella, porque nadie se daba tiempo para los otros lujos.

Las llevaban a misa de once. Cruzaban el Paseo Bravo con las mantillas sobre los hombros, en fila, de dos en dos, sin permiso para mirar las jaulas de los changos con sus sonrisas obscenas o levantar la cabeza hasta la punta de la rueda de la fortuna y dejarla ahí dando vueltas.

Ella siempre aprovechaba ese tiempo para romper el ayuno con un chicle, tres cacahuates o cualquier cosa que significara un castigo menos grave que la excomunión derivada de comulgar con el sexto mandamiento metido en todo el cuerpo.

Pero después de cuatro veces de ponerla a escribir todo un cuaderno con "No debo romper el ayuno", su maestra caminó junto a ella por el parque fijándose muy bien que no se metiera nada en la boca.

Entonces alegó no estar confesada y se paró en la punta de la fila más larga junto al confesionario. Para su suerte, había muchas niñas urgidas de confesar lo de siempre: engaños a los papás y pleitos con los hermanos. Ella les cedió su lugar cinco veces y cuando llegó la hora de comulgar, se había librado del confesionario por falta de tiempo.

Trucos de esos encontró durante un año, pero hasta su audacia imaginaba que se le acabarían alguna vez. Por eso sintió un brinco de gusto cuando supo que había llegado a la parroquia de su barrio un padrecito nuevo que venía de la sierra. Hablaba un español tropezado y su despeinada cabeza le inspiró confianza.

La iglesia de Santiago era un esperpento de yesos cubiertos con dorado y santos a medio despostillar. La misma mezcla de viejos ricos y eternos pobres se amontonaba en sus democráticas y cochambrosas bancas. Los confesionarios eran de madera labrada y tenían tres puertas: por la de en medio entraba el cura, las otras dos formaban pequeños escondrijos en los que cabía un reclinatorio bajo la única ventana, que era una rejilla directa sobre la oreja del confesor. Ahí se hincaban las niñas, ponían la boca contra la pestilente rejilla y descargaban su conciencia. Luego recibían una dosis de Avesmarías y se iban con la misma intranquilidad a seguir peleando con los hermanos y asaltando la despensa.

La tía Verónica supo que el recién llegado estaba justo frente al confesionario en el que se sentaba el eterno padre Cuspinera, el que la bautizó, le dio la primera comunión y le pellizcaba las mejillas en el atrio mientras repetía los mismos saludos para su mamá. Ella no podía permitirse lastimar los oídos del padre Cuspinera, el ronco y redondo monseñor, Prelado Doméstico de su Santidad, que era como un pariente sin hijos, como un tío empeñado en construirle una iglesia a la Virgen del Perpetuo Socorro con la misma terquedad con que ella persistía en sus pecados nocturnos. Lo mejor —volvió a pensar— era el recién llegado. Así todo quedaría entre desconocidos.

Entró al confesionario, atropelló el *Yo pecador* y dijo:

—Pequé contra el sexto.

—¿Sola o acompañada? —le preguntó el nuevo vicario.

Hasta entonces supo la tía Verónica que tal asunto se podía practicar acompañada. "¿Cómo sería eso?" se preguntó mientras contestaba: "Sola". Era tal su sorpresa que se ahorró la desobediencia y las otras minucias y dijo suavemente: "Nada más, padre".

Después oyó la penitencia: tenía que salir del confesionario, rezar otra vez el *Yo pecador* y luego irse a su casa deteniéndose en el camino frente a cada poste que encontrara, a darse un tope al son de una Salve.

Cosa más horrenda no pudo haber imaginado como penitencia. Ella estaba dispuesta a cualquier dolor que fuera tan clandestino como su pecado, pero ir dándose de topes en cada poste con la turba de sus hermanos riéndose tras ella, le daba más miedo que irle a contar todo al padre Cuspinera.

Lo miró sentado en el confesionario de enfrente, con su gesto de niño aburrido, harto de que la tarde fuera tan igual a otras tardes, dormitando entre beata y beata. De repente empujó la puerta que lo medio escondía y miró la fila de mujeres esperando su turno:

—Todas ustedes —les dijo— ya se confesaron ayer. Si no traen algo nuevo, hínquense porque les voy a dar la absolución.

Sin levantarse de su asiento empezó a bendecirlas mientras murmuraba algo en latín. Después las mandó a su casa y redujo su tarea de confesor a la corta hilera de hombres que se fueron arrodillando frente a él.

Cuando terminó con el último, oyó que la puerta de las mujeres se abría despacio. Sintió un cuerpo breve caer sobre el reclinatorio y un aliento joven contra la rejilla. Suspiró mientras oía el *Yo pecador* repetido por una voz que sonaba al cristal de sus copas alemanas.

—He pecado contra el sexto —dijo el sonido a punto de romperse.

No necesitó más para levantarse de la silla y caminar hasta la puerta contigua. La abrió. Ahí estaba la delgada figura de la tía Verónica, con sus enormes ojos oscuros, su boca como un desafío, su cuello largo, su melena corta.

—¿Tú, creatura? —dijo el padre Cuspinera, con su voz de campanario—. No sabes lo que estás diciendo.

Luego la tomó de la mano, la llevó a sentarse junto a él en una banca vacía, le pellizcó los cachetes, le dio una palmada en el hombro, sonrió desde el fondo de su casto pasado y le dijo:

—Echale una miradita al Santísimo, y vete a dormir. Mañana comulgas que es Viernes Primero.

Desde entonces la tía Verónica durmió y pecó como la bendita que fue.

Tía Eugenia

La tía Eugenia conoció el Hospital de San José hasta que parió a su quinto hijo. Después de luchar veinte horas ayudada por toda su familia, aceptó el peligro de irse a un hospital, dado que nadie sabía qué hacer para sacarle al niño que se le cuatrapeó a media barriga. La tía les tenía terror a los hospitales porque aseguraba que era imposible que unos desconocidos quisieran a la gente que veían por primera vez.

Ella era buena amiga de su partera, su partera llegaba siempre a tiempo, limpia como un vaso recién enjabonado, sonriente y suave, hábil y vertiginosa como no era posible encontrar ningún médico. Llegaba con sus miles de trapos albeantes y sus cubos de agua hervida, a contemplar el trabajo con que tía Eugenia ponía sus hijos en el mundo.

Sabía que no era la protagonista de esa historia y se limitaba a ser una presencia llena de consejos acertados y aún más acertados silencios.

La tía Eugenia era la primera en tocar a sus hijos, la primera que los besaba y lamía, la primera en revisar si estaban completos y bien hechos. Doña Telia la confortaba después y dirigía el primer baño de la creatura. Todo con una tranquilidad contagiosa que hacía de cada parto un acontecimiento casi agradable. No había gritos, ni carreras, ni miedo, con doña Telia como ayuda.

Pero por desgracia, esa mujer de prodigio no era eterna y se murió dos meses antes del último alumbramiento de la tía Eugenia. De todos modos, ella se instaló en su recámara como siempre y le pidió ayuda a su hermana, a su mamá y a la cocinera. Todo habría ido muy bien si al niño no se le ocurre dar una marometa que lo dejó con la cabeza para arriba.

Después de algunas horas de pujar y maldecir en la intimidad, todo el que se atrevió pudo pasar entre las piernas de la tía a ver si con sus consejos era posible convencer al mocoso necio de que la vida sería buena lejos de su mamá. Pero nadie atinó a solucionar aquel desbarajuste. Así que el marido se puso enérgico y cargó con la tía al hospital. Ahí la pobrecita cayó en manos de tres médicos que le pusieron cloroformo en la nariz para sacarla de la discusión y hacer con ella lo que más les convino.

Sólo varias horas después la tía recobró el alma, preguntando por su niño. Le dijeron que estaba en el cunero.

Todavía hay en el hospital quien recuerda el escándalo que se armó entonces. La tía tuvo fuerzas para golpear a la enfermera que salió corriendo en busca de su jefa. También su jefa recibió un empujón y una retahila de insultos. Mientras caminaba por los pasillos en busca del cunero la llamó cursi, marisabidilla, ridícula, torpe, ruin, loca, demente, posesiva, arbitraria y suma, pero sumamente tonta.

Por fin entró a la salita llena de cunas y se fue sin ningún trabajo hasta la de su hijo. Metió la cara dentro de la cesta y empezó a decir asuntos que nadie entendía. Habló y habló miles de cosas, abrazada a su niño, hasta que consideró suficiente la dosis de susurros. Luego lo desvistió para contarle los dedos de los pies y revisarle el ombligo, las rodillas, la pirinola, los ojos, la nariz. Se chupó un dedo y se lo puso cerca de la boca llamándolo remilgoso. Y sólo respiró en orden hasta verlo menear la cabeza y extender los labios en busca de un pezón. Entonces lo cargó dándole besos y se lo puso en la chichi izquierda.

—Eso —le dijo—. Hay que entrar al mundo con el pie derecho y por la chichi izquierda. ¿Verdad, mi amor?

La jefa de enfermeras tenía unos cuatro o cinco años, seis hijos y un marido menos que la tía Eugenia. Desde la inmensa sabiduría de sus vírgenes veinticinco, juzgó que la recién parida pasaba por uno de los múltiples trances de hiperactividad y prepotencia que una madre necesita para sobrellevar los primeros días de crianza, así que decidió tratar el agravio con el marido de la señora. Se tragó los insultos y le preguntó a la tía si quería que la ayudara a volver a su cuarto. La tía dijo no necesitar más ayuda que sus dos piernas y se fue caminando como una aparición hasta el cuarto 311.

El marido de Eugenia era un hombre que con los ojos negaba sus irremediables cuarenta años, que tenía la inteligencia hasta en el modo de caminar, y las ganas de vivir cruzándole la risa y las palabras de tal modo que a veces parecía inmortal.

Llegó una tarde a visitar a su mujer cargado con las flores de siempre, un dibujo de cada hijo, unos chocolates que enviaba su madre y las dos cajas de puros que distribuiría entre las visitas para celebrar que el bebé fuera un hombre. Caminaba por el pasillo divirtiéndose con sólo pensar en lo que serían los mil defectos propios de los hospitales que de seguro había encontrado su esposa, esa mujer a su juicio extraña y fascinante con la que había jurado vivir toda la vida no sólo porque en algún momento le pareció la más linda del mundo, sino porque supo siempre que con ella sería imposible aburrirse.

En mitad del pasillo, lo detuvo la impredecible boca de Georgina Dávila. Había oído hablar de ella alguna vez: mal, por supuesto. A la gente le parecía que era una muchacha medio loca, rica como todas las personas de las que se habla demasiado y extravagante porque no podía ser más que una extravagancia meterse a estudiar medicina en vez de buscarse un marido que le diera razón a su existencia. No le había importado la amenaza de perder hasta la hermosa hacienda de Vicencio, ni la pena infinita que le causaba a su madre saberla entre la pus y las heridas de un hospital, como si su familia no tuviera dónde caerse viva. En realidad, era una vanidosa empeñada en tener profesión como si no tuviera ya todo. Hasta el padre Mastachi le había hablado de los riesgos de la soberbia, pero ella no quería oír a nadie. Se limitaba a sonreír, enseñando a medias unos dientes de princesa, manteniendo firmes los ojos de monja guapa que tantos corazones habían roto. Se consiguió una sonrisa suave y cuidadosa que esgrimía frente a quienes se empeñaban en convencerla de cuán bella y altruista profesión era el matrimonio, una risa que quería decir algo así como:

—Ustedes no entienden nada y yo no me voy a tomar la molestia de seguir explicándoles.

Está claro que a Georgina Dávila le costaba suficiente trabajo mantenerse en el lugar que le había buscado a su vida, como para perderlo frente a una parturienta lépera. De modo que en cuanto vio al marido le cayó encima con una lista de los desacatos que había cometido la tía Eugenia y terminó su discurso pidiéndole que controlara a su señora.

—Mire usted —dijo el hombre, con el brillo de una ironía— no me pida imposibles.

Ella accedió a entenderlo con sus helados ojos azules y el marido de la tía se enamoró de aquella frialdad con la misma fuerza intempestiva con que amó siempre la calidez de su esposa.

—Voy por su hijo— acertó a decir la doctora Dávila, extendiendo una mano que no sintió suya.

Tenía una palpitación en el sitio que con tanto cariño había cuidado en otras mujeres y padecía la pena horrible de ver llegar el deseo por el mismo lugar que las otras.

Al poco tiempo entró a la recámara cargando a un niño con la cara de papa cocida que tenían los demás recién nacidos, pero al que de pronto ella veía como un ser luminoso y adorable. Lo puso en los brazos de la mamá.

—Viene completo— dijo.

—Perdón por el escándalo de hoy en la mañana— pidió la tía Eugenia mirando a Georgina Dávila con agrado.

—No hay nada que perdonar— se oyó decir Georgina.

—Lo volvería a hacer— completó la tía Eugenia.

—Tendría usted razón— le contestó Georgina.

Luego dio la vuelta y se fue rápido a examinar la sensación de ignominia que le recorría el cuerpo. Había cruzado cuatro palabras con el marido de esa señora y ya le parecía una tortura dejarlo con ella.

—Soy una estúpida. Me hace falta dormir— se dijo mientras caminaba hacia el cuarto de una mujer que en lugar de vientre tenía un volcán adolorido.

Cerca de la media noche volvió donde la tía en busca del bebé que había engendrado el hombre aquel, tan parecido a su abuelo materno. Su abuelo fue el único adulto al que ella vio desnudo bajo la regadera en que se bañaban juntos, su abuelo de piernas largas que le enseñaba el pito con la misma naturalidad con que la dejaba tocar las grandes venas que se endurecían en sus manos, su abuelo que le contaba las vértebras bajo el agua.

—Eres un montón de huesitos —le decía—. Te debes llamar *Huesitos.*

Cuando entró al cuarto 311, la tía Eugenia dormía como un ángel exhausto. Su marido no se había atrevido a mover el brazo sobre el cual ella recargó durante un largo rato su incansable vehemencia, hasta irla perdiendo en la del sueño.

Georgina le quitó al niño del regazo y lo miró para no mirar al hombre que le estaba robando la paciencia.

—Son un milagro— oyó que decía su voz en la penumbra.

—Todo— contestó ella, abrazando al niño que se llevaba.

Tres días después, la tía Eugenia salió del hospital con su quinto hijo y la mitad de su marido.

De un día para otro, el hombre aquel había perdido la certidumbre de su dicha sin agujeros, la fuerza que alguna vez lo hizo inmortal, el control de sus días y de sus sueños.

Desde entonces vivió en el infierno que es disimular un amor frente a otro, y ya nada fue bueno para él, en ninguna parte estuvo a gusto, y se le instaló en los ojos una irremisible nostalgia.

Toda la pasión con que alguna vez anduvo por la vida se le partió en dos y ya no fue feliz, y ya no pudo hacer feliz a nadie.

Por eso cuando en medio de una comida familiar, su corazón debilitado no pudo seguir con la vida en vilo de esos años, la tía Eugenia lo llevó sin la menor duda al Hospital San José. Porque ahí estaría Georgina.

—¿Se va a morir?— preguntó la tía Eugenia en cuanto estuvieron solas.

—Sí— le contestó Georgina.

—¿Cuándo?— preguntó la tía Eugenia.

—Al rato, mañana, el jueves— dijo la doctora y se encajó los dientes en el labio inferior.

La tía Eugenia caminó los cuatro pasos que las separaban para abrazarla. Georgina Dávila se dejó mecer y acariciar como una huérfana.

Una semana después, el cambio de enfermeras las sorprendió a las dos llorando sobre el mismo cadáver. Entre las dos habían velado sus últimos sueños, le habían quitado los harapos al ir y venir de su mirada, habían puesto sosiego en sus manos, palabras de amnistía en sus oídos. Cada una le había dado como último consuelo la certidumbre de que era imposible no querer a la otra.

—Nadie pudo ser mejor compañía. Nadie era tan infeliz como yo, más que Georgina— contaba la tía Eugenia años después, al recordar los orígenes de su larga hermandad con la doctora Dávila.

Tía Natalia

Un día Natalia Esparza, mujer de piernas breves y redondas chichis, se enamoró del mar. No supo bien a bien en qué momento le llegó aquel deseo inaplazable de conocer el remoto y legendario océano, pero le llegó con tal fuerza que hubo de abandonar la escuela de piano y lanzarse a la búsqueda del Caribe, porque al Caribe llegaron sus antepasados un siglo antes, y de ahí la llamaba sin piedad lo que nombró el pedazo extraviado de su conciencia.

El llamado del mar se hizo tan fuerte que ni su propia madre logró convencerla de esperar siquiera media hora. Por más que le rogó calmar su locura hasta que las almendras estuvieran listas para el turrón, hasta que hubiera terminado el mantel de cerezas que bordaba para la boda de su hermana, hasta que su padre entendiera que no era la putería, ni el ocio, ni una incurable enfermedad mental lo que la había puesto tan necia en irse de repente.

La tía Natalia creció mirando los volcanes, escudriñándolos en las mañanas y en las tardes. Sabía de memoria los pliegues en el pecho de la Mujer Dormida y la desafiante cuesta en que termina el Popocatépetl. Vivió siempre en la tierra oscura y el cielo frío, cocinando dulces a fuego lento y carne escondida bajo los colores de salsas complicadísimas. Comía en platos dibujados, bebía en copas de cristal y pasaba horas sentada frente a la lluvia, oyendo los rezos de su mamá y las historias de su abuelo sobre dragones y caballos con alas. Pero supo del mar la tarde en que unos tíos de Campeche entraron a su merienda de pan y chocolate, antes de seguir el camino hacia la ciudad amurallada a la que rodeaba un implacable océano de colores.

Siete azules, tres verdes, un dorado: todo cabía en el mar. La plata que nadie podría llevarse del país: entera bajo una tarde nublada. La noche desafiando el valor de las barcas, la tranquila conciencia de quienes las gobiernan. La mañana como un sueño de cristal, el mediodía brillante como los deseos.

Ahí, pensó ella, hasta los hombres debían ser distintos. Los que vivieran junto a ese mar que ella imaginó sin tregua a partir de la merienda del jueves, no serían dueños de fábricas, ni vendedores de arroz, ni molineros, ni hacendados, ni nadie que pudiera quedarse quieto bajo la misma luz toda la vida. Tanto habían hablado su tío y su padre de los piratas de antes, de los de ahora, de Don Lorenzo Patiño abuelo de su madre, al que entre burlas apodaron Lorencillo cuando ella contaba que había llegado a Campeche en su propio bergantín. Tanto habían dicho de las manos callosas y los cuerpos pródigos que pedían aquel sol y aquella brisa; tan harta estaba ella del mantel y del piano, que salió tras los tíos sin ningún remordimiento. Con los tíos viviría, esperó su madre. Sola, como una cabra loca, adivinó su padre.

No sabía por dónde era el camino, sólo quería ir al mar. Y al mar llegó después de un largo viaje hasta Mérida y de una terrible caminata tras los pescadores que conoció en el mercado de la famosa ciudad blanca.

Eran uno viejo y uno joven. El viejo, conversador y marihuano; el joven, considerando todo una locura. ¿Cómo volvían ellos a Holbox con una mujer tan preguntona y bien hecha? ¿Cómo podían dejarla?

—A ti también te gusta —le había dicho el viejo— y ella quiere venir. ¿No ves cómo quiere venir?

La tía Natalia había pasado toda la mañana sentada en la pescadería del mercado, viendo llegar uno tras otro a hombres que cambiaban por cualquier cosa sus animales planos, de huesos y carne blanca, sus animales raros, pestilentes y hermosos como debía ser el mar. Se detuvo en los hombros y el paso, en la voz afrentada del que no quiso regalar su caracol.

—Es tanto o me lo regreso— había dicho.

"Tanto o me lo regreso", y los ojos de la tía Natalia se fueron tras él.

El primer día caminaron sin parar, con ella preguntando y preguntando si en verdad la arena del mar era blanca como el azúcar y las noches calientes como el alcohol. A veces se sentaba a sobarse los pies y ellos aprovechaban para dejarla atrás. Entonces se ponía los zapatos y arrancaba a correr repitiendo las maldiciones del viejo.

Llegaron hasta la tarde del día siguiente. La tía Natalia no lo podía creer. Corrió al agua empujada por sus últimas fuerzas y se puso a llorar sal en la sal. Le dolían los pies, las rodillas, los muslos. Le ardían de sol los hombros y la cara. Le dolían los deseos, el corazón y el pelo. ¿Por qué estaba llorando? ¿No era hundirse ahí lo único que deseaba?

Oscureció despacio. Sola en la playa interminable tocó sus piernas y todavía no eran una cola de sirena. Hacía un aire casi frío, se dejó empujar por las olas hasta la orilla. Caminó por la playa espantando unos mosquitos diminutos que le comían los brazos. No muy lejos estaba el viejo con los ojos extraviados en ella.

Se tiró con la ropa mojada sobre la blanca cama de arena y sintió acercarse al anciano, meter los dedos entre su cabello enredado y explicarle que si quería quedarse tenía que ser con él porque todos los otros ya tenían su mujer.

—Con usted me quedo— dijo y se durmió.

Nadie sabe cómo fue la vida de la tía Natalia en Holbox. Regresó a Puebla seis meses después y diez años más vieja, llamándose la viuda de Uc Yam.

Tenía la piel morena y arrugada, las manos callosas y una extraña seguridad para vivir. No se casó nunca, nunca le faltó un hombre, aprendió a pintar y el azul de sus cuadros se hizo famoso en París y en Nueva York.

Sin embargo, la casa en que vivió estuvo siempre en Puebla, por más que algunas tardes, mirando a los volcanes, se le perdieran los sueños para írsele al mar.

—Uno es de donde es —decía, mientras pintaba con sus manos de vieja y sus ojos de niña—. Por más que no quieras, te regresan de allá.

Tía Clemencia

El novio de Clemencia Ortega no supo el frasco de locura y pasiones que estaba destapando aquella noche. Lo tomó como a la mermelada y lo abrió, pero de ahí para adelante su vida toda, su tranquilo ir y venir por el mundo, con su traje inglés o su raqueta de frontón, se llenó de aquel perfume, de aquel brebaje atroz, de aquel veneno.

Era bonita la tía Clemencia, pero abajo de los rizos morenos tenía pensamientos y eso a la larga resultó un problema. Porque a la corta habían sido sus pensamientos y no sólo sus antojos los que la llevaron sin dificultad a la cama clandestina que compartió con su novio.

En aquellos tiempos, las niñas poblanas bien educadas no sólo no se acostaban con sus novios sino que a los novios no se les ocurría siquiera sugerir la posibilidad. Fue la tía Clemencia la que desabrochó su corpiño, cuando de tanto sobarse a escondidas sintió que sus pezones estaban puntiagudos como dos pirinolas. Fue ella la que metió sus manos bajo el pantalón hasta la cueva donde guardan los hombres la mascota que llevan a todas partes, el animal que le prestan a uno cuando se les pega la gana, y que luego se llevan, indiferente y sosegado, como si nunca nos hubiera visto. Fue ella, sin que nadie la obligara, la que acercó sus manos al aliento irregular de aquel pingo, la que lo quiso ver, la tentona.

Así que el novio no sintió nunca la vergüenza de los que abusan, ni el deber de los que prometen. Hicieron el amor en la despensa mientras la atención de todo el mundo se detenía en la prima de la tía Clemencia, que esa mañana se había vestido de novia para casarse como Dios manda. La despensa estaba oscura y en silencio al terminar el banquete. Olía a especias y nuez, a chocolate de Oaxaca y chile ancho, a vainilla y aceitunas, a panela y bacalao. La música se oía lejos, entrecortada por el griterío que pedía que se besaran los novios, que el ramo fuera para una pobre fea, que bailaran los suegros. A la tía Clemencia le pareció que no podía haber mejor sitio en el mundo para lo que había elegido tener aquella tarde. Hicieron el amor sin echar juramentos, sin piruetas, sin la pesada responsabilidad de saberse mirados. Y fueron lo que se llama felices, durante un rato.

—Tienes orégano en el pelo —le dijo su madre cuando la vio pasar bailando cerca de la mesa en la que ella y el papá de Clemencia llevaban sentados cinco horas y media.

—Debe ser del ramo que cayó en mi cabeza.

—No vi que te tocara el ramo —dijo su madre—. No te vi siquiera cuando aventaron el ramo. Te estuve gritando.

—Me tocó otro ramo —contestó Clemencia con la soltura de una niña tramposa.

Su mamá estaba acostumbrada a ese tipo de respuestas. Aunque le sonaban del todo desatinadas, las achacaba al desorden mental que le quedó a su niña tras las calenturas de un fuerte sarampión. Sabía también que lo mejor en esos casos era no preguntar más, para evitar caer en un embrollo. Se limitó a discurrir que el orégano era una hierba preciosa, a la que se le había hecho poca justicia en la cocina.

—A nadie se le ha ocurrido usarlo en postres —dijo, en voz alta, para terminar su reflexión.

—Qué bonito baila Clemencia —le comentó su vecina de asiento y se pusieron a platicar.

Cuando el novio al que se había regalado en la despensa quiso casarse con la tía Clemencia, ella le contestó que eso era imposible. Y se lo dijo con tanta seriedad que él pensó que estaba resentida porque en lugar de pedírselo antes se había esperado un año de perfúmenes furtivos, durante el cual afianzó bien el negocio de las panaderías hasta tener una cadena de seis con pan blanco y pan dulce, y dos más con pasteles y gelatinas.

Pero no era por eso que la tía Clemencia se negaba, sino por todas las razones que con él no había tenido nunca ni tiempo ni necesidad de explicar.

—Yo creía que tú habías entendido hace mucho —le dijo.

—¿Entendido qué? —preguntó el otro.

—Que en mis planes no estaba casarme, ni siquiera contigo.

—No te entiendo —dijo el novio, que era un hombre común y corriente—. ¿Quieres ser una puta toda tu vida?

Cuando la tía Clemencia oyó aquello se arrepintió en un segundo de todas las horas, las tardes y las noches que le había dado a ese desconocido. Ni siquiera tuvo ánimo para sentirse agraviada.

—Vete —le dijo—. Vete, antes de que te cobre el dineral que me debes.

El tuvo miedo, y se fue.

Poco después, se casó con la hija de unos asturianos, bautizó seis hijos y dejó que el tiempo pasara sobre sus recuerdos, enmoheciéndolos igual que el agua estancada en las paredes de una fuente. Se volvió un enfurecido fumador de puros, un bebedor de todas las tardes, un insomne que no sabía qué hacer con las horas de la madrugada, un insaciable buscador de negocios. Hablaba poco, tenía dos amigos con los que iba al club de tiro los sábados en la tarde y a los que nunca pudo confiarles nada más íntimo que la rabia infantil que lo paralizaba cuando se le iban vivos más de dos pichones. Se aburría.

La mañana de un martes, diecinueve años después de haber perdido el perfume y la boca de la tía Clemencia, un yucateco se presentó a ofrecerle en venta la tienda de abarrotes mejor surtida de la ciudad. Fueron a verla. Entraron por la bodega de la trastienda, un cuarto enorme lleno de semillas, sacos de harina y azúcar, cereales, chocolate, yerbas de olor, chiles y demás productos para llenar despensas.

De golpe el hombre sintió un desorden en todo el cuerpo, sacó su chequera para comprar la tienda sin haberla visto entera, le pagó al yucateco el primer precio, y salió corriendo, hasta la casa de tres patios donde aún vivía la tía Clemencia. Cuando le avisaron que en la puerta la buscaba un señor, ella bajó corriendo las escaleras que conducían a un patio lleno de flores y pájaros.

El la vio acercarse y quiso besar el suelo que pisaba aquella diosa de armonía en que estaba convertida la mujer de treinta y nueve años que era aquella Clemencia. La vio acercarse y hubiera querido desaparecer pensando en lo feo y envejecido que él estaba. Clemencia notó su turbación, sintió pena por su barriga y su cabeza medio calva, por las bolsas que empezaban a crecerle bajo los ojos, por el rictus de tedio que él hubiera querido borrarse de la cara.

—Nos hemos hecho viejos —le dijo, incluyéndose en el desastre, para quitarle la zozobra.

—No seas buena conmigo. He sido un estúpido y se me nota por todas partes.

—Yo no te quise por inteligente —dijo la tía Clemencia con una sonrisa.

—Pero me dejaste de querer por idiota —dijo él.

—Yo nunca he dejado de quererte —dijo la tía Clemencia—. No me gusta desperdiciar. Menos los sentimientos.

—Clemencia —dijo el hombre, temblando de sorpresa—. Después de mí has tenido doce novios.

—A los doce los sigo queriendo —dijo la tía Clemencia desamarrándose el delantal que llevaba sobre el vestido.

—¿Cómo? —dijo el pobre hombre.

—Con todo el escalofrío de mi corazón —contestó la tía Clemencia, acercándose a su ex novio hasta que lo sintió temblar como ella sabía que temblaba.

—Vamos —dijo después, tomándolo del brazo para salir a la calle. Entonces él dejó de temblar y la llevó de prisa a la tienda que acababa de comprarse.

—Apaga la luz —pidió ella cuando entraron a la bodega y el olor del orégano envolvió su cabeza. El extendió un brazo hacia atrás y en la oscuridad reanduvo los veinte años de ausencia que dejaron de pesarle en el cuerpo.

Dos horas después, escarmenando el orégano en los rizos oscuros de la tía Clemencia, le pidió de nuevo:

—Cásate conmigo.

La tía Clemencia lo besó despacio y se vistió aprisa.

—¿A dónde vas? —le preguntó él cuando la vio caminar hacia la puerta mientras abría y cerraba una mano diciéndole adiós.

—A la mañana de hoy —dijo la tía, mirando su reloj.

—Pero me quieres —dijo él.

—Sí —contestó la tía Clemencia.

—¿Más que a ninguno de los otros? —preguntó él.

—Igual —dijo la tía.

—Eres una . . . —empezó a decir él cuando Clemencia lo detuvo:

—Cuidado con lo que dices porque te cobro, y no te alcanza con las treinta panaderías.

Después abrió la puerta y se fue sin oír más.

La mañana siguiente Clemencia Ortega recibió en su casa las escrituras de treinta panaderías y una tienda de abarrotes. Venían en un sobre, junto con una tarjeta que decía: "Eres una terca".

Tía Fátima

Fátima Lapuente fue novia de José Limón durante diez años. Desde antes de que él se lo pidiera ella había comprometido su cuerpo lleno de luciérnagas con el hombre que se las había puesto en revuelo.

Todo empezó la noche de una fiesta en el campo. Desde el final de la tarde, prendieron una fogata enorme en el centro de la casa. Uno de esos patios que tienen las casas de cuatro lados, para abrir sobre ellos balcones y barandales ávidos de luz y temerosos del campo abierto. Alrededor de la lumbre se fueron sentando los invitados, después de padecer una corrida de toros.

José Limón tenía una guitarra. Empezó cantando la historia del jinete que vaga solo en busca de su amada y nada más eso necesitó la tía Fátima para prendarse de él. Nunca le habían gustado los tipos alegres, así que aquel colmo de penas la fascinó. Estaba sentada enfrente de su voz y lo veía moverse tras la lumbre, brincando: "Toda la vida quisiste, mi bien, con dos barajas jugar", cantó.

"No puedes jugar con una, mi bien, y quieres jugar con dos"

—coreó Fátima y José dio la vuelta a la fogata para instalarse junto a ella.

La fiesta era en un rancho al que una vez al año estaban invitados todos los amigos de la familia Limón, con todos sus hijos y si era necesario sus padres, a celebrar el cumpleaños del viejo abuelo, que era un hombre de pistola y memoria precisas. Junto con su nieto José, era el único habitante del único rancho que la revolución reciente le dejó a su familia. Ese día el viejo y el nieto arreglaban camas en todos los cuartos y hasta en el establo dormían los más jóvenes, mezclados con los más borrachos.

La comida se ponía en el patio y los invitados comían con los dedos, arrancando la barbacoa de los animales que exhibían su muerte guisada entre pencas de maguey bajo la tierra. También había mole y chiles rellenos, nopales con cebolla, salsas de colores, pulque o curado de piña y apio. Las viejas hermanas Limón pasaban varios días haciendo galletitas de Santa Clara, turrón y dulce de leche, para quitar el sabor del chile y la sal antes de que la tarde, con peleas de gallos y corrida de toros, cayera eufórica y lenta entre sangre, tragos y maldiciones. Esa noche perdían los modales hasta los Caballeros de Colón y en el desbarajuste se llegaba a permitir que las mujeres amanecieran cantando con algún hombre, sin que fuera preciso que se casaran al día siguiente.

Por eso José y Fátima pudieron ir a ver cómo paría una vaca que no respetó la noche de asueto. José y tres peones jalaron al becerro ante el infranqueable horror que Fátima sentía en la garganta. Todavía estaba oscuro cuando salieron del establo rumbo a la casa. Las estrellas se apretujaban en el cielo y ella se acurrucó en el abrazo de ese hombre arisco que la madrugada había convertido en un refugio cálido y persuasivo.

Quién sabe cuál habrá sido su preciso encanto. La tía Fátima nunca pudo explicarlo con claridad, pero supo siempre que lo de sus luciérnagas no tenía remedio y que el vértigo que le provocaban valía la pena de ver cómo sus amigas se casaban una y otra, tenían hijos, cosían y usaban las camas de sus recámaras llenas de encajes y cojines, sólo para intentar alguna vez el juego al que ella y Limón se entregaban, muchas tardes, en el catre desordenado que él tenía en la hacienda.

—José Limón es incasable —le decía su madre todo el día.

—Ya lo sé —contestaba ella todo el día.

La gente decía que era terco y distante, ensimismado, iracundo, egoísta y soberbio. Cuentan también que tenía un cuerpo fuerte y las manos muy grandes, que miraba como quien guarda un secreto y que siendo dueño de fábricas y tiendas se empeñaba en vivir atado a la obligación de cuidar la hacienda, consintiendo las locuras de su abuelo, como si la vida no le ofreciera caminos más cómodos y menos peligrosos.

Entonces los noviazgos eran largos, pero nunca del largo que alcanzó el de la tía Fátima. Después de los primeros dos años, tras la muerte del abuelo que parecía el único pretexto para no deshacerse del rancho y volver a la ciudad en busca de la vida en sosiego y la novia que lo esperaba desde hacía años, todo el mundo empezó a preguntarse y preguntar cuándo era la boda.

Sólo la tía Fátima supo siempre que no había para cuándo. Que Limón era inasible, que no le pondría nunca una casa ni a ella ni a nadie, que tenía otro pleito en la vida, que ni siquiera debía lamentar haberlo querido sin vueltas desde el principio, porque de no ser así no hubiera sido nunca. Con él hacerse del rogar habría sido inútil, quizá la pérdida de todo lo que les pasaba. Porque les pasaban cosas a ellos dos juntos. Cosas que no tenían nada que ver ni con la paz ni con la cordura a la que otros aspiraban, sino con la guerra que hace a unos cuantos solitarios y desasosegados.

Llevaban diez años de escandalizar con su eterno noviazgo, cuando a José Limón lo mataron los agaristas. Al menos eso se dijo en la ciudad. Que habían sido los agraristas y nadie más que los agraristas que lo odiaban porque tenía la hacienda dividida entre los nombres de todos sus parientes.

—No fueron los agraristas —dijo la tía Fátima con firmeza, antes de ir a besar el cadáver que aún nadie había movido del piso. Se hincó junto a él, acariciándolo con una mano y apoyando la otra en la humedad de los ladrillos. Lo alzó sin ayuda de nadie, como si estuviera acostumbrada al peso de aquel cuerpo enorme. Lo peinó, le cerró los ojos, le acarició mucho rato las mejillas heladas. Pidió a los peones que cavaran un hoyo abajo del fresno, junto a la casa. Mandó comprar un petate para envolver su tesoro, y lo veló como si fuera un indio, rodeado de velas y lágrimas, durante toda la noche.

Al día siguiente caminó frente a los amigos que lo cargaron y lo echaron a la tierra oscura, como si las órdenes de la novia fueran las de una viuda con todos los derechos. Nadie: ni los hermanos, ni los tíos, ni siquiera la madre, pudo intervenir en el orden de tal ceremonia.

Más tarde la tía Fátima escribió en su diario:

"Hoy enterramos el cadáver de José, llorando y llorando, como si su muerte fuera posible. Para mañana sabremos que él nunca ha estado más vivo, y que jamás podrá morirse antes que yo. Porque no alcanzaría la tierra para cubrir la luz de su cuerpo a media tarde, ni el peor viento para acallar su voz hablando bajo. José me pertenece. Me atravesó la vida con su vida y no habrá quién me lo quite de los ojos y el alma. Aunque se pretenda muerto. Nadie puede matar la parte de sí que ha hecho vivir en los otros".

Nunca se casó. A nadie quiso y a nadie se le ocurrió intentar quererla. A los niños les parecía encantadora y extraña. No tenía hijos, no tomaba partido en los pleitos, nunca la oyeron gritar ni carcajearse. Jamás la vieron llorar ni en la iglesia, ni en los entierros, ni en el teatro, ni en la Navidad. En cambio la oyeron cantar con frecuencia. Durante las tardes de mayo llevaban a los niños a ofrecer flores y la tía Fátima cantaba desde el coro con su voz intensa y triste. Lo que hubiera sido un ritual de medio tono, hecho de niños en fila que le pegan con la flor al de adelante, se convertía con su canto en una ceremonia para privilegiados. Aún ahora, al evocar su voz, las luciérnagas de otros cuerpos se revuelven.

Cuando murió la tía Fátima, cincuenta años más tarde que José Limón, la enterraron bajo el mismo fresno que a él. La noche del día en que se acostó para morirse escribió en su diario:

"Creo que el amor, como la eternidad, es una ambición. Una hermosa ambición de los humanos".

Tía Magdalena

Un día el marido de la tía Magdalena le abrió la puerta a un propio que llevaba una carta dirigida a ella. Nunca habían tenido secretos y era tal la simbiosis de aquel matrimonio que ahí las cartas las abría uno aunque fueran dirigidas al otro. Nadie consideraba eso violación de la intimidad, menos aún falta de educación. Así que al recibir aquel sobre tan blanco, tan planchado, con el nombre de su mujer escrito por una letra contundente, lo abrió. El mensaje decía:

Magdalena:
Como siempre que hablamos del tema terminas llorando y te confundes en la locura de que nos quieres a los dos con la misma intensidad, he decidido no volver a verte. No creo imposible deshacerme de mi deseo por ti, alguna vez hay que despertar de los sueños. Estoy seguro de que tú no tendrás grandes problemas olvidándome. Acabar con este desorden nos hará bien a los dos. Vuelve al deber que elegiste y no llames ni pretendas convencerme de nada. Alejandro.

PD. Tienes razón, fue hermoso.

El marido de la tía Magdalena guardó la carta, le puso pegamento al sobre y lo dejó en la charola del correo junto con el recibo del teléfono y las cuentas del banco. Estaba furioso. La rabia le puso las orejas coloradas y los ojos húmedos. Entró a su despacho para que nadie lo viera, por más que no había nadie en la casa. Su mujer, las nanas y los niños, se habían ido al desfile del 5 de mayo para celebrar el recuerdo del día en que los "zacapoaxtlas le restaron prestigio a Napoleón".

Sentado en la silla frente a su escritorio, el hombre respiraba con violencia por la boca. Tenía las manos sobre la frente y los brazos alrededor de la cara. Si algo en la vida él quería y respetaba por encima de todo, eran el cuerpo y la sabiduría de su mujer. ¿Cómo podía alguien atreverse a escribirle de aquel modo? Magdalena era una reina, un tesoro, una diosa. Magdalena era un pan, un árbol, una espada. Era generosa, íntegra, valiente, perfecta. Y si ella alguna vez le había dicho a alguien te quiero, ese alguien debió postrarse a sus pies. ¿Cómo era posible que la hiciera llorar?

Bebió un whisky y luego dos. Pegó contra el suelo con un palo de golf hasta desbaratarlo. Se metió veinte minutos bajo la regadera y al salir puso en el tocadiscos al Beethoven más desesperado y cuando su mujer y los niños entraron a la casa, dos horas después, estaba disimuladamente tranquilo.

Se habían asoleado, todos tenían las cabezas un poco desordenadas y las mejillas hirviendo. La tía Magdalena se quitó el sombrero y fue a sentarse junto a su marido.

—¿Te sirvo otro whisky? —dijo tras besarlo como a un hermano.

—Ya no, porque vamos a comer en casa de los Cobián y no me quiero emborrachar.

—¿Vamos a comer en casa de los Cobián? Nunca me dijiste.

—Te digo ahorita.

—"Te digo ahorita". Siempre me haces lo mismo.

—Y nunca te enojas, eres una esposa perfecta.

—Nunca me enojo, pero no soy una esposa perfecta.

—Sí eres una esposa perfecta. Y sí tráeme otro whisky.

La tía caminó hasta la botella y los hielos, sirvió el whisky, lo movió, quiso uno para ella. Cuando lo tuvo listo, volvió junto a su marido con un vaso en cada mano. De verdad era linda Magdalena. Era de esas mujeres bonitas que no necesitan nada para serlo más que levantarse en las mañanas y acostarse en las noches. De remate, la tía Magdalena se acostaba a otras horas llena de pasión y culpa, lo que en los últimos tiempos le había dado una firmeza de caminado y un temblor en los labios con los que su tipo de ángel ganó justo la pizca de maldad necesaria para parecer divina. Fue a sentarse a los pies de su marido y le contó los ires y devenires del desfile. Le dio la lista completa de quienes estaban en los palcos de la casa del círculo español. Después le dibujó en un papelito un nuevo diseño para vajilla de talavera que podría hacerse en la fábrica. Hablaron largo rato de los problemas que estaban dando los acaparadores de frijol en el mercado *La Victoria*. Durante todo ese tiempo, la tía Magdalena se sintió observada por su marido de una manera nueva. Mientras hablaba, muchas veces la interrumpió para acariciarle la frente o las mejillas, como si quisiera detenerle cada gesto de júbilo.

—Me estás mirando raro —le dijo ella una vez.

—Te estoy mirando —contestó él.

—Raro —volvió a decir la tía.

—Raro —asintió él y continuó la conversación. ¿Cómo había alguien en el mundo capaz de permitirse perder a esa mujer? Debía estar loco. Empezó a enfurecerse de nuevo contra quien mandó esa carta y de paso contra él, que no la había escondido siquiera hasta el día siguiente. Así su mujer la encontraría durante la mañana, cuando ni él ni los niños estorbaran su tristeza. Entonces se levantó del sillón alegando que ya era tarde y mientras la tía Magdalena iba a pintarse los labios, él caminó al recibidor y quitó la carta de la charola del correo. La mesa sobre la que estaba era una antigüedad que había pertenecido a la bisabuela de la tía Magdalena. Tenía un cajón en medio al que la polilla se colaba con frecuencia. Ahí metió la carta y respiró, feliz de postergarle el problema a su mujer. Gracias a eso pasaron una comida apacible y risueña.

El lunes, antes de irse a la fábrica, puso la carta encima de todas las demás.

La tía Magdalena había amanecido radiante.

—Debe ser porque nos vamos —pensó el marido.

Y en efecto, a la tía Magdalena le gustaban los días hábiles, Quién sabe a qué horas ni cómo se encontraba con el torpe aquel, pero de seguro era en los días hábiles. Cuando se despidieron, él dijo como de costumbre: "Estoy en la fábrica por si algo necesitas" y la besó en la cabeza. Entonces ella dio el último trago a su café y mordió la rebanada de pan con mantequilla del que siempre dejaba un pedacito, atendiendo a quién sabe qué disciplina dietética. Luego levantó y fue en busca del correo.

Entonces dio con la carta. Se la llevó al baño de junto a su recámara que todavía era un caos de toallas húmedas y piyamas recién arrancadas. Sentada en el suelo, la abrió. No le bastaron las toallas para secarse la cantidad de lágrimas que derramó. Se tuvo lástima durante tanto rato y con tal brío que si la cocinera no la saca del precipicio para preguntarle qué hacer de comida hubiera podido convertirse en charco. Contestó que hicieran sopa de hongos, carne fría, ensalada, papas fritas y pastel de queso, sin dudar ni desdecirse y a una velocidad tal que la cocinera no le creyó. Siempre pasaban horas confeccionando el menú y ella había contagiado a la muchacha de sus manías:

—La sopa es café y la carne también —dijo la cocinera segura de que habría un cambio.

—No importa —le contestó la tía Magdalena, aún poseída por un dolor de velorio.

Su marido regresó temprano del trabajo, como cuando estaban recién casados y a ella le daba catarro. Llegó buscándola, seguro de que la pena la tendría postrada fingiendo algún mal. La encontró sentada en el jardín, esperando su turno para brincar la reata en un concurso al que sus dos hijas y una prima le concedían rango de olímpico. Estaba contando los brincos de su hija que iba en el ciento tres. Las otras dos niñas tenían la reata una de cada punta y la movían mientras contaban, perfectamente acopladas.

—Juego de mujeres —dijo el marido, que nunca le había encontrado chiste a brincar la reata.

La tía Magdalena se levantó a besarlo. El puso el brazo sobre sus hombros y la oyó seguir contando los brincos de la niña:

—Ciento doce, ciento trece, ciento catorce, ciento quince, ciento dieciséis . . . ¡Pisaste! —gritó riéndose—. Me toca.

Se separó de su marido y voló al centro de la cuerda. Le brillaban los ojos, tenía los labios embravecidos y las mejillas más rojas que nunca. Empezó a brincar en silencio, con la boca apretada y los brazos en vilo, oyendo sólo la voz de las niñas que contaban en coro. Cuando llegó al cien, su voz empezó a salir como un murmullo en el que se apoyaba para seguir brincando. El marido se unió al coro cuando vio a la tía Magdalena llegar al ciento diecisiete sin haber pisado la cuerda. Acunada por aquel canto la tía brincó cada vez más rápido. Pasó por el doscientos como una exhalación y siguió brinca y brinca hasta llegar al setecientos cinco.

—¡Gané! —gritó entonces—. ¡Gané! —y se dejó caer al suelo alzándose un segundo después con el brío de una llama. —¡Gané! ¡Gané! —gritó corriendo hasta donde estaba su marido.

—Afortunada en el juego, desfortunada en el amor —dijo él.

—Afortunada en todo —contestó ella jadeante—. ¿O me vas a salir tú también con que ya no me quieres?

—¿Yo también? —dijo el marido.

—Esposo, eres un violador de correspondencia y usaste un pésimo pegamento para disimularlo —dijo la tía Magdalena.

—En cambio tú disimulas bien. ¿No estás muy triste?

—Algo —dijo la tía Magdalena.

—¿Si yo me fuera podrías brincar la reata? —preguntó el.

—Creo que no —dijo la tía Magdalena.

—Entonces me quedo —contestó el marido, recuperando su alma. Y se quedó.

Tía Cecilia

Junto a casa de la tía Cecilia se murió una viejita. La tía vio salir su caja de aquel caserón de piedra tan parecido al de ella, y la recordó conversando con sus gatos y podrida en mugre como había vivido los últimos años. Se rascaba la cabeza que alguna vez peinó unos rizos claros, aún brillantes en los retratos sepia de la sala.

Iba y venía por su casa, en la que se apretujaban los tibores chinos y los cristales de bacará, las pinturas virreinales, los santos lacerados, las lámparas de cristales azules, los candiles franceses, las sillitas doradas y los sillones de asientos tiesos y brazos angostos, las vitrinas hartas de porcelanas, las mil carpetitas tejidas por su aburrida juventud, las alfombras persas, las chinas, las camas de latón con sus colchones de plumas oliendo a polvo de tres generaciones, los roperos de madera labrada, las cómodas de Bull y las mesas de incrustaciones, las sillas de mimbre austriaco y el corredor con sus vitrales, la gran colección de relojes acomodada en la sala para marcar el tiempo con campanas de todos los tiempos.

Ahí, frente a los relojes, pasaba muchas horas. Ahí la encontraba la tía Cecilia con más frecuencia que en ningún otro sitio, y ahí se quedaba a platicar con ella de las cosas que le iban pasando por la cabeza y que la hacían la colección de historias más atractiva que la tía Cecilia había oído en su vida. Eran historias que muchas veces no tenían fin, que empezaban narrando el espantoso trato que le daba la cocinera a su servicio y terminaban describiendo la hermosura del emperador Maximiliano o la idiotez de un novio que llamó vejestorio a una pintura de *Adán y Eva*, colgada entre los cuadros de la antesala para disimular su condición de tesoro del siglo XVI, quizá uno de los primeros cuadros que se pintaron en la Nueva España.

Eran historias que hablaban de cosas que ella no había oído jamás entre los sanos miembros de su familia. A la tía le gustaba oír una que ponía a la viejita roja de furia: la del hermano descarriado que se metió con una piruja con la que engendró tres hijas a las que ella no había visto ni quería ver jamás.

Hablaba la viejita de su hermano alto, muy guapo, que cometió la barbaridad de meterse con una de la calle a la que por supuesto no llevó a su casa. El hermano había muerto arrepentido de su perdición y preso de los espantosos dolores con que Dios apenas lo castigó por su descarrío.

Ella no hubiera permitido jamás que una mala pasión la perturbara. Las malas pasiones se quitan con agua fría, con un cordón apretado a las piernas durante la misa de madrugada y en el mejor de los casos —reía la vieja con sus dos dientes— con una sopa de pescado y un vaso de ostiones frescos antes del desayuno:

—Queda una asqueada de todo.

La mamá de la tía Cecilia consideraba que la viejita era un olvido del diablo sobre la tierra y le tenía prohibidas las visitas a su casa. Alguna vez la tía Cecilia trató de convencerla describiéndole lo abandonada y purulenta que estaba, pero no suscitó en su madre ni un ápice de compasión.

—Apenas lo que se merece —dijo sólo su madre, mujer piadosa y caritativa como pocas.

—De todos modos la tía Cecilia aprovechaba cualquier oportunidad para escaparse a casa de la viejita y recorrerla, metiendo la nariz bajo las camas, tratando de saber qué habría guardado en los roperos para que valiera la pena sentarse a cuidarlos tanto. Nunca pudo saberlo, pero la viejita vivía para ese cuidado. De tanta mugre, tanta pena y tantas cosas se murió por fin a los 97 años.

Por una puerta salieron sus polvorientos huesos y por la misma entraron las hijas del hermano con sus maridos, sus hijos y sus nietos, a sacar todo para venderlo en veinticuatro horas a los anticuarios de todas partes.

—La culpa la tuvo ella —dijo la mamá de la tía Cecilia y enumeró los pecados de alguien por primera vez en su vida—: Por amedrentar al hermano. Por enloquecer a la hermana. Por guardar y guardar y guardar, como si pudiera uno llevarse los jarrones puestos al purgatorio.

—No, mamá —dijo la tía Cecilia, recordando la única vez que vio llorar a la viejita—: La culpa la tuvo el tipo que no supo reconocer una pintura del siglo XVI.

Con el paso de los años y el cambio de los tiempos, la tía Cecilia, hija única, se casó con un hombre conversador y generoso que resultó un desastre para los negocios y un genio para la fertilidad, de modo que en menos de una década le hizo a la tía seis hijos y le gastó su herencia. Cuando ya no les quedaba sino la casa de Reforma, se mudaron a las afueras y la tía Cecilia abrió una tienda de antigüedades. Empezó vendiendo las de su familia al montón de nuevos ricos en busca de abolengo que asolaban la ciudad, y terminó con una cadena de bazares por toda la república.

Cuando se puso a comprar cosas para abrir la sucursal de San Francisco, en California, llegó a su tienda de Reforma una adolescente de rizos claros que llevaba en la cajuela de su coche una colección de relojes antiguos, un candil de vidrios azules, un marco con la figura sepia de una mujer, y el *Adán y Eva* del siglo XVI.

La tía la vio llegar y sintió que tenía los cuarenta años más viejos de la tierra.

—¿Cuánto nos da por estas cháchara? —preguntó el muchacho, que llevaba a la adolescente de la cintura y la besaba de vez en cuando.

—¿De dónde sacaste las "cháchara"? —preguntó la tía Cecilia, dirigiéndose a la muchacha.

—Estaban en la casa de mi abuela —dijo la muchacha—. Creo que fueron de una tía maniática. No sé. Oí hablar de ella poco y mal. Por eso las quiero vender, no tiran buenas vibras.

—Pero se pagan bien ¿verdad? —preguntó el muchacho.

—Sí, se pagan bien —contestó la tía Cecilia.

—¿Debería guardarlas? —preguntó la muchacha, con un asomo de indecisión.

—No, hija —dijo la tía Cecilia y quiso decirle, pero sólo pensó: "Más vale mal acompañada que sola".

Porque evocó la imagen de la viejita, entre cuadros y gatos, sucia y desmemoriada, prometiéndole a ella, con la avidez de un limosnero: "Si regresas mañana, te regalo el relojito azul".

El brillante relojito azul que ahora tenía en sus manos.

Tía Mari

Era tan precavida la tía Mari que dejó comprado el baúl de olinalá en el que deberían poner sus cenizas. Y ahí estaba, en mitad del salón hasta donde todos los que la quisieron habían llegado para pensar en ella.

Tía Mari tuvo una amiga de su corazón. Una amiga con la que hablaba de sus pesares y sus dichas, con la que tenía en común varios secretos y un montón de recuerdos, una amiga que estuvo sentada junto al cofrecito sin hablar con nadie durante todo el día y toda la noche que duró el velorio. Al amanecer, se levantó despacio y fue hasta él. Cuando estuvo cerca, sacó de su bolsa un frasco y una cuchara, alzó la tapa de madera perfumada y con la cuchara tomó dos tantos de cenizas y los puso en el frasquito. Hizo todo con tal sigilo que quienes estaban en la sala imaginaron que se había acercado para rezar.

Sólo fue descubierta por un par de ojos, a su dueña le rindió cuentas tras verlos brincar de sorpresa:

—No te asustes —le dijo—. Ella me dio permiso. Sabía que me hará bien tener un poco de su aroma en la caja donde están las cenizas de los demás. Siempre que puedo me llevo un poco de los seres a los que seguiré queriendo después de muerte, y lo mezclo con los anteriores. Ella me regaló la caja de marquetería donde los guardo a todos. Cuando yo me muera, me pondrán ahí adentro y me confundiré con ellos. Después, que nos entierren o nos echen a volar, pero juntos.

Tía Rebeca

A los ciento tres años Rebeca Paz y Puente no había tenido en su vida más enfermedad que aquella que desde un principio pareció la última.

Le quedaban vivos cinco hijos de los trece que parió entre los diecisiete y los treinta años. Había enterrado a su marido hacía casi medio siglo, y alrededor de su cama iban y venían setenta y dos nietos. Llevaba seis meses tan grave que cada noche se decía imposible que llegara a la mañana, cada mañana que moriría como a las cuatro de la tarde y cada tarde que sería un milagro si alcanzaba la medianoche. De la frondosa y sonriente vieja que llegó a ser, ya no quedaba sino el pálido forro de un esqueleto. Había sido bella, como ninguna mujer de la época juarista, pero de eso ya no había nadie que se acordara, porque todos sus contemporáneos murieron antes de la revolución contra Porfirio Díaz. Así que el perfume de su cuerpo liberal, sólo ella lo recordaba: todos los días, y con el mismo brío que durante el sitio a la ciudad la sacó de su casa a disparar una pistola de la noche a la mañana y hasta la rendición.

Respiraba diez veces por minuto y parecía haberse ido hacía semanas. Sin embargo, una fuerza la mantenía viva, huyendo de la muerte como de algo mucho peor.

A ratos los hijos le hablaban al oído, buscando su empequeñecida cabeza en medio de una melena blanca cada día más abundante.

—¿Por qué no descansas, mamá? —le preguntaban, exhaustos y compadecidos.

—¿Qué quieres? ¿Qué esperas aún?

No contestaba. Ponía la mirada en los vidrios de colores que formaban el emplomado de un balcón frente a su cama y sonreía como si temiera lastimar con sus palabras.

Entre los nietos había una mujer que todas las tardes se sentaba junto a ella y le platicaba sus penas, como quien se las platica a sí misma.

—Ya no me oyes, abuela. Mejor, para oír amarguras haces

bien de estar sorda. ¿O sí me oyes? A veces estoy segura de que me oyes. ¿Ya te dije que se fue? Ya te lo dije. Pero para mí, como si aún estuviera porque lo ando cargando. ¿Es verdad que tú perdiste un amor en la guerra? Eso me hubiera gustado a mí, que me lo mataran antes de que a él le diera por matarme. En lugar de este odio tendría el orgullo de haber vivido con un héroe. Porque tu amor fue un héroe ¿verdad? ¿Abuela, cómo le hiciste para vivir tanto tiempo después de perderlo? ¿Por qué sigues viva aunque te mataron a tu hombre, aunque mi abuelo te haya regresado a golpes del lugar en que se desangró? Te habían casado a la fuerza con mi abuelo ¿verdad? Cómo no me atreví a preguntártelo antes, a ti tan elocuente, tan hermosa. Ahora ya de qué sirve, ahora no sabré nunca si fueron ciertos los chismes que se cuentan de ti, si de veras abandonaste a toda tu familia para seguir a un general juarista. Si lo mató un francés o si lo mató tu marido un poco antes de que terminara el sitio.

La abuela no respondía. Se concentraba en respirar y respiraba entre suspiros largos y desordenados. Dos veces había estado el señor obispo a confesarla y cuatro a darle la extremaunción, hasta que de tanto verla agonizar, sus descendientes se acostumbraron a vivir con ella muriéndose.

—Está mejorando —decía su nieta. A ella le daba pánico que su abuela se muriera, se quedaría sin confidente y cuando falta el amor la única cura son las confidencias.

—Ay, abuela —le dijo una tarde—. Tengo el cuerpo seco: secos los ojos, la boca, la entrepierna. Así como ando, mejor querría morirme.

—Tonta —dijo la vieja, interrumpiendo un año de silencio—. No sabes de qué hablas. —Su voz se oyó como estremecida por otro mundo.

—¿Tú conoces la muerte, abuela? Tú la conoces ¿verdad?

Por todo respuesta doña Rebeca se perdió entre soplidos y respiraciones turbias.

—¿Por qué peleas, abuela? ¿Por qué no te has muerto? ¿Quieres tu relicario? ¿Quieres cambiar la herencia? ¿Qué pendiente tienes?

La vieja movió una de sus manos para pedirle que se acercara y la nieta acercó un oído a su boca trastabillante.

—¿Qué te pasa? —le preguntó, acariciándola. Ella se dejó estar así por un rato, sintiendo la mano de su nieta ir y venir por su cabeza, su mejilla, sus hombros.

Por fin dijo con su voz en trozos:

—No quiero que me entierren con el hombre.

Media hora después los hijos de doña Rebeca Paz y Puente le prometieron enterrarla a sus anchas, en una tumba para ella sola.

—Me voy con una deuda —le dijo a la nieta, antes de morirse por última vez.

Al día siguiente su influencia celestial hizo volver al esposo perdido de la nieta. El hombre entró a su casa con un desfile de rosas, una letanía de perdones, juramentos de amor eterno, elegías y ruegos.

Todas las lenguas le habían dicho que su mujer era un guiñapo, que las ojeras le tocaban la boca y que los pechos se le habían consumido en lágrimas, qué de tanto llorar tenía ojos de pescado y de tanto sufrir estaba flaca como perro de vecindad. Encontró a una mujer delgada y luminosa como una vela, con los ojos más tristes pero más vivos que nunca, con la sonrisa como un sortilegio y el aplomo de una reina para caminar hacia él, mirarlo como si no tuviera cuatro hijos suyos y decirle:

—¿Quién te llamó a un funeral? Saca tus flores y vete. Yo no quiero que me entierren contigo.

Tía Laura

Al marido de Laura Guzmán le gustaba que su recámara diera a la calle. Era un hombre de costumbres cuidadosas y horarios pertinentes que se dormía poco después de las nueve y se levantaba poco antes de las seis. Nada más era poner la cabeza sobre la almohada y trasladar su inconsciente a un sitio en el que permanecía mudo durante toda la noche, porque si de algo se jactaba aquel hombre era de no cansar su ocupada mollera con el desenfreno de los sueños. Jamás en su vida había soñado, y tenía la certidumbre de que jamás pasaría por su vida tan insana sorpresa. Despertaba un poco antes de las seis y se volvía hacia el despertador suizo que todas las noches colocaba con precisión:

—Te gané otra vez —le decía, orgulloso del mecanismo interior que su madre le había instalado en el cuerpo. Entonces se oía el silbato del tipo que entregaba el periódico, la escoba del hombre que barría la banqueta, la primera conversación de dos obreros rumbo a la fábrica de Mayorazgo, el chisme de unas comadres que iban por las tortillas, los gritos con que la vecina de enfrente despedía a sus hijos rumbo a la escuela y el paso de los primeros automóviles. Todo eso despertaba a Laura Guzmán de su reciente agonía y sin remedio iba lastimando todos los sueños que le hacían falta antes de las once de la mañana.

Al contrario de su marido, ella era una desvelada de oficio. Le gustaba darse quehaceres cuando la casa por fin estaba quieta, ir y venir del sótano a la cocina, de la cocina al costurero y de ahí a la despensa en donde todas las noches escribía un diario minucioso de lo que le iba pasando por la vida. Había llevado una serie de cuadernos que guardaba junto a los libros de cocina al terminar el rito de cada jornada. Luego se le podía ocurrir cortarse las uñas, cepillarse el pelo, oír bajito un disco de cuplés que su marido tenía prohibido tocar entre las paredes de su casa, revisar que cada niño estuviera bien tapado y en su cama, sentarse a inspeccionar que no pasaran ratones de la cocina al comedor, salir al patio a bañarse con la luna, rumiar acurrucada en su sillón junto al gato. El caso era irse a la cama tarde, nunca antes de las tres de la mañana, hurgar al máximo en el tiempo de soledad que le regalaría la noche. Por supuesto, a las seis de la mañana era un guiñapo al que le faltaban casi cuatro horas de sueño para convertirse en esposa. Pero a las siete era imposible seguir durmiendo y entonces ella juraba por todas las biblias que ya siempre se dormiría antes de las nueve y metía la cabeza bajo la almohada intentando reconstruirse mientras contaba hasta sesenta.

Sin embargo, ni siquiera ese minuto era de paz. Afuera la guerra había empezado desde las cinco de la mañana y no existía Dios capaz de pararla. Muchas veces ella la había seguido desde su primer ruido. Una o dos horas después de acostarse despertaba con el susto de algún sueño no escrito el día anterior, y no volvía a dormirse sino hasta pasado el mediodía, hecha un tres bajo el sol de su refugio en la azotea. En la recámara, jamás. La recámara parecía un mercado durante todo el día, todo el que pasaba por la calle pasaba encima de su cama, lo que fuera: coche, perro, niño, vendedor o borracho se oía sobre la almohada como un pregón. Y eso sólo lo sabía ella, porque sólo ella había perdido tiempo intentando dormir en ese cuarto durante el día.

En la suma de todos esos tiempos aprendió el vocabulario alterno que no le habían enseñado ni en su casa ni en la escuela, que no usaban ni su marido, ni sus padres, ni sus amigas, ni cualquiera de las personas con las que vivía. Un vocabulario que ella aprendió a utilizar de modo tan correcto, que le daba a las noches con sus cuadernos un tono audaz y rendentor.

En ese lenguaje los tontos se llamaban pendejos y sólo por eso eran más tontos, lo mismo que eran más malos los cabrones y más de todo los hijos de la chingada. No era sólo de palabras aquel lenguaje, también estaba hecho de tonos. Ella vivía en un mundo en que los peores agravios se decían con suavidad y por lo mismo parecían menos dichos. En cambio en la calle, cualquier cosa podía sonar procaz, hasta el nombre de aquel a quien no debía mencionarse en vano. Laura tenía sobre los tímpanos el agudo grito de un borracho en la madrugada que no podía olvidar: "Aay Dioooss Míííoˮ. La voz de aquel hombre se le metió entre sueño y sueño como la más ardiente pesadilla. Era una voz chillona, desesperada y furibunda. La voz de un infeliz harto de serlo que cuando llama a Dios lo insulta, lo maldice, le reclama. A la tía Laura le daba miedo aquel recuerdo: miedo y éxtasis. "¡Ay Diooos Mííío!" Sonaba en su cabeza y sentía vergüenza, porque aquel sonido le producía un placer inaudito.

—Soy horrenda —decía en voz alta y se llenaba de quehaceres ruidosos.

¿Por qué vivía ella con aquel marido hecho de tedio y disciplina? Quién sabe. Ella no lo sabía y según sus reflexiones nocturnas ya tampoco tenía mucho caso que lo investigara. Iba a quedarse ahí, con él, porque así lo había prometido en la iglesia, porque tenía devoción por sus hijos, y porque así tenía que ser. Ella no era Juana de Arco, ni tenía ganas de que la quemaran viva. Después de todo, sólo en sueños conocía un mejor sitio que su casa. Y su casa sólo era su casa porque se la prestaba el señor con el que dormía.

De entre los variados problemas que le daba aquel matrimonio de conveniencia, uno de los peores era recibir elogios en público. Su marido era experto en eso. Podía pasar semanas lejos, visitando negocios o mujeres más ordenadas, podía vivir en su casa un día tras otro sin hablar mayor cosa, mudo de la cama al comedor y del comedor a la oficina.

Presidía meditabundo la comida mientras sus hijos se codeaban para pedirse la sal sin hacer ruido, luego se iba a jugar cubilete al Círculo Español y de ahí volvía a poner el despertador y meterse a la cama entresacando de su mutismo un arrastrado buenas noches. Días idénticos podía pasar sin fijarse ni de qué color estaba vestida su mujer. Pero no fuera a haber una cena de esas que los hombres acuerdan "con señoras", porque entonces la miraba cuidadoso desde que ella con toda su lentitud cepillaba su pelo imaginando un buen peinado. La veía meterse en un fondo de encajes, recorrer el armario buscando vestido, meterse en las medias que él compraba como tributo por sus estancias en la capital, poner chapas en sus mejillas y pintarse los labios de rojo y las pestañas de azul. La miraba crecer con los tacones de razo oscuro y buscarse los hoyitos de los oídos para entrar en los aretes que él sacaba de la caja fuerte. Luego, terminada la faena del arreglo, ella lo oía:

—No pude elegir mejor, eres perfecta.

Le cubría los hombros con el abrigo y la tomaba del brazo hasta subir al coche.

Durante el camino iba diciéndole lo mucho que la quería, sus ganas de viajar con ella por Italia, los problemas enormes que daban las fortunas, lo agradable que le resultaba su compañía esa noche. Aquello era nada más el principio, y la tía ya estaba casi acostumbrada a sobrellevarlo con paciencia. Lo difícil venía luego: ser liberal con los liberales y conservador con los conservadores, anticomunista frente a don Jaime Villar y proyanqui en casa de los Adame. Apacible en casa de los Pérez Rivero, y activa en casa de los Uriarte. En cualquier caso, su marido declamaba sus virtudes en público y según las preferencias de la dueña del hogar ella era excelente lectora y pianista sensible, o gran repostera, madre sacrificada, esposa de suaves y aristocráticas costumbres.

Su marido sabía siempre cuál de sus cualidades exaltar frente a quién. No era difícil. La ciudad estaba dominada por un aliento conservador y perezoso y la gente que nacía en un bando casi nunca se enteraba de lo que pasaba en el otro. Hubiera sido imposible que en algunas casas se aceptara el invento de la educación laica, lo mismo que se consideraría una locura la idea de hablar mal del general Calles en algunas otras.

Una noche cenaron en casa de los Rodríguez para conocer a unas personas de la Mitra con las que el marido de la tía Laura tenía planeado hacer varios negocios.

La pareja Rodríguez gozaba de gran prestigio entre el señor Arzobispo, el señor Obispo, el Prelado Doméstico de su Santidad y todos los demás inversionistas místicos reunidos ahí. Asistían a misa diaria en catedral con toda su familia, tenían trece hijos y estaban dispuestos a seguir teniendo todos los que Dios en su infinita misericordia quisiera enviar a la fervorosa matriz de la señora Rodríguez, quien además de ser una tenaz creyente era una madre ejemplar que vivía con la sonrisa como una flor, en medio de pañales, desveladas y jaculatorias.

A pesar del agobio de tanto nuevo cristiano, había preparado una cena opulenta para los cristianos mayores, se esmeraba en besar debidamente los anillos encaramados en las manos de los representantes de la Santa Madre y era de una suavidad que rayaba en la idiotez o, como pensó la tía, de una idiotez disfrazada de suavidad, muy propia de su especie.

La tía Laura sobrellevó con heroísmo la conversación sobre la santidad de su Santidad el Papa, y las explicaciones teológicas que hacían plausible la venta de unos terrenos y la compra de otros que figurarían como patrimonio de su marido para que el gobierno, que era tan perverso, no se los fuera a quitar a la Iglesia. La Iglesia no podía tener nada que no le quisiera quitar el gobierno. Por aquel favor, que más que eso debía considerarse una obra pía, la Iglesia le proporcionaba al marido una bendición papal, tres rosarios de pétalo de rosa, una astilla de la cruz de Jesucristo, un clavo tocado en los clavos sagrados y 500 metros de los veinte mil que quedarían a su nombre.

El cónyuge de la tía estaba tan encantado con aquel negocio, que esa noche exageró las virtudes de su mujer. Con gran paciencia ella escuchó el recuento de sus cualidades cristianas y en algunos momentos hasta le resultó agradable saber que su marido se daba cuenta de lo generosa que ella era en el trato con los demás, de la devoción infinita con que acudía a la misa obligatoria y del tiempo que dedicaba a las obras de caridad. Pero lo que en la sopa y la carne fue la descripción de alguien más o menos parecido a la tía Laura, al llegar al postre de fresas y crema era el dibujo de una mojigata insufrible. Según su marido ella iba a misa dos veces diarias, rezaba un rosario a las cinco de la mañana y otro a las seis de la tarde, enseñaba catecismo, asistía a cien niños pobres, visitaba un hospital y un manicomio, se había convertido en la luz de un asilo de ancianos y tenía una devoción de tal magnitud por el Beato Sebastían de Aparicio que a veces el Beato la visitaba en las noches, cuando todos los demás dormían. De esto último el marido se daba cuenta porque la cocina se iluminaba con el brillo celestial de una aureola y desde su recámara podía oír la voz del santo bendiciendo a su esposa.

Para esas horas, los cognacs se habían apoderado de las devotas gargantas de los obispos y todos estaban dispuestos a deslumbrarse con la discreta piedad de la tía Laura. Entonces ella, que había decidido soportar hasta el fin esa tortura, se refugió en el postre como en el único escondite posible. Pero, para su desgracia, la ocupada maternidad de la anfitriona le había impedido darse cuenta de que la crema estaba rancia y un sabor a pocilga se desprendía de aquel postre bajo el cual la tía no pudo esconderse.

—¡Ay Dios míooo! —gritó la tía Laura escupiendo las fresas, aventando la cuchara, llenando el aire con el furor y el éxtasis que aquel grito le producía.

Doña Sara Rodríguez cayó de rodillas con los ojos llorosos:

—Perdónala Señor —dijo transida.

—No tiene nada que perdonarme —aclaró la tía Laura quien ya con la boca desata se siguió de frente con el vocabulario callejero que había tenido trabándole la lengua toda la noche.

Sin detenerse ni a respirar acribilló la lista de sus atributos piadosos y calificó a su marido, a los Rodríguez y a los obispos con todos y cada uno de los memorables adjetivos que había colocado en el centro de sus entrañas el impío balcón de su recámara. Luego salió corriendo hasta su casa y se acostó a dormir en aquel cuarto lleno de improperios y bulla sin levantar la cabeza en diez horas de olvido.

El único negocio que la Mitra aceptó hacer con su desconcertado cónyuge fue el costoso trámite de su anulación matrimonial.

Tía Pilar y Tía Marta

Tía Pilar y tía Marta se encontraron una tarde varios años, hijos y hombres después de terminar la escuela primaria. Y se pusieron a conversar como si el día anterior les hubieran dado el último diploma de niñas aplicadas.

La misma gente les había trasmitido las mismas manías, el mismo valor, los mismos miedos. Cada una a su modo había hecho con todo eso algo distinto. Las dos de sólo verse descubrieron el tamaño de su valor y la calidad de sus manías, dieron todo eso por sabido y entraron a contarse lo que habían hecho con sus miedos.

La tía Pilar tenía los mismos ojos transparentes con que miraba el mundo a los once años, pero la tía Marta encontró en ellos el ímpetu que dura hasta la muerte en la mirada de quienes han pasado por un montón de líos y no se han detenido a llorar una pena sin buscarle remedio.

Pensó que su amiga era preciosa y se lo dijo. Se lo dijo por si no lo había oído suficiente, por las veces en que lo había dudado y porque era cierto. Después se acomodó en el sillón, agradecida porque las mujeres tienen el privilegio de elogiarse sin escandalizar. Le provocaba una ternura del diablo aquella mujer con tres niños y dos maridos que había convertido su cocina en empresa para librarse de los maridos y quedarse con los niños, aquella señora de casi cuarenta años que ella no podía dejar de ver como a una niña de doce: su amiga Pilar Cid.

—¿Todavía operan lagartijas tus hermanos? —preguntó Marta Weber. Se había dedicado a cantar. Tenía una voz irónica y ardiente con la que se hizo de fama en la radio y dolores en la cabeza. Cantar había sido siempre su descanso y su juego. Cuando lo convirtió en trabajo, empezó a dolerle todo.

Se lo contó a su amiga Pilar. Le contó también cuánto quería a un señor y cuánto a otro, cuánto a sus hijos, cuánto a su destino.

Entonces la tía Pilar miró su pelo en desorden, sus ojos como recién asombrados, y le hizo un cariño en la cabeza:

—No tienes idea del bien que me haces. Temí que me abrumaras con el júbilo del poder y la gloria. ¿Te imaginas? Lo aburrido que hubiera sido.

Se abrazaron. Tía Marta sintió el olor de los doce años entre su cuerpo.

Tía Celia

Se encontraron en el vestíbulo del Hotel Palace en Madrid. La tía Celia estaba pidiendo las llaves de su cuarto y lo sintió a sus espaldas. Algo había en el aire cuando él lo cortaba y eso no se olvida en quince años.

Oyó su voz como traída por un caracol de mar. Tuvo miedo.

—¿Quién investiga en tus ojos? —dijo rozándole los hombros. Y ella volvió a sentir el escalofrío que a los veinte años la había empujado hacia él. Fue un domingo. La tía Celia estaba sorbiendo una nieve de limón, idéntica a la de las otras mujeres con las que revoloteaba por la plaza haciendo un ruido de pájaros. El se acercó con el novio de alguna y quedó presentado como Diego Alzina, el primo español que pasaba por México unas semanas. Saludó deslumbrando a cada una con un beso en la mano, pero al llegar a la tía Celia tropezó con su mirada y le dijo: "¿Quién investiga en tus ojos?"

Entonces ella los mantuvo altos y contestó con la voz de lumbre que le había dado la naturaleza:

—Todavía no encuentro quién.

Se hicieron amigos. Iban todos los días a jugar frontón en la casa de los Guzmán y bailaron hasta la madrugada en la boda de Georgina Sánchez con José García el de los *Almacenes García*. Lo hicieron tan bien que fueron la pareja más comentada de la boda después de los novios, y al día siguiente, la pareja más comentada de la ciudad.

Entonces los españoles eran como diamantes, aun cuando hubieran llegado con una mano atrás y otra en la valija de trapo, a patear un veinte para completar un peso, trabajando contra del mostrador sobre el que dormían. Así que cuando llegó Diego Alzina, que no conforme con ser español era rico y noble, según contaban sus primos, puso a la ciudad en vilo, pendiente de si se iba o se quedaba con alguna de las niñas que aprendían a cecear desde pequeñas para distinguir la calidad de su origen.

La tía Celia empezó a tejer una quimera y Alzina a olvidarse de regresar a España en tres semanas. Estaba muy a gusto con aquella sevillana sin remiendos que por casualidad había nacido entre indios, cosa que la hacía aún más encantadora porque tenía actitudes excéntricas como llorar mientras cantaba y comer con un montón de chiles que mordía entre bocado y bocado. "Gitana" le puso, y se hizo de ella.

Salían a caminar mañanas enteras por el campo que rodeaba la ciudad. La tía Celia lo hacía subir hasta la punta de lomas pelonas que según ella se volverían pirámides con sólo quitarles la costra. La tenía obsesionada un lugar llamado Cacaxtla sobre el que se paraba a imaginar la existencia de una hermosa civilización destruida.

—Devastada por los salvajes, irresponsables y necios de tus antepasados —le dijo a Diego Alzina un mediodía de furia.

—No digas que fueron mis antepasados —contestó Alzina—. Porque yo soy el primer miembro de mi familia que visita este país. Mis antepasados no se han movido nunca de España. *Tus* antepasados en cambio Gitana, los tuyos sí eran unos destructores. Andaluces hambrientos que para no morirse entre piedras y olivos, vinieron a ver qué rompían por la América.

—Mis antepasados eran indios —dijo la tía Celia.

—¿Indios? —contestó Alzina—. ¿Y de dónde sacaste la nariz de andaluza?

—Tiene razón Diego —dijo Jorge Cubillas, un amigo de la tía Celia que caminaba cerca de ellos—. Nosotros somos españoles. Nunca nos hemos mezclado con indios. Ni es probable que nos mezclemos alguna vez. ¿O te casarías con tu mozo Justino?

—Ese no es un indio, es un borracho —dijo la tía Celia.

—Por indio, chula, por indio es borracho —replicó Cubillas—. Si fuera como nosotros, sería catador de vinos.

—Siempre me has de contradecir. Eres desesperante —le reprochó la tía Celia—. Tú y todos me desesperan cuando salen con su estúpida veneración por España. España es un país, no es la luna. Y los mexicanos somos tan buenos para todo como los españoles.

—Quedemos en que fueron tus antepasados —dijo Alzina—. Pero ¿por qué no coincidimos en que si algo se destruyó es una lástima y me das un beso de buena voluntad para cambiar de tema?

—No quiero cambiar de tema —dijo la tía Celia, tras una risa larga. Luego besó muchas veces al hombre aquel que de tan fino no parecía español sino húngaro.

Jorge Cubillas y los otros invitados al campo pregonaron al día siguiente que la próxima boda sería la de ellos dos.

Entonces la mamá de la tía Celia pensó que por muy español que fuera el muchacho, sería mejor mandar a sus hijas menores como acompañantes, cada vez que Celia paseara con Alzina. No les fue difícil colocar a las niñas en el cine Reforma, con tres bolsas de palomitas cada una, y caminar todas las tardes por quién sabe dónde.

—¡Qué bien follan las indias! —dijo él una vez, en la torre del campanario de la iglesia de la Santísima.

Desde entonces encontraron en los campanarios el recoveco que necesitaban a diario. Y caminaron hasta ellos de la mano y besándose en público como lo harían todos los jóvenes cuarenta años después.

Pero en esa época hasta por el último rincón de Puebla empezó a hablarse de los abusos de Alzina y la pirujería de la tía Celia.

Un día Cubillas encontró a la mamá de la tía llorando a su hija como a una muerta, después de recibir a una visita que, con las mejores intenciones y sabiendo que ella era una pobre viuda sin respaldo, tuvo la amabilidad de informarle algunas de las historias que iban y venían por la ciudad arrastrando la reputación y devastando el destino de Celia.

—A la gente le cuesta trabajo soportar la felicidad ajena —le dijo Cubillas para consolarla—. Y si la felicidad viene de lo que parece ser un acuerdo con otro, entonces simplemente no es soportable.

Así estaban las cosas cuando en España estalló una guerra. La célebre república española estaba en peligro, y Alzina no pudo encontrar mejor motivo para escaparse de la dicha que aquella desgracia llamándolo a la guerra como a un entretenimiento menos arduo que el amor.

Se lo dijo a la tía Celia de golpe y sin escándalo, sin esconder el consuelo que sentía al huir de la necesidad que ella le provocaba. Porque el apuro por ella lo estaba volviendo obsesivo y celoso, tanto que contra todo lo que pensaba, se hubiera casado con la tía completa en menos de un mes, para que en menos de seis la rutina lo hubiera convertido en un burócrata doméstico que de tanto guardar una mujer en su cama termina viéndola como si fuera una almohada.

Hacía bien en irse y así se lo dijo a la tía Celia, quien primero lo miró como si estuviera loco y luego tuvo que creerle, como se cree en los temblores durante los minutos de un temblor. Se fue sobre él a mordidas y rasguños, a insultos y patadas, a lágrimas, mocos y súplicas. Pero de todos modos, Diego Alzina logró huir del éxtasis.

Después, nada. Tres años oyó hablar de la famosa guerra, sin que nadie nombrara jamás la intervención de Alzina. A veces lo recordaba bien. Iba despacio por las calles que cada tanto interrumpe una iglesia, y a cada iglesia entraba a rezar un Ave María para revivir la euforia de cada campanario. Se volvió parte de su mala fama el horror que provocaba mirarla, hincada frente al Santísimo, diciendo oraciones extrañas, al mismo tiempo que su cara toda sonreía con una placidez indigna de los místicos.

—Mejor hubiera hecho quedándose —decía la tía Celia—. Nada más fue a salar una causa noble. Quién sabe ni qué habrá sido de él. Seguro lo mataron como a tantos, para nada. Pero la culpa la tengo yo por dejarlo ir vivo. Cómo no le saqué un ojo, cómo no le arranqué el pelo, el patriotismo —decía llorando.

Así pasó el tiempo hasta que llegó a la ciudad un pianista húngaro dueño de unas manos hermosas y un gesto tibio y distraído.

Cuando la tía Celia lo vio entrar al escenario del Teatro Principal arrastrando la delgadez de su cuerpo infantil, le dijo a su amigo Cubillas:

—Este pobre hombre, está como mi alma.

Diez minutos después, la violenta música de Liszt lo había convertido en un gran señor. La tía Celia cerró los treinta y cuatro años de sus ojos y se preguntó si aún habría tiempo para ella. Al terminar el concierto, le pidió a Jorge Cubillas que le presentara al hombre aquel. Cubillas era uno de los fundadores de la Sociedad de Conciertos de Puebla. Para decir la verdad, él y Paco Sánchez eran la Sociedad de Conciertos misma. Su amistad con la tía Celia era una más de las extravagancias que todo el mundo encontraba en ellos dos. Tenían distinto sexo y la cabeza les funcionaba parecido, eran tan amigos que nunca lo echaron a perder todo con la ruindad del enamoramiento. Es más, Cubillas se había empeñado en contratar al húngaro que conoció en Europa porque tuvo la certidumbre de que haría un buen marido para Celia.

Y tuvo razón. Se casaron veinte días después de conocerse. La tía Celia no quiso que la boda fuera en Puebla porque no soportaba el olor de sus iglesias. Así que le dio a su madre un último disgusto yéndose de la ciudad con el pianista que apenas conocía de una semana.

—No sufra, señora —le decía Cubillas, acariciándole una mano—. En seis meses estarán de regreso y el último de los ociosos habrá abandonado el deber de preocuparse por la reputación y el destino de Celia. A las mujeres casadas les desaparece el destino. Aunque sólo fuera por eso, estuvo bien casarla.

—Te hubieras casado tú con ella —dijo la madre.

—Yo todo quiero menos pelearme, señora. Celia es la persona que más amo en el mundo.

La tía Celia y el húngaro regresaron al poco tiempo. Pasaron el verano bajo la lluvia y los volcanes de Puebla y luego volvieron al trabajo de recorrer teatros por el mundo. Ni en sus más drásticas fantasías había soñado algo así la tía Celia.

En noviembre llegaron a España, donde los esperaba Cubillas con una lista de los últimos bautizos, velorios y rompimientos que habían agitado a la ciudad en los cuatro meses de ausencia. Fueron a cenar a *Casa Lucio* y volvieron como a la una de la mañana. A esa hora, el buen húngaro besó a su mujer y le pidió a Cubillas que lo perdonara por no quedarse a escuchar los milagros y la vida de tanto desconocido.

A Jorge y la tía Celia les amaneció en el chisme. Como a las seis de la mañana el pianista vio entrar a su mujer brillante de recuerdos y nostalgias satisfechas.

Al principio se comunicaban en francés, pero los dos sabían

que algo profundo del otro desconocerían hasta no hablar su lengua. La tía que era una memoriosa aprendió en poco tiempo un montón de palabras y hacía frases y breves discursos mal construidos con los que seducía al húngaro concentrado casi siempre en aprender partituras. Hacían una pareja de maneras suaves y comprensiones vastas. La tía Celia descubrió que había en el mundo una manera distinta de buscarse el aliento:

—Digamos que menos enfática —le confesó a Cubillas cuando cerca de las cuatro de la mañana la conversación llegó por fin a lo único que habían querido preguntarse y decir en toda la noche.

—Ya no lo extraño ni con aquí ni con acá —dijo la tía Celia señalándose primero el corazón de arriba y después el de abajo—. Cuando me entere de dónde está enterrado voy a ir a verlo sólo para darle el disgusto de no llorar una lágrima. Tengo la paz, ya no quiero la magia.

—Ay, amiga —dijo Cubillas—. Donde hay rencor hay recuerdo.

—Te vemos felices —dijo el húngaro cuando ella se metió en la cama pegándose a su cuerpo delgado.

—Sí, mi vida, me veo feliz. Estoy muy feliz. Boldog vagyok —dijo, empeñada en traducirse.

Doce horas después, la tía regresaba de hacer compras cargando un montón de paquetes y emociones frívolas, cuando oyó a sus espaldas la voz de Alzina. Decía su padre que el tiempo era una invención de la humanidad: nunca creyó ese aforismo con tantas fuerzas.

—¿Quién investiga en tus ojos? —sintió la voz a sus espaldas.

—No te acerques —dijo ella, sin voltear a mirarlo. Luego soltó los paquetes y corrió, como si la persiguieran a caballo. "Si volteas para atrás te conviertes en estatua de sal", pensó mientras subía por las escaleras al cuarto de Cubillas. Lo despertó en lo más sagrado de su siesta.

—Ahí está —le dijo, temblando—: Ahí está. Sácame de aquí. Llévame a Fátima, a Lourdes, a San Pedro. Sácame de aquí.

Cubillas no le tuvo que preguntar de quién hablaba.

—¿Qué haremos? —dijo tan horrorizado como la tía Celia—. ¿Qué se le ofrece?

—No sé —dijo la tía Celia—. Escapé antes de verlo.

Mientras ellos temblaban, Alzina recogió los bultos tirados por la tía Celia, preguntó el número de su habitación y fue a buscarla.

El húngaro abrió la puerta con su habitual sosiego.

—¿En qué puedo servirle? —preguntó.

—Celia Ocejo —dijo Alzina.

—Es mi esposa —contestó el húngaro.

Sólo entonces Alzina se dio cuenta de que su amor por la Gitana llevaba años en silencio y que era más o menos lógico que ella se hubiera hecho de un marido.

—Me ofrecí a subir sus paquetes. Somos amigos. Lo fuimos.

—Tal vez está con Cubillas. ¿Usted conoce Cubillas? —dijo el húngaro en español—. Es un poblano amigo nuestro que llegó apenas ayer, creo que aún no terminan de chismear —agregó en francés, con la esperanza de ser entendido.

Alzina entendió *Cubillas* y pidió al húngaro que le escribiera el número de su cuarto en un papel. Luego le entregó los paquetes, le sonrió y se fue corriendo.

Tocó en la puerta del cuarto 502 como si adentro hubiera sordos. Cubillas le abrió rezongando.

—¡Qué escándalo! Te vas quince años y quieres regresar en dos minutos —dijo.

Alzina lo abrazó viendo sobre sus hombros a la tía Celia que estaba tras de Cubillas con los ojos cerrados y las manos cubriéndole la cara.

—Vete, Alzina —dijo—. Vete que si te miro perjudico lo que me queda de vida.

—India tenías que ser —le dijo Alzina. Y con eso bastó para que la tía se fuera sobre él a patadas y rasguños con la misma fiereza que si hubieran dormido juntos durante quince años.

Cubillas escapó. Un griterío de horror salía del cuarto estremeciendo el pasillo. Se dejó caer de espaldas a la puerta y quedó sentado con las piernas encogidas. No entendía gran cosa porque los gritos se encimaban. La voz de la tía Celia a veces era un torbellino de insultos y otras un susurro atropellado por la furia hispánica de Alzina.

Como una hora después, los gritos fueron apagándose hasta que un hálito de paz empezó a salir por debajo de la puerta. Entonces Cubillas consideró una indiscreción quedarse escuchando el silencio y bajó al segundo piso en busca del pianista.

Estaba poniéndose el frac, no encontraba la pechera y se sentía incapaz de hacerse la corbata.

—Esta mujer me ha convertido en un inútil —le dijo a Cubillas—. Tú eres testigo de que yo salía bien vestido a mis conciertos antes de conocerla. Me ha vuelto un inútil. ¿Dónde está?

Cubillas le encontró la pechera y le hizo el moño de la corbata.

—No te preocupes —inventó—. Se fue con Maicha su amiga y con ella no hay tiempo que dure. Si no llegan pronto, nos alcanzan en el concierto.

El pianista oyó la excusa de Cubillas como quien oye una misa en latín. Se peinó sin decir palabra y sin decir palabra pasó todo el camino al concierto. Cubillas se dio la responsabilidad de llenar el silencio. Años después todavía recordaba, avergonzado, la sensación de loro que llegó a embargarlo.

El último Prokofiev salía del piano, cuando Celia Ocejo entró al palco en que estaba Cubillas. Segundos después, todo el teatro aplaudía.

—Mil gracias —le dijo la tía Celia a su amigo—. Nunca voy a tener con qué pagarte.

Desde el escenario los ojos de su marido la descubrieron como a un refugio, ella le aplaudió tanto que lo hizo sentarse a tocar el primer *encore* de su vida.

—Me lo podrías contar todo —dijo Cubillas—. Sería un buen pago.

—Pero no puedo —contestó la tía Celia con la boca encendida por quién sabía qué.

—Cuéntame —insistió Cubillas—, no seas díscola.

—No —dijo la tía levantándose para aplaudir a su marido.

Jamás en 40 años volvieron a tocar el tema. Sólo hasta hace poco, cuando los antropólogos descubrieron las ruinas de una civilización enterrada en el valle de Cacaxtla, la tía le dijo a su amigo mientras paseaban sobre el pasado:

—Escríbele a Diego Alzina y cuéntale hasta dónde yo tenía razón.

—¿Cuál Diego? —preguntó el húngaro, en perfecto español.

—Un amigo nuestro que ya se murió —contestó Cubillas.

La tía Celia siguió caminando como si no hubiera oído.

—¿Cómo lo supiste? —preguntó después de un rato con la cabeza llena de campanarios.

—Ustedes —dijo el húngaro— se van a morir jaloneándose un chisme.

—No creas —le dijo la tía Celia, en perfecto húngaro—. Yo acabo de perder la guerra.

—¿Qué le dijiste? —le preguntó Cubillas a la tía Celia.

—No te lo puedo decir —contestó ella.

Tía Mónica

A veces la tía Mónica quería con todas sus ganas no ser ella. Detestaba su pelo y su barriga, su manera de caminar, sus pestañas lacias y su necesidad de otras cosas aparte de la paz escondida en las macetas, del tiempo yéndose con trabajos y tan aprisa que apenas dejaba pasar algo más importante que el bautizo de algún sobrino o el extraño descubrimiento de un sabor nuevo en la cocina.

La tía Mónica hubiera querido ser un globo de esos que los niños dejan ir al cielo, para después llorarlos como si hubieran puesto algún cuidado en no perderlos. La tía Mónica hubiera querido montar a caballo hasta caerse alguna tarde y perder la mitad de la cabeza, hubiera querido viajar por países exóticos o recorrer los pueblos de México con la misma curiosidad de una antropóloga francesa, hubiera querido enamorarse de un lanchero en Acapulco, ser la esposa del primer aviador, la novia de un poeta suicida, la mamá de un cantante de ópera. Hubiera querido tocar el piano como Chopin y que alguien como Chopin la tocara como si fuera un piano.

La tía Mónica quería que en Puebla lloviera como en Tabasco, quería que las noches fueran más largas y más accidentadas, quería meterse al mar de madrugada y beberse los rayos de la luna como si fueran té de manzanilla. Quería dormir una noche en el Palace de Madrid y bañarse sin brasier en la fuente de Trevi o de perdida en la de San Miguel.

Nadie entendió nunca por qué ella no se estaba quieta más de cinco minutos. Tenía que moverse porque de otro modo se le encimaban las fantasías. Y ella sabía muy bien que se castigan, que desde que las empieza uno a cometer llega el castigo, porque no hay peor castigo que la clara sensación de que uno está soñando con placeres prohibidos.

Por eso ella puso tanto empeño en hacerse de una casa con tres patios, por eso inventó ponerle dos fuentes y convertir la parte de atrás en casa de huéspedes, por eso tenía una máquina de coser en la que pedaleaba hasta que todas sus sobrinas podían estrenar vestidos iguales los domingos, por eso en invierno tejía gorros y bufandas para cada miembro respetable o no de su familia, por eso una tarde ella misma se cortó el pelo que le llegaba a la cintura y que tanto le gustaba a su amoroso marido. Tan amoroso que para mantenerla trabajaba hasta volver en las noches con los ojos hartos y una beatífica pero inservible sonrisa de hombre que cumple con su deber.

Nadie ha hecho jamás tantas y tan deliciosas galletas de queso como la tía Mónica. Eran chiquitas y largas, pasaba horas amasándolas, luego las horneaba a fuego lento. Cuando por fin estaban listas las cubría de azúcar y tras contemplarlas medio segundo se las comía todas de una sentada.

—Lo malo —confesó una vez— es que cuando me las acabo todavía tengo lugar para alguna barbaridad y me voy a la cama con ella. Cierro los ojos para ver si se escapa, pero no. Entonces hablo con Dios: "Tú me la dejaste, te consta que he soportado todo el día de lucha. Esta va a ganarme y a ver si mañana me quieres perdonar".

Luego se dormía con la tentación entre los ojos, como una santa.

Tía Teresa

El amante de la tía Teresa era un hombre de maneras suaves y ojos férreos. Alternaba el uso de una y de otros según lo necesitara la situación.

Era correcto como el mediodía o desatado como el mar en la noche. Tenía un sonrisa blanca y cautivadora que casi nunca hacía juego con sus ojos. Los ojos los ponía en otra parte, porque estaban pensando en otras cosas. Sólo de vez en cuando se unían a la claridad de su gesto y entonces era irresistible.

Al menos eso creía la tía Teresa, que fue juntando con avaricia cada una de estas magníficas alianzas, cada atisbo de cercanía, para después contemplarlos como grandes tesoros: el momento precario en que había dicho su nombre con necesidad, la frase suelta que habló de un hijo mutuo, la desesperación con que quiso tocarla una noche de lluvia, el ansia con que la besó después de un viaje.

Cien noches intentó descifrarlo. Parecía inasible. Quién sabe, a la mejor alguna vez lo tuvo completo y no se dio cuenta, bendito habría sido Dios si ella lo hubiera sabido a los ochenta años, cuando deliraba buscando llaves y corbatas por toda la casa.

Se veían en un sitio escondido por donde entonces estaba el fin de la ciudad. La tía Teresa Gaudín Lerdo era una de las cinco mujeres que tenían y manejaban un coche en Puebla. Así que al cruzar el puente de la carretera a Cholula, dentro de sí les pedía disculpas a las otras cuatro por estar arriesgando el buen nombre de las cinco.

Su amante se llamaba Ignacio Lagos y tenía un Packard con su correspondiente chofer, en el que viajaba revisando papeles.

La tía Teresa no pudo olvidar el resto de su vida el temblor con que se bajaba de su Chrysler azul para entrar al cuarto de la colonia Resurrección. Era miedosa como buena Gaudín y desaforada como buena Lerdo. Iba a encontrarse con el hombre de sus obsesiones, muerta de pavor y fingiendo aplomo. Cuando la puerta se abría y atrás estaba él dispuesto a cederle la mirada y la boca al mismo tiempo, todos los riesgos dejaban de serlo y el mundo era un escarabajo hasta que ambos se hubieran reclamado sus ausencias, su desconfianza, su odio, su pedregoso amor de veinte suelas.

Después, cuando ella apenas empezaba a cobijarse en su abandono, él decidía correr porque ya era tarde. Había que alcanzar al eterno enemigo agazapado en la cabeza de otros que es el tiempo. Pero Teresa se quedaba en la cama mientras él, bajo cualquier clima, se daba un baño que a ella la hacía sentirse podrida por dentro. Cuando reaparecía brillante y perfumado, la tía Teresa brincaba de la cama a recoger la ropa que había ido tirando por todo el cuarto y se vestía de prisa, sintiendo sobre sí la mirada, otra vez ajena, de aquel señor.

Salían a la calle tratando de fingir que nunca se habían visto. El tenía las llaves del lugar, con ellas deshacía las siete vueltas del cerrojo y dejaba que ella saliera dando unos pasos lentos que a esas horas lo desesperaban. Dos minutos después él salía, cerraba y se metía en su automóvil con la rapidez de un fugitivo.

Una noche perdieron las llaves.

—Tú las tienes —dijo él viendo las que ella mecía en sus manos.

—Estas son las de mi coche —explicó moviéndolas frente a sus ojos.

Era tan guapo Ignacio jugueteando la corbata entre las manos, con su gesto de eficiencia perturbada, que la tía Teresa hubiera empezado todo otra vez.

—¿Entonces dónde están? Guárdame esto —dijo Ignacio, poniendo sobre los hombros de la tía Teresa la corbata que le estorbaba entre las manos. Era una corbata de seda azul que ella sintió alrededor de su cuello como un abrazo en mitad de la calle.

Con las manos desocupadas, Ignacio hurgó de prisa en las bolsas de su pantalón y entre las sábanas revueltas. Encontró las llaves que había tirado ahí al llegar, cuando no le importaba otro futuro que el ferviente cobijo de Teresa. La hizo salir. Su coche acudió dócil como un caballo a la disposición de su amo. Con la mano hizo un adiós silencioso y quedó a resguardo mientras la tía caminaba hasta su Chrysler, pasando por la oscuridad con el terror de siempre. Ni el luminoso recuerdo del cielo en las mañanas, que se ponía en la cabeza para ese momento, le quitó el miedo. Temblaba. La fiesta había terminado y ella no se atrevía a tararear una canción. Aún veía lejos su coche cuando oyó una voz tras ella. Una voz de metal llamándola. Fingió que no la oía. Hasta el último resquicio de su cuerpo, todavía enfebrecido, se arrepintió de estar ahí.

—Me puede matar —pensó—. Pero esto me pasa por necia.

La abrumó la visión de su cuerpo tirado a media calle: inerte, despojado, frío. Nunca tuvo más frío que cuando imaginó aquel frío. Su coche estaba a tres pasos eternos, la voz seguía llamándola. Sintió unas manos apoyarse sobre sus hombros. Un vómito de horror le subió a la garganta:

—Mi corbata, querida —dijo la voz de Ignacio a sus espaldas—. Te llevabas mi corbata.

Jaló la corbata sin cuidado y la tía Teresa la sintió correr como un látigo sobre su cuello. Luego, sin decir ni darse cuenta de más, Ignacio Lagos volvió al auto detenido enfrente, y se fue.

La tía Teresa llegó a su coche tiritando, como si estuviera desnuda. Manejó hacia la ciudad, cruzó el puente, entró a su casa. No hubo aquella noche soledad más grande que la suya.

Nunca volvió a encontrarse con Ignacio Lagos. Muchos años después, cuando la cordura se desvaneció en su inquieta cabeza envejecida, empezó a soñar con la colonia Resurrección, con los ojos y la inclemente boca de aquel amor empedernido. Le dio entonces por buscar llaves entre las sábanas de toda la casa, y no había ropero que no hurgaran sus desesperadas manos en pos de una corbata. Las hijas acordaron ponerle cerca llaveros y corbatas viejas, y quienes iban a visitarla sabían que no podían llevarle mejor regalo que un atado de llaves y una corbata de seda clara.

—Ahora sí, señor —decía la anciana tía Teresa, desvariando, con las dos cosas en la mano—. Ahora sí ya podemos irnos juntos.

Tía Mariana

A la tía Mariana le costaba mucho trabajo entender lo que le había hecho la vida. Decía *la vida* para darle algún nombre al montón de casualidades que la habían colocado poco a poco, aunque la suma se presentara como una tragedia fulminante, en las condiciones de postración con las cuales tenía que lidiar cada mañana.

Para todo el mundo, incluida su madre, casi todas sus amigas, y todas las amigas de su madre —ya no digamos su suegra, sus cuñadas, los miembros del Club Rotario, Monseñor Figueroa y hasta el Presidente municipal—, ella era una mujer con suerte. Se había casado con un hombre de bien, empeñado en el bien común, depositario del noventa por ciento de los planes modernizadores y las actividades de solidaridad social con los que contaba la sociedad poblana de los años cuarenta. Era la célebre esposa de un hombre célebre, la sonriente compañera de un prócer, la más querida y respetada de todas las mujeres que iban a misa los domingos. De remate, su marido era guapo como Maximiliano de Habsburgo, elegante como el príncipe Felipe, generoso como San Francisco y prudente como el provincial de los jesuitas. Por si fuera poco, era rico, como los hacendados de antes y buen inversionista, como los libaneses de ahora.

Estaba la situación de la tía Mariana como para vivir agradecida y feliz todos los días de su vida. Y nunca hubiera sido de otro modo si, como sólo ella sabía, no se le hubiera cruzado la inmensa pena de avizorar la dicha. Sólo a ella le podía haber ocurrido semejante idiotez. Tan en paz que se había propuesto vivir, ¿por qué tuvo que dejarse cruzar por la guerra? Nunca acabaría de arrepentirse, como si uno pudiera arrepentirse de lo que no elige. Porque la verdad es que a ella el torbellino se le metió hasta el fondo como entran por toda la casa los olores que salen de la cocina, como la imprevisible punzada con que aparece y se queda un dolor de muela. Y se enamoró, se enamoró, se enamoró.

De la noche a la mañana perdió la suave tranquilidad con que despertaba para vestir a los niños y dejarse desvestir por su marido. Perdió la lenta lujuria con que bebía su jugo de naranja y el deleite que le provocaba sentarse a planear el menú de la comida durante media hora de cada día. Perdió la paciencia con que escuchaba a su impertinente cuñada, las ganas de hacer pasteles toda una tarde, la habilidad para hundirse sonriente en la tediosa parejura de las cenas familiares. Perdió la paz que había mecido sus barrigas de embarazada y el sueño caliente y generoso que le tomaba el cuerpo por las noches. Perdió la voz discreta y los silencios de éxtasis con que rodeaba las opiniones y los planes de su marido.

En cambio, adquirió una terrible habilidad para olvidarlo todo, desde las llaves hasta los nombres. Se volvió distraída como una alumna sorda y anuente como los mal aconsejados por la indiferencia. Nada más tenía una pasión. ¡Ella, que se dijo hecha para las causas menores, que apostó a no tener que solucionar más deseos que los ajenos, que gozaba sin ruido con las plantas y la pecera, los calcetines sin doblar y los cajones ordenados!

Vivía de pronto en el caos que se deriva de la excitación permanente, en el palabrerío que esconde un miedo enorme, saltando del júbilo a la desdicha con la obsesión enfebrecida de quienes están poseídos por una sola causa. Se preguntaba todo el tiempo cómo había podido pasarle aquello. No podía creer que el recién conocido cuerpo de un hombre que nunca previó, la tuviera en ese estado de confusión.

—Lo odio —decía y tras decirlo se entregaba al cuidado febril de su uñas y su pelo, a los ejercicios para hacer cintura y a quitarse los vellos de las piernas, uno por uno, con unas pinzas para depilar cejas.

Se compró la ropa interior más tersa que haya dado seda alguna, y sorprendió a su marido con una colección de pantaletas brillantes, ¡ella que se había pasado la vida hablando de las virtudes del algodón!

—Quién me lo iba a decir —murmuraba, caminando por el jardín, o mientras intentaba regar las plantas del corredor. Por primera vez en su vida, se había acabado el dineral que su marido le ponía cada mes en la caja fuerte de su ropero. Se había comprado tres vestidos en una misma semana, cuando ella estrenaba uno al mes para no molestar con ostentaciones. Y había ido al joyero por la cadena larga de oro torcido, cuyo precio le parecía un escándalo.

—Estoy loca —se decía, usando el calificativo que usó siempre para descalificar a quienes no estaban de acuerdo con ella. Y es que ella no estaba de acuerdo con ella. ¿A quién se le ocurría enamorarse? ¡Qué insensatez! Sin embargo se dejaba ir por el precipicio insensato de necesitar a alguien. Porque tenía una insobornable necesidad de aquel señor que, al contrario de su marido, hablaba muy poco, no explicaba su silencio y tenía unas manos insustituibles. Sólo por ellas valía la pena arriesgarse todos los días a estar muerta. Porque muerta iba a estar si se sabía su desvarío. Aunque su marido fuera bueno con ella como lo era con todo el mundo, nada la salvaría de enfrentarse al linchamiento colectivo. Viva la quemarían en el atrio de la catedral o en el zócalo, todos los adoradores de su adorable marido.

Cuando llegaba a esta conclusión, detenía los ojos en el infinito y poco a poco iba sintiendo cómo la culpa se le salía del cuerpo y le dejaba el sitio a un miedo enorme. A veces pasaba horas presa de la quemazón que la destruiría, oyendo hasta las voces de sus amigas llamarla "puta" y "mal agradecida". Luego, como si hubiera tenido una premonición celestial, abría una sonrisa por en medio de su cara llena de lágrimas y se llenaba los brazos de pulseras y el cuello de perfumes, antes de ir a esconderse en la dicha que no se le gastaba todavía.

Era un hombre suave y silencioso el amante de la tía Mariana. La iba queriendo sin prisa y sin órdenes, como si fueran iguales. Luego pedía:

—Cuéntame algo.

Entonces la tía Mariana le contaba las gripas de los niños, los menús, sus olvidos y, con toda precisión, cada una de las cosas que le habían pasado desde su último encuentro. Lo hacía reir hasta que todo su cuerpo recuperaba el jolgorio de los veinte años.

—Con razón sueño que me queman a media calle. Me lo he de merecer —murmuraba para sí la tía Mariana, sacudiéndose la paja de un establo en Chipilo. El refrigerador de su casa estaba siempre surtido con los quesos que ella iba a buscar a aquel pueblo, lleno de moscas y campesinos güeros que descendían de los primeros italianos sembradores de algo en México. A veces pensaba que su abuelo hubiera aprobado su proclividad por un hombre que, como él, podría haber nacido en las montañas del Piamonte. Hacía el regreso, todavía con luz, en su auto rojo despojado de chofer.

Una tarde, al volver, la rebasó el Mercedes Benz de su marido. Era el único Mercedes que había en Puebla y ella estuvo segura de haber visto dos cabezas cuando lo miró pasar. Pero cuando quedó colocado delante de su coche, lo único que vio fue la honrada cabeza de su marido volviendo a solas del rancho en Matamoros.

—De qué color tendré la conciencia —dijo para sí la tía Mariana y siguió el coche de su marido por la carretera.

Viajaron un coche adelante y otro atrás todo el camino, hasta llegar a la entrada de la ciudad, en donde uno dio vuelta a la derecha y la otra a la izquierda, sacando la mano por la ventanilla para decirse adiós en el mutuo acuerdo de que a las siete de la tarde todavía cada quien tenía deberes por separado.

La tía Mariana pensó que sus hijos estarían a punto de pedir la merienda y que ella nunca los dejaba solos a esas horas. Sin embargo, la culpa le había caído de golpe pensando en su marido trabajador, capaz de pasar el día solo entre los sembradíos de melón y jitomate que visitaba los jueves hasta Matamoros, para después volver a la tienda y al club Rotario, sin permitirse la más mínima tregua. Decidió dar la vuelta y alcanzarlo en ese momento, para contarle la maldad que le tenía tomado el corazón. Eso hizo. En dos minutos dio con el tranquilo paso del Mercedes dentro del cual reinaba la cabeza elegante de su marido. Le temblaban las manos y tenía la punta de una lágrima en cada ojo, acercó su coche al de su esposo sintiendo que ponía el último esfuerzo de su vida en la mano que agitaba llamándolo. Su gesto entero imploraba perdón antes de haber abierto la boca. Entonces vio la hermosa cabeza de una mujer recostada sobre el asiento muy cerca de las piernas de su marido. Y por primera vez en mucho tiempo sintió alivio, cambió la pena por sorpresa y después la sorpresa por paz.

Durante años, la ciudad habló de la dulzura con que la tía Natalia había sobrellevado el romance de su marido con Amelia Berumen. Lo que nadie pudo entender nunca fue cómo ni siquiera durante esos meses de pena ella interrumpió su absurda costumbre de ir hasta Chipilo a comprar los quesos de la semana.

Tía Inés

Había una luna a medias la noche que desquició para siempre los ordenados sentimientos de la tía Inés Aguirre. Una luna intrigosa y ardiente que se reía de ella. Y era tan negro el cielo que la rodeaba que adivinar por qué no pensó Inés en escaparse de aquel embrujo.

Quizás aunque la luna no hubiera estado ahí, aunque el cielo hubiera fingido transparencia, todo habría sido igual. Pero la tía Inés culpaba a la luna para no sentirse la única causante de su desgracia. Sólo bajo esa luna pudo empezarle a ella la pena que le tenía tomado el cuerpo. Una desdicha que, como casi siempre pasa, se le metió fingiendo ser el origen mismo de la dicha.

Porque la noche aquella, bajo la luna, el hombre le dio un beso en la nuca como quien bebe un trago de agua, y fue una noche tan lejos de la pena que nadie hubiera podido imaginarla como el inicio de la más mínima desgracia. Apenas había llegado la luz eléctrica y las casas bajo el cerro parecían estrellas. En alguien tuvo que vengar esa luna el dolor que le dieron las casas encendidas, las calles bajo el cobijo de aquella luz comprada y mentirosa, la ingratitud de toda una ciudad anocheciendo tranquila, sin buscar el auxilio de su fulgor. De algo tenía que servir ella, alguien tendría que recordar su luz despidiendo la tarde, y ese alguien fue Inés Aguirre: la luna la empujó hasta el fondo de unos brazos que la cercarían para siempre aunque fueran a irse temprano.

Al día siguiente, la tía Inés no recordó un ruego, menos una orden, pero tenía una luz entre ojo y ojo ensombreciendo toda su existencia. No podía ya olvidar el aliento que le entibió los hombros, ni desprender de su corazón la pena que lo ató a la voluntad sagrada de la luna.

Se volvió distraída y olvidadiza. Pedía auxilio para encontrar el lápiz que tenía en la mano, los anteojos que llevaba puestos, las flores que acababa de cortar. Del modo en que andaba podía derivarse que no iba a ninguna parte, porque después del primer paso casi siempre olvidaba su destino. Confundía la mano derecha con la izquierda y nunca recordaba un apellido. Terminó llamando a sus tíos con el nombre de sus hermanos y a sus hermanas con el nombre de sus amigas. Cada mañana tenía que adivinar en cuál cajón guardaba su ropa interior y cómo se llamaban las frutas redondas que ponía en el jugo del desayuno. Nunca sabía qué horas eran y varias veces estuvo a punto de ser atropellada.

Una tarde hacía el más delicioso pastel de chocolate y a la semana siguiente no encontraba la receta ni sabía de qué pastel le hablaban. Iba al mercado para volver sin cebollas, y hasta el Padre Nuestro se le olvidó de buenas a primeras. A veces se quedaba mirando un florero, una silla, un tenedor, un peine, una sortija y preguntaba con la ingenuidad de su alma: —¿Para qué sirve ésto?

Otras, escribía en cualquier cuaderno toda clase de historias que después no podía leer porque con el punto final olvidaba las letras.

En uno de estos cuadernos escribió la última vez que supo hacerlo: "Cada luna es distinta. Cada luna tiene su propia historia. Dichosos quienes pueden olvidar su mejor luna".

Tía Ofelia

Hay gente con la que la vida se ensaña, gente que no tiene una mala racha sino una continua sucesión de tormentas. Casi siempre esa gente se vuelve lacrimosa. Cuando alguien la encuentra, se pone a contar sus desgracias, hasta que otra de sus desgracias acaba siendo que nadie quiere encontrársela.

Esto último no le pasó nunca a la tía Ofelia, porque a la tía Ofelia la vida la cercó varias veces con su arbitrariedad y sus infortunios, pero ella jamás abrumó a nadie con la historia de sus pesares. Dicen que fueron muchos, pero ni siquiera se sabe cuántos, y menos las causas, porque ella se encargó de borrarlos cada mañana del recuerdo ajeno.

Era una mujer de brazos fuertes y expresión juguetona, tenía una risa clara y contagiosa que supo soltar siempre en el momento adecuado. En cambio, nadie la vio llorar jamás.

A veces le dolían el aire y la tierra que pisaba, el sol del amanecer, la cuenca de los ojos. Le dolían como un vértigo el recuerdo, y como le peor amenaza, el futuro. Despertaba a media noche con la certidumbre de que se partiría en dos, segura de que el dolor se la comería de golpe. Pero apenas había luz para todos, ella se levantaba, se ponía la risa, se acomodaba el brillo en las pestañas, y salía a encontrar a los demás como si los pesares la hicieran flotar.

Nadie se atrevió a compadecerla nunca. Era tan extravagante su fortaleza, que la gente empezó a buscarla para pedirle ayuda. ¿Cuál era su secreto? ¿Quién amparaba sus aflicciones? ¿De dónde sacaba el talento que la mantenía erguida frente a las peores desgracias?

Un día le contó su secreto a una mujer joven cuya pena parecía no tener remedio:

—Hay muchas maneras de dividir a los seres humanos —le dijo—. Yo los divido entre los que se arrugan para arriba y los que se arrugan para abajo, y quiero pertenecer a los primeros. Quiero que mi cara de vieja no sea triste, quiero tener las arrugas de la risa y llevármelas conmigo al otro mundo. Quién sabe lo que habrá que enfrentar allá.

Tía Marcela y Tía Jacinta

Aquellas dos mujeres eran cada una el gajo de una trenza. Desde que iban a un colegio de monjas escondido bajo un túnel y varias escaleras, en tiempos de la persecución a los cristeros, hasta que en los años cuarenta fueron al primer baile de la universidad a encontrarse con esos seres extravagantes y remotos que eran los hombres. No los hombres de sus casas, que eran a veces como muebles y a veces como frazadas, sino los que las miraban con ojos de codicia y curiosidad. Los que pensaban en ellas con todo y sus piernas, en ellas con todo y el hueco bajo sus cinturas, en ellas como algo también impredecible y turbador.

Las dos encontraron la misma noche a los encendidos corazones que les tomarían la vida y el vientre para llenárselos con sus apellidos, sus obsesiones, sus hijos. Las dos cursaron por noviazgos más o menos decorosos, las dos terminaron casándose más o menos por los mismos años, las dos compartieron la inquietud de sus barrigas preñadas por primera vez, las dos tuvieron un pleito infernal antes de que pasaran dos días de luna de miel y las dos aprendieron que tras la pena de apariencia fatal que tiene cada pleito, llegan después horas de gloria y frases de intimidad que le dan al patético carácter de irreversible que tiene el pacto conyugal, la sensación de que no se puede haber hecho mejor pacto en la vida. Las dos guisaban con tantos parecidos de cebolla y hasta sus pasteles despedían un olor igual, aunque se hornearan en hornos y horarios muy distintos. No conformes con eso, las dos tuvieron cinco hijos cada una.

Pasaban las tardes cosiéndoles vestidos en serie y cuidando a los diez juntos, como si fueran pastoras del mismo rebaño. Eran idénticas las gemelas Gómez, sólo las distinguía la precisión de algunos gestos. Sin embargo, esa diferencia en sus rostros era la exacta medida de la diferencia entre sus espíritus. La tía Marcela tenía en los ojos la luz de quienes le buscan a la vida su mejor lado, la de quienes para su desgracia no accedieron a la felicidad que sólo pueden disfrutar los tontos, pero que están dispuestos incluso a parecerlo con tal de asirse a la punta de alguna dicha. Por eso canturreaba siempre, para dormir a los niños y para despertarlos, para ensartar una aguja, para rogarle al cielo que los huevos del desayuno no se pegaran al sartén, para pedirle a su marido que la mirara como al principio y hasta para acompañar el soliloquio de sus largas caminatas.

La tía Jacinta heredó de su madre una melancolía extenuante. A veces se quedaba mirando al infinito como si algo se le hubiera perdido, como si el infinito mismo no le bastara a su anhelo de absoluto. A veces la entristecía no haber nacido en Noruega una noche de tormenta, no conocer el Congo, ni saberse capaz de viajar por la India. Estaba segura de que nunca vería Egipto, de que jamás podría recorrer la sierra de Chihuahua, de que el mar con sus traiciones y sus promesas no sería nunca su compañero de todos los amaneceres. Desde niña había leído con pasión, pero de cada historia que leía no sacó nunca la certidumbre de estar dentro de ella que sienten muchos lectores. Al contrario, cada historia, cada lugar, cada personaje había servido siempre para que ella se hundiera en la nostalgia de sólo ser ella. No sería jamás una suicida como Ana Karenina, ni una borracha como Ava Gardner, ni una loca como Juana de Orléans, ni una invasora como Carlota Amalia, ni una cantante desaforada como Celia Cruz.

Tenía cinco hijos, nunca podría saber lo que era tener dos ni lo que sería tener diez. Tenía una casa mediana y un marido comerciante, nunca sabría de los palacios, ni del hambre. Su marido tenía el pelo castaño y dócil, ella jamás entendería lo que era acariciar un pelo hirsuto y negro como el de Emiliano Zapata, una cabeza dorada como la de Henry Fonda o una por completo calva como la del Obispo Toríz.

A veces su hermana interrumpía una canción para preguntarle en qué pensaba, por qué en los últimos quince minutos no había dado un pespunte. Entonces la tía Jacinta le contestaba cosas como:

—¿No te hubiera gustado pintar la Mona Lisa? ¿Te imaginas si hubiéramos aprendido baile con Fred Astaire? ¿Evita Perón será una mentirosa? ¿De qué número calzará Pedro Infante? Dicen que hay una playa en Oaxaca que se llama Huatulco y es el paraíso. Y tú y yo aquí metidas.

—A mí me gusta aquí —decía la tía Marcela, mirando el campo a su alrededor y los volcanes a lo lejos. Ese campo nunca era el mismo. Cada estación lo iba cambiando de colores y sólo porque los hábitos decían que esas montañas se llamaban siempre igual era posible verlas como lo mismo cuando a veces brillaban de verde y a veces la sequía los dejaba grises y polvorientos.

En esa época que todo lo resecaba, hasta la piel de las manos y los párpados, en ese tiempo que el sol picaba en las mañanas y se iba temprano para dejarle paso a un viento de hielo, en aquellas tardes que les llevaban a los niños unas fiebres atroces, que les herían la garganta hasta hacerlos toser como perros, en esos días aún cercanos a la Navidad pero que pasada la esperanza de las fiestas eran largos como misas de tres padres y odiosos como sermones de Cuaresma, la tía Marcela se descubrió una bolita en el pecho izquierdo.

Estaban cosiendo unos vestidos blancos con puntos rojos para que las niñas recibieran al domingo de Pascua.

—No sé para qué inventamos esto de ponerles tanto olán —dijo la tía Jacinta deteniéndose en un pliegue.

—Tengo una bolita medio rara en el pecho izquierdo —le contestó su hermana, la tía Marcela.

—Qué? —dijo Jacinta aventando un vestido—. Déjame ver, déjame ver. —Jaló el suéter de su hermana y metió su mano hasta tocarle el pecho: ahí estaba, dura como un champiñón, sin poder sentirse exactamente redonda. Buscándole la vuelta a la evidencia, la tía Jacinta tocó más arriba y sintió una igual, más abajo y otra. Toda ella tembló de terror ante la sola idea de que eso pudiera ser malo. Su hermana la vio palidecer mientras intentaba un tono despreocupado.

—No creo que sea importante, pero habrá que ir al doctor —dijo—. No le digas a tu marido, ya sabes lo escandalosos que son los hombres.

—¿Por qué te pusiste pálida? Se parecen a las de mi mamá ¿verdad? —preguntó la tía Marcela.

—Ya no me acuerdo. Fue hace casi veinte años.

—Yo sí me acuerdo —dijo la tía Marcela extendiendo una sonrisa que de tan bella la hacía maligna—. Eran iguales.

—¿No pensarás morirte sin conocer Egipto? —dijo la tía Jacinta jugando con los olanes de un vestido.

—De ningún modo —le contestó su hermana, la tía Marcela.

La tarde siguiente visitaron al doctor. Era un hombre como de cincuenta años al que le gustaban los buenos vinos y la música de Brahms. Lo conocían desde que tenían memoria. Alguna vez tuvo el pelo castaño y completo, pero sólo hasta entonces la tía Jacinta le conoció el gesto de misericordia que de pronto le embellecía los ojos.

Mientras la tía Marcela se dejaba revisar los pechos intentando concentrarse en la idea de que eran sus rodillas, de que por eso no tenía que sentir vergüenza, porque hasta las niñas enseñan sin rubor los moretones de una rodilla, el pobre hombre miró a la tía Jacinta disculpándose por ser él quien debía decirlo. La tía Jacinta se mordió los labios. Para entonces, la tía Marcela había abierto los ojos y miraba el gesto de su hermana. Con la rapidez de una niña, levantó su espalda de la mesa de auscultación y le dijo, esgrimiendo la maligna sonrisa del día anterior:

—No te preocupes, nos alcanza el tiempo para conocer Alejandría.

La tía Jacinta la miró como si ella misma fuera el infinito. La tía Marcela siguió hablando, se levantó y fue a vestirse al cuarto de junto. Los oyó cuchichear.

—No me hagan trampas —dijo, saliendo con los últimos botones de la blusa sin abrochar—. Quiero estar en la película de mi muerte haciendo algo más que morirme a espaldas de todo el mundo.

—Jaime te propone una operación —dijo la tía Jacinta—. Quizá no esté tan ramificado.

—¿Me dejarías plana? —le preguntó la tía Marcela al doctor.

—Sí —dijo el hombre.

—¿Y tú quieres que yo cumpla cuarenta años sin pechos?

—Hermana, es que si no, puedes no cumplirlos —dijo la tía Jacinta.

—Será un alivio —contestó la tía Marcela—. Bastante tiene uno con tener cáncer, para además tener que cumplir cuarenta años.

Desde entonces, la tía Jacinta no dejó sola a su hermana ni un minuto. Fue con ella a la operación y a los tratamientos, a los chocheros, a los médicos de agüitas, a los brujos de la sierra, a las iglesias y a Rochester.

—Vas a saber lo que es tener diez hijos —le dijo la tía Marcela una tarde, al salir de Santo Domingo—. Yo no sé por qué Dios se empeña en sacarme de la fiesta.

La oyó repetir eso en "La Santísima", hincadas una junto a la otra en los reclinatorios forrados de terciopelo rojo que están frente al altar: "Dios, Dios, Dios, ¿por qué te empeñas en sacarme de la fiesta?" Su cuerpo de hombros erguidos y piernas largas se había ido empequeñeciendo. Caminaba apoyada en un bastón y había perdido la frescura de su piel y el ímpetu de los ojos, pero aún regía en su gesto la implacable bondad de su sonrisa.

Sólo habían pasado nueve meses desde la tarde en que visitaron al médico. Y octubre estaba encima con los inevitables cuarenta años.

—¿Por qué no hacemos nuestra fiesta en el albergue del volcán? —dijo la tía Marcela una tarde de niños alborotando.

—Donde tú quieras —contestó la tía Jacinta, que había perdido su eterna condición de añorante. No gastaba ya ni un segundo en desear otros sitios. Cuidaba diez niños, dos casas, un marido, un cuñado y una ciega esperanza. Ese era su modo de exorcizar la lenta ceremonia de la muerte. Pero sabía que la tía Marcela estaba harta, que cientos de pequeños y grandes dolores la cruzaban, que ya no valía la pena ni disimular, y que muy pronto se cansaría de fingir. Iba por la calle señalando para sí a las personas que podrían morirse en lugar de su hermana, señalando a los perversos, a los inútiles, a los indeseables, hasta que tras mucho señalar terminaba señalándose a sí misma como la pieza más injusta de todas. Al principio, jugaba con su hermana a hablar del futuro, hacían planes para viajar, para ir de compras, para inscribirse en las clases de francés de Madame Girón, para aprender a nadar antes de ir a Cozumel. Con el tiempo habían dejado de hacerlo, como si ambas hubieran acordado suspenderle a la otra esa tortura. Entonces la tía Marcela dedicó muchas horas a describir las virtudes y las debilidades de sus hijos, a contarlos tanto y de tantas maneras que su hermana pudiera reconocerlos y predecirlos hasta en el último detalle.

—Acuérdate de que Raúl finge dureza para disimular alguna pena, no se te olvide que Mónica es tímida, no descuides la vocación artística de Patricia, no dejes que Juan crezca con miedos, acaricia con mucha frecuencia a Federico. Tú ya sabes ¿no?

—Sí, hermana. Ya sé. Aunque también sé que tú serías mucho mejor mamá de los míos y que Dios está loco.

—No digas eso hermana —le contestó Marcela que también había pensado muchas veces que Dios estaba loco, que ni siquiera estaba, pero que sabía perfectamente la falta que algo como Dios le haría a su hermana cuando ella se muriera—. Dios sabe por qué hace las cosas, escribe derecho en renglones torcidos, nos quiere, nos cuida, nos protege.

—Sí, hermana, sí. Por eso te vas a morir, cuando más haces falta. No hay que engañarse, ¿para qué?

—¿Para qué? Hermana, tú para seguir viva, yo para morirme sin tantísimo desconsuelo. No te niegues a las ideas de tu tiempo. Y no se te ocurra enseñarles a mis hijos ni uno solo de nuestros disparates.

Hicieron una fiesta en el albergue nevado del volcán. Las hermanas soplaron sus cuarenta velas y los hijos adolescentes inventaron una caminata. La tía Marcela se dispuso a seguirlos.

—¿A dónde vas, Marce? Todavía no estás bien —le dijo su marido, con el que la tía Marcela aún jugaba a que alguna vez se aliviaría.

—Nada más a que me pegue el aire.

—Voy contigo —dijo la tía Jacinta ayudándola a levantarse. Afuera hacía un frío de los que se meten por la nariz hasta el último lugar del cuerpo.

—Me va a odiar por traicionarlo —dijo la tía Marcela—. Para él voy a ser siempre la mujer que lo dejó a medio camino. ¿Y qué le digo? ¿Que no sea injusto, que me tenga más lástima de la que siente por él, que me perdone, que yo no tengo la culpa, que por favor no me olvide, que se case con otra, que me cuente lo atractiva que le parezco, que durante el siguiente mes me diga "Mi vida", en lugar de "Oye Marce"?

La tía Jacinta le pasó un brazo sobre los hombros y no le contestó. Se quedaron así hasta que los maridos se acercaron. Durante un rato hablaron de la belleza del volcán, de cómo hacía brillar la nieve, de la primera mañana que estuvieron ahí juntos. Luego, volvieron los hijos, colorados y ardientes, contando hazañas.

—Vámonos, cuarentonas —dijo el marido de la tía Marcela acariciándole el cuello. La ayudó a bajar hasta el coche y la instaló adentro, arropándola como a una niña.

La tía Jacinta se acercó a darle un beso.

—Conste que te acompañé a cumplir años —le dijo la tía Marcela.

Al día siguiente no quiso levantarse: "Me están pesando los cuarenta", coqueteó con la tía Jacinta cuando la vio llegar con el aliento entreverado de angustia.

Dos días después el médico se decidió a ponerle morfina.

—Ayer soñé con Alejandría —le dijo la tía Marcela a la tía Jacinta cuando despertó de alguno de los trances en que la colocaba la droga—. Con razón quieres ir. ¿Qué vas a hacer con tus deseos, hermana?

—Los voy a heredar —dijo la tía Jacinta con la pena en los labios.

—Habría que ir también a Dinamarca y a Italia, a Marruecos y a Sevilla, a Cozumel y China —volvió a decir la tía Marcela—. Me estoy volviendo como tú. ¿Qué vas a hacer con tus deseos, hermana?

Hacía un año que todos sus deseos eran el solo deseo de no perderla, hacía mucho que su hermana se había vuelto París y Nueva York, Estambul y las Islas Griegas, el más largo resumen de imposibles con que la hubiera torturado la vida.

La noche del día en que enterraron a su hermana Marcela, la tía Jacinta exhausta de velar durante meses, poseída por una pena que ya era parte de su cuerpo, se quedó dormida sobre un sillón de la sala. Al poco rato despertó con frío y una sonrisa extravagante palpitando en su boca.

—¿Qué pasó? —le preguntó su marido que estaba cerca, mirándola.

—Soñé con Marcela —dijo la tía Jacinta—. Está en el cielo.

—¿Y qué dice? —preguntó el hombre, que conocía los riesgos de perturbar aquella pena.

—Dice que es como aquí, y está contenta. Ya sabes que a ella nunca le gustó viajar —contestó tía Jacinta caminando hacia su cuarto—. Vamos, ven a la cama. Hay que dormir para ver qué más vemos.

Tía Elvira

De niña, a la tía Elvira le daba miedo la oscuridad. Creían sus hermanas que porque en lo oscuro no se puede ver nada, pero la razón de su miedo era exactamente la contraria: ella en lo oscuro veía de todo. De lo oscuro salían arañas y vampiros gigantes, salía su mamá en camisón abrazada a un crucifijo, salía su papá en cuatro pies contemplando un cometa verde, mientras el abuelo y los tíos pasaban encima de él a toda carrera, abriendo sus bocas moradas para aullar sin que nadie los oyera. En lo oscuro había una niña amarrada al barandal de la escalera con un listón de satín que le sacaba sangre. No decía nada la tía Elvira, pero movía los labios como si dijera: "Hay leones y pájaros flotando muertos en sus peceras".

—No inventes, Elvira —le decían sus hermanas—. En la oscuridad no hay nada más que lo mismo que cuando hay luz.

Sin embargo, aún habiendo luz la tía Elvira no veía las mismas cosas que sus hermanas. Ella era capaz de convertir el piano en lagarto, la despensa en cueva de Alí Babá, la fuente en el Mar Negro y el agua de jamaica en sangre de fusilados.

Decían que la tía Elvira estaba siempre un poco fuera de la realidad, pero en los ratos que le dedicó aprendió a bordar como cualquier otra señorita que se respetara, a tocar el piano sin aporrearlo, a cantar todo el cancionero decente, incluídas las nueve más hermosas versiones del Ave María.

Cocinaba de todo, menos bacalao. Su abuela materna se había empeñado en que sus hijas y nietas no aprendieran ese guiso, porque en España era comida de pobres, y si ella había pasado tantos trabajos para vivir en México, no iba a ser para que sus descendientes acabaran comiendo pescado seco, como cualquier andaluz muerto de hambre.

La tía Elvira tenía los ojos negros de su mamá y la boca imprudente de su padre. Una boca conversadora y leguleya sin la cual se podría haber casado antes de los veinte años con cualquier criollo de cincuenta generaciones, o con uno de esos españoles recién llegados de la pobreza, que hacían la América con tan buena fortuna. O bien, en caso de enamoramiento inevitable, y dado que su papá practicaba una tolerancia racial que en realidad era indiferencia, con algún libanés trabajador y abusado. Cualquiera de estos hombres esperaba, como todos los otros, fincar con una mujer que no anduviera opinando, ni metiéndose en las pláticas de los señores, ni aconsejando cómo solucionar el problema de la basura o la epidemia de los gobernadores. Las mujeres no estaban para hablar de temas que no fueran domésticos, y entre menos hablaran mejor. Las mujeres, a coser y cantar, a guisar y rezar, a dormir y a despertarse cuando era debido.

Se sabía en la ciudad que la tía Elvira Almada no sólo estaba más llena de opiniones que un periódico contestatario, sino que también tenía prácticas raras. Algunas tan raras como mantenerse despierta hasta las tres de la mañana y no ser capaz de levantarse a tiempo ni para ir a la misa de nueve que era la última. A las nueve y a las diez, la tía Elvira dormía como el bebé que nadie iba a hacerle bajo el ombligo, justo porque a ella no le importaba dónde había que tener el ombligo a cada instante. Las damas de entonces cuidadan muy bien de llevar sus ombligos a la misa de ocho y de regresarlos a la casa en cuanto terminaba para que nadie fuera a pensar que andaban paseándose como viejas cuzcas. De ahí hasta la hora de la comida, guisaban o hacían jardinería, ayudaban a sus madres o escribían cartas púdicas para ensayar hasta la perfección su letra de piquitos. Las más disipadas echaban chisme o memorizaban un poema con lágrimas.

En cambio, la tía Elvira y su ombligo iban despertando por ahí de las once. Pasaban la mañana leyendo novelas y teorías sociales, hasta que la fiereza con que el ombligo sentía hambre indicaba la hora de entregarse al uso de jarras y palanganas para irse lavando todo el cuerpo de un modo disperso pero acucioso. Primero la entrepierna y sus pelitos, en los que la horrorizaba la idea de un piojo llegado durante la noche de algún rincón; después las axilas, a las que ella les depilaba los vellos con la misma obstinación de una mujer actual; luego la cuenca del ombligo y al final los pies y las rodillas. Ya bien bañada, se ponía loción de rosas en los diez puntos que consideraba cardinales y betabel en las mejillas. Hacía esto último con tal habilidad y desde tan niña, que hasta su madre estaba segura de que su hija Elvira tenía un espléndido rubor natural.

Llegaba al comedor siempre al último, pero siempre a tiempo.

—Buenos días, chulita —decía su mamá, que vivía angustiada con el comportamiento de aquel pedazo suyo al que veía, como todos, destinado a la soledad.

—Buenos días —contestaba ella, con el alma tranquila de quien se levanta a desayunar a las seis de la mañana. La comida era siempre su primer alimento y aunque el destino la colocó en días aciagos y desmañanados, nunca supo comer antes de las dos y media de la tarde. A esa hora su papá volvía de emprender negocios y fracasos todos los días.

A la tía Elvira le gustaba llevar la conversación para ese lado. El mundo de su padre estaba lleno de proyectos y espejismos y ella era feliz intentando que todos en la familia navegaran por ese mar. No hubo negocio infausto que no emprendiera su padre. Había comprado una fábrica en quiebra, que le costó lo mismo que una nueva, y que debía de impuestos al fisco más de lo que costó. El gobernador acabó decidiendo que pasara a manos de los obreros y el papá de la tía Elvira aceptó la decisión sin chistar. Con lo que le quedó, compró las acciones de una mina de sal que en realidad era una compañía formada por dos genios fracasados en su intento de desalinizar el agua del mar. Importó después vajillas alemanas y chinas. Para venderlas, puso una tienda de regalos que al poco tiempo se convirtió en el centro de plática más atractivo de la ciudad. Siempre había café y cigarros para todos los que manifestaran algún interés por la compra, venta o uso de la porcelana.

Al año de instalado, el comercio quebró y hubo que cerrarlo, pero la gente se había acostumbrado de tal modo a pasar ahí las horas del café y el chisme, que un turco lo compró para volverlo taquería y se hizo rico en las narices del buen don José Antonio Almada.

Frente a tal decepción, el señor Almada viajó hasta Guerrero en busca de tierras y volvió de allá convertido en el dueño de unos terrenos a lo largo de la costa en un puerto llamado Acapulco, que a decir suyo se convertiría en una de las playas más famosas del mundo. Esa vez intervino su esposa y ella, que nunca se hubiera atrevido a mencionar tal palabra, se dispuso al divorcio si su marido no vendía cuanto antes las cinco hectáreas de aquella playa inhóspita. Puestas las cosas de aquel modo, el papá de Elvira vendió su playa y perdió lo que hubiera sido el único buen negocio de su vida.

—Algo malo va a salir de todo esto —dijo la tarde que le compraron sus terrenos—. No se puede despreciar tal maravilla sin pagarlo.

Gastadas todas sus fantasías empresariales, el señor Almada entró a la política con la misma vehemencia y la misma ignorancia con que había ido por el mundo de los negocios. Como si no supiera todo el mundo que con el gobierno era mejor no ponerse, el papá de la tía Elvira tuvo a bien desempolvar su carrera de abogado para defender a un torero que no había podido cobrarle al gobernador su trabajo en la corrida de toros en que lidió seis bestias con los cuernos sin rasurar, e hizo una faena tras otra en honor a los valientes del 5 de mayo.

Al papá de la tía Elvira, que había visto la corrida con la misma devoción con que otros oyen misa o van al banco, le pareció el colmo. Una cosa era que el gobernador llevara la autoridad de su investidura hasta manejar las finanzas públicas como si fueran las suyas, y otra que con toda su calma le negara el salario a un artista, porque al último toro no lo había matado en el primer intento.

—Aquí el circo es gratis —le dijo el gobernador—. Te puedo dar pan y mujer, pero billetes ni los sueñes. Además, te portaste como un carnicero.

El torero había demostrado su valor durante tres horas seguidas y no tuvo manera de guardárselo. Se puso a llamar tirano, asesino y ladrón al gobernador quien, en su turno, lo mandó encerrar.

No tardó el papá de la tía Elvira en salir rumbo a la cárcel a ofrecerle sus servicios al torero.

Puso una demanda contra el jefe del gobierno, acusándolo de robo y abuso de autoridad. Para la hora de la comida, estaba casi seguro de que ganaría el pleito. Se había hecho ayudar por sus amigos de la prensa, que tanto café le debían y a quienes les pareció un litigio de tamaño tolerable para tenerlo con el gobernador. Dedicaron largas prosas a dudar de que un señor tan magnánimo y aficionado a la fiesta brava como era el gobernador, hubiera podido maltratar a un torero. Seguro no sería así, pero que si algún malentendido había, ahí estaba ese hombre de bien llamado don José Antonio Almada.

Comían el postre cuando un ayudante llegó con el aviso de que el torero iba a salir libre. La tía Elvira le dio tres cucharadas a su natilla y se fue corriendo tras su papá. Llegaron a tiempo para presenciar la firma de libertad y fue tal el gusto de su padre que se llevó a la tía Elvira a una cantina a la que poco a poco fueron llegando celebradores. Se armó una fiesta de brandy y anises, música y leperadas de la que no se repuso nunca la reputación de Elvira Almada. Había bailado con el torero hasta que ambos cayeron sobre una mesa desvencijados del cansacio. Había bebido chinchón y usado palabras de hombre con tal descaro y habilidad que todos los presentes llegaron a olvidarse de que estaba entre ellos una de las recatadas señoritas Almada. No se acordaron de que ella era ella, sino hasta la mañana siguiente. Entonces la tía Elvira y su padre volvieron a la casa canturreando *Estrellita* y declarándose su amor.

—Oyelo bien, niña —le dijo su padre—. Yo soy el único hombre de tu vida que te va a querer sin pedirte algo.

—Y yo la única mujer que te va a seguir queriendo cuando seas un anciano y te hagas pipí en los pantalones —le contestó la tía Elvira.

Entraron riéndose al patio alumbrado por un sol tibio. En el centro, detenida como un fantasma, estaba la madre de la tía Elvira.

—¿Te das cuenta de lo que has hecho? —le gritó a su marido.

Iba cobijada por la mantilla con que salía a la iglesia. Había llorado, no entendía de qué podían reirse aquel par de irresponsables. Claro que no se daban cuenta de lo que habían hecho. La gente feliz es ciega y sorda.

—Saqué al torero de la cárcel —dijo el hombre—. ¿Tú dormiste mal? Te ves desmejorada.

Le dio luego un beso a su mujer de mejilla con mejilla y subió las escaleras pensando en su almohada.

La tía Elvira supo que si permanecía un segundo a solas con su mamá, el cielo podría caerle en la cabeza, así que corrió a la cocina en busca de una quesadilla con epazote.

Durante unos días su madre no les habló ni a ella ni a su marido, pero después se dejó reconquistar por ambos y su existencia volvió a ser sobria y grata. Fuera de la incapacidad de su marido para los negocios, la vida había sido amable con la mamá de la tía Elvira. Pero su corta imaginación le daba para creer a pie juntillas la versión salesiana de que el mundo es malo cuando no es bueno. Y la tía Elvira tenía desde pequeña una enorme propensión a no respetar lo que todo el mundo considera bueno.

Como bien adivinó la gente, no fueron las diligencias legales y periodísticas del señor Almada las que pusieron al torero en libertad, sino el simple hecho de que el Ciudadano Gobernador recordó con placer, al día siguiente de la corrida, los momentos de valor que había tenido el hombre. Mejorado su buen ánimo, consideró una injusticia mantenerlo encerrado sólo por haber extendido su bravura hasta él. Incluso le mandó pagar como era debido y volvió a tener con el torero algo que es difícil llamar amistad, pero que se le parece en los modos.

Total, como en todos sus negocios, el único que había quedado mal parado era el papá de la tía Elvira, quien por supuesto no se enteró de nada. Por eso al poco tiempo se entusiasmó con la solicitud de unos obreros en huelga a los que el gobierno había instado a volver a su trabajo por la buena, lo que significaba simplemente volver sin más. Qué salarios, qué prestaciones ni qué ocho cuartos, lo importante era restablecer la productividad.

Como si algo le faltara para tomar aquella causa con pasión, lo de la productividad terminó de empujar al papá de la tía Elvira. Ninguna buena persona tenía que ser por fuerza productiva y menos aún empeñarse en que otros lo fueran. Declaró a los periódicos todo lo que pudo en contra de quienes pretenden que la productividad sea el único criterio para juzgar a los seres humanos, aprovechó para criticar a quienes lo único que buscan en la vida es el poder y el dinero, y volvió a poner un amparo contra el gobernador y sus aliados.

Todas estas cosas, dichas en la casa o con sus amigos, le ganaban los elogios y la admiración de medio mundo. Pero puestas en papel y tinta sonaban a locura, a suicidio, al peor negocio que don José Antonio Almada hubiera emprendido en su cálida y generosa existencia.

Al gobernador le había llegado la historia de la celebración con el torero. Quien se la contó había descrito a la tía Elvira como el lujo de pasión y belleza que irradió aquella noche.

—A cada quien por donde le duela —dijo el gobernador muerto de risa—. Y éste la pone fácil, porque deja su dolor en libertad. Sólo a un tarugo buen hombre como él se le ocurre.

Después de comer, la tía Elvira y su hermana Josefina acostumbraban caminar por la avenida de La Paz rumbo al cerro de San Juan. Eran dos mujeres que parecían opuestas y quizá se adoraban precisamente por eso. Josefina iba a casarse con el mejor partido de la ciudad, un hombre prudente y rico que, a decir de la tía Elvira, hubiera sido hasta guapo si no tuviera el gesto como amarrado.

Pasada la mitad del camino, casi donde terminaba la ciudad, estaba la gran casa del novio, más grande aún porque tenía junto el molino de harina del que salía parte de la fortuna familiar. Ahí se quedaba Josefina para estar un rato con su suegra, que la esperaba en la puerta y dedicaba las siguientes dos horas a ir entrenando a la muchacha en los exactos manejos y los precisos gustos domésticos de la familia, a la que habría de entrar con toda su suavidad, su inteligencia y su perfecta cintura.

La tía Elvira seguía sola el camino hasta el cerro al que subía como una chiva mordiendo el tallo de alguna flor y sujetándose al pasto y la tierra con sus pies conocedores y firmes. Al llegar a la punta se arrellanaba para mirar la puesta de sol con la devoción de quienes conocen rezos de privilegio. Algún antepasado cholulteca la empujaba a ese rito de contemplar el sol y los volcanes.

De esa ceremonia la robaron una tarde. Le vendaron los ojos y empezaron a bajarla del cerro pegando unos gritos que nadie oía. Su hermana estaba a dos kilómetros de distancia aprendiendo deshilado fino, su mamá hacía galletas de naranja, su papá había prendido un puro sobre una taza de café libanés y comentaba con sus amigos el desastre de seguir viviendo en una sociedad maniquea como la poblana, que era como la mexicana, que al fin y al cabo era igual a la de cualquier parte.

Fue hasta que anocheció cuando su hermana Josefina empezó a preguntarse por la demora de la tía Elvira. Era una loca audaz, pero como todos sabían, no le gustaba andar en la oscuridad. Al principio Josefina disimuló su aflicción porque le daba vergüenza molestar a su próxima familia política preocupándola con las locuras de su hermana Elvira que no había sido capaz de caer en líos siquiera después de la boda. Pero cuando, acompañada por el novio y la suegra, subió y bajó del cerro desnudando con la vista todos los alrededores y llamándola a gritos desde el coche sin la menor respuesta, una angustia como podredumbre le corrió del estómago a la boca y dejó de hablar. Tuvo que rendirse a la certidumbre de que Elvira no estaba en los alrededores y volver a la casa junto al molino conteniendo las lágrimas en un gesto de niña golpeada.

Al llegar ahí encontró reunida a toda la familia de su novio. El suegro, las tías, la cuñada, el cuñado y la mamá, abandonaron su habitual prudencia y en un gesto de cordialidad y buen tino se pusieron a hilvanar historias de mujeres raptadas, violadas, muertas y descuartizadas, durante los últimos treinta años. Su suegra había perdido en la revolución todos los bienes que su marido obtuvo por la misma época. Le echaba la culpa al gobierno de todos y cada uno de aquellos actos de barbarie, incluyendo el de la niña que se fue a un pozo mientras su mamá se distrajo un segundo.

Don José Antonio Almada llegó a su casa a las ocho en punto y encontró a su mujer decorando galletitas y repitiendo "La Magnífica" detrás de una sonrisa. Cuando el señor Almada preguntó por las niñas ella interrumpió su oración para afirmar que no habían llegado y el hombre se le fue encima diciéndole que también ella estaba chiflada, que no luego dijera que la locura de Elvira nada más era herencia de su lado, que si no se había dado cuenta de la hora que era.

—Sí, ya me dí cuenta —dijo la mujer—. Pero no escandalizo porque como siempre me dicen que exagero, estoy haciéndome el propósito de no gritar para no parecer ¿cómo dices?

—Maniquea, esposa, maniquea. Pero es que nunca tardan tanto.

—Eso pienso yo. Pero yo siempre he dicho que no me gusta que caminen solas en la tarde, que Elvira se trepe al monte, que se le haga de noche. Y tú dices que soy una posesiva, que en Nueva York así es, que ya hace rato que empezó el siglo veinte y que . . .

No pudo seguir y se puso a llorar despavorida.

—Voy a buscarlas —avisó temblando don José Antonio.

Toda la tarde había oído en el café advertencias mucho más exageradas que las que nunca se hubiera atrevido a hacer su esposa sobre lo arriesgado que era enfrentarse a la autoridad cuando uno tenía hijas.

Se fue por la calle rumbo al molino diciendo improperios contra sus hijas, que de seguro estaban ahí tomando churros muy tranquilas. Contra su mujer que siempre acababa teniendo razón, y a quien por contradecir había dejado él que sus hijas anduvieran por el mundo como personas y no como las joyas que eran. Y también contra los toreros y contra los trabajadores en huelga, contra el gobernador, y sobre todo contra sí mismo.

Hacía el último frío de marzo y él temblaba resintiéndolo más que ningún otro. Cuando llegó al molino, su hija mayor lo abrazó como si él también tuviera la certidumbre de que la tía Elvira se había perdido para siempre.

El novio de Josefina se acercó a saludar, con la mezcla de bondad y perfección que después su mujer detestaría.

—Sé que es una imprudencia recordarle que le advertí los

peligros de meterse a defender trabajadores levantados —le dijo al señor Almada.

—Si lo sabe, por qué me lo recuerda —contestó el señor Almada aparentemente recobrado del primer miedo. Tenía el brazo sobre los hombros de su hija Josefina, que al oírlo se preguntó si estaría escogiendo un buen marido.

Antes de que nadie se preocupara por ella, la tía Elvira había empezado a bajar el cerro con las manos atadas y la boca libre. Después de los primeros gritos, dejó de oponerle resistencia a su secuestrador. Al contrario de lo que éste esperaba, ella contuvo su garganta en cuanto se dio cuenta de que nadie la oiría. Desde que le contaron en la escuela la tragedia de la Santa María Goretti, una adolescente que se dejó matar antes que dejarse poseer por un villano, había pensado que la santa cometió un error garrafal, y que si alguna vez su cuerpo corría un riesgo parecido, haría todo menos oponerse a los designios de la vida. Así que cuando se vio atrapada por aquel hombre de brazos fuertes y expresión bruta, le dijo:

—Si lo que quieres es llevarme, voy contigo. Pero no me maltrates.

El tipo lo pensó un segundo y le pidió después que extendiera las manos para atárselas.

—No me vayas a tapar la boca porque me angustio y me desmayo —informó la tía Elvira—. Te prometo no gritar. Pero no te preocupes si no cumplo mi promesa, de todos modos no hay quien pueda oírme.

El tipo era menos bruto de lo que se veía y aceptó la propuesta de Elvira, con tal de no cargarla desmayada hasta el coche en que los esperaba su jefe inmediato, un hombre cincuentón, afodongado y eternamente crudo que lo había hecho subir solo porque, según dijo, estaba harto de cargar viejas asustadas.

Empezaron a bajar.

—¿Tú con quién trabajas? —preguntó la tía Elvira después de un rato.

—Con Tigre —dijo el muchacho, que no se aguantó las ganas de presumir.

—¿Y ese qué conmigo? —dijo ella.

—Yo qué sé.

—¿Eres de los que obedecen sin preguntar? —dijo la tía Elvira.

—Oí que eres hija de un tipo Almada —contestó el muchacho irritándose.

—¿Y eso qué? ¿Cuánto te pagan?

—Mucho. ¿Qué te importa? Ni que yo te fuera a mantener. Te llevo y allá te dejo con ellos.

—¿Quién me va a mantener?

—Depende. Estás bonita. Adivinar quién te quiera. Allá se ven puras bonitas.

—Las verás tú, otros no nada más las ven —dijo la tía Elvira.

El muchacho se acercó furioso, le pellizcó los brazos y la besó como en las películas.

—Así serás valiente, con la vieja amarrada —dijo la tía Elvira—. ¿Vienes solo o te mandaron con otro?

—Claro que vengo con otro. El otro trae el coche y la pistola

—dijo el joven buscando con la mirada el auto de su amigo en las faldas del cerro.

Por el camino llegaba otro auto y el viejo tendría que alejarse para que no sospecharan de él. Eso estaba planeado. Si alguien se acercaba, el muchacho tendría que esconder a la hija de Almada en la pequeña cueva que se abría a medio cerro, al otro lado de la vereda por la que la gente acostumbraba subir, y justo por el que bajaban la tía y su apresador. Ella la conocía como conocía todo el monte, pero no entraba nunca, porque era un lugar oscuro y pestilente, lleno de telarañas y ratones.

El joven tapó la boca de Elvira y la arrastró a la cueva sin encontrar demasiada resistencia.

La muchacha tenía tanto empeño en huir como él. Se tiró al suelo, le hizo señas para que también él se arrastrara y se metió a la pequeña cueva con más rapidez y habilidad que el muchacho. Oscurecía. La tía Elvira oyó a lo lejos los gritos de Josefina y sintió pena por ella. Pero pensó que si la encontraban los Miranda amarrada a un vago pestilente, la vida que su hermana soñaba por las tardes se iría a la basura sin mayor trámite. Por fin los gritos se apagaron. El muchacho miró a la tía Elvira. Se hacía de noche, pero su cuerpo iluminaba la creciente oscuridad.

—¿Por qué no gritaste? —le preguntó.

—Para que no te lastimaran —contestó la tía Elvira.

—Pinche vieja, me quieres meter en un lío —dijo acercándose a tentarla despacio.

—Si yo me robara algo, me lo robaría para mí —dijo la tía Elvira.

La noche se había cerrado sobre ellos y sintió que sería mejor acogerse a la idea de que estaba soñando. El tipo volvió a besarla y a sobarse contra ella, enfebrecido.

—Así, quién no es valiente —dijo la tía Elvira, arrastrándose otra vez hacia afuera de la cueva. El joven la siguió. Sintieron al aire pegarles en el cuerpo como otra caricia. El le desamarró las manos y ella se las echó al cuello. Su piel olía raro. La tía Elvira pensó que nunca había tenido tan cerca una piel no emparentada con la suya. Luego cerró los ojos y con las manos libres acarició al desconocido como si tuviera que grabárselo en la memoria de sus yemas. Le fue desabrochando la camisa poco a poco hasta que se la quitó. Luego le tapó los ojos con un cariño y se fue sobre el cinturón con una soltura que cualquiera diría que hacía tiempo practicaba. Lo fue tocando todo y en todo fue hábil y buena, hasta en los dedos de los pies que le sobó como quien compone las flores de un adorno. No dejó en aquel cuerpo ningún recelo. Lo apaciguó a fuerza de hablarle cosas en los oídos y en todas las partes por las que pasaron sus labios.

—Yo sabía que las ricas eran tontas en esto —dijo el muchacho desde su apaciguada y ferviente desnudez.

—Somos —dijo Elvira cuando sintió moverse la mano de él entre sus piernas de virgen intrépida—. Somos, somos —murmuró arrancando a correr como un gato asustado. Dejando tras de sí el primer cuerpo desnudo que le mandó el azar.

Abrazaba el monton de ropa del muchacho y corría hacia el molino impetuosa y desesperada. En las faldas del cerro estaba un coche con el gordo de la pistola dormido como el ángel que no fue jamás. Había vuelto en cuanto el coche con Josefina y el novio abandonó el lugar, y cuando vio que su pupilo tardaba en bajar imaginó que algo bueno le estaría pasando y se dio permiso para una siesta. Le había parecido correcto esperar a que el muchacho hiciera su primer trabajo ganándoles un poco de mujer a sus patrones.

La tía Elvira pasó cerca del coche sin voltear a mirarlo. La movía una excitación desconocida. ¿Qué hubiera venido después? le preguntó un instante a su cuerpo. Pero en lugar de contestar, siguió corriendo.

Entró al molino con los ojos de luna y la boca de una muerta. El portero la vio subir la escalera todavía como un animal perseguido. Luego entró a la sala y abrazó a su papá que de mirarla viva sintió su corazón reventarse y su cuerpo desfallecer.

—Todo esto fue por vender Acapulco —dijo el señor Almada varias veces, en su agónico delirio de los siguientes días—. ¿Para qué me salí de los negocios? —le preguntaba a todo el que iba a visitarlo al hospital.

La tía Elvira lo besaba y lo besaba con la cara marchita de llanto y desesperanza.

—No te aflijas, papá. Lo volveremos a comprar, pero no te me mueras. No te mueras.

Siguió rogándole que no se muriera mucho tiempo después de haberlo enterrado. Porque la tía Elvira en realidad no enterró nunca a su padre. Pasó el resto de su larga vida haciendo negocios en su honor. Su madre le entregó la administración de la ladrillera de Xonaca, que era lo último que les quedaba, para ver si haciéndola sentir imprescindible lograba sacarla del pozo al que se había tirado.

Y eso la entretuvo para siempre. Empezó por convencer a la mitad de los constructores del estado de que sus tabiques estaban mejor hechos que ningunos y acabó dueña de una verdadera mina de sal, dos de los primeros cinco aviones que cruzaron el cielo mexicano, tres de los primeros veinte rascacielos y cuatro hoteles sobre la costera de Acapulco.

—Ya ves, papá —decía al final de su vida, cada tarde frente al mar—. Volvimos a comprar Acapulco.

Tía Daniela

La tía Daniela se enamoró como se enamoran siempre las mujeres inteligentes: como una idiota. Lo había visto llegar una mañana, caminando con los hombros erguidos sobre un paso sereno y había pensado: "Este hombre se cree Dios". Pero al rato de oírlo decir historias sobre mundos desconocidos y pasiones extrañas, se enamoró de él y de sus brazos como si desde niña no hablara latín, no supiera lógica, ni hubiera sorprendido a media ciudad copiando los juegos de Góngora y Sor Juana como quien responde a una canción en el recreo.

Era tan sabia que ningún hombre quería meterse con ella, por más que tuviera los ojos de miel y una boca brillante, por más que su cuerpo acariciara la imaginación despertando las ganas de mirarlo desnudo, por más que fuera hermosa como la virgen del Rosario. Daba temor quererla porque algo había en su inteligencia que sugería siempre un desprecio por el sexo opuesto y sus confusiones.

Pero aquel hombre que no sabía nada de ella y sus libros, se le acercó como a cualquiera. Entonces la tía Daniela lo dotó de una inteligencia deslumbrante, una virtud de angel y un talento de artista. Su cabeza lo miró de tantos modos que en doce días creyó conocer cien hombres.

Lo quiso convencida de que Dios puede andar entre mortales, entregada hasta las uñas a los deseos y ocurrencias de un tipo que nunca llegó para quedarse y jamás entendió uno solo de todos los poemas que Daniela quiso leerle para explicar su amor.

Un día, así como había llegado, se fue sin despedir siquiera. Y no hubo entonces en la redonda inteligencia de la tía Daniela un solo atisbo capaz de entender qué había pasado.

Hipnotizada por un dolor sin nombre ni destino se volvió la más tonta de las tontas. Perderlo fue una pena larga como el insomnio, una vejez de siglos, el infierno.

Por unos días de luz, por un indicio, por los ojos de hierro y súplica que le prestó una noche, la tía Daniela enterró las ganas de estar viva y fue perdiendo el brillo de la piel, la fuerza de las piernas, la intensidad en la frente y las entrañas.

Se quedó casi ciega en tres meses, una joroba le creció en la espalda, y algo le sucedió a su termostato que a pesar de andar hasta en el rayo del sol con abrigo y calcetines, tiritaba de frío como si viviera en el centro mismo del invierno. La sacaban al aire como a un canario. Cerca le ponían fruta y galletas para que picoteara, pero su madre se llevaba las cosas intactas mientras ella seguía muda a pesar de los esfuerzos que todo el mundo hacía por distraerla.

Al principio la invitaban a la calle para ver si mirando las palomas o viendo ir y venir a la gente, algo de ella volvía a dar muestras de apego a la vida. Trataron todo. Su madre se la llevó de viaje a España y la hizo entrar y salir de todos los tablados sevillanos sin obtener de ella más que una lágrima la noche en que el cantador estuvo alegre. A la mañana siguiente, le puso un telegrama a su marido diciendo: "Empieza a mejorar, ha llorado un segundo". Se había vuelto un árbol seco, iba para donde la llevaran y en cuanto podía se dejaba caer en la cama como si hubiera trabajado veinticuatro horas recogiendo algodón. Por fin las fuerzas no le alcanzaron más que para echarse en una silla y decirle a su madre: "Te lo ruego, vámonos a casa".

Cuando volvieron, la tía Daniela apenas podía caminar y desde entonces no quiso levantarse. Tampoco quería bañarse, ni peinarse, ni hacer pipí. Una mañana no pudo siquiera abrir los ojos.

—¡Está muerta! —oyó decir a su alrededor y no encontró las fuerzas para negarlo.

Alguien le sugirió a su madre que ese comportamiento era un chantaje, un modo de vengarse en los otros, una pose de niña consentida que si de repente perdiera la tranquilidad de su casa y la comida segura, se las arreglaría para mejorar de un día para otro. Su madre hizo el esfuerzo de creerlo y siguió el consejo de abandonarla en el quicio de la puerta de Catedral. La dejaron ahí una noche con la esperanza de verla regresar al día siguiente, hambrienta y furiosa, como había sido alguna vez. A la tercera noche la recogieron de la puerta de Catedral con pulmonía y la llevaron al hospital entre lágrimas de toda la familia.

Ahí fue a visitarla su amiga Elidé, una joven de piel brillante que hablaba sin tregua y que decía saber las curas del mal de amores. Pidió que la dejaran hacerse cargo del alma y el estómago de aquella náufraga. Era una creatura alegre y ávida. La oyeron opinar. Según ella el error en el tratamiento de su inteligente amiga estaba en los consejos de que olvidara. Olvidar era un asunto imposible. Lo que había que hacer era encauzarle los recuerdos, para que no la mataran, para que la obligaran a seguir viva.

Los padres oyeron hablar a la muchacha con la misma indiferencia que ya les provocaba cualquier intento de curar a su hija. Daban por hecho que no serviría de nada y sin embargo lo autorizaban como si no hubieran perdido la esperanza que ya habían perdido.

Las pusieron a dormir en el mismo cuarto. Siempre que alguien pasaba frente a la puerta oía la incansable voz de Elidé hablando del asunto con la misma obstinación con que un médico vigila a un moribundo. No se callaba. No le daba tregua. Un día y otro, una semana y otra.

—¿Cómo dices que eran sus manos? —preguntaba. Si la tía Daniela no le contestaba, Elidé volvía por otro lado.

—Tenía los ojos verdes? ¿Cafés? ¿Grandes?

—Chicos —le contestó la tía Daniela hablando por primera vez en treinta días.

—¿Chicos y turbios? —preguntó la tía Elidé.

—Chicos y fieros —contestó la tía Daniela, y volvió a callarse otro mes.

—Seguro era Leo. Así son los Leo —decía su amiga sacando un libro de horóscopos para leerle. Decía todos los horrores que pueden caber en un Leo. —De remate son mentirosos. Pero no tienes que dejarte, tú eres Tauro. Son fuertes las mujeres de Tauro.

—Mentiras sí que dijo —le contestó Daniela una tarde.

—¿Cuáles? No se te vaya a olvidar. Porque el mundo no es tan grande como para que no demos con él, y entonces le vas a recordar sus palabras. Una por una, las que oiste y las que te hizo decir.

—No quiero humillarme.

—El humillado va a ser él. Si no todo es tan fácil como sembrar palabras y largarse.

—Me iluminaron —defendió la tía Daniela.

—Se te nota iluminada —decía su amiga cuando llegaban a puntos así.

Al tercer mes de hablar y hablar la hizo comer como Dios manda. Ni siquiera se dio cuenta de cómo fue. La llevó a una caminata por el jardín. Cargaba una cesta con frutas, queso, pan, mantequilla y té. Extendió un mantel sobre el pasto, sacó las cosas y siguió hablando mientras empezaba a comer sin ofrecerle.

—Le gustaban las uvas —dijo la enferma.

—Entiendo que lo extrañes.

—Sí —dijo la enferma acercándose un racimo de uvas—. Besaba regio. Y tenía suave la piel de los hombros y la cintura.

—¿Cómo tenía? Ya sabes —dijo la amiga como si supiera desde siempre lo que la torturaba.

—No te lo voy a decir —contestó riéndose por primera vez en meses. Luego comió queso y té, pan y mantequilla.

—¿Rico? —le preguntó Elidé.

—Sí —contestó la enferma empezando a ser ella.

Una noche bajaron a cenar. La tía Daniela con un vestido nuevo y el pelo brillante y limpio, libre por fin de la trenza polvosa que no se había peinado en mucho tiempo.

Veinte días después ella y su amiga habían repasado los recuerdos de arriba para abajo hasta convertirlos en trivia. Todo lo que había tratado de olvidar la tía Daniela forzándose a no pensarlo, se le volvió indigno de recuerdo después de repetirlo muchas veces. Castigó su buen juicio oyéndose contar una tras otra las ciento veinte mil tonterías que la habían hecho feliz y desgraciada.

—Ya no quiero ni vengarme —le dijo una mañana a Elidé—. Estoy aburridísima del tema.

—¿Cómo? No te pongas inteligente —dijo Elidé—. Este ha sido todo el tiempo un asunto de razón menguada. ¿Lo vas a convertir en algo lúcido? No lo eches a perder. Nos falta lo mejor. Nos falta buscar al hombre en Europa y Africa, en Sudamérica y la India, nos falta encontrarlo y hacer un escándalo que justifique nuestros viajes. Nos falta conocer la Galería Pitti, ver Florencia, enamorarnos en Venecia, echar una moneda en la fuente de Trevi. ¿No vamos a perseguir a ese hombre que te enamoró como a una imbécil y luego se fue?

Habían planeado viajar por el mundo en busca del culpable y eso de que la venganza ya no fuera trascendente en la cura de su amiga tenía devastada a Elidé. Iban a perderse la India y Marruecos, Bolivia y el Congo, Viena y sobre todo Italia. Nunca pensó que podría convertirla en un ser racional después de haberla visto paralizada y casi loca hacía cuatro meses.

—Tenemos que ir a buscarlo. No te vuelvas inteligente antes de tiempo —le decía.

—Llegó ayer —le contestó la tía Daniela un mediodía.

—¿Cómo sabes?

—Lo vi. Tocó en el balcón como antes.

—¿Y qué sentiste?

—Nada.

—¿Y qué te dijo?

—Todo.

—¿Y qué le contestaste?

—Cerré.

—Y ahora? —preguntó la terapista.

—Ahora sí nos vamos a Italia: los ausentes siempre se equivocan.

Y se fueron a Italia por la voz del Dante: "Poi piovve dentro a l'alta fantasia".

Tía Amalia

Amalia Ruiz encontró la pasión de su vida en el cuerpo y la voz de un hombre prohibido. Durante más de un año lo vio llegar febril hasta el borde de su falda que salía volando tras un abrazo. No hablaban demasiado, se conocían como si hubieran nacido en el mismo cuarto, se provocaban temblores y dichas con sólo tocarse los abrigos. Lo demás salía de sus cuerpos afortunados con tanta facilidad que al poco rato de estar juntos el cuarto de sus amores sonaba como la Sinfonía Pastoral y olía a perfume como si lo hubiera inventado Coco Chanel.

Aquella gloria mantenía sus vidas en vilo y convertía sus muertes en imposible. Por eso eran hermosos como un hechizo y promisorios como una fantasía.

Hasta que una noche de octubre el amante de tía Meli llegó a la cita tarde y hablando de negocios. Ella se dejó besar sin arrebato y sintió el aliento de la costumbre devastarle al boca. Se guardó los reproches, pero salió corriendo hasta su casa y no quiso volver a saber más de aquel amor.

—Cuando lo imposible se quiere volver rutina, hay que dejarlo —le explicó a su hermana, que no era capaz de entender una actitud tan radical—. Uno no puede meterse en el lío de ambicionar algo prohibido, de poseerlo a veces como una bendición, de quererlo más que a nada por eso, por imposible, por desesperado, y de buenas a primeras convertirse en el anexo de una oficina. No me lo puedo permitir, no me lo voy a permitir. Sea por Dios que algo tiene de prohibido y por eso está bendito.

Tía Amanda

Durante mucho tiempo se dijo que Amanda Rodoreda era hija de Antonio Sánchez, el compadre de su papá. Y ni su propia madre pareció saber de dónde le había llegado a la barriga aquella niña tan poco parecida a los dos hombres que para su desgracia le cruzaron la vida. Decían que cuando la soltó al mundo, su corazón todavía estaba ardiendo por la boca y las manos de Antonio Sánchez, aunque su cabeza descansara como siempre en el regazo de su apacible Rodoreda.

Varios años había convivido con ambos de la mañana a la noche, oyéndolos inventar negocios y fundarlos, viéndolos tener éxitos y fracasos entre conversaciones eternas y extenuantes borracheras. Lo mismo a uno que al otro los había recogido del suelo como fardos, los había puesto en sus camas y cobijado al llegar la madrugada. Para los dos había preparado chilaquiles y café negro, a los dos les había organizado las maletas cuando se iban a recorrer el rancho de Tlaxcala y con uno y el otro se había puesto a cantar en las noches sin luz eléctrica que se ciernen sobre los alrededores del cerro La Malinche. Estaba casada con uno de ellos, muy bien y desde siempre lo había querido como se debe. Al otro empezó queriéndolo como una extensión de ese amor y acabó enamorándose de su voz y de las cosas que con ella decía. Pero no fue su culpa. En realidad no fue culpa de nadie. Así sucede a veces y no vale la pena desvelarse investigando por qué.

Supongo que algo de eso pensó Antonio Sánchez cuando decidió irse a quién sabe dónde sin dejar un aviso ni reclamar un centavo de todos los que tenía metidos en la sociedad con Rodoreda. Se fue la mañana siguiente a la noche en que su compadre le notificó que su señora estaba embarazada, y lo dejó todo, hasta las tijeras con que cortaba la punta de sus puros. No más de tres camisas y un pantalón faltaban en sus cajones, así que Daniel Rodoreda pensó que algo urgente se le había cruzado y que volvería al terminar la semana. Pero pasaron más de seis meses sin que se oyera de él y Rodoreda empezó a extrañarlo como un perro. Le urgía su presencia sonriente y audaz, le hacían falta sus observaciones, su ingenio, la compañía de tiempo completo a la que estaba acostumbrado, su complicidad. Sobre todo en esos últimos meses del embarazo que había convertido a su alegre y despabilada mujer en un bulto que apenas hablaba, que podía pasarse horas sin decir palabra, que lloraba con cualquier pregunta y con dificultad comía tres cucharadas de sopa para alimentar a la maravilla que llevaba dentro.

Amanda no había nacido todavía, cuando su futura abuela paterna tuvo la delicadeza de preguntarle a su hijo si estaba seguro de que por el vientre de su mujer no había pasado más que el esperma Rodoreda. Con esa sola pregunta derribó la torre de naipes que era ya la vida de aquel marido, empeñado en no ver la pena que su señora tenía en los ojos. Rodoreda volvió a su casa a tirarse en una cama para tratar de morirse. Estuvo dos semanas con fiebre, echando espuma por la boca y un líquido azulado por los ojos, con la piel ceniza y el pelo encaneciendo de uno en uno, pero a tal velocidad que cuando volvió en sí tenía la cabeza blanca. Su mujer estaba junto a él y lo vio abrir los ojos por primera vez para mirar, no sólo para perderse en un horizonte inalcanzable.

Lo vio mirarla y una paz que jamás imaginó la hizo sonreir como la primera vez.

—Perdóname —dijo.

—No tengo nada que perdonar —contestó él.

Nunca se habló más del asunto.

Un mes después nació una niña de ojos claros que Daniel Rodoreda bautizó como suya y con la cual terminó de perder el poco juicio que le quedaba. Aseguró que sería imposible encontrar nada más hermoso en el mundo y la vio crecer prendado hasta de la ira que le llenaba los ojos ante cualquier contratiempo.

Cuando murió su madre, Amanda tenía diez años y la furia más que la tristeza se le instaló en los ojos durante meses. Lo mismo le pasó a Rodoreda, así que estuvieron viviendo juntos más de un año sin hablarse. Un día Rodoreda se la quedó mirando mientas ella escribía su tarea empinada sobre un cuaderno.

—¿A quién te pareces tú? —le preguntó acariciándola.

—A mí —le contestó Amanda—. ¿A quién quieres que me parezca?

—A mi abuela —dijo Rodoreda y empezó a contar cosas de su abuela en Asturias hasta que la conversación se instaló de nuevo en la casa.

Diez años más tarde Antonio Sánchez regresó a la ciudad, hermoso y devastador como siempre. A los cuarenta y cinco años era tan idéntico a sí mismo que volvió a fascinar a Rodoreda. Había ido a buscarlo, le había pedido perdón por irse sin avisar, le había dado un largo abrazo y no le había pedido cuentas al preguntar sobre la situación de los ranchos y la tienda a los que llamó tus negocios, nunca los nuestros. Sólo al hablar de Amanda notó en su voz algo más que el interés de un tío ausente y descuidado. Entonces Rodoreda la mandó llamar, feliz y temeroso de enseñarle aquel tesoro.

Amanda entró a la sala con su cabeza llena de rizos y un lápiz en la boca.

—Papá, estoy estudiando —dijo, con la voz de prisa y disgusto que a él le caía tan en gracia.

—Tú perdones los modos —pidió Rodoreda a Antonio Sánchez—. En febrero entra a la universidad y es una niña muy obsesiva.

—¿Va a la universidad? —preguntó Antonio Sánchez, deslumbrado con aquel monstruo que sonreía con la misma impaciencia disimulada de su papá.

—Sí —dijo Rodoreda—. Por fin alguien en la familia podrá ser intelectual de tiempo completo.

—¿Y qué estudias? —le preguntó Antonio Sánchez al ángel ensoberbecido que tenía enfrente.

—Derecho —contestó ella—. ¿Y usted quién es?

—Me llamo Antonio Sánchez —dijo él, mirándola como si toda ella fuera la Vía Láctea.

—Ah, ya. De usted es de quien se supone que soy hija —dijo Amanda en el tono con que se comenta el buen clima—. ¿Y a qué ha vuelto? ¿A casarse conmigo? Porque yo de hija suya no tengo ni la estampa, ni las ganas.

Daniel Rodoreda se quitó los anteojos y mordió una de las patitas hasta arrancarla.

—¿Qué dices tú? —le preguntó a su hija.

—No lo digo yo, papá. Todo el mundo comenta. ¿Por qué nosotros no? ¿El señor me engendró? ¿De ninguna manera? ¿Quién sabe?

—Quién sabe —dijo Antonio Sánchez.

—¿Quién sabe? —preguntó Rodoreda—. Yo sé. Tú eres hija mía como que te pareces a mi abuela materna hasta en los dobleces del cuello, como que sabes cantar como mi padre y enojarte como sólo yo.

—Muy bien. Qué bendición. Soy tu hija. Entonces me quiero casar con tu amigo.

—Amanda, no me vuelvas loco.

—¿Cómo? Si lo que pretendo es que dejes de estar loco. Demuéstrame por una vez que de verdad puedes creer con todo tu cuerpo eso que dices con tanto ruido: Amanda es mi hija. ¡Claro que soy tu hija! Daniel Rodoreda, tu esposa no se acostó nunca con tu amigo. ¿Verdad?

—Verdad —dijo Sánchez.

—Y Amanda no es un regalo de Dios, ni un golpe de suerte, ni una furia que recogió tu generosidad. Amanda es tu hija y por eso se va a casar con su otro papá. Para que se acaben los chismes, para que se traguen sus elucubraciones los papás de mis compañeras de colegio, mis nanas, mi abuela, las maestras, el cura de San Sebastían, el Señor Arzobispo y el perro de la esquina.

—¿A eso volviste? —le preguntó a su amigo.

Un año después Daniel Rodoreda desfiló por el pasillo central de Santo Domingo llevando del brazo a su hija Amanda. La entregó en matrimonio a Don Antonio Sánchez, su mejor amigo.

La noche de bodas la pasaron los tres en el rancho de Atlixco, muertos de risa y paz.

Tía Jose

Tía Jose Rivadeneira tuvo una hija con los ojos grandes como dos lunas, como un deseo. Apenas colocada en su abrazo, todavía húmeda y vacilante, la niña mostró los ojos y algo en las alas de sus labios que parecía pregunta.

—¿Qué quieres saber? —le dijo la tía Jose jugando a que entendía ese gesto.

Como todas las madres, tía Jose pensó que no había en la historia del mundo una creatura tan hermosa como la suya. La deslumbraban el color de su piel, el tamaño de sus pestañas y la placidez con que dormía. Temblaba de orgullo imaginando lo que haría con la sangre y las quimeras que latían en su cuerpo.

Se dedicó a contemplarla con altivez y regocijo durante más de tres semanas. Entonces la inexpugnable vida hizo caer sobre la niña una enfermedad que en cinco horas convirtió su extraordinaria viveza en un sueño extenuado y remoto que parecía llevársela de regreso a la muerte.

Cuando todos sus talentos curativos no lograron mejoría alguna, tía Jose, pálida de terror, la cargó hasta el hospital. Ahí se la quitaron de los brazos y una docena de médicos y enfermeras empezaron a moverse agitados y confundidos en torno a la niña. Tía Jose la vio irse tras una puerta que le prohibía la entrada y se dejó caer al suelo incapaz de cargar consigo misma y con aquel dolor como un acantilado.

Ahí la encontró su marido que era un hombre sensato y prudente como los hombres acostumbran fingir que son. Le ayudó a levantarse y la regañó por su falta de cordura y esperanza. Su marido confiaba en la ciencia médica y hablaba de ella como otros hablan de Dios. Por eso lo turbaba la insensatez en que se había colocado su mujer, incapaz de hacer otra cosa que llorar y maldecir al destino.

Aislaron a la niña en una sala de terapia intensiva. Un lugar blanco y limpio al que las madres sólo podían entrar media hora diaria. Entonces se llenaba de oraciones y ruegos. Todas las mujeres persignaban el rostro de sus hijos, les recorrían el cuerpo con estampas y agua bendita, pedían a todo Dios que los dejara vivos. La tía Jose no conseguía sino llegar junto a la cuna donde su hija apenas respiraba para pedirle: "no te mueras". Después lloraba y lloraba sin secarse los ojos ni moverse hasta que las enfermeras le avisaban que debía salir.

Entonces volvía a sentarse en bancas cercanas a la puerta, con la cabeza sobre las piernas, sin hambre y sin voz, rencorosa y arisca, ferviente y desesperada. ¿Qué podía hacer? ¿Por qué tenía que vivir su hija? ¿Qué sería bueno ofrecerle a su cuerpo pequeño lleno de agujas y sondas para que le interesara quedarse en este mundo? ¿Qué podría decirle para convencerla de que valía la pena hacer el esfuerzo en vez de morirse?

Una mañana, sin saber la causa, iluminada sólo por los fantasmas de su corazón, se acercó a la niña y empezó a contarle las historias de sus antepasadas. Quiénes habían sido, qué mujeres tejieron sus vidas con qué hombres antes de que la boca y el ombligo de su hija se anudaran a ella. De qué estaban hechas, cuántos trabajos habían pasado, qué penas y jolgorios traía ella como herencia. Quiénes sembraron con intrepidez y fantasías la vida que le tocaba prolongar.

Durante muchos días recordó, imaginó, inventó. Cada minuto de cada hora disponible habló sin tregua en el oído de su hija. Por fin, al atardecer de un jueves, mientras contaba implacable alguna historia, su hija abrió los ojos y la miró ávida y desafiante, como sería el resto de su larga existencia.

El marido de tía Jose dio las gracias a los médicos, los médicos dieron gracias a los adelantos de su ciencia, la tía abrazó a su niña y salió del hospital sin decir una palabra. Sólo ella sabía a quiénes agradecer la vida de su hija. Sólo ella supo siempre que ninguna ciencia fue capaz de mover tanto, como la escondida en los ásperos y sutiles hallazgos de otras mujeres con los ojos grandes.

Tía Concha

Al final de su vida cultivaba violetas. Tenía un cuarto luminoso que fue llenando de flores. Llegó a crecer las más extravagantes y le gustaba regalarlas para que todo el mundo tuviera en su casa el inquebrantable aroma de Concha Esparza.

Murió rodeada de parientes sin consuelo, metida en su bata de seda azul brillante, con los labios pintados y un enorme disgusto porque la vida no quiso darle más de ochenta y cinco años.

Nadie sabe cómo no estaba cansada de vivir, había trabajado como un arriero durante casi toda su existencia. Pero algo tenían las generaciones de antes que aguantaban más. Como todas las cosas de antes, como los autos, los relojes, las lámparas, las sillas, los platos y los sartenes de antes.

Concepción Esparza tuvo, igual que todas sus hermanas, las piernas flacas, grandes los pechos y una sonrisa inclemente para mirar y mirarse, una absoluta incredulidad en los santos de yeso y una fe ciega en los espíritus y sus chocarrerías.

Era hija de un médico que participó en la revolución de Tuxtepec, fue diputado federal en 1882 y se unió al antirreeleccionismo en 1908. Un hombre sabio y fascinante que le permeó la vida con su gusto por la música y las causas difíciles.

Pero como al destino le gusta emparejar sus dones, a Concha le sobró padre pero le faltó marido. Se casó con un hombre de apellido Hiniesta cuyo único defecto era parecerse tanto a sus hijos que ella tuvo que tratarlo siempre como a un niño más. No era muy apto para ganar dinero y la idea de que los hombres mantienen a su familia, tan común en los años treinta, no le regía la existencia. Conseguir la comida, tener casa y cobijas en las camas, pagar el colegio de los niños, vestirlos y otras nimiedades fueron siempre asunto de Concha su mujer. Mientras, él inventaba cómo hacer grandes negocios que nunca se hacían. Para cerrar uno de estos negocios fue que se le ocurrió dar un cheque sin fondos por tal cantidad que le dictaron orden de aprehensión y la policía se presentó a buscarlo en su casa.

Cuando Concha supo de qué se trataba dijo lo primero que se le ocurrió:

—Lo que pasa es que este hombre está loco. Perdido de loco está.

Con ese argumento lo acompañó al juzgado, con ese argumento le impidió intentar una defensa que lo hubiera hundido por completo y con ese argumento evitó que lo metieran a la cárcel. A cambio de tan horrible destino, con ese argumento Concha Esparza organizó que su marido fuera a dar a un manicomio cercano a la pirámide de Cholula. Era un lugar tranquilo, vigilado por frailes, en las faldas del cerro.

Agradecidos con las visitas médicas del padre de Concha, los frailes aceptaron ahí al señor Hiniesta mientras se olvidaba el asunto del cheque. Claro está que Concha debía pagar cada mes el mantenimiento de aquel cuerdo entre los impávidos muros del manicomio.

Seis meses hizo ella el esfuerzo de costear la estancia. Cuando sus finanzas no pudieron más decidió recoger a su marido tras conseguir la anuencia pública para hacerse cargo de él y sus desatinos.

Un domingo fue a buscarlo a Cholula. Lo encontró desayunando entre los frailes a los que hacía reir con la historia de un marinero que se tatuó una sirena en la calva.

—A usted padre no le quedaría mal una —le decía al más sonriente.

Mientras conversaba el señor Hiniesta vio acercarse a su mujer por el corredor que conducía al refectorio. Siguió hablando y riendo durante todo el tiempo que la tía Concha empleó en llegar hasta la mesa en que él y los frailes departían con ese regocijo infantil que sólo tienen los hombres cuando se saben rodeados de hombres.

Como si no conociera las reglas de tal privacía Concha Esparza caminó alrededor de la mesa haciendo sonar los zapatos de tacón alto que sólo sacaba del ropero en ocasiones a su juicio memorables. Cuando estuvo frente a su marido saludó al grupo con una sonrisa.

—¿Y tú qué andas haciendo por aquí? —le preguntó el señor Hiniesta más incómodo que sorprendido.

—Vine a recogerte —le respondió tía Concha hablándole como se les habla a los niños a la hora de recogerlos en la escuela, jugando a entregarles el tesoro de su libertad a cambio de un abrazo.

—¿Por qué? —dijo Hiniesta mortificado—. Aquí estoy seguro. No conviene que salga de aquí. Además la paso bien. Se respira un aire de jardines y paz que le va de maravilla a mi espíritu.

—¿Qué? —preguntó Concha Esparza.

—Lo que te digo, de momento no estoy mal aquí. No te preocupes. Tengo buena amistad con los cuerdos y no la llevo mal con los locos. Algunos tienen ratos de excepcional inspiración, otros son excelentes interlocutores. Me está cayendo bien el descanso porque en este lugar hasta los que gritan hacen menos ruido que tus hijos —dijo como si él no tuviera nada que ver con la existencia de tales hijos.

—Hiniesta ¿qué voy a hacer contigo? —le preguntó al aire Concha Esparza. Después dio la vuelta y caminó hasta la reja de salida.

—Por favor, padre, explíquele usted —le dijo al fraile que la acompañaba—, que sus vacaciones cuestan, y que yo no le voy a pagar un día más.

Adivinar qué le habrá explicado el padre aquel al señor

Hiniesta, el caso fue que el lunes en la mañana el cerrojo de la casa de tía Concha sonó lento como lo hacía sonar la calma con que lo empujaba su marido.

—Ya vine, madre —dijo Hiniesta con una tristeza de velorio.

—Qué bueno, hijo —le contestó su mujer sin mostrar asombro—. Te está esperando el señor Benítez.

—Para proponerme un negocio —dijo él y recuperó la viveza de su voz—. Verás, verás qué negocio, Concha. Ahora vas a ver.

—Así era ese hombre —comentaba la tía muchos años después—. Toda la vida fue así.

Para entonces ya la casa de huéspedes de la tía Concha había sido un éxito y le había dejado los ahorros con los que puso un restaurant que después le dejó tiempo para comerciar con bienes raíces y hasta le dio la oportunidad de comprarse un terreno en Polanco y otro en Acapulco.

Cuando sus hijos crecieron y tras la muerte del señor Hiniesta, ella aprendió a pintar las olas de "La Quebrada" y a comunicarse con el espíritu de su padre. Poca gente ha sido tan feliz como ella entonces.

Por eso la enojó tanto la vida, yéndose cuando apenas empezaba a gozarla.

ABOUT THE AUTHOR

Ángeles Mastretta is the author of the novels *Tear This Heart Out* and *Lovesick*, a winner of the prestigious Rómulo Gallegos Prize. She lives in Mexico City.